I0544682

Carpathian Vampire

...when you've never known love...

by

Lumi Laura

Translated
from the Romanian by
Dragoş Tătărescu

Tragedy's Workshop
Healdsburg, CA

Copyright 2014 by Luminiţa Laura
All rights reserved. Published in the United States
by Tragedy's Workshop, Healdsburg, CA
ISBN-13: 978-0-9829534-9-5
ISBN-10: 0-9829534-9-6

Cover illustrations and design
by Richard Sheppard
www.artstudios.com

Publisher Web site:
www.TragedysWorkshop.com

Author Web site:
www.LumiLaura.com

Book Web site:
www.CarpathianVampire.com

For

My father, Romond Laura

Acknowledgements

Many people have helped me with this book and through life, too many to thank publicly, but here are some of the more important ones: the Roma family who for most of the writing of this book made my life on Earth possible; my mother and father who gave me life, I love you; Dragos Tătărescu, my translator who understands my immature Romanian and is awesome with English.

A very special thank you to David Kennedy of Edinburgh, Scotland and his family, who have sheltered, provided for and loved me during the last year of bringing this work to print. Words cannot express the affection I have for all of you.

Finally, to the anonymous person in America who accepted at face value a request from a derelict Romanian girl he'd never met, expressed his confidence in her, accepted the financial risks, and made this publication a reality, I owe a debt of gratitude that I can only hope my writing will repay.

Author's Note

For those who might wonder about such things as the origin of the idea for this work of fiction, let it be known that this volume came into the world as a result of a discussion I had with friends concerning the nature of immortality. I decided on the spot that I would write a vampire novel. The thought of doing this greatly excited me, and I dove into the task with boundless energy. I wanted to set the novel in the Carpathian Mountains in my native Romania, and since the Roma clan I'd come to live among a couple of years before had once taken me during the summer months to the small mountain town of Sinaia, which has exotic castles and an old monastery, I decided to set my story there. My subsequent researches into the history of the town led naturally to its connection with Queen Marie of Romania (1875-1938), who frequently visited the area and lived there at times. The fact that the Queen did actually have an affair that resulted in an illegitimate child who quickly disappeared from public knowledge was a great piece of actual history with which to connect my fictional work, and I decided to make my story about that forbidden child, a girl I supposed, and her offspring. My fictional take on this actual person is that she should be the great grandmother of the protagonist of my story, which is set in current day Romania.

One must keep in mind that vampires are not real and that this is a fictional story that I have intentionally intertwined with the lives of real historical people and events. In the same vein, I make use of, but only briefly, the fact that a Ms Maruka Cantacuzene, who was an actual friend of Queen Marie, had an aversion to light and lit her home with oil lamps, but only faintly, and to the point of which visitors to her home did stumble over furniture in the dark. I fictionally attributed this aversion to vampirism, although one must remember, again, that vampires are not real and that this person was never a vampire and did not undergo a cure later in life, as I claim in my story. Although curiously, she did lose her aversion to light. A more accurate view of even the actual people I mention in my story is that they also are fictional characters with only a referential connection to the names of those actual people who lived in this world. I would compare them to the character presented as an American president in the rather recent movie, "Abraham Lincoln, Vampire Hunter."

Let it also be known that, although this is a totally fictional story of vampires, legends of such date to prehistoric times. Even as late as the nineteenth century, vampirism was a great fear in some communities, causing the raising of the dead to remove the deceased's head to extinguish the possibility of vampirism. But then again, mine is a fictional tale, and the vampires as well as the divine beings I've depicted, came solely from my imagination.

The sins of an author in constructing a fictional narrative are, as they say, many and varied. I've constructed a mythology for my race of vampires, and just as I've coupled my story with actual historical figures, I've also interconnected it with both existing religions and ancient mythologies. I've even linked religion with mythology, which within itself is not unusual. Of course, everyone knows the story of the Garden of Eden from Genesis, and I've also made generous use of the connection between Christ's cross and the Tree of Life. The most thorough explanation I've found of this actual history is contained in *A Heritage of Holy Wood, The Legend of the True Cross in Text and Image* by Barbara Baert, 2004.

Those familiar with Greek mythology will recognize the Centaur Cheiron and the god Prometheus, both of whom play a role in my mythology concerning the origin of vampirism. To the myth of Cheiron, I've added a method concerning how he received his wisdom and immortality, one that reflects back to Genesis. I've also used his painful wound and the fact that he gave up his immortality to Prometheus to my advantage in providing attributes to my own brand of vampirism. Even though some will view my uninhibited use of such religious and mythological details as regrettable, it was great fun to uncover the connections and make such a consistent and, some might even believe, believable story.

As I've already stated, my tale originated in a discussion of worldly immortality versus divine immortality. Such subjects are real and alive in the world today and will undoubtedly become more popular in the future as people strive to live longer lives. Once started, I found my story to have a life of its own, and I had but to follow where it led. Perhaps that is the reason vampirism has become so prevalent in popular culture. As soon as you say that someone is immortal in the natural world, they attain a stature, albeit a fictional one, that exceeds that of all mortal others. These contrivances allow us to consider issues of great philosophical interest and explore hidden ramifications of our most cherished beliefs and philosophical conflicts while indulging in fanciful adventures.

Those I've allowed to peruse these pages during its creation have generally, except for my publisher, been unappreciative and accused me of all forms of religious and secular offenses, up to and including crimes against humanity.

Proceed at your own risk.

*

Those who participate in such things as social networking may wish to follow me on twitter: @LumiLaura, although I'm not a frequent tweeter. If you're into reading personal blogs, take a look at mine at www.LumiLaura.com. You'll surely find more information about me there than you wish to know.

Table of Contents

Carpathian Vampire

...when you've never known love...

And the LORD God said, Behold, the man is become as one of us, to know good and evil: and now, lest he put forth his hand, and take also of the tree of life, and eat, and live for ever: Therefore the LORD God sent him forth from the garden of Eden, to till the ground from whence he was taken. So he drove out the man; and he placed at the east of the garden of Eden Cherubims, and a flaming sword which turned every way, to keep the way of the tree of life. —Genesis 22-24

Verily, verily, I say unto you, except a corn of wheat fall
into the ground and die, it abideth alone: but if it die,
it bringeth forth much fruit. —John 12:24

Surely this world, stored outwardly with shapes and influences of beauty and good, is peopled in its intellectual life by myriads of loving spirits that mould our thoughts to good, influence beneficially the course of events, and minister to the destiny of man. —Mary Shelley, *The Letters*

1

The First Vampire: How It Happened

Some time before 1200 BC

Alucius Kardasian was a mountain man. He loved the lakes and streams of the high country. In the colors of the sky at sunrise and sunset, he found great beauty, and at such times, he'd climb the hillside to peer down upon the villages in the valleys below bathed in pinks and golds. He'd become the leader of a clan at a young age and had several women and a horde of offspring. He kept them all within his dwelling made of animal bone and stretched hides. Life was good for Alucius, and he was a great believer in the gods. He was kind to people, and they loved him for his benevolence and his knowledge of seed-planting and crop-growing, a new way of life for human beings. He was known far and wide, and many a medicine man and sorcerer came to live in his village because he showed them respect and used their esoteric knowledge to help the tribe. He worshiped the twin gods Before and After because they understood the significance of everything, thinking before the act, and considering its consequences afterward. Thus, one could project one's self from the past into the future at considerably reduced risk.

All this thinking had its benefits, and lately his tribe had developed a use for fire that could melt rocks and cause the tears of the gods to pour forth from the Divine World into the real world. Once cooled, these holy tears became solid and could be pounded into any shape imaginable. Alucius made weapon tips and long-bladed knives from these celestial tears with which to slaughter his enemies.

Alucius was, in fact, so fond of this world that he came to despise the priests of his clan who talked of how the human soul left the body after death and found its way into the Divine World where it lived forever. Alucius had no desire to leave. He loved the smell and feel of a woman and didn't mind watching them perform their amorous arts on each other either. He realized that the Divine World had its sad points, including limited carnality. The priests didn't think much of copulating and talked of moderation in all things. Imagine.

Then one evening while sitting before a fire in the Carpathian Mountains with a few of his many women cuddled around and he thinking how horrible death could take all this from him, Alucius spotted a stranger standing in the shadows just out of the flickering firelight, and he called to the man to see if he was in need of a place to pass the night. It wasn't until the man approached the fire that Alucius came to see that he was of uncommon size and carried weapons unfamiliar to his tribe. The man joined them, without a word, and sat alongside him at the fire. Then, also without a word, the man placed a wondrous object before them — a shiny container that allowed one to see through it but was firm and held its shape. Inside the container was a red liquid that looked both familiar and strange. Could it be blood? Yet, it was a brighter red than he'd ever seen.

The large man spoke his first words. "Eternal life," he said, as if the jar contained the concept incarnate.

"Don't we wish," said Alucius.

"No," said the man, as he pushed the jar closer to the fire, and he repeated the words. "Eternal life."

Alucius didn't have to be told three times, and he reached for the jar, whereupon the man grabbed his wrist with such strength that Alucius was helpless.

"Are you sure?" the man asked and with such force that Alucius was taken aback, but he thought, What could possibly be wrong with eternal life? So he said, "I am."

"Then drink."

What Alucius didn't realize, and wouldn't consider until later, is that the being with whom he'd just made a pact was the god Before, and what he would have realized had he known his identity is that After wasn't with him.

It looked like a lot to drink. At first whiff, Alucius realized that it was blood, some animal's blood, but he was willing to choke it down, if it'd do the job. Twice he had to lower the jar to catch his breath, but he got it done.

The man kept looking at him, as if expecting some radical change, but Alucius remained the same.

"Hump," the man said, and at the same time, a huge animal stepped into the firelight.

"I thought I'd killed him," the man said, then stood up, as if surprised that an act he'd performed didn't turn out as planned.

The animal was a Centaur. Alucius had heard of such mythical beings, having the body of a horse with the torso and head of a human, but never thought they were real until now. And this one looked pissed off. The man walked to the Centaur and the two exchanged heated words. Finally, the man motioned Alucius over.

Alucius wasn't very fond of Centaurs. They'd been the subject of some negative gossip of late — something about being violent and uncivilized — and Alucius had no intention of getting mixed up in a pissing contest with one. But the man was insistent, and Alucius drifted over beside him but tried to keep his distance from the Centaur who appeared to be in considerable pain, stamping his hooves and shuffling about uncontrollably.

"This is an immortal being," the man said to Alucius. "However, he's been injured and wishes to give up his immortality. I've brokered this deal for you, where you may take it on for yourself."

Immortality suddenly didn't seem quite the gift he'd imagined, and Alucius thought maybe he'd made a bad bargain in the first place, and that he'd just walk away and let this Centaur keep his deathlessness, but he didn't want to seem ungrateful. "At what cost?" he responded.

"I am already immortal in the Divine World myself," the man said, "or I'd take it on. I've always been a benefactor of mankind and since you're appreciative of the gods, I've negotiated this deal for you."

"But at what cost?" Alucius again asked. He'd already noticed a certain contrariness having come to his nature since drinking the crimson liquid from the jar.

At which point, the immortal man seemed confused. He shrugged his shoulders, as if to say, How should I know? He finally found a few words. "You'd turn down immortality? A little more blood and the deed is done."

Alucius knew the man was right. He also realized that the blood he'd just drunk from the jar was from the Centaur and that drawing the blood was supposed to have killed him, and that when Alucius drank the blood from the jar, it should have made him immortal, but didn't. What the heck, he thought. I've already gorged myself. What's a little more?

Alucius had envisioned the man opening a Centaur vein and refilling the jar, but it seemed the process had evolved.

The Centaur bent down and motioned to his neck.

Alucius turned from the Centaur to the man. "What's he want?"

"Bite him," said the man.

Alucius had his reservations about biting a pissed off Centaur. "On the neck?" he asked.

The man nodded. "Drink the blood."

The Centaur stamped his hooves and again lowered his head and shoulders, and Alucius came up to him and inspected the location where he was expected to place his mouth. He couldn't quite bring himself to do it.

"Bite him!" ordered the man again.

Alucius still wouldn't do it and started to back away, but the Centaur was in enough pain to want to get the show on the road, so he grabbed Alucius about the shoulders with his unusually large and powerful arms. "I'll show him," said the Centaur with a gravely voice that seemed to come from some ancient echo chamber within his horse body. And then the Centaur did. He bit Alucius on the neck, and it hurt so bad that he screamed and emitted an unholy epithet about the beast. But he couldn't shake himself loose, and he became afraid that he'd be drained of all his blood and encounter hated death instead, so he used the only weapon available: his own teeth. He lunged forward, bit into the neck of the Centaur and sucked ferociously, tearing at the wound and growling as he slurped, and the Centaur's blood flowed freely and copiously, and Alucius strangled, recovered and continued to guzzle, thinking that surely the Centaur would weaken soon. And soon he did. He stopped sucking on Alucius and fell from his hooves to his knees and then rolled over on the ground, all the while holding Alucius to his neck with all the strength he had remaining.

"That's it! That's it! You've gotten the hang of it," said the immortal man.

As the Centaur's life faded, so Alucius gained new vitality. No longer did he struggle at the open wound but sucked so hard that the Centaur's body began to wither, the hide collapsing upon the bones, its frame shrinking. Then the flow of blood stopped, the Centaur's remaining strength waned, his arms falling from around Alucius, and thus he was released.

Alucius rose from his victim in a daze. His entire body seemed supercharged. He leaned his head back, growled into the heavens, and a bright flash of white light emanated from his eyes that momentarily put out the brightest of stars. He then turned to the man who had given him this immortality.

"What's your name?" he asked.

"I'm Before, one of two gods of Thought," he said. "Enjoy this immortality, and remember me, the god who gave it to you, in your prayers and sacrifices."

As it turned out, Before and After, the two gods of Thought that Alucius worshiped, had had a falling out. The two brothers argued, and it was over this Centaur-type immortality. After Thought didn't think it wise to disrupt the methods adopted ever since mankind was created. But impulsive Before Thought didn't much give a rat's ass and told After Thought as much, whereupon After Thought washed his hands of the whole affair.

That brings us to these two gods, as we in modern times have come to know them. In the ancient Greek, After Thought is Epimetheus; and Before Thought, or simply Fore Thought, is Prometheus. The god who had given mankind fire and caused so much consternation in the

Divine World had just usurped the Powers-That-Be again and created his own form of immortality for mankind right here on Earth. The row over Prometheus giving mankind fire never approached the likes of the turmoil this new immortality thing generated. The divine dust has still not settled and isn't likely to, ever.

Not long after becoming immortal, Alucius came to notice a burning pain throughout his body and a craving for blood that was beyond all telling. Since no more Centaurs existed in the world, he tried other animals but found them deficient in both taste and efficacy. The pain became unbearable, and he came to equate it with that of the Centaur, a realization that caused him to be less than pleased with Prometheus. Alucius termed it the "Curse of Cheiron."

Then one day, one of his clansmen showed undue affection for one of Alucius' wives, and he pounced on the man. He found that his teeth had now become his primary weapon, and he bit him, sucked him within a hair of his life before letting go. But while watching the man die, one of his most fearsome warriors, he experienced regret, and in a frantic attempt to revive him, placed the man's mouth on his own neck and made him suck. To his chagrin and consternation, the man also showed renewed strength and hostility shortly thereafter and had acquired his own taste for blood. Whereupon, Alucius turned all his wives, and thus began the race of immortal vampires.

Among the many things that Prometheus didn't tell Alucius was that another god had also been in agreement with Epimetheus and against Prometheus giving immortality to human beings. This was the sun god, Helios. Helios tried to prevent Prometheus from giving away Cheiron's immortality, but Prometheus did it under the cover of darkness, while Helios was away on the other side of the world and unaware of what was taking place. When Helios learned what had happened in his absence, he commanded that this new form of immortality be unable to tolerate his rays. They would of necessity become creatures of the night.

Thus, when Alucius discovered that his new lifestyle included an aversion to sunlight, he went underground during the day and became nocturnal for his above-world activities. He came to appreciate the deep recesses of the underworld, and particularly partook of the beauty of stalactites and stalagmites. Some of his flocks congregate in caverns to this day.

Once Bram Stoker came along and made vampirism cool, Alucius Kardasian became an aficionado and liked the name Dracula so much that he kept fiddling around with the letters of his own name and one day realized that if he shortened both his first and last names to the form Alu Kard and then joined the two words into Alukard, he could spell his name backwards to get Drakula. The "k" instead of a "c" was a bit problematic, but close enough. Since then he has proudly proclaimed his name to be Alu Kard. Of course Alu's detractors have taken the word Centaur, spelled it backwards to get Ruat Nec, which sounds a little like "rat neck" which describes some of the people off of whom Alu has fed through the millennia. You'll hear the disparaging epithet applied even among Alu's own flock of bloodsuckers when times get tough.

2

In the beginning...

A Testimonial

I, Catalin of the City of God and Counselor of many Caretakers of Earth's Spiritual Realm, was walking amongst the trees of the Garden when God evicted Adam and Eve for eating fruit from the Tree of Knowledge. He realized that they could no longer be trusted and had taken positive measures to keep them from eating fruit from the Tree of Life, which would have made them immortal. God sought to protect mankind from becoming eternal on Earth. By dying, the soul is released and allowed to go to Heaven. Many saw the eviction as a punishment, and certainly that was Adam and Eve's opinion, but it was actually a blessing because, by dying, mankind gained eternal life in the Divine World where they could live among divine beings.

Divine beings such as myself are among the ancient Watchers, who provide guidance to spirits of the natural world. We observe but do not generally interfere in the affairs of God's Earth. We do, however, take an interest in all beings that occupy our realm.

Seth, Adam and Eve's third son, had the Archangel Michael fetch a branch of the Tree of Life from the Garden of Eden and plant it on his father's grave. It grew into a gigantic tree. Much later, Solomon cut down the tree for use in his temple, but found the wood unsuitable. He discarded it. The Romans then used that wood for Christ's cross when they crucified him.

As a divine being, I was amongst those present at the Crucifixion. Although I was there only to observe, I quickly became interested in another of the witnesses, one Alucius of Kardacia, a mortal, or at least I initially thought he was mortal. Although no longer in existence, Kardacia was then a small village in the Carpathian Mountains of Romania. Alucius had traveled all the way from there by foot. He had sometime before received what he perceived as a great gift from the minor immortal called Prometheus. Prometheus had negotiated the gift with the Centaur Cheiron. Centaurs were a race of earthly beings that, because of their violent and uncivilized behavior, came to be viewed as a mistake of Creation and were allowed to dwindle into nonexistence. All except Cheiron.

Cheiron, presumptuous and self-aggrandizing, had committed the same transgression as had Adam and Eve, but instead of just tasting fruit from the Tree of Knowledge, Cheiron had in fact gorged himself on it. Cheiron became the wisest of all beings, earthly that is. But Cheiron had done Adam and Eve one better. He'd also eaten fruit from the Tree of Life and had in fact become immortal. Because of this, God expelled Cheiron from the Garden, as he had Adam and Eve, and shouted a disparaging epithet after him. However, Cheiron's immortality was not for the Divine World, but for the "real" world here on Earth. Cheiron valued his immortality immensely until one day he was accidentally injured by Heracles and suffered a wound that would not heal. Thus stuck with his immortality, he was destined for eternal agony. At which point, Prometheus entered the picture.

Prometheus wanted Cheiron's immortality but not for himself. Prometheus offered it to Alucius, and he readily accepted because he loved life on Earth and thought the promise of life after death in the Divine World a risky proposition, particularly if one's actions were to be judged prior to being allowed entry into Heaven. No one really wanted to talk about what happened if you didn't make it. Alucius took on Cheiron's immortality by sharing blood with the Centaur, not realizing that Cheiron's pain came with it. He also appreciated the extra kick his intelligence received because he'd never been accused of being the sharpest arrow in the quiver. Alucius felt no pain for periods of time while still under the influence of fresh blood, but once the effect wore off, it had to be renewed, and renewed again and again. Only human blood would satisfactorily suppress the affliction. Good thing violence and uncivilized behavior were a part of the Centaur's gift package, thought Alucius.

When Alucius had just been turned into a vampire, although a shudder had been sent through the Divine World, we initially suspected only minimal damage to the Divine Plan. After all, he was just one man. We didn't understand the pain that Alucius would suffer and that he would discover a way to alleviate the pain, and that it would cause his immortality on Earth to spread. Even then few in the Divine World thought that any human being would covet such a disgusting affliction.

Alucius valued immortality but soon grew tired of the trouble to obtain human blood. He'd also developed a profound adverse reaction to sunlight and was forced to spend his active hours during the dark of night. The gift that just keeps giving, he thought. Having soured on earthly immortality, he became interested in Christ's promise of a better life in the Divine World, and attended the Crucifixion to see what he offered. He didn't hear the Sermon on the Mount because that was during the day. But he did hear of it, and wrote down the words so as to better understand this young man's meaning. "Blessed are the meek, blessed are the pure in heart," well he'd find ways around all that.

Alucius was a servant at the Last Supper. He heard Christ's words for himself, his promise of eternal life, and was taken in by his soft-spoken manner and congeniality. He thought about the bread being Christ's body and the wine being his blood, but was particularly interested in the sharing of such. He didn't attend Christ's trial, but knew that he would be convicted, for he was far too good a man to let live. Yet, nothing prepared him for the way Christ died.

Alucius was there at the Crucifixion and saw, from his hideaway out of sunlight, Christ carry his own cross. Later on that evening, Alucius had the opportunity to witness the Crucifixion up close. Alucius already knew that blood could alleviate the vampire's pain, so the carnage at Golgotha exhilarated rather than repulsed him. And he made the mistake of tasting Christ's blood while Christ was on the cross because he, Alucius, thought that Christ's blood might cure all his ills. After all, Christ was a healer.

Now, Cheiron's pain had come from a poisoned arrow that Heracles dropped on the Centaur's hoof. Not a major injury, but painful beyond all telling because the venom was from the gall of the Hydra. By tasting Christ's blood, Alucius not only hadn't rid himself of the Centaur's pain but had in fact acquired the pain from all Christ's wounds as well: the whip lashes, crown of thorns, spikes through the palms and feet. A sword in the side. Plus, he felt the debilitating, profound fatigue Christ experienced climbing Golgotha while carrying his own cross. Not only had Alucius inherited Cheiron's pain, but now he had absorbed an entire catalogue of new agonies, Christ's Stigmata. He, and all those turned since, experience the Stigmata and fatigue when only, simply, viewing a cross.

Vampire women cannot conceive. Therefore, vampires must always add to their species by turning humans. Alucius also came to realize that vampires could be killed. The ways were rather specialized and gory — beheading, excessive sunlight, or a wood stake through the heart — all would do the job. Then life was over. Completely over. No Afterlife awaits a vampire. Or at least, so we of the Divine World thought.

3

To Grandmother's House

Present Day — Sinaia, Romania

Alex never cried, and she'd never known love. It wasn't because of the fact that she was a little tall and deficient in the cleavage department. Well, maybe some cleavage, not enough, but she'd just turned eighteen, and other girls her age were in and out of love daily. She attributed it to her family. No, not the breasts, but staying to herself. She had been a family afterthought, accident actually, with an older brother and sister, both planned. Her brother was seventeen and her sister fifteen years older. Alex had come along when no one was expecting her — this rude intrusion into her parents' post-kids plans, disrupting both their hopes for financial stability and her mother's professional ambitions. The lawyer syndrome, Alex called it. Gavril was off to Braşov in Transylvania working political angles, not married. Sonya was married with four kids, but she lived with her wealthy husband on the other side of Bucharest. Their mother and father had always worked, and her two siblings had raised Alex — got her dressed in the morning, fed her breakfast and put her out the door. One day they just walked out and didn't come back — off to college and then to live their own lives, leaving Alex in the lurch.

And then there was school. She was quite the intellectual, or so the other kids said, accusingly. Yes, she got good marks, always had, and she loved to read. Mostly European stuff and in English. She had been hooked on psychological novels, but lately had moved on to ancient military, and had a soft spot for lieutenants and colonels. Anyone in uniform who could manage a sword. She told her friends, if you could call them friends, that she was saving herself for a military man. She loved war. She wanted a large family, several kids. She'd treat hers differently, she promised, give each all the attention she could muster.

She'd been asked out on dates, more than her share, she'd heard, been on quite a few, but couldn't really get into being that close to someone. She'd tried making out but what was the point of gnawing on someone's face and drinking a bunch of their spit? "Plictisit acum," is the expression she used when someone mentioned a boy she might date.

"You're too British," one boy complained. "You've read too many English novels." Another claimed she must be Scottish. Several girls laughed at her for appearing American. Alex took it as a compliment.

She'd had a tutor, many of the better-off kids did, and her after-school hours had been spent with the retired English schoolteacher. Not a bad old lady, but not someone you could brag about to friends. Alex didn't have much of a taste for television and only occasionally saw a movie — a dud pretty much in anyone's world. But now she'd be off to college, and she was eager to leave secondary school behind. She wanted a new start in an intellectual circle.

It wasn't as if Alex was content with herself. She felt empty, and she didn't believe it was entirely her lack of a love life. And it wasn't as if she didn't have something she desperately wanted. It was more like a vacancy, a vacuum within her where something should be but just wasn't. Perhaps I'm a crippled person, she thought at times, someone who is outwardly fine but inside, missing a metaphorical arm or leg.

She didn't much care for her name either. Alexandra was alright, but everyone called her Alex. Alex pronounced it Al-Ex and said it was Arabic, or half Arabic. She translated it as meaning "The ex-person, she who had at one time been real."

Dance was the one thing Alex did like. While the other girls wanted to be gymnasts, the fame of Nadia Comăneci, Sandra Izbașa and Cătălina Ponor ever occupying their minds, Alex want to be a ballerina. The problem, of course, was that she wasn't good at it. She had quickness and power but no coordination. She lacked control and seemed to have no feel for music and its rhythms. Yet, she never gave up, persistence her one virtue, and practiced in her room during her long hours alone. She loved the clothes, the tiny shoes, the tights, the little skirts and tops. She had the body for it, sleek and tall. It just never quite jelled. She loved classical music that her friends thought morbid: the dark moods of Mussorgsky's Night on Bald Mountain, and Rachmaninov's The March of the Dead. She was captivated by the last two movements of Berlioz's Symphony Fantastique: "March to the Scaffold" and "Dream of a Witches' Sabbath." Yet, she could never consummate her compulsion for music with emotional surrender. She reached for the ecstatic heights where she knew it could take her, but she could never quite rise to its level. One by one, her ballet instructors abandoned her.

And now comes the best part, or perhaps the worst, depending on how she looked at it. She was with her mother in the car headed north to visit Alex's grandmother, her bunică, or at least Alex was going to visit. Her mother would unload Alex in Sinaia, pass a couple of hours with her mother, and return to litigating. Alex would be there for some weeks. The DN1 expressway hillsides outside Bucharest were lined with massive firs, linden, apple orchards. Red-tile roofs and whitewashed walls dotted the green fields. Alex could breathe better once they got through Ploiesti, the farmlands beyond stretching to the horizon.

They started up the winding road into the mountains. She saw an old horse-drawn wagon with two men and two boys in sheepskin vests. The boys waved as she passed, their smiling faces, and this was as close as she came to feeling affection. She had to turn away her own irrepressible smile. She was much more interested in the boys, and the towering walls of mountains rising up on both sides of Prahova Valley that separates the southern from the eastern Carpathian Mountains, than anything in Bucharest.

Alex heard a "beep" from her cellphone, checked the text message and deleted it rather than respond. She was through with secondary school and looking, skeptically, forward to a more adult environment at university. She hoped her hopeless social network would collapse in her absence, and this was her first strike against it. In the fall, she'd be off to Christ Church, Oxford, the realization of which made her "friends" at school standoffish even before the year was out. She'd applied at the insistence of her grandmother, who undoubtedly used her influence to facilitate Alex's acceptance. Herself, Alex wasn't so excited. Just more classrooms, professors, and writing papers, papers, papers. Still, it offered an excellent curriculum in European history, the one subject she felt she could tolerate.

Her grandfather had died five years before, and every summer sense, Alex had spent much of it with her grandmother, to keep the old lady company and help run her rather large home, the "Estate" Alex exaggerated, but the "Cottage" as it was known to her family. Her grandmother had a couple of workmen who performed outdoor chores, and inside she had a maid, but her grandmother let people run over her and didn't make them work as they should. On the other hand, Alex had a mean streak. She liked to boss people, particularly men, and they seemed to enjoy the adolescent's sassy attitude.

But the situation was more than that for Alex. She had been born in little Sinaia and loved the thought of being "home" again — its stone buildings, massive forests, and towering mountains, the cold summer nights. Peleş Castle was there, built by King Carol I, and although Alex never rubbed shoulders with them, dignitaries and royalty from all over the world congregated in Sinaia to argue the great issues of the times. Foreign dignitaries such as American presidents Richard Nixon and Gerald Ford, along with terrorists Muammar al-Gaddafi, and Yasser Arafat had been guests there. These were the movers and shakers, the Masters of the Universe, who determined the fate of the world, and it was all happening a short walk from her grandmother's home.

Alex's grandmother always paid attention to her. She could peruse her grandmother's treasure trove of books, and she loved working in the garden. It was her grandmother's influence that created her interests. Throughout her childhood, her grandmother would come to their home in Bucharest and stay a week or two, probe into Alex's classes, and query her about her homework. It didn't matter if it were maths, science or history, she had something helpful to say about everything. And then in the summer months, Alex would to go to Sinaia to stay with her bunică for several weeks. These were magical times, walks through the forest, singing songs of love and war. Her grandfather had been the great hiker, and had taken her deep into Sinaia's forests and up the steep mountains of Prahova Valley.

After Alex's grandfather had passed, her grandmother was more anxious than ever for Alex to stay with her. The joy had gone out of her grandmother's life, and now their times together were even more intimate. Her grandmother never talked much about the family, but about things concerning the divine, she was all aflutter. She was not religious, but quite spiritual and claimed to have seen an angel hovering above her own property years ago, the night Alex was born. They talked about dreams they'd had recently, or memorable ones they'd had perhaps years before and what they possibly meant. She'd tell Alex stories of royalty, what the kings and queens were like, the messes they made of their lives, and how they ruled over countries. Alex wondered how she knew such things.

Her mother turned off the highway and took Bulevardul Carol to the traffic circle at the center of Sinaia. From there she turned left onto Strada Aosta and through a series of loops and switchbacks, which put them among tall pines, ended up on a mountainside halfway between Sinaia Monastery, from which the city got its name, and Peleş Castle, the main tourist attraction.

The one last reason Alex was anxious to again be in Sinaia was to see the one person her age she liked. When Alex was at home in Bucharest, she wondered if the girl was real or perhaps an apparition. While there at her grandmother's, Alex at times played by herself outside amongst the trees and bushes at the edge of the Estate. When she did, a girl would join her in the deep shadows or just at twilight. Alex couldn't remember when the girl first came to visit and play with her. She'd always been a part of the landscape and never seemed to age. She came out of nowhere and dissolved into the forest when she left. She was a curious girl, dressed in boys clothes, and she talked about the strangest things, wondering mostly about Alex's life, her friends at school, and what it was like to have a family. At times, she seemed to be older than her years, much older, but at heart, she was just a teenage girl and liked to play and laugh. She would never tell Alex her name. "Call me Ariel," she said. Alex asked her grandmother about her mysterious neighbor, but she knew of no such girl.

Her grandmother must have heard the car coming up the short drive. She was standing in the doorway, a white cat at her feet. Her grandmother's scowl masked an excitement that she'd only reveal later, after Alex's mother had left. A metal cross escaped her blouse and flickered sunlight as it pendulumed across her breasts. She curiously tucked it back inside. She betrayed nothing as she kissed her daughter, calling her Madalina, and took the hands of her grandchild, studying Alex's face as if deciphering an ancient scroll. Alex wondered what it was that could demand such acute attention. Perhaps she had a zit. Nălucă, the cat, ran for cover once he saw Alex. He'd never liked her.

Her mother gone, Alex unpacked, but it was evening by the time she'd settled into her bedroom. With the maid also gone, she helped her grandmother fix the evening meal of bread, cheese, and a little sausage left over from lunch, her grandmother apologizing for not having something special for their first evening alone together. They sat for a while next to the fire drinking hot tea, Sinaia's perennial evening chill settling over the old home. Her grandmother questioned her about her studies wearing a perpetual smile that gave away her great pleasure at having her granddaughter alone with her again. The white cat hopped up into her grandmother's lap, and she cuddled it while they talked.

"Your face is changing, child," she said. "You're finally coming into your looks. You're a beautiful young woman." Her grandmother was staring off into the fire, a distant look in her eyes, as if remembering something or someone from times past. She looked up at Alex. "All that hair. I'll need to brush it to bring back the luster."

Alex had let her hair grow, but all that bushy stuff was a nuisance, and she'd considered getting it cut. She thought that her grandmother seemed more tired and older than when last she'd seen her. She didn't get around as well.

After warming her feet, her grandmother was off to bed, leaving Alex up with the cat. "Don't let Nălucă out," she called over her shoulder. "He fights with skunks."

Alex fondled a few books in the library and then went to bolt the backdoor. She opened it a second to feel the cold mountain air and peer into the darkness, but as she did, the stupid cat squeezed out and scurried off. Alex ran after him, wishing she'd grabbed a sweater first, but thinking she'd only be out a second.

4

Velinar: First Bite

Alex was just in time to see the white cat exit the yard and scamper up the mountainside into the forest. She felt the cold and hugged her arms to her sides as she became enveloped in darkness. She would have hated to disappoint her grandmother if anything should happen to her cat, so she skipped across the grass yard and up through the trees into the gloom, a little apprehensive because she was close to the family graveyard.

She was about to turn back — the cold really was a little frightening — when she saw the cat up ahead, its face turned back as if beckoning her onward. Alex's eyes adjusted enough to the darkness to make out a clearing and an outline of a building, a gazebo, she could tell as she got closer. As a kid, she'd played there on an old foundation of what her grandmother described as a once-marvelous structure built by previous occupants. The foundation had been familiar territory, one of her favorite summer reading spots, and now allayed her fear.

This was the one place her mysterious friend would never go.

Her grandmother's description of the gazebo in its heyday had given it a mystical significance that even now the moonlight magnified. She wondered why her grandmother hadn't mentioned that she'd rebuilt it. It cast a pale shadow as moonlight filtered through. She felt less exposed beneath this magnificent structure, lunar beams setting her white blouse aglow.

The cat was nowhere in sight. "Here kitty," she called, but the sound of her voice seemed to make her more vulnerable. "Nălucă, you little moron." She walked to the edge of the gazebo and peered into the trees where he'd disappeared. A foul odor rose up to meet her, and instead of the cat, she saw something among the dead leaves, a body lying on the ground outside the gazebo and at the edge of the family graveyard. Startled at first, she started to run but caught herself. Must be a dead animal mostly covered by matted leaves and tall grass, couldn't possibly be a body. She stepped off the gazebo, approached it and reached to see if it was her imagination drawing a false image in the pale light. She wondered if it could be her mysterious childhood friend come to a bad end. But this was real, and it was a woman, not a girl, the dead body of a woman.

The blood in her veins had turned to ice. Still, Alex held her nose and touched it. Quick as a snake strike, a hand clasped her wrist, and the feminine shape rose up from within the leaves to stand amongst the tombstones. The woman was dressed in a flowing gown, all ruffles and pleats, once elegant but now covered in grime. A delicate shawl circled her neck and fell to her belted waist. She was old, tall and stank as if she'd been dead a while.

Alex screamed and tried to jerk free, but the woman's grip was like an animal trap. She pulled Alex to her, and Alex struggled to push her away, the woman's skeletal frame cold and damp against her. Her eyes were bloodshot and sunk back into their sockets, darkened skin chalky and scaly. Her smell was like the fumes of a rotted animal Alex had once buried.

Alex tried to fight free but couldn't overcome the woman, who brought her even closer with an embrace that scared Alex so much that she thought she might faint. She heard the woman sniff her neck, then felt her push her away to get a better look. "Dear Lord, forgive me," the woman said in a gravely voice, then lunged forward, planting her mouth firmly against Alex's neck. They struggled and stumbled back into the gazebo just as she felt the woman's teeth break her skin.

Alex heard a muffled voice from behind.

"Velinar!" it shouted.

It was a man's voice, but Alex couldn't turn to see whose. The splitting pain in her neck subsided as the woman sucked, as if extinguished by some awful anesthetic. The man tried to push her off Alex, but his hand seemed to pass right through her, as if he were but a nălucă, ghost. The woman held to her neck like she'd grown there and sucked at her ferociously.

"That's enough," the man said. "Her strength is failing."

And indeed, Alex's strength was gone, the world itself fading before her. She faltered, and when the woman stepped away, Alex fell to her knees on the cold hard gazebo floor and looked up into the face of the man who'd saved her. She still felt faint, her vision blurred, but he seemed a marvelous being, luminescent in moonlight.

"My God!" he said. "Marie?"

Heart pounding, Alex crawled on all fours away from them, to sit on a section of stone bench looking up at her assailant. The woman had been transformed into an iridescent being, no longer old and cadaverous, but young, angelic, even seemed to project internal light as did her companion. Alex believed she must be hallucinating.

The woman stepped toward her and stooped to look at Alex's face. She now seemed kind, gentle, and her expression reminded Alex of her grandmother's earlier that day.

"She can't be," the woman said to her companion, then turned back to Alex. "I'm terribly sorry," she said, her voice ringing like an angel's. She backed away and faded into the night.

Alex struggled to her feet, wishing the man would help her, but he did nothing. Still weak, she reached out to hold onto him, but nothing was there. He was an apparition.

"This'll not happen again," he said. "Velinar was simply beyond herself. Terrible, but nothing can be done now. I must go after her. I'll return tomorrow evening, and perhaps I can explain. I'm called Catalin. You'll need help through this."

With that, he also vanished.

Alex slumped to the floor, then rolled out of the gazebo onto the cold soft ground between the gazebo and the graveyard. This time, she did faint, the world fading away in spite of her fear that something else might come for her. She descended into a heavy sleep and dreamed first of a dark shape hovering over her trying to wake her, something wet and sticky in her mouth, then saw scenes of far-off places, had profane visions of Heaven and Hell. Dark, quarreling shapes, silhouetted against a bright background, milled about. Finally, a benevolent light descended on her. She felt love, contentment, peace.

Sometime before dawn, Alex woke, unaccountably recovered although she still trembled. Nălucă was cuddled against her. Most unusual. "You little rodent," she said. "Look what you've done to me." She felt something in her mouth. She removed a small red seed, and with her finger pushed it into the soft wet earth. A fog had filtered in between trees, but she could make out a faint pre-dawn glow in the distance. She'd better return quickly, or her grandmother would find her missing.

Alex staggered back into the house carrying Nălucă. It was still dark and quiet when she entered. She dropped the cat, and he scurried upstairs to her grandmother. She dragged herself upstairs and entered the bathroom, struggled to stand and then washed the blood from her neck and marveled at how faint were the bite marks, two pinpricks four centimeters apart. She had black blood in one corner of her mouth. She shivered at the memory of what had happened. She entered her bedroom, fell between covers and again fainted dead away.

5

Royalty's Dark Side

Alex was awake enough to know it was raining, and she thought, through remnants of some strange dream of being lost in a deep darkness, that the booming she heard was thunder. But then she realized it was her grandmother banging on her bedroom door. She rose, struggled to escape the dream, and unlocked the door, still in her nightgown.

Her grandmother was in a state. "I thought you'd died in there," she said. "How could you sleep through all the racket I was making? And what did you drag through the house last night?"

Alex stepped out into the hall, looked back toward the stairs, and saw a string of leaves and mud trailing up from the entryway. She mustn't tell her grandmother what had happened after she'd been warned to watch the cat. She didn't even believe it herself.

"I found blood on the bathroom sink. Are you injured?"

Alex refused to panic, but thought a partial confession might be best. "I'm sorry, Bunică," she said, "but the kitty escaped out the backdoor. I had to chase him down."

Her grandmother frowned. "You aren't to go out at night, Alex. This isn't Bucharest. And the blood?"

"I had a nosebleed. Must be the altitude," she lied.

"Get dressed and come downstairs," her grandmother said,

obviously not believing a word. "Eat your breakfast."

Alex dressed noticing she felt unusually strong but was still confused about the events of the previous evening concerning the woman and man. She wondered if anything at all had happened. She saw in the hall mirror that the marks on her neck had almost disappeared. Or, were they ever even there? Nălucă circled her feet, rubbing against her legs. Why this new affection?

She followed her grandmother into the kitchen where her obviously cold breakfast of mortadella, fried egg, cheese slices and tea were all laid out on the breakfast table. Her grandmother had already eaten.

"I'm sorry," Alex said, again.

"Don't apologize until you've told the truth."

Perhaps a little more confession would be in order. "I did chase Nălucă into the trees," she offered. "I found him inside the gazebo."

"That old foundation? And the leaves?"

"I fell running from someone. Did bump my nose." After all, she couldn't tell the whole truth. "I hit it on one of the gazebo benches running from a man. But Bunică, why didn't you tell me you'd rebuilt it."

"What are you talking about, child? The gazebo hasn't been rebuilt."

"Of course it has. I was inside it last night." She rose from her breakfast and went into the living room where the bay window looked out over the backyard. The rain had stopped. "I can't see it from here, but I'm sure it's there."

Her grandmother had already started outside, and Alex followed her through the wet grass, sidestepping puddles, but the gazebo was nowhere to be found.

"It was right here," Alex said, walking into the little clearing. But the ruins were just the same as they'd always been, the circular cement foundation now rain soaked. "I don't understand," she said. "That wasn't a dream."

"Where did you see the man?"

"He was right here." She walked to the far side.

"Did he chase you?" her grandmother asked.

"No. He wasn't after me. It was a chance encounter. I found the kitty and returned."

Her grandmother still didn't seem satisfied. "We've had a series of rapes in Sinaia and other small mountain towns to the north over the last few months," she said.

"He made no aggression toward me." But Alex had her own question about last night, and she thought her grandmother might have an answer. "This man. He thought he recognized me. I surprised him, and he called me Marie."

This seemed to please her grandmother no end. "Did he then, really?" She came up close to Alex and looked her over carefully. "You've seen an apparition," she said. "And inside the gazebo. Remarkable."

"It was so real." She still didn't want to tell her about the woman. "How could someone in Sinaia know my other given name? No one outside my family knows it."

"This would be a real mystery then," her grandmother said, and her mood changed instantly. "You do favor her, you know."

"No, I don't know. Whom are you talking about?"

"Marie, Queen of Romania. She had the gazebo built many years ago."

"That couldn't be who he meant. I believe he was referring to some woman living today."

"Possibly. But still, you do favor her."

"Bunică, I don't look like a queen."

"Let's go back in the house. Finish breakfast, and I'll tell you a story." Her grandmother turned to go. "Perhaps you fell asleep on the sofa and had a powerful dream."

"And all the leaves I tracked in?"

They walked back across the wet grass, reentered the house, and Alex returned to her breakfast. Nălucă jumped up in her lap and purred while she ate.

Her grandmother sat opposite her at the kitchen table. "Perhaps this is the time I should divulged my little secret. Now that you've told me yours, I'll tell you mine. I've been keeping this one for decades, and it's time I told someone who can pass it down. You've read of

Queen Marie in the history books?"

"Yes, of course. She was the great savior of Romania during World War One. She attended the troops as a Red Cross nurse."

"Yes, she even had her own regiment of hussars. Marie was the architect of modern Romania," her grandmother said. "She was a warrior woman, of sorts, but her husband King Ferdinand was a coward, and if it hadn't been for her leadership during the War, Romania wouldn't exist today. And now I'm going to tell you something that I'm guessing wasn't in your history books. Marie, though married to the King, had an affair with one of her hussars. Something about loving the sight of a military man on horseback. And she had a child."

Alex looked up from her breakfast. "How do you know this, Bunică?"

"Firsthand knowledge, my dear. Firsthand. Marie, Queen of Romania, told me that when the child, a girl, was born they made her shuffle it off to a family who adopted it without knowing its lineage. But Marie loved that illegitimate child as much as she did all those she had by the King, perhaps more. And she never forgot her."

"You knew the Queen?"

"Yes. And you'll come to understand why in just a moment."

This much of her story told, the old lady got up from the breakfast table with a groan and took Alex into the living room where they looked out through the wall of windows. They viewed the countryside that cascaded down below them revealing the red-tile tops of buildings in the town of Sinaia, the ribbons of Highway E60, the railway, and the Prahova River that cut through the valley, all trailing north to Braşov, where Alex's brother Gavril lived. On the other side of the little city, the mountains once again rose up to form the valley's far side.

"That illegitimate child," she said, "was my mother. Marie was my grandmother."

"But then, am I even related to you?"

Alex was having difficulty with the bright sunlight now peeking through the cloud cover. It blinded her. That dream-like encounter the night before had set her mind a drift, and now these revelations seemed to be more important than she could withstand. Her head was spinning, but she didn't want to stop her grandmother, who obviously had been keeping a secret for years that she was about to share with her.

"Yes. Your mother really is my daughter. Look Alex. Have you ever noticed anything special about your name?"

"No."

"Before Marie married Ferdinand, she was called Marie Alexandra of Edinburgh. Your two given names are the reverse of hers. What led me to believe that someone in your family would be special is your father's name, Eidyn. Eidyn is the ancient form of the word 'Edinburgh.' You essentially have the same three names, as did Marie before she married. Yes, Marie was your great great grandmother, and you share her name."

"But my family name, it's coincidental."

"No. Your mother and father, theirs was an arranged marriage. I was involved up to my ears in the planning of it. Your father is also an illegitimate castoff of royalty in Edinburgh. When your sister was born, I loved her, but in my heart of hearts, I was so disappointed because I knew she wasn't the one I expected. She wasn't special. I was waiting for the daughter that would fulfill my every wish. Years passed. I'd given up. And then you came along. Instantly, I knew it was you. I insisted on your naming. "

"I was an accident. My parents never wanted me."

Nălucă jumped up onto the back of the sofa and purred loudly into Alex's ear, as if he were trying to tell her something. She brushed him away, he was becoming a nuisance, but he returned immediately. He was making her dizzy.

"But the gods did, child. The ancients tell us that Divine Will works within the element of chance."

"You're saying that I'm descended from royalty, that I am royalty? And that some divine force caused my birth? That can't be true."

It wasn't just her grandmother's revelations that troubled Alex. When the cat purred into her ear, her eyes blurred. It seemed that a great darkness came and went, her dreams once again invading her psychic space. Nălucă purred again, and she saw shapes traveling a dark mysterious road.

"Yes. We are all royalty. Though denied, hushed up, hidden from the public, we are all direct descendants of Queen Victoria, grandmother of Queen Marie of Romania. Even your father's touch of royalty is through Queen Victoria."

"So this is the reason I was admitted to Oxford," Alex said, her head spinning and not quite able to grasp this new social order.

"Let's just say, it didn't hurt. You'll be looked after there too, so nothing to worry about."

The vertigo wouldn't turn loose of Alex. She fell against the side of the sofa, rolled off onto the floor, and fainted dead away. Again, she saw dark shapes clustered about her. She stumbled off the dark psychic road and wandered alone in a barren landscape. She fell onto the dark earth and was lost in the wilderness of her dreams with ominous, quarreling shapes coming to fight over her.

When she came to, she was still stretched out on the floor with her head in her grandmother's lap and Nălucă sitting on her chest.

"Now it's my turn to apologize, child. Never did I imagine that such a revelation would hit you so hard. I'm thinking I should take you to the doctor."

"Oh, please, Bunică. I'll be okay. It's just that I was so sure of the gazebo, but perhaps I was dreaming. I don't know what happened just now," Alex said. "It was as if a dark cloud enveloped me."

Her grandmother got Alex back up on the sofa and went to fix them both another cup of tea. "Something to wake you," she said.

"Coffee," said Alex. "I need coffee." She had to shake the dreams or she'd lose her mind.

Alex had developed a chill. She had her grandmother draw the curtains, and they moved to the chair before the fireplace. Nălucă again found her lap. Then, at Alex's insistence, her grandmother continued her story.

"Did you understand what I told you?"

"Oh yes. I'm the direct descendent of Queen Victoria, from both sides of my family. We're a bunch of royal castoffs?"

"I guess that's one way of putting it. But to me, we're simply the hidden royalty, the invisible royalty. We are the dark side of royal reality. They are the light; we are the darkness. I have something special for you, Alex," she said, and off the mantle she took a rather new volume that had seen a lot of use. "This you must take with you. It's a biography. Something special, at least to me."

Alex took it from her, opened it and turned to the title page. It was a biography of Queen Marie of Romania, in English.

Her grandmother continued, "All the forces at work in the universe are not of this world. Some poor souls here on Earth have destinies, just as some events are fated. I've wondered for a while if you might. And then that apparition mistook you, at least in my mind, for Queen Marie. I wouldn't worry over this. It is a coincidence, but some coincidences have an acausal connection."

Alex then curled up on the sofa, her grandmother piled pillows around her, and she set to reading about Queen Marie. For the first time, she felt more than an interest, a real kinship, with someone in a book. She seemed to gravitate to every detail of the woman's life, her children, her lovers. She wondered about the baby girl that Queen Marie had given away, Alex's great grandmother. She wished the book said more about her. From what her grandmother had said years before, her name was Catherine, and that when she was grown, she'd not been the one to raise her own baby, Alex's grandmother. Alex couldn't remember why.

But Alex also felt something strange, alien waken inside her. The fainting and shadow visions were part of it. The queen's extramarital affairs radiated a sexual yearning that Alex hadn't known. Forbidden love, she thought.

That evening, after her grandmother went to bed, she got restless and needed to get out of the house. Also, Catalin had said that he'd meet with her again in the ruins of the gazebo, but Alex wasn't about to chance the forest with that serial rapist still lurking about. Still, she had to get out, so she decided a little trek into the center of Sinaia was just what she needed. She made sure Nălucă stayed behind.

It had always been against her nature to walk the streets of Sinaia, but then, she didn't feel her normal self tonight. Not at all.

6

Jaklin and Mikhail

Once she stepped outside, Alex realized that her relationship with the night had changed. As she walked the side of the winding street toward the center of town, her eyes adjusted more quickly than normal to the lack of light. In her peripheral vision, she saw evanescent outlines that dissolved when she looked directly at them. Though largely without color, each object seemed internally radiant. Her relationship with the heavens had also changed. She saw deep into the firmament, the pin pricks of light, saw a glowing Milky Way that beckoned her into its sparkling depths.

Alex wondered if she wasn't changing too. Her breasts itched and seemed a little larger, felt puffy, as they sometimes did around her period. Which, by the way, was now officially late, just a day, but that hadn't happened in a while.

As Alex came into town, she noticed an excitement to the nightlife for the first time. Voices from restaurants and pubs seemed to pull her in. She wanted to speak to those voices, have them respond to her. She heard laughter, felt a thrill ripple through her. This must be what her friends back in Bucharest felt when they talked about their love of nightlife, something until now, Alex couldn't share.

Alex walked by a pub and noticed the music and laughter spilling out into the street. She decided to go inside and was aghast at the mash of bodies writhing to the pounding music. She heard someone mention the rapist, and pushed her way through the mass of humanity, unexpectedly relishing other bodies rubbing against hers, the smell of cologne and perfume. She stood at the bar, shrugged off the bartender, not really wanting a drink. She seemed to have a purpose, to be actively looking for something, someone, although she couldn't imagine what or who.

She wedged a path into the dark reaches of the room and spotted a girl in the corner who looked sullen, perhaps even morose. Alex felt drawn to her, as if caught in some sci-fi tractor beam. The girl smiled as she approached. It was the goth that attracted her, the dark lipstick, deep-set shadowed eyes. Those large bulbous whites seemed to glow in the dark. Her hair fell in soft ringlets about her shoulders, and black bangs covered her forehead. The girl was a little older and apparently not with anyone, although another chair at her table sat empty. The girl motioned her to take it, and Alex surprised herself by slipping into the warm seat. At least the girl didn't have any piercings.

"Buna Ziua," said Alex.

"Vorbiţi bulgară?" the girl asked in Romanian. She was brunette, full-figured, prominent clivaj. Though sullen, she seemed to have a sense of eternal optimism about her, covered by a scowl.

"Engleză şi un rus puţin," Alex replied.

"Mikhail will love you," the girl said, and looked down.

Alex was enchanted. "Oh god! I'm going for the goth."

"You like goth?" The girl seemed peevish but wiggled in her chair.

"I do now." Alex loved those sparkling dark eyes.

"We're preparing ourselves for Braşov, if we can ever tear ourselves away from Sinaia. We love this place."

Alex couldn't take her eyes off the girl's cleavage. Her throat looked even more inviting. "Who's Mikhail?"

"My friend from Russia."

"Russian? You like Russians?"

"You don't?"

"Fifty years of communist suppression? I guess not."

"I met him a couple of weeks ago. I'm Jaklin." She squinted and looked at Alex as though she'd seen her before. An orchestral interlude started the next song. "Dance?" she asked.

Alex was taken aback. A girl asking her to dance? But one girl couple was already on the dance floor. She rose and walked toward it with Jaklin following. Once there, they danced apart, but Alex couldn't take her eyes off this dark beauty from Bulgaria. She was shorter than Alex, with a self-conscious, perhaps self-inhibited smile. The song was Lana Del Rey's "Born to Die," a recent international hit that she'd not been fond of but now seemed particularly appealing. The drummer's steady beat projected a sense of urgency that drove her body movement. *Choose your last words, This is the last time, Cause you and I, we were born to die...*, Lana's contralto vocal reverberated sending a chill up Alex's back. *...born to die..., born to die...* echoed in her mind. Jaklin looked so familiar. Alex realized she had been ... *Lost but now I am found, I can see but once I was blind...* How true, so very true.

Alex could hardly keep her hands off Jaklin. She leaned forward and spoke into her ear over the music, "You're Bulgarian?"

"Came here for a part-time job with the Bulgarian Consulate. Decided to stay." Jaklin took her hand. Black fingernail polish.

Alex flinched, but let her keep it. It was warm and smooth, silky soft. *...the road is long, we carry on...* That line reminded Alex of the psychic road she saw when she'd fainted.

The song changed to Del Rey's "Blue Jeans" just as a tall young man with black curly hair started dancing alongside them. "This is Mikhail," Jaklin said in her ear. He was less goth, with rimless glasses. Quite handsome. Well, yes, Alex thought. This Russian, I can stand to be around a while. They became a threesome, the perception flowering and pulling them together. Del Rey's voice animated the three of them. *I will love you till the end of time...* The rest of the dance floor seemed to disappear, the three alone, immediate friends in a euphoric dance of life and death. This is it, Alex thought. This is my life. *...till the end of time...* They are my life. But how silly to know someone for five minutes and be so... attached.

Alex leaned toward Jaklin again. "You two seem familiar, but we've never met, have we? I come here every summer." Her hair smelled like a field of wildflowers.

"Isn't this dreadful?" Jaklin said. "Dreadfully good."

Alex looked up at Mikhail, loved that scrubby little beard, and caught herself singing along with Lana. *I know that love is mean, and love hurts...* Me singing? How can this be? And singing to a young Russian with a short black beard. He was singing to her also. *...love hurts...* A magnificent feeling enveloped her. Just now, she felt as though she could suck whatever she wanted out of the Universe. *I would wait a million years...*

The song ended and Mikhail disappeared. So disappointing. She followed Jaklin back to her table in the corner. The magic had evaporated with Mikhail's departure.

Once in their seats, Alex leaned forward, asked in Jaklin's ear, "How long will you be here?"

Jaklin turned her head so that their cheeks touched. "Who are you?" she asked. "You feel like a lover." She kept turning until the corners of their mouths touched. They kissed, a faint touch of tongues. Alex felt a charge of electricity ripple through her.

"What are you two doing?" It was the young man, Mikhail, and as the girls separated, he pulled another chair up between them. He had a soft creamy complexion that Alex wanted to touch, and that grizzly little beard that she wanted to scrape her palm across. Neither answered, but Alex felt her own body warm. What is happening to me? she wondered. I'm not like this. This is not my body. She felt her nipples tingle.

"I'm Missy," she said, pulling back to get a better look at him. She'd quickly adopted Queen Marie's nickname. "So you're the Russian?"

"What did Jaklin say about me?" Mikhail looked defensive, and rather cute with that bit of beard and glasses.

Alex actually liked guys in glasses, the studious type. He'd be a great boyfriend at Oxford, she thought. "Nothing you'll have to live down," she said. "At least you speak English, if not Romanian." But Alex was wondering what she was doing. She'd never kissed a girl before. That was not something a good Romanian girl would even consider. And now this dark Russian looked even more delicious.

"Why did you decide to stay in Sinaia?" asked Alex.

Jaklin and Mikhail looked at each other. "Something inexplicable," said Mikhail. "Perhaps it's because Sinaia is so international, and we're close to royalty, Peleş Castle just up the hill."

"Well, that's not quite the whole story," said Jaklin. "I have a part-time job at Casino Sinaia. You do know it's not actually a casino?"

"Of course. It's the ICC, International Conference Centre. How did you land a job like that?"

"The Bulgarian Consulate. I just graduated with a degree in international relations."

Alex was intimidated. Here she was just about to enter university, and Jaklin had already graduated. Yet, she had a real affinity for these two. She seemed to read them as she'd never been able to her friends in Bucharest.

"How about you, Mikhail? You work there also?"

"No way. I came here with a study abroad class. Once I met Jaklin, I decided to stay a while. I was planning to start graduate school, but now I'm not so sure."

"Also in international relations?"

"Heavens no. Nothing that practical. I majored in literature. I'll have to teach, so I have several years yet at university."

"In the fall, I'm off to Oxford. Not that I'm particularly excited about it."

"An intellectual," said Mikhail. "You'll be famous."

Alex was surprised at how instantly at home she was with these two university-educated foreigners. "I don't have any friends," she confessed. "Never have. Why is it that I like you two so much?"

"Just something in the air," added Jaklin.

"Something darkly spiritual," said Mikhail.

"You're into religion?" asked Alex.

"Not really," they said simultaneously, then frowned at their synchronicity.

"He's royalty," said Jaklin.

"Just a distant descendant of royalty," objected Mikhail. "Jaklin's heritage is the closest."

"You wish," she countered. "We're both offshoots of the Cantacuzene family. Mikhail from the Russian branch and me the Bulgarian, through some bizarre marital twists that no one will confirm."

"Then we are all three some dark side of royalty," said Alex. "Just today, I learned that I'm a descendent of Queen Marie of Romania, but through illegitimate birth."

"That's rank and file," said Jaklin. "We are a royal trinity. Makes me tingle." She squiggled in her chair again, and her eyes roamed Alex's face, settled on her lips. "You know of the Cantacuzenes?"

"Never heard of them," said Alex.

"You should have," said Mikhail. "The Sinaia Monastery was founded by a Cantacuzene."

"I'll have to ask Bunică. She knows the history of Sinaia."

"So you're from Sinaia? Lived here all your life?" asked Jaklin.

Alex laughed out loud, something she rarely did. "Heavens no! I was born here, but raised in Bucharest. I'm just spending the summer."

Jaklin whispered something in Mikhail's ear, and he whispered back.

"What's the secret?" Alex asked.

"No," Mikhail said to Jaklin.

"What?" asked Alex.

Mikhail smiled at her. "She's a kinky Bulgarian girl," he said. "She wants me to kiss you."

"Just a little affection to consummate our royal kinship," added Jaklin.

Alex instinctively leaned toward Mikhail and pulled his face to hers. She just had to get her hand on that bit of beard. A spark of static electricity made her flinch, then their lips met. She closed her eyes and drifted into a few seconds of bliss. He tasted like salami and pepperoni pizza, a dash of olive, felt the brush of beard across her cheek.

"Break it up, you two," said Jaklin. "Now, I'm jealous." She gave Mikhail a quick kiss then pushed him forward over the table and leaned behind him and toward Alex.

Alex took the cue. Their lips met again, and this time it was tongue wrapped around tongue. With her hand on Mikhail's shoulder and his back up against her breasts, the heat of the two of them was a rage inside her. "Delicious" didn't begin to describe Jaklin. She tasted like blackberry cobbler.

A strange sexual yearning enveloped Alex, and she pushed back. "I don't know what I'm doing," she said, alarm in her voice. "What is happening to me?" She felt panic. She didn't know either of them, yet she had an out-of-control yearning. With that, she jumped to her feet, ran from the table.

"Missy!" they called after her.

Alex pushed her way through the crowd and out of the pub, leaving her two new friends behind.

What had frightened her more even than what she was doing was the blossoming thought: the three of them together, in bed, a ménage à trois.

7

Catalin: "You'll be alright."

Once outside, Alex shouted into the night air, arms raised. "What's happening to me?" And then to herself, Am I a lesbian? Have I always been? Bisexual? Already, she regretted abandoning her two friends. She felt lonely. "Imagine! Me, lonely."

She roamed the main street through Sinaia watching people and tried to come to terms with herself. She had a feeling she was being followed. She turned to look behind several times, but at first could see no one suspicious. It was as if she had a new sixth sense. Then she saw him. A strange man in a cloak or robe. Or was it an animal? What was not right about him, she couldn't quite determine. Yet, she sensed something scary, and it wasn't just that his clothes were a couple hundred years out of fashion. She decided she'd experienced enough nightlife.

She'd been avoiding returning to the gazebo where Catalin had asked her to meet him, but now she realized she had to. That bite on the neck had done something. And that woman, Velinar, had actually fed on her, sucked her blood. The reality and seriousness of it finally hit home.

Once back at her grandmother's, Alex entered by the front door, walked straight through the living room, and exited out the backdoor as she had the night she chased Nălucă into the woods. Tonight, it was much darker, the moon not up yet, and she almost turned back to get a flashlight, but noticed that her night vision had adjusted quickly.

She was disappointed to see that the gazebo was not there, and wondered if she'd dreamed the entire episode. She started to turn back again but knew she had to find out what was happening to her. Catalin had said that he could help. She then noticed a small green shoot at the very spot where she'd shoved the small seed into the ground. She bent to touch it. Remarkable, she thought.

She waited at the ruins, where she last saw Catalin, and called. Standing alone in the dark, she was afraid she would run into Velinar again. Just as she was about to leave, someone came walking out of the darkness. She jumped, but then saw that it was Catalin.

"I'd been waiting and had given up," he said.

"Where's the gazebo? The dark is frightening."

"The apparition was Velinar's doing. I don't have the strength she can muster even when close to death. I can't constellate the gazebo. All I can generate is the faint glow of my presence."

"I've started changing. I want to know what that woman did to me. Who is she?"

Catalin hesitated, as if sifting what he could tell her from what he shouldn't. "Velinareina, Velinar we call her, is still very ill."

That response made Alex angry. "Do I now have some terminal affliction?"

Catalin shook his head no. "She is in fact a divine being. She had come to Earth, taken on mortal form, to accomplish a task, but while here, a vampire bit her. As an immortal, she needed the blood of a mortal to regain the strength to return."

"What are you talking about? A divine being? Get serious."

"I'm just an apparition myself. Try to touch me, if you don't believe me."

Alex did more than that. She tried to slap him, and then tried to hit him in the chest with her fist. But her hand and fist just passed through him.

"You don't have to be so belligerent," he said. "I'm not your enemy."

"But you let that creature attack me."

"Yes. And unfortunately, in biting you, she has in fact infected you."

"So I'm now a vampire, and that's why I've been acting and feeling strange?"

"No. Well... yes. But it isn't a normal vampire infection. Obviously, you'll take on some shades of vampirism, but they should not be serious, and they will pass. You didn't suck her blood."

"If what I'm now experiencing is only a shade, the full monty must be something to talk about."

"Monty? Not familiar with that."

"No flicks where you come from?" He was even more hopeless than she. "Full experience."

"Yes, I'm afraid it is. But you could never become one from being bitten by Velinar."

"Is Velinar some sort of disgusting daemon?"

"No," said Catalin. "She was here on a mission. She got bit by a vampire, and became sort of a vampire herself."

"Sort of a vampire? Can't you do better than that?"

"Well, yes, a vampire. She was then trapped here on Earth. She was too weak to cast off the mortal form and leave behind the earthly vampire she'd become. She had to feed to get the strength to become divine again. Even in divine form, a remnant of what happened to her will remain, the taint of vampirism, but at least she got back to Heaven, thanks to you. But she can never again take on mortal form."

"Who bit her?" Alex had gone into interrogation mode as she'd frequently seen her mother.

"I don't know that I should get into that. She'd resigned herself to die here on Earth, her soul forever condemned to the Great Void. You came along when she was on the verge of death and an emotional wreck. She feels bad about what she did, but she found you irresistible. She sent me to tell you this. She wishes she could have come herself. It would have been the right thing to do."

This guy is really good at sidestepping a question, she thought. She wondered if he was a lawyer in the Divine World. "How can I trust you about this? Who are you?"

At first, Catalin didn't seem to know how to answer, or perhaps his integrity had never been questioned. "I was her guardian while she was here," he said, finally. "I failed to protect her. I knew she'd come to Earth but didn't know the full extent of her mission. I would have never let her attempt such a dangerous task. She is the Great Velinar, one of the most magnificent divine souls, a wondrous being and the sweetest entity I've ever known. Now she has been forever crippled."

Sidestepping again. This guy was incorrigible. "She's great, sweet, but she made me a vampire."

"Stop that! I told you. You are not a vampire and neither is she, now, thanks to you. Since she is in her very essence an immortal, you will not become a vampire. You will take on some of the characteristics for a while, but will not become one." He halted and became unsure of himself.

"So my situation is temporary?"

"There is one way you could become a vampire, and only one. But this possibility, if I can even call it that, is so remote that I hate to mention it."

"Indulge me."

Catalin looked away, slumped in irritation, then turned back to her. "If you ever, yourself, kill someone by drinking their blood, then you will become a vampire. But that is not something you have to worry about because you won't have the craving."

"This still isn't right," she said. "This should not have happened to me. I've done nothing wrong."

"I realize that. Yet, it is what it is. I will help all I can. But I can't always be here for you either. You have to understand. Coming here is incredibly difficult and immensely dangerous. I can't take on corporeal form as did Velinar. Even an apparition is a stretch for me. I will meet with you once more, if you should need me. But use me sparingly. My ability to take on this limited, visual form has already weakened me."

Before Alex could let him go, she had another question. "Why did you call me Marie? Last night, when you first saw me."

"I'm a caretaker of this entire region of Earth, the Carpathian Mountains. I've been doing this since the mountains formed. I'm not the caretaker of the people but the mountains themselves, its wildlife and foliage. All that nature provides. I watched Queen Marie throughout her life. She was one of my favorite mortals. It was a shock to see someone who favors her so."

"I'm a descendent of hers, at least that's what my grandmother told me."

"That would explain it. But you're not one of the royalty?"

"No. I'm descended from a string of illegitimate royal children."

"Really? This might change things. You may have a destiny. I'll have to check into this. We should meet again. It will be the last time."

"You're beginning to sound like my grandmother. I'm not interested in a destiny. I'm concerned about how I've changed since Velinar bit me. It's disgusting. I think I'm bisexual. I'm horny as hell."

Catalin roared with laughter. "Don't worry. You'll be fine. "

"Seriously! I'm ill-equipped to handle these feelings. I've not been wondering about sex since I was five like most girls. This is an internal world I've never experienced. I don't recognize myself."

"Be patient. You'll recover. You'll be fine."

"I'll be fine? I'm already not fine."

"That's not vampirism but a property of the divine." He shook his head and smiled broadly. "I suppose you picked up a little of that from Velinar also. In the Divine World, we're all bisexual, or at least have a semblance of it. We take more liberties. Go easy on yourself," he said, still lighthearted. "It may take a while, but it'll wear off. Stay home. Being out at night makes it worse."

He walked away from her and disappeared into the darkness.

*

Once in bed, Alex couldn't get to sleep. She wondered if Oxford offered separate housing for vampires. Then, this second encounter with Catalin weighed heavily. When she'd first seen him coming toward her, it was as if he just appeared out of nothing. No, that's not quite it, she thought. His presence was as if she'd just remembered that he was already there, as if he'd always been there. When he disappeared, it was as if she lost the memory of his presence, as if she forgot how to remember he was still there. Are these spirits around us all the time, but we just can't remember that we see them? she wondered.

In the middle of the night, Alex dreamed that angels fluttered around her like butterflies about a flower. They seemed to be trying to tell her something, something crucial. Although she could see them vividly in her dream, she could not hear them. Their presence was like a video clip with the audio muted. They urgently needed to tell her something; just what, she couldn't hear.

I'll be fine? she said to herself while trying to get back to sleep. Oh yes, I'll be just fine.

8

Father Zosimos

The next morning, Alex needed to talk to her grandmother. She was not feeling right, and it was not just one thing but several. She liked sunlight even less than the day before, and she still hadn't started her period. She wondered if female vampires had periods. Oh yes, she wasn't a vampire. Not quite, anyway.

Alex got out of bed late, walked through the house and found that her grandmother wasn't home. She anguished over what had happened with Jaklin and Mikhail. She obsessed over seeing them again, lots of lewd fantasies, and that worried her, a lot. The thought of them all three being royalty, sort of, was a powerful aphrodisiac.

When her grandmother finally returned from the market with seedlings for the garden, Alex cornered her. "I'm not feeling well," she told her. "And I'm getting scared."

"What's the matter, child? What would bother you so?"

"I'm ashamed that I didn't tell the complete truth about what happened two nights ago, when I saw that man in the forest."

"I thought so. Tell me everything. I'll do whatever I can to make it right."

Alex pulled the curtains, and they sat facing each other on the sofa.

"To begin with, it wasn't just a man. I saw a woman on the ground by the graveyard. I thought she was dead, but when I tried to roll her over, she grabbed me. Oh, Bunică! How can I say this? She bit me on the neck. I think I've become a vampire."

"Nonsense, girl. Don't let me hear you say that again. So you made up the man?"

"Oh no! He was there too. He did think I looked like Queen Marie. I went again last night because he said he could help me. He says I'll be okay. But I don't trust him. What have I gotten myself into?"

"Don't know, child. But I know someone who can help. A local priest."

"Oh no, Bunică. I couldn't look a priest in the eyes."

"Don't worry. I won't let him scold you." With that, she left.

Alex set on the sofa with her head in her hands. She became drowsy and thought that now she seemed to want to sleep more in daytime than night. She fidgeted and paced the floor to keep awake. She couldn't stand waiting for the priest. Soon she heard a car in the driveway and muffled voices and footsteps outside the front door. They entered, the priest in his black cassock and cylindrical flat hat, and carrying a small wooden box. He had a full gray beard. She heard him call her grandmother by her given name, Margareta. Alex's grandmother hung back and the priest introduced himself.

"I'm Father Zosimos," he said. "Tell your problem, and I'll provide a prayer to remedy the situation, hopefully."

Her grandmother sat with him on the sofa, and Alex sat in a chair opposite. The priest held his wooden box in his lap. Alex told him what happened to her in the forest, the woman biting her. She also told him of her second meeting with Catalin. She closed with, "He said she was a very good person, in spite of what she'd done."

"Yes," said Father Zosimos, shaking his head no. "A good apparition who bites people on the neck and sucks their blood? I don't think so."

"Yes, that's very much the point," she said. "He said that Velinar was not an angel."

"You mean, not a very nice person?"

"No. I had asked him if she were an angel," and then her voice got quiet, and she said slowly, almost a whisper. "He said she was a divine being who'd taken on mortal form. She was on a mission to..."

Zosimos held up a hand to stop her. "Divine beings..." he shook his head again. "Your neck. Let me see."

She pulled her hair back and leaned her head to the side.

He pursed his lips. "Nothing."

Alex looked at her grandmother. "He'll never believe me. I'm not sure I do myself."

"Did you suck this woman's blood?" the priest asked.

"No!" said Alex, offended. "Of course not. She stank."

"I know these evil beings do exist," he said. "A few are right here in Sinaia. One must take care, but generally they stay off to themselves and don't bother the population."

"Then that concerns me even more," Alex said. "I've been bitten."

"Vampires generally come from Royalty. Something about interbreeding weakening royal bloodlines. Let me see your teeth."

This was the first Alex realized that her mouth had felt a little different. Opening it for this priest to look inside felt like a violation of her person.

"Wider," said Zosimos, pushing back her lips to see her gums. "Hmmm. Canines not extended. Although they do have a curious length and are rather sharp."

Alex closed her mouth and shrunk back from him.

"Look," said the priest. "The crucial issue, whether I believe you or not, is: Are you a vampire? That's easy to determine, young lady." With that he pushed the box from his lap to his knees. "Close your eyes."

Against her better judgment, she obeyed. She heard him rustling about.

"Now open them," he said.

Alex jerked her head back. The priest had open the box and was holding it close to her face. It was filled with crosses.

"Not good," the priest said. "Do they frighten you?"

"No," she said slowly. "You startled me."

"Yes. Well, we'll see about that," he said. "Touch them, please. Pick up one."

She admitted to herself — but would never have told him — that she didn't like the looks of them much, and she was afraid of what would happen when she touched them. But slowly, she put her hand into the box. Her fingers tingled, and the sensation ran up her arm to her elbow. She said nothing of this, but she did pick up a cross, although it wasn't very pleasant.

"Well then," said the priest. "This is a good sign. Your grandmother tells me that you don't wear a cross. Why is this, girl? Do you not believe in our Lord?"

"Well, yes, I do, Father. I've just never felt the need for an ostentatious display of faith."

He snorted. "Perhaps you do now," he suggested. "Select one you like, and I'll let you have it free. It's just that you must promise to wear it."

"Oh," Alex said, "I'd love to have one." If it would ward off the Forces of Darkness she'd gladly wear it. She looked through the box, pushed them around with her fingers. They were all gold and silver, some inlaid with jewels. These seemed pretentious, inappropriate. Besides, she didn't think she could take the tingling. Then she noticed one with diamonds. "Wow!" she said. "That one is beautiful."

"Yes," he said. "Just as I expected. The most expensive the Church has."

"Well," Alex admitted, "although it is beautiful, I'm still not interested in wearing it. I don't see anything I really like. None seem as though they would belong to me, if I claimed one."

Her grandmother finally spoke up. "Please, child. You must select one."

"Ah," she said. "What's this?" She held up a rather small wooden cross. It looked old and worn. "I'm in love."

"I'd meant to discard that one," he said, leaning back and looking out the window. "I would have, except for the legend."

"What legend?"

"Well, one can't put any confidence in such things, particularly one that came to us through an old Rom. He wasn't even a believer."

"A Gypsy? Please, tell me anyway," said Alex. "I'd like to know."

"So the story goes," he said, looking up at her, a little embarrassed, and then back at the cross, "St. John at the Crucifixion broke off a piece of Christ's cross and carried it always. He took it with him during his exile on Patmos where he wrote Revelation, and later at Ephesus, where he died. From John, the cross was supposedly passed from priest to priest and worn during the Second World War, where it came into the hands of a homeless Rom who was given it by a dying priest." Father Zosimos stopped his story there. "Like I said, not much to recommend it, coming from a Rom. Yet, I've kept the aged cross out of respect to the dying priest who gave it to him, so the Rom said. I had to pay him a leu for it. But that was forty years ago. Little to give a young girl to carry with her the rest of her life."

"Oh, but I disagree!" said Alex. "I find it immensely satisfying." And she was really, quite unaccountably, thrilled. That old rugged cross meant something to her.

"You can't be serious," said the priest. "It's a trivial keepsake. Not much of a devotional relic. It has no polish. I like those that radiate with internal light, enlightenment."

"Was Christ's cross not of wood?" Alex replied.

"Yes, yes, yes. Have it your way. At least you've selected one, and the rest of these have proven that you're not a vampire. A good days work for an old priest," he said, still obviously not satisfied with her.

"Thank you," Alex said. "And I promise to wear it always. It has warmed to my hand already."

"Here. Let's do this properly," he said, taking it from her. He crossed himself first and then her, both times saying, "In the Name of the Father, the Son, and the Holy Spirit." He then placed the chain over her head and let it fall around her neck. "If it comes apart on you, call on me for another."

"Christ's cross would never fail the wearer, now would it, Father?"

Finally, he smiled at her. "And now that the old priest has received his catechism from the child, he shall withdraw to his solitary chamber."

Alex glanced at her grandmother, saw her scowl.

"I'm sorry, Father," Alex said. "I'm just pleased with your gift."

"Then so am I," he replied with complete conviction. "And may it serve you well."

Her grandmother walked the priest to the door, and they

whispered in private for longer than Alex would have expected. She heard him call her "Marg" with marked familiarity.

When he was gone, Alex went to her bedroom to look at the cross all on her own. It was simple and carved from a single piece of wood with great care. She teared up at that. The wood was old beyond imagining. "And the legend is that it was carved from Christ's own cross," she said aloud. Alex couldn't imagine that anything would offer her more protection from a vampire. Perhaps it'll also cure this dreadful passion I have for Jaklin and Mikhail.

That night when she slept, she again dreamed of being lost in a dark place where others milled about beside her. She held her cross close, and the dreams dissolved.

9

An Unfortunate Encounter

The next evening, Alex put on a long skirt and went out wearing the cross inside her blouse. She thought to herself, If these tits don't quit growing, they'll become a nuisance. She wanted to find her two friends, Jaklin and Mikhail. She couldn't suppress thoughts of smooching with them. Perhaps if she could just see them again, her recollection would loosen it's power over her. Memory does embellish the spell, she thought. And then there was the influence of the cross. She recalled that Catalin had advised her to stay home at night, but now she imagined that it would protect her from all harm.

Alex was again surprised to learn that she'd become fond of the dark and felt that it was her friend. She enjoyed its subdued hues and hidden secrets. She even noticed a sense of being a predator and relished the act of seeing but not being seen. She hid in the shadows, moved covertly among the bushes, lurked at the edge of visibility. She hid behind trees in Dimitrie Ghica Park and spied on young lovers practicing dry sex in the shadows. She was a shade, shifting among misty nocturnal shapes.

Her heightened senses caught a foreign scent wafting among that of pine needles and humus, the faint body odor of a man. She played with this smell, letting it roll around in her nostrils as something new, exotic. She thought it came from someone in front of her, but the breeze had subtly shifted. She heard a shuffling behind her, and started to turn, but quite suddenly, he was upon her. The fear that flashed inside her was not panic. Although he was a large man, she knew she could break free, or at least she thought she could.

She didn't cry out, but he was bigger, much bigger, and stronger, much stronger, than she'd first thought. One arm, he planted around her waist and the other hand he held firmly over her mouth and nose. Not only could she not scream, she could not breathe. He made no attempt to keep her upright but fell on her, taking her breath. He then rolled her over and spread her legs, pushed up her skirt and ripped her panties. He was in sweatpants and had them down in an instant, but as he did so, Alex broke free. She was also stronger than either of them realized, but he had her by the ankle and dragged her back to him. With the other foot, she kicked him in the chest, and again rose to her feet, then faced her assailant front on and hit him with her fist square on the nose. He grabbed her again with a grip that was overpowering and shoved her up against a tree. Now, he was between her legs. His lips sought hers again, and Alex smelled blood from his nose. She'd broken it, and the taste was startling. Fresh human blood, something sexual about it. He mouthed her, found her lips, but she bit him, again drawing blood, until he pulled back. He cursed her, and finding her pelvis with his erect phallus, entered her.

The violation, splitting pain and blunt-force trauma became an explosion of hatred. He was hot and stank. As he pushed deeper, Alex exploded with rage. No longer was she the victim, and the taste of blood was the fuel that set her ablaze. She wrapped her legs around him, drew him even deeper inside her and tightened on him until he cried out. She clawed at him, ripped though his shirt and into his flesh, raking her fingernails into him.

She leaned back, took in the full view of him, his eyes wild with ecstasy, and then she drove her head into his neck, sunk her teeth into his flesh, and for the first time felt hot human blood gush into her mouth. He cried out again, not from having his pleasure, but from pain. He tried to push her away, but her legs and arms were locked around him, as if she'd grown to his body. Her teeth chewed for the juggler, found it, fondled it with her tongue. As she gnawed it in two, her tongue wrapped around it, and she sucked it loose, and like a large straw, she had access to the entire pool of fluid filling him. As his frightened heart pumped spurts into her mouth, so she sucked, gorging on his life as her pelvis beat on him, her sexual energy overflowing. He went limp. She didn't know if her eyes were open or closed, but the world exploded with light, her rapture driven into a convulsion of spasms by the man's death. The smell of his blood, the taste like cinnamon in spasmodic gulps, the feel of trembling flesh as his heart began to fail. His death, his life leaving his body, flowed into her, fueling her nonstop ecstasy.

She sucked him as her fingernails scraped against his rib bones. Her fingers dug deep, beneath his rip cage, and lacerated his liver. More, she needed more blood. All of it. Any drop that might be left in his corpse. He slumped to the ground and fell backward into pine needles, but she was still on top of him, still gnawing his carcass. She bit the other side of his neck, searching for more blood, but his body was empty, drained. She broke open his ribcage with a crack and licked the lungs, broke the heart loose, squeezed it to pump the last crimson fluid into her mouth. The light, burning in her eyes like the midsummer sun, started to fade. Her assailant was now a lifeless hunk of worthless flesh, disgusting, nasty, bloodless.

Alex rose up from him on all fours, staring off into the darkness between trees. A thought came to her instantly, without malice but with need, hunger. Perhaps another one, another body full of blood, a sack of ichorous fluid. She rose up to view her surroundings, now the determined predator, the animal with only carnal needs, the merged feelings of lust and gluttony united into one powerful compulsion.

She saw a man walk into the darkness of the trees, her darkness, her forest. He stopped and urinated on a tree, like a dog, she thought, as she moved through the forest toward him. His pants were already open, and she wanted him, wanted to plant her teeth in his neck. Like a large cat, she moved in behind him, and just as he finished relieving himself, she was on him. He'd turned toward her, just as her body collided with his, and she had him on the ground. This man was smaller, not erect. She wanted him, needed him, but he filled with terror, the sharp, sweaty scent of panic. She was much stronger, and although he tried to push her off, she clung to him. She sunk her teeth into his neck, and again the flow of fresh blood gushed into her mouth, down her throat. Never had she savored such a rich beverage.

"Please, don't kill me," he whispered. "I have kids."

Alex was in a euphoric, murderous rage and couldn't come down, but knew this was wrong. A spark of humanity returned, just the faintest glimmer of compassion. She stopped, and the man broke free, rolled away and ran like a rabbit from her, jumped the iron-barred fence and fell into the street.

Alex woke from her homicidal frenzy feeling vulnerable, hunted. She leapt from the ground, fled farther up the mountainside and into the forest, deeper into darkness, her mind still a whirr, not of murderous thoughts, but for the taste of blood. She ran among the trees.

She'd killed a man, and almost killed another.

Her stomach was distended from gorging on the two men, but her body demanded more, her flesh scintillating, tingling, sparkling with expectation. She ran deeper into the forest, moonlight creating dim patches that guided her. She needed another kill, anyone, anything. Her heart raced, pounded her chest. Her breaths were deep, strong and rapid. She licked the blood off her arms, hands. Delicious corpuscular blood. Her front was covered with it. She sucked her blouse, pulling the last drops from it.

She rousted a deer from the bushes, and chased it up the hill. It bounded and zigzagged, but she was faster, quicker. She grabbed it by the antlers, and bulldozed it to the ground. She clamped her mouth to its neck like a mountain lion, searching for the jugular. Blood gushed into her mouth, awful blood, animal blood. She spat it out, and turned loose of the trembling animal. The stag was instantly on its feet again and disappeared into the forest. She needed a human. Someone fresh.

Her pupils dilated far beyond normal. The moon went behind a cloud, yet she could still see in complete darkness. She was an owl, bird of the night, felt as though she could fly. She saw two people walking together up the mountainside. This calmed her, but still the desire for blood was overwhelming, so she slid from tree to tree following them. They looked different, something strange about them, the graceful elegance of their gait like that of the caped figure she'd seen after meeting Jaklin and Mikhail. And then she realized — they were vampires. A sickening feeling came over her. She almost vomited but looked away. She needed more blood, but not used blood from a vampire. That'd be like drinking urine. She needed a fresh human.

Stinking vampires. Bloodsuckers. But that's me. I'm a vampire. My cross. She felt for it. Why does it not burn me? How could this be? Did the cross not work? Was the priest right? Was it, after all, not a true cross?

Alex followed the vampires up the mountainside. She saw them disappear into the side of the cliff, as if they'd walked through solid granite. She walked to the spot where they'd disappeared and found a depression behind bushes, but no cave entrance.

She heard rock grating against rock. The depression moved. Someone was coming out. She backed away. But some form of courage told her she could handle this vampire. As he came in her direction, she hid behind a tree, and when he got close, Alex stepped out into his path. At first he was surprised but then came for her. She heard him sniff the air. She reeked of blood. Why had he not recognized her as a vampire? Alex pulled her cross from within her blouse and held it before him. He humped over in pain, hissed and retreated. She went toward him. He turned and fled down the mountainside.

Alex walked what was a much longer distance to her grandmother's home than she'd thought. Had she really run that far up the mountain? She didn't go inside. Instead, she went around back and lingered in the shadows cast by moonlight. She went to the outdoor hearth and stripped off her clothes, struck flame to them and watched them burn. The sharp smell of leather singed her nostrils. She worked over them, ensuring all were ashes. She gathered branches and sticks to add to the fire and turned the coals until her clothes, bra, socks and shoes were gone. Just the metal shoestring eyes remained. She doused the coals with water.

Though nude except for her cross and chain, she felt no chill. The cold Alex did feel ran much deeper and was that of the soul. She had killed a man and almost killed another. Her life was forever marked. She had no intention of turning herself in to the police. He had raped her. Her primary concern was what Catalin had told her. He had said, "If you ever kill anyone by sucking their blood, you will become a vampire." She was not supposed to have had the craving. Yet at the first scent of it on the rapist, she went crazy. It was the violation, pain and rage that had brought out the animal in her. No, not the animal, the vampire.

She found the garden hose, turned on the faucet, and washed herself from head to foot with cold water. Even her hair. All the blood had to come off. She no longer felt a craving, but she did feel different. Her relationship with the world had changed. She was immortal. How could that be? How could one live forever? But now she would have to feed off humans. Could she bring herself to do that, again? How strong would the craving have to be before she would violate another human being? If she did, would they become a vampire? The man who got away from her tonight, would he now be a vampire? An immortal being? And the man she killed, would he rise from the grave?

All the history of the world, the Earth, now seemed to stretch out before her. She was a cosmic creature. She'd live through centuries of human history, as had Catalin. Perhaps millennia. But he was a divine creature of the spirit world. She was still a being of Earth. What would her life be like? What did it mean to be a vampire?

Before she'd been friendless, or at least felt as though she were, but now, she was utterly alone. She needed her mother. She wanted to be held as if she were a child. She needed her father. Although this was something he certainly couldn't fix. And what would Gavril and Sonya think? They'd been her surrogate parents. She thought of Jaklin and Mikhail, two people she hardly knew, but now needed, craved, and felt less guilt over lusting after them. She felt afloat in the ocean, a thousand miles of water to the nearest shore. Would anyone care for her if they knew what she had become?

Something shifted in the darkness at the edge of the forest in the direction of the gazebo. A black shape. Was it just a moon shadow? It moved toward her. A man, the dark shape of a man. She'd seen him before. That strange caped figure, after she met Jaklin and Mikhail. She turned to run into the house, but something stronger than fear impelled her to look back. Her hand immediately went to her cross. She raised it until it came between her and the dark figure.

He stopped, folded his hands and blood dripped from them. His thin voice said, "You need me. Come, when you're ready," just a gracile line of words strung along a whisper. "I thought I'd failed." He grabbed his side and bent over.

The voice momentarily froze her. Then Alex quickly walked to the backdoor, turned to see him limp away. Something she'd done seemed to cripple him. She opened the door, stepped inside, and bolted it. She stood before the door listening, but could hear nothing.

She walked upstairs to the bathroom, ran the tub full. Remembering how Father Zosimos had examined her, she looked at her face in the mirror, pulled up her lips to expose her gums. Nothing unusual. Then she bared her teeth and made a threatening face. She jumped back from the mirror. This was not good.

As she soaked in the tub, staring blindly into the darkness, it suddenly came to her. She would never have her own children. It felt like a body blow that took her breath. She would never hold her own children in her arms, watch them grown into adults. She could never right the wrongs that had been her lot. This type of thing is supposed to happen in Braşov where legend said that Dracula, Vlad the Impaler actually, had his castle, where Gavril now lives, not in Sinaia.

She stepped dripping out of the tub, dried off, and walked into her bedroom. She slipped between the covers and slept the sleep of the dead. Except that she did dream. She dreamt of a magnificent city among the heavens. She heard the flutter of angel wings.

10

Bounty Hunter

Next morning Alex woke remarkably refreshed, and with considerable less guilt over the murder than she'd imagined. Sunlight bothered her more than yesterday but still, it was tolerable. Local television was a continuous stream of reports concerning a murdered man found by two lovers inside Dimitrie Ghica Park. The man appeared to have been mauled by a large animal, perhaps a bear. Another man, also attacked, claimed it wasn't an animal, but a woman, a wild vampire woman. Snickers and guffaws ensued.

Over breakfast, Alex watched the news with her grandmother, who said, "Good. The bastard's in the ground. Now, people will sleep easier."

The police had confirmed that the dead man was the rapist. The man's widow was also on TV, and she had somewhat of a different opinion. Through tears, she said, "He was a wonderful husband. A big woolly bear, gentle, sensitive. Couldn't have been the rapist."

Alex made an excuse to her grandmother, left the house and walked downtown. Just off the main street, she noticed a group of people and went to investigate. She saw that the police had cordoned off an area just inside the trees. Alex walked up to a man and asked what was going on.

"Murder," he said.

"Is it the man on TV?"

"Killed by an animal. Or, if you're the sensational type, a vampire." He laughed.

Alex liked this guy's sense of humor. "Are you the sensational type?"

"I'll wait until he's buried. If he rises again..."

"Is that the lore? If killed by a vampire, you become one and live forever?"

"Well... it's not quite that easy. Once bitten, you have to suck the vampire's blood before you can turn. Not something they're anxious to let just anyone do. Vampires value their lofted state and consider themselves special, above mortals."

"They see it as a privilege?"

"Exactly. Both the vampire and the victim have to consent. Otherwise," he shook his head, "it's a no-go."

"That's a comforting thought. They won't spread very fast."

"Yes, but unfortunately lately we've heard reports, not yet verified, that some vampires can turn an individual just by biting them, and the transformation is quick. Really scary, if true."

"Apparently, you believe all this vampire nonsense."

"Young lady," he said, eyeing her from head to toe, "I am Stefan Stanescu, vampire hunter extraordinaire!" Stefan was taller than anyone she'd ever known. He had dirty blond hair and a ruddy complexion overrun with freckles.

"Now that sounds sensational." She couldn't repress a laugh. "They should have had you on TV this morning." She was amazed at her own audacity, talking to a man about her own crime without a shred of nervousness. He would put her in the ground if he knew.

He laughed too. "I'm not big on publicity."

"The deceased was the rapist?"

"Petru Balc. Married son of a Bucharest physician. He'd been under surveillance for a month, but eluded police last night, or perhaps they'd have caught his assailant. Apparently, he raped her too, without knowing she was a vampire."

"And paid the ultimate price."

"That's the vampire's other victim over there," he said, pointing toward an older man gesticulating at two police officers. His neck was bandaged.

Alex stepped back to put Stefan between the man and her. "And he'll be a vampire too, if this new theory pans out?"

"Radu Cuza. He's hysterical over the thought. Won't quit asking questions about vampires. He has a wife and four kids, two boys and two girls. I think he's safe. If he had anything to worry about, he'd have turned by now."

Alex fell silent. What if she hadn't quit when she did? Orphaned kids and a widow? She must talk to Catalin again.

Stefan looked at her suspiciously. "I don't remember seeing you before. From around here?"

"Bucharest. Visiting my grandmother. Do you hunt vampires on your own?"

"I work for the Monastery. I'm a bounty hunter, so called by some," he said scratching a freckled forearm.

"Oh! Father Zosimos?" Immediately, Alex knew she'd made a mistake.

"You know him?"

"Yes. Well... know of him. My grandmother knows him."

"What are you hiding behind that blush?" Stefan asked.

She look away and wouldn't answer.

"So you're back to Bucharest this fall?"

"No, I'm off to Oxford. More intellectual punishment."

"Really..."

But before Stefan could respond, someone tugged on Alex's sleeve, and she turned to see Jaklin and Mikhail.

"Hi, Missy," said Jaklin, her face beaming. "I've been calling you. Don't you recognize your own name?"

Alex was immensely glad to see her two friends. Jaklin's fake sour face made her feel warm inside. Mikhail was striking in his black leather jacket, short-cropped beard and glasses. "I'm sorry I left so suddenly the other night. I wasn't myself." She'd thought that if she saw them in daylight it would lessen the intrigue and her attraction. Not a chance.

"I understand," said Mikhail. "We were freaked out by our

behavior too."

Alex took both their hands, held them longer than she should. She was glad they broke up her conversation with Stefan. She walked off with her arms around the two of them. She called back to Stefan, "Good luck catching your vampire."

"At least I know it wasn't you. You're out in daylight, and you wear a cross. On the other hand," he said, "the murderer always returns to the scene of the crime."

Alex walked with Jaklin and Mikhail away from the crowd, and they stood near a large oak looking at each other.

"What's that about a vampire?" asked Jaklin.

"One man killed and another injured," Alex answered. "Stefan thinks it was a vampire, but then he's a vampire hunter, so he would."

"He's kidding, right?" said Mikhail. "Vampires? That's just Bram Stoker fiction. All this goth craze is fun but nonsense."

"Not sure myself." Although it was only her second time seeing them, they still seemed like old friends, and more adorable than before. "What is it about you two?" she asked. "I'm not like this with anyone."

"We've been talking about you too, about the three of us, together," said Mikhail, he looked down bashfully, wouldn't meet her eyes.

"I know," said Alex. "I'm beginning to realize that something has happened to me, and you two seem to have been drawn into it."

"What happened?" asked Jaklin. "You've brought Mikhail and me closer together too." She glanced at Mikhail and then back at Alex. "We can't quit thinking and talking about you. It's as if we're distant cousins."

"Perhaps not even that distant," added Mikhail.

"Stranger things have happened to me lately," said Alex. "Perhaps I can tell you more tomorrow. I'll be busy this afternoon and tonight."

"So will I," said Jaklin. "We have a conference, and I have to work three to midnight, but let's get together tomorrow evening. Know a place?"

"Restaurant Bucegi," suggested Alex. "Just down the street, past the traffic circle. We'll try to figure out what's happening to us over pizza."

"It's just good old physical attraction," said Mikhail with an infectious smile.

"Might be. Could be bigger than you realize," said Alex. "I can't tell you everything I suspect now. Perhaps I can tell you more tomorrow night."

She kissed Jaklin on the cheek, smiled at Mikhail, and walked away. She had to get back to her grandmother.

11

The Gazebo

Alex found her grandmother in the garden. Nights were still cold, but the sun warmed the ground enough during the day to plant seedlings. Her grandmother was planning a large garden with tomatoes, cucumbers, artichokes, squash, carrots, beats, turnips, onions, radishes, and bell peppers. Alex took a deep breath. Who's going to eat all this? she wondered, as she eagerly pitched in. Sunlight seemed to be bothering her less this afternoon. While they covered the roots of the tiny plants, Alex pumped her grandmother for more information about the gazebo.

"Who built the gazebo? What happened to it?"

Her grandmother fell silent and continued working. She didn't answer for a long time and when she did, her voice was soft and far off. "The gazebo was built at the direction of Queen Marie herself. She used to take my mother there when she'd come visit. They'd spend a little time alone together. Years later, she came to visit me."

Her grandmother told Alex that the gazebo had been a nonagon, a nine-sided, airy structure open in all directions. At each of its nine corners, thin vertical columns supported the roof. Inside stood short stone benches, five sections circling a pentagonal stone table.

"But why there, next to the family graveyard?"

"I believe partially for privacy. After my mother was no longer with us and I was a little older, Queen Marie wanted just the two of us together when she came on her rare visits. But she was a spiritual woman, and used to tell me that the entire human race was one big family. She said that all religions worshiped but one god. I sensed something going on beneath the surface of our conversations, which caused me to question my entire upbringing. Something was wrong, and it had to do with my mother."

"Do you know anything about the Cantacuzene family of Sinaia? I've heard that they have a connection to the Monastery."

"Why sure, child. Prince Mihail Cantacuzino founded the Monastery after a pilgrimage to Mount Sinai in the Holy Land. The man Queen Marie had an affair with was Zizi Cantacuzene, a descendent of the prince. Zizi is mentioned in the biography I gave you. He was my biological grandfather. It's an ancient family originating in Smyrna, Greece, which is now a part of Turkey. You and I both have Cantacuzene blood flowing in our veins." She seemed to want to ask a question but fell silent.

"How old were you when your mother died?" Alex had a faint memory of the story of her grandmother's mother. No one talked much about her. She'd been raised by another family, several families, actually. She'd been passed from one to another.

"That's one of the mysteries we must discuss while you're here."

"A mystery? How did she die?"

"That's just it, you see. She didn't. She disappeared."

"They never found her? Did the police look?"

"I've not been able to learn the full story myself. I was still a child and hardly even remember my mother. The Cantacuzenes not only wouldn't discuss her, they wouldn't have anything to do with me after she disappeared. Queen Marie did visit, not too often, but as much as she could. Whenever she was at Peleş Castle, she'd come down here once a week. She didn't regret her little extra-marital indiscretions. When she died, I was eight. She came to Peleş to die, so she could see me one last time. She called the gazebo her sacred space. She was a great believer in God, but didn't much care for Romanian Orthodoxy. Later in life, she embraced the Baha'i faith, which believes in the spiritual unity of all religions and mankind. That's why she had the gazebo built as a nonagon, which is a symbol of the Baha'i."

"What happened to it?" asked Alex. "A structure like that should have lasted a long time."

"And it would have, if it hadn't been for the Communists after the Second World War. The follower of Baha'i believes in the worth of the individual, which is not a Communist ideal. They tore it down."

Alex walked out of the garden and to the hearth where she'd burned her blood-soaked clothing, scooped the black ashes into a bucket, then returned, and while sprinkling them along a row of tomatoes, she again addressed her questions to her grandmother.

"Have you considered rebuilding it?"

"Many times. The Monastery is against it."

"Father Zosimos?"

"He's a good man, but not tolerant of other religions, even one that accepts his."

"Why not do it anyway?" Alex asked, then wished she hadn't.

Her grandmother didn't answer.

*

Late that afternoon, they came in from working in the garden, bathed, ate dinner, and sat before the fire. Her grandmother loved to brush Alex's hair, and Alex had mountains of it, a great mass of golden hair, of which her grandmother was tremendously proud. Nălucă came to sit in Alex's lap and purr.

"I've never seen it so radiant," her grandmother said, running the brush from her scalp down to the end of her flowing mane below her shoulders. "What a glorious gift."

Alex loved a fire, but sundown brought apprehension, not from fear of the dark but because of her attraction to it. She felt a wildness growing inside.

Her grandmother again broke the silence. "I have some things in the attic I need to show you. Something strange has gone on up there in years past. Your grandfather and I could never figure it out. It's always been another of our big family secrets. Let's wait while. I can't face this all at once."

While her grandmother brushed her hair, Alex thought of Jaklin, her mounds of chocolate hair, and Mikhail's small beard and short black hair, the one curl that fell onto his forehead.

Alex asked her grandmother, "Do I seem different? Have I changed?"

"I must say, you do seem more yourself, more an extrovert. You are not the lost little girl I've known you to be in the past."

"That's me. I know who I am now, and it's frightening. It happened all at once."

"Don't worry about growing up. That's a good thing."

"I made some friends a couple of nights ago, Bunică. They make me so happy when I'm with them."

"My one concern when you stay with me has always been your solitude. How happy it makes me to know that you've found friends here. You're a grown woman. Have fun with them. Youth is such a fleeting state."

"They are also descendants of the Cantacuzene family. We're distant cousins."

"As is half of Romania, or so it seems. But that's wonderful. You'll have to bring them to meet me. Queen Marie once told my mother that we should be glad to not be a recognized part of the royal family. 'Your life will be your own,' she said. 'What a treasure!' Take her advice, Alexandra. Enjoy life, dear girl. Enjoy your friends in whatever way you choose. Just live it with passion and without regret."

They didn't speak for a while, the crackle of fire the only sound in the room other than the whisper of the brush through Alex's hair. She wondered what her grandmother would think of her friends if she knew they weren't Romanian, one a Russian and the other a Bulgarian.

"We can think about rebuilding the gazebo," her grandmother said, quietly. "I've been missing it lately myself."

12

Catalin: The Cross

That evening, Alex walked out the backdoor. Her wounds from the rapist had already healed. She wasn't even sore, but still, she wanted to talk to Catalin. She blamed him. If he'd looked after Velinar as he should, none of this would have happened. He'd said so himself.

Her eyes rapidly adjusted to the night. She could feel something new in the air, something strange and wonderful. She coveted the darkness, and loved the points of light in the distance, the brightness that pricked the night. She seemed at one with nature and felt a cosmic connection, sensed continent grind against continent pushing the Carpathians ever higher. She felt Earth turn on its axis.

She reached the clearing and the ruins of the ancient gazebo, all shrouded in darkness. The object she noticed first was the tree shoot from her seed. It had already grown into a small but sturdy sapling. How could that be? she wondered. It's been but a couple of days.

She stepped onto the foundation, but saw only darkness. Catalin was nowhere in sight. She waited, staring off into the surrounding gloom. She noticed that she cast a faint shadow and hearing something behind her, she flinched, and turned to see Catalin standing facing her.

"Sorry I frightened you," he said. "I'd given up on you coming, again." His form did glow a little in the deep darkness.

"You should be more careful."

"I've come to tell you more about your 'condition'," he said. "Velinar is sure you'll gradually return to the way you were. She..." He stopped. "What's wrong with you? Something has changed." He'd become course, agitated. He backed away. "What in Heaven's Name! You're a vampire." His face showed great fear.

"Yes," Alex said. "What you said couldn't happened."

"What did you do? Stay back! Don't come near me. Even to an apparition, you can cause trauma."

"I was raped. I fought him with all the strength I could muster."

"The strength and ways of a vampire. Did you kill him?"

"I lost control." She sighed. Surely he'd understand.

Catalin showed no sympathy. "I can't help you. Not after this." He turned to go. "Being around you is too risky, especially for me."

"But this isn't my fault. It's yours and Velinar's."

He glanced back at her. "It isn't about fault. This is the way of the world, your world, and it's your problem."

"But please..."

Again he turned to go but stopped. He looked more closely at her. "What's that under your blouse?"

"Well, yes. The breast augmentation is great. Small consolation though."

"No, that around your neck. Please tell me it's a cross."

Alex pulled the chain from within her garment. "The priest offered several, but only this felt right."

"A vampire can't wear a cross," he said, his fear easing. "As a matter of fact, you shouldn't even be able to enter the gazebo. How can you be a vampire?"

"That's my question," she said. "I can wear one of gold or silver, but with a certain amount of pain. This old wooden one fits me perfectly."

"Where did you get it?"

"Father Zosimos. He said it wasn't worth much."

"I'm going to ask a question. Please answer truthfully and completely. Were you wearing the cross when you were raped? When you became a vampire?"

She thought a moment. "Well, yes. That was the first night I wore it."

"Was it around your neck?"

"I've already answered that. When I changed, I witnessed a flash of light that blinded me momentarily."

"I... this... can't be. I've heard rumors, hints concerning such a... transformation."

"Powerful but not very pleasant," she said.

"Yes. I can imagine, or really can't, I suppose."

"I became an animal. Lost all control and sense of who I am. 'Frightening' is the word. Terrifying."

"I've heard prophecies of a vampire, both gifted and tragic, a good vampire with special abilities. She will wield a divine force on Earth, a vampire who will wear Christ's cross. But this is only prophecy, even in the Divine World."

"Father Zosimos told of a legend about this cross, one he did not believe. The legend says that it is made from Christ's cross."

Catalin walked toward her with tears in his eyes. "Oh dear Lord in Heaven. Never have I thought that even in my divine lifetime would I meet such a person. I must tell you the full story of this cross, and also tell you who you are, for the world has been waiting millennia."

Alex looked at him with her nose all wrinkled. "Don't tell me..."

He smiled through tears. "No, you are not the Second Coming." And then he told her that he might be able to confirm the priest's legend, "...whether the wood really is from Christ's cross," he said. "Even in the Divine World, much is secret. I must go for now, but I'll return with the truth and perhaps a word or two about what this means."

But she couldn't let him go. "Just another question, please. I'm greatly troubled by my attachment to two friends I've just made. I'm attracted to them in ways I've never been before, not to anyone."

"Do they share this attraction?"

"Yes, very much. It's as if we've known each other for years. We're actually distant cousins from an legendary family, the Cantacuzenes."

"Yes, a family with an ancient and dark history. If what I believe to be true is, then you are all captives of a myth, one that lives human beings. In your world it's called the Eternal Return and repeats many times throughout human existence. Essentially, you have known them before." He shook his head, stopped. "This is nonsense. I must learn more of this mystery. Ordinarily, we wouldn't involve ourselves in your world, but what Velinar did places some responsibility on me. I can't determine or affect your fate, but perhaps I can help you understand it and who you've become."

"I'm still remembering what happened to me that night," she said. "After Velinar bit me, I collapsed here at the gazebo and dreamed of crossing a river on a ferry at night. Then a few nights later, after killing the man who raped me, I dreamed of being escorted around a marvelous little city with children playing in a park. The buildings were made of some exotic material, and the entire city was a cathedral."

Catalin smiled, and Alex again saw tears in his eyes. "The City of God," he said.

"An angel-like figure allowed me to see the City, but I couldn't stay."

"Enough! We mustn't go too far with this until I learn more."

Alex could tell that this last revelation was greatly troubling. A dark cloud seemed to descend over Catalin. She wished she'd kept her mouth shut.

"I must return to the Divine World for advice," he said. "Our next meeting will be the last. In the meantime, here is another warning. Heed it this time. You'll now be susceptible to evil. You'll know many things that you've not known before, and some will have to do with evil. Be suspicious. Trust no one."

And then he disappeared.

His sudden departure left Alex angry. She'd wanted to tell him about the dark shape she'd seen the night she was raped, the man who'd asked her to come to him.

13

The Vampire Den

The next morning, Alex was still worried at having told Stefan she knew Father Zosimos. If the two talked, Stefan could learn about her thinking she might be a vampire. But right now, she had something else on her mind. She wanted to find out what was going on in the vampire lair, what her "compatriots" were up to. She considered Catalin's warning, but just had to do this. She had her protection.

Alex put her cross in her handbag, told her grandmother she was going for a walk, and went into the mountains in the direction she believed she'd run after killing Radu Cuza. But that night, everything had been surreal, a black-and-white world with sinister implications behind every tree. Today, the forest seemed so friendly, the smell of pine needles assaulting her senses with affection. The dappled sunlight casting shadows on the soft duff made her want to lie down and be part of it. She heard children laughing in the distance and thought of the City of God. She felt at peace with herself, something she realized that she'd never before experienced.

Even being on this mountainside, as she'd been many times with her grandfather, seemed such a new experience that she revelled in its grandeur. She noticed the high-pitched drawn-out whistle of the wallcreeper as it flashed its crimson wings. She saw the virginal white hellebore and the bright-blue bellflower and smelled the sweet perfume of all the wildflowers lofting about her. The deep violet of the alpine primrose was so beautiful and touched her so deeply that it almost hurt. How could she be this sensitive now and so blasé before?

Just as she thought she'd lost her way ruminating over the flora and fauna, she recognized the stone cliff where the vampires had disappeared. It still took a while to locate the recess, and she was surprised at how well it was hidden within a deep depression. She'd had great courage hunting the lair, coming alone all the way up the mountain, yet, once she stood before the giant rock, she trembled. This was both an acknowledgement of her own condition, and an admission that she was one of them. She now realized that she would have to at least appear to accept them.

Alex tapped a couple of times on the rock surface, but nothing happened. She'd expected to hear the grinding of rock against rock, and the great stone move. She examined the stone cliff closer but could see no separation to indicate an opening. Perhaps she'd been mistaken about the location. She heard a noise behind her, but before she could turn around, two men grabbed her, one with his cold hand over her mouth, so she could not scream, which she would have because she was terrified. Her heart was about to beat out of her chest. They said nothing to her, but tapped a complex code on the stone surface, and instantly it began to move. The two men pushed her inside, into complete darkness, and the stone again groaned to. They released her.

The silence and darkness were more terrifying than being held, and although she actually heard nothing, she had the immediate impression of being in an enormous cavern. She smelled something akin to bat guano overlaid with a trace of death, rot.

One of the men spoke first and not to her. "She's the one who was here two nights ago. I told you she saw the entrance. No telling who she's told."

A deep-throated female voice responded. "Has she been turned, or is she one of them?"

"She's definitely human, Cosmina," he said. "Warm as baked bread fresh from the oven. And besides, the sunlight thing. She was walking on the mountainside."

"Why did you come here?" said Cosmina, angrily. "Speak up, girl.

Who are you?"

Alex as aghast at how unprepared she was, and decided to play it straight. "I believe the gentleman is mistaken," she said, to quiet snickers. "I am a vampire. I've killed a man."

"Here in Sinaia, two nights ago?"

"Yes, and almost killed another."

"And caused more trouble for us than you can imagine," the other man said.

Alex's eyes had adjusted to the point where she could make out faint shapes around her. She also detected a glow on the far side of the cavern, which now appeared even larger than she'd suspected, and hints of exotic geological treasures.

"Perhaps she's the one Alu asked us to watch for," said Cosmina. "She's about the right age. Are you Alexandra?"

Alex didn't answer, just turned her head to the side hoping they'd let it go.

"Test her, Rutfen," said Cosmina.

"Why me?" he asked. "Why is it always me? Vampire blood is garbage."

"Shut up and do it," she said. "You out-of-town vampires need to earn your keep."

"Hold still, young lady," Rutfen said. "This might hurt a little, but not for long."

Alex calmed. Somehow she welcomed this testing. And although the man's hands were cold, his touch was soft, gentle. "I always get the dirty work," he said. "You know how I hate biting vampires."

"Don't be ridiculous," Cosmina said. "You'd bite anything with a pulse. Almost as bad as Old Rat Neck himself." She was a tall, heavyset woman with sandy hair chopped short.

Rutfen brought Alex toward him like a lover, his body touching her from knees to breasts. She leaned her head to the side, and his cold lips kissed her neck, as if marking the spot, and when his teeth broke her skin, the pain sent a sexual surge that caused her to go limp in his arms. She sighed as he sucked her and felt great affection for him.

"Enough," said the woman. "You'll have to turn her, if she's not already."

"Sweet, delicious," said Rutfen. "Yet a flavoring of vampire, but not like anyone I've tasted. You try her Cosmina. See what you think."

"No. Your companion can do it. Emelia, get up here."

"Come here, girl," said Emelia and took Alex by the hand. She was a little thing, skin and bones. "Let me smell you," she said. She leaned toward Alex, sniffed, slowly licked the blood from her neck, and then bit into her, sucked.

Alex had to pushed her off.

Emelia smacked. "Tasty, appetizing, but, yes, a warm, tangy vampire."

But Alex thought Emelia seemed confused. She stepped back with Rutfen. Emelia then slinked off into the shadows with him.

"Who turned you, girl?" Cosmina asked. Her aroma wafted around Alex, a mixture of earth and pine needles, perhaps a tinge of ashes.

Alex again realized that she was in a bad position. She didn't want to lie, and yet she couldn't tell them about Velinar, not until she felt she could trust them. "I don't know. I was caught by surprise and passed out."

"Well, perhaps someday we'll get the truth about that also. We understand the secrecy. We've all been through it at first. Where are you from?"

"Bucharest, just here visiting when that rapist assaulted me. That's when I found out that I'm a vampire. I know I'm not the same person I used to be. I just need someone to help me into this. I don't know what to do with myself."

"Well spoken," said the woman. "Alu must meet you, but first we need to show you around. What's your name?"

Alex was in another spot. She didn't want to give up her identity, and she certainly wasn't going to give them the same name she gave Jaklin and Mikhail. "Call me Marie," she said.

"Yes. Well, Ishmael, that'll do until we've gained your trust." She took Alex's warm hand in her cold one and led her down a slope out of the entryway. "Get this straight though," Cosmina said. "You are the same person. You're not a daemon or a phantom or a zombie. You are one of the Undead but still the same person."

As the cavern opened up into a magnificent chamber, Cosmina said, "This is where most of us stay. We call it the Cathedral." Huge stalactites hung from the ceiling, some slim spikes, others rippled pillars from ceiling to floor. "We've excavated paths and social quarters to make it comfortable for the few who actually live here." Her deep voice echoed.

Alex noticed that a crowd had converged on them. She hadn't been aware that she'd generated so much curiosity. She walked amongst them, male and female, and they gathered closely about her. One wanted to touch her, "So warm," he said. They were all kind, gentle.

"Don't be afraid," one old vampire told her, touching her arm. "We're all one here, even if you are a little different."

"Are you Alu?"

"No, no, lady," he said. "Just an old vampire infatuated with your youth and freshness. All that blond hair. I've never met a warm sprite like you."

She continued walking through the crowd, and they gathered about her like ants drawn to honey. She started touching them, feeling their cold bodies, and they seemed to crave her. Some would rub shoulders with her, some kissed her cheek, something that pleased her greatly. A woman touched her golden hair and sighed. This felt like a homecoming. She'd not dreamed she'd receive such affection.

Sooner than she would have liked, it was over, the crowd dispersed, and Cosmina showed her around the Cathedral. "This isn't a permanent place to set up residence," she said as they passed a group talking softly among themselves. "It's a congregation of scholars."

"You mean like college professors?"

Cosmina chuckled, her body shaking all over. "Imagine professors who've been studying civilization for hundreds and for some even a thousand years. Learning never stops here. No university professor has the wisdom of the least among us."

Alex didn't know what to say. "I'd have never guessed."

"Unlearn everything you've ever heard about vampires," Cosmina said. "Truth is, we're the cornerstone of civilization. Breakthroughs in science, economics, politics, it all originates here. We come up a little short on healthcare, but we're working on it."

They passed a corridor that split off from the main cavern, and Alex peeked inside. What she saw was at once confusing and shocking. Half a dozen bodies were naked together, writhing on an overlarge bed of stone with a soft covering. They reminded her of a mass of earthworms all sticky and intertwined, humping. Alex caught her breath realizing that it was a vampire orgy.

"Perhaps you're not ready for that, yet," said Emelia, trying to lead her away.

Alex couldn't quit staring. It created a sexual longing in her that was much different than anything she'd ever felt. She caught herself panting, and yet it was disgusting.

"Are they all making love?" she asked.

"That's not love, honey. It's lust. We've broken new ground in that arena too."

They walked on.

"So, am I immortal? Will I live forever?"

"No. Few make it past two hundred years. Something always seems to happen. The Undead can be killed with the right technique. Some tire of vampire life and chose to end theirs. We do have a few lucky ones who've lived to be over a thousand. One of us has lived over two millennia. You won't age though. That's a plus."

"And who might that be who's lived two-thousand years?" Alex asked.

"I'm taking you to him now."

14

Alucius Kardasian

At the far side of the Cathedral, Alex and Cosmina came upon another passageway, a tunnel that led into a less-spacious cavern, although even taller. The walls were made of rippled flowstones that emerged from the ceiling like draperies that glistened in the soft light. Their footsteps reverberated, and Alex heard the tinkling echo of dripping water. But the great beauty of the place was at the far end, where all the natural formations gave way to what could only be described as a megaron. The majesty of it reminded her a little of her dream of the City of God, as Catalin had called it. It was lit inexplicably by some enchanted source that brought forth both a red glow and a deepening darkness. All of it illuminated one object at its center: a huge stone seat, a throne, which now stood empty.

Alex sensed great evil lurking there. What had Catalin said? That she'd be susceptible to evil now that she was a vampire?

"This is Alu Kard's chamber, the Throne Room," Cosmina said. "His rule and power over his people emanates from here."

Alex took a step back and started to run. This evil had no place in her life, regardless if she lived forever. "I'll be leaving now," she said. She felt her handbag for her cross.

"Don't be afraid, Marie," Cosmina said. "The original vampire is kind and generous. He offers eternal life, one without illness or disease, a life that fulfills your every wish without regret or guilt."

But Alex had already quit listening because she'd caught sight of movement beyond the throne, a dark shape that she'd seen before outside her grandmother's home. Here was evil incarnate. Her hand found her cross. It felt warm and comforting. She tried to retreat, but Cosmina used her bulk to block Alex's way.

"Give him a chance," she said in Alex's ear. "Speak with him." But Cosmina's presence had changed also. No longer did she seem so benign.

Conversation with Alu was not something Alex wished. Yet, the closer he got, the less apprehensive she became. He removed the black cape from his shoulders and draped it across his left forearm. She released her cross and removed her hand from her handbag.

"You've come to us, as I suggested you might," he said, his voice as she remembered, distant, thin, scratchy. "Yet, you're reluctant to stay. Spend some time with me. Let us talk as equals." His hair and eyebrows were coal black, his lips deep berry red like a bruise.

"If I'd known it was you I was to meet, I'd not troubled you."

"You have no reason to fear us. We're a part of the world. Have been for three millennia. You are one of us now. You were born here in the Carpathians. Were you not?" Alu's eyes were sunk back into his skull like a dead man's. They had no whites. And yet, her gut instinct had changed. Something about him was appealing. Although, that he knew her birthplace seemed a personal violation.

"Here in Sinaia." She instantly hated that she'd verified it for him and wondered how he knew.

He moved to his throne and stood before it, placed his cape over one of the stone arms. The back of the throne extended far above his head. "In the ancient tongue, Sinaia was called Theos Koilas, Sacred Vale. The monastery has spoiled many such traditions. The Church cares little of this existence and ancient traditions or how precious life is. Its priests know nothing of the great forces that shape human destiny."

Alex wasn't going to let him get away with this. "Yet, you are parasites."

"A quite offensive characterization. The single shortcoming of our existence. Yet, we give back tenfold. All we do here is not distasteful, is it?"

"I have found friendship and affection. I'll not deny that. Yet, I've not seen love."

Alu laughed, snickered. "A truly disgusting, trouble-causing emotion."

Yes, thought Alex. This is the crucial issue. "Yet, for humans, the great pleasure and meaning of life." She wondered why she'd suddenly become so concerned about something that had never been her focus.

Alu finally seated himself on his throne, looked down upon her. "Such naivety. Stay with us. Learn our ways. We contemplate the great philosophical issues of the times, plant ideas to improve society, and have a longterm commitment to human existence. We see the world with a millennial perspective, something people who live only a normal life span cannot. If you become one of us, you can have all the riches of the world and a community that respects and adores you."

"Eternal lust and greed is what you're talking about. What about morality, right and wrong?"

"Outdated concepts. The old world is being swept away and the notion of morality with it. It's a new cosmic connection. You've spent a little time with the men and women following me today. I've sensed you lusting after them. That is real, the sense of community, the commitment to one another and this world we're building. We are the true civilization of the future."

"Yes, I have sensed a great arrogance among your people."

"It's not arrogance, if you are truly superior."

"Arrogance is always arrogance, and pride comes before the fall."

Alu laughed. "A clichéd observation, yet I admire your inclination to question authority." Then he leaned forward and became stern. "I will tell you the difference between our world and that of mundane mortals."

Alex turned to go again. "I'm not sure I care to hear such blasphemy."

Alu had a great laugh. "This Catalin who has come to you recently, you value his council?"

Alex turned back. Was this ancient vampire spying on her every move? "How do you know of him?"

"I've known him, and this Velinar spirit you've encountered, for centuries. He's offered you council, but without knowing your own full story. Velinar it was who did this to you, made you a vampire. This you know. Do you not?"

Alex remained silent.

"But let me tell you this, young lady. You died that night at the gazebo, and it was neither she nor he who brought you back to life. It was me. I thought I had failed because you did not respond immediately as you should have. But I know this for fact. You owe your existence on this planet, not to them, but to me. Alucius Kardasian."

Alex faltered. This was deeply troubling. "I fainted, and have no memory of it, if it did happen as you say."

"Let's be honest with each other, Miss Eidyn." He shook his head. "Honesty — something which you have in short supply. It may seem a dream, but it is there in your memory. You know it."

Alex remembered some dark creature hovering about while she lay on the ground beside the gazebo, but she also remembered a benevolent spirit who came afterward bringing feelings of infinite peace and wellbeing.

Alu was quiet a moment and then shook his head. "That's enough. You are to see Catalin again. Bring this up. See if he's capable of telling the truth."

"He's never lied."

Alu laughed again. "And you would know? Velinar did this to you, both of them left you to die, and yet they are your prize counselors? When you return to us, and you will," he said, "leave your cross at home. Yes, I know you have it tucked away in your purse. Quite a stench it makes in my chamber. You used it on me the first time we met. The others may not sense it, but it's an old rank object that I'll not have in my house again. Let Miss Eidyn out, would you please, Cosmina. I've tired of her."

Alex noticed that his palms had started bleeding again. He rose and stepped away from the throne, turned and walked back behind it and disappeared. He seemed to be limping.

Cosmina kept her distance from Alex. "Shame on you!" she said. "Bringing such an object in here. Out with you. If the others should learn of this, they would not go as easy on you as did Alu. How can you be one of us and harbor such a thing?"

"It's a part of who I am," said Alex.

"I don't understand the respect and difference Alu shows you. He's more sensitive to the cross than any of us. Why the honor? Who are you girl?"

"Just a teenager trying to find a place in the world."

Cosmina ushered Alex back through the tunnel and into the community cavern, the Cathedral. Alex looked for Emelia and Rutfen and wondered what had happened to them. They were nowhere in sight. Cosmina shoved her out the way she'd come in.

15

Lives at Stake

Alex walked back to her grandmother's home in a daze. The bright sun, peeking around puffy white clouds, hurt her eyes, and the sharp smell of the pine forest assaulted her senses. She was shaken by the scolding Alu had given her and trembled all the way back through the forest. She felt attached to those inside the cavern, if not Alucius Kardasian. However, she also sensed a strange attraction for him, and it frightened her. Catalin had said she'd be vulnerable to evil, and she knew that this was what he meant.

Once home, she sought out her grandmother, and although she wouldn't say why, held her close for several moments and even shed tears. Nălucă came to sniff her clothing and rub against her leg.

"Perhaps you should meet with Father Zosimos again," her grandmother suggested. "He isn't what you might think. He is a wise man and will understand, perhaps even be able to help. He is dogmatic in many ways, but his knowledge goes far beyond that of the Church."

"Perhaps another time."

"Have your friends upset you?" her grandmother asked.

"No, Bunică," she answered. "I've not seen them since yesterday."

"If you won't tell me, and you're not interested in seeing Father Zosimos either, go to them. That's what friends are for."

Alex bathed, put on a low-cut blouse — new cleavage playtime — short skirt, just a little above the knee.

Her grandmother saw her to the door. "Be careful out this evening," she said. "The people of Sinaia have reached a point of near hysteria. First, the rapist on the loose for weeks rattled not only Sinaia but also small communities all along the Vale. And now the news that he has been killed by a vampire and another man attacked have brought this community close to the edge."

Alex felt worse about her ordeal with Alu and was somewhat less than concerned about the vampire scare. She scurried out the door in a hurry to meet her friends. She tried to push back the arousal she still felt from seeing all those vampire bodies locked in passion. I'm just a royal bitch in heat, she thought.

No one was there to meet her outside Bucegi. She stood out front waiting, but heard a ruckus down the street, and shouts of "Vampire!" Moving quickly along the sidewalk, she noticed a sizable group gathered to watch what she thought was a fistfight. She pushed her way through the crowd. At the center of the commotion was Stefan Stanescu and another man, who had two people, a man and a woman, in handcuffs face down on the ground. Stefan had his knee in the back of the man and appeared ready to drive a stake through him. The crowd urged him on.

Alex stepped out from the crowd and stood over Stefan. "You can't do this!" she shouted. "I won't let you!" Alex recognized the two, realized that they were vampires, and yet wasn't convinced they should be killed. They were Rutfen and Emelia, the two who'd tasted her in the cavern.

"Stake her too," someone shouted from the crowd. "Yeah, take out the vampire lover," another added. They had reached a point of murderous frenzy.

Alex realized that she'd acted on impulse. Now her life was also in danger. Why had she stepped forward so quickly? Had she already assimilated into the vampire community?

Stefan looked up at Alex. "I've been chasing these two for years. They are vampires."

Stefan's colleague turned to face Alex. "Cuff her, Stefan," the man said. "She's a vampire too."

The man was Radu Cuza, her second victim the night she killed the rapist. She looked away. If he recognizes me, I'm doomed, she thought.

"No," said Stefan. "I've talked to Zosimos about her. He's tested and found her clean. I've seen her out in daylight."

Emelia looked up at Alex. "We are not vampires," she said. "Help us, Marie. Help us." She lowered her voice. "We're no longer vampires."

More shouts of condemnation came from the bloodthirsty crowd. Alex wondered how she'd ever get herself out of this mess. She heard more in the crowd mumbling for murder.

Then a different voice, a familiar one, came from close behind Alex. It was directed at the crowd. "No! You can't do this. You'll have to go through us too." It was a tall young man in a leather jacket, shortcut beard. Mikhail, thought Alex. A girl stood alongside him. Jaklin. Both facing the crowd.

"Two more goth creatures!" someone shouted. "Stake them also, particularly that goth Ruski!"

Alex knew she had to think fast, for her own life, for those of Rutfen and Emelia, and now for Jaklin and Mikhail. She knew that Emelia and Rutfen had been vampires when she met them in the cavern. What could have changed them?

"Test them," said Alex. "If they are vampires, we'll walk away." The presence of her two friends greatly bolstered her confidence.

"Do what you want?" asked Stefan. "I'm not turning them loose, Oxford or no Oxford."

Alex pulled her wooden cross from within her blouse. "Kiss the cross," she commanded.

Emelia grabbed it with both hands, slobbered all over it, and held it to her breast. "Christ Almighty! Save us!" she yelled.

A little over the top, Alex thought and wondered, What on Earth is going on? She had to pull it from Emelia's hands. She handed it to Rutfen.

His head jerked back, obviously afraid.

"Stake him!" shouted someone.

Alex hoped it was just a reflex. "Take it!" she looked daggers at him.

And he did. He took the cross, first with one hand, timidly, and then with the other.

"Kiss it!" she commanded.

He gave it a big smack, held the cross up for the crowd to see, and then handed it back to Alex.

Stefan stood staring at Alex. "What is this?" he said. "What sort of wizardry are you working?" He looked at the crowd. "Another cross!" he shouted. "Who has another cross?"

An old lady stepped forward with a silver one the size of a platter. Alex took it from her, felt its weight and wondered how she could carry such a thing. Alex kissed her on the cheek, and raised the shiny cross high in the air for the crowd to see, her own hand tingling at its touch. Light flashed off it. Already, the crowd had begun to quieten.

Alex turned to Emelia and Rutfen. Then as she'd seen priests do in church services, she touched the cross to Rutfen's forehead and had him kiss it. She did the same with Emelia. "Now rise," she said. Alex turned to the crowd. "This gentleman has made a mistake. An understandable one, but this should be a lesson to all here. Life is precious. Judgment and execution are not for a mob. Leave prosecution to the authorities."

Alex handed the cross back to the old woman and turned on Stefan. "How many mistakes have you made in the past?"

"But I knew they were vampires. Why were you so sure they weren't?"

"Because they said they weren't."

Stefan and Radu removed the handcuffs, and Emelia and Rutfen quickly disappeared down the street. But Stefan wasn't through with Alex. "There's something strange about you, girl. I don't know what yet, but something's not right about you."

"I'm not as much a mystery as you think."

Radu said, "Then tell me why the female called you by name?"

"Marie is not my name," she lied.

"We'll see about that," said Stefan. "A lot of strange goings on here. Radu has been bitten again, but he still hasn't changed. He thinks he's invincible."

"Sounds like a good deal to me," said Alex.

"The rapist, Petru Balc, has been watched closely in the morgue," said Stefan. "He hasn't changed into a vampire either."

"I thought they also had to feed on the vampire."

Stefan faltered. "Well, yes. But the one that got Radu the second time was one of those new feral vampires. He should have changed anyway."

Alex turned her back on both bounty hunters and quickly left with Jaklin and Mikhail in tow. All the while, she was pondering what Stefan had just said about Petru and Radu. She'd bitten both, and Emelia and Rutfen had tasted her blood as well, and pronounced her a vampire, but somehow with a warm, spicy edge. And now neither was a vampire. Alex agreed that something strange was happening, and to her chagrin, she seemed to be right in the middle of it.

16

Passion

Before they entered Bucegi, Alex stopped and hugged both Jaklin and Mikhail. "Thank you," she said, taking a hand of each, "for standing by me. I was in way over my head until you two stepped forward."

"You know," said Mikhail, "I'm the biggest coward in the world, but when I saw you standing there alone, I knew my place was beside you, Missy."

"I've never felt so brave, either," said Jaklin, "The sight of you before the crowd, ready to take on the world, was my inspiration. I felt invincible."

They walked through the opening in the stone fence and inside the restaurant patio, took a table in the front where they could watch pedestrians along the street. The waiter came and took their order.

"What's all this talk of vampires?" asked Jaklin. "Surely, the rumors and news reports can't be true."

"Unfortunately," said Alex, "it's all true. I've had a couple of experiences that make it undeniable."

"Like what?" asked Mikhail. "I've been wanting a first-hand report."

"I've seen them. Talked to them," she said.

"You've got to be joking. How can any of this be little more than superstition."

"Those two whose lives we saved tonight, Emelia and Rutfen? I've spoken to them before. They were vampires then, but have become human again."

Jaklin put her hand on Alex's arm to quieten her and nodded toward other patrons at tables in the patio. All eyes were fixed on the three of them. "Not so sure this is the place for this discussion," she said.

"I've urged you on. I'm always running my mouth when I should be listening," said Mikhail.

Alex had never met a guy who was so naturally self-effacing. Most young men were braggarts, always concerned about their position in the world, but Mikhail's self-critiquing was natural and quite endearing.

What Jaklin said was true. Alex could see out the corner of her eye that all faces were turned toward their table. "I have a lot more to tell," she whispered. "Let's eat and get out of here."

*

Jaklin and Mikhail took Alex back to their flat. When they entered, Alex asked them to keep the lights off. Enough streetlight filtered in through the windows, and she liked the dark shadows and soft glow of their faces in pale light. They had one large bed in the middle of the room. The three of them lay down on it facing each other.

"What we're into," Alex said, "has cosmic implications. I've heard that vampires, since they are immortal, are at the cutting edge of civilization. But I also sensed great evil when I was among them."

"Even having seen them, what makes you believe they were vampires?" asked Mikhail. Mikhail had inquisitiveness with a touch of pessimism, a sense of not quite knowing what was happening. Alex wondered what lay beyond that eternal question that was always lurking beneath his speech. That sense of confusion made him tentative and he defer to Jaklin. This guy was irresistible, yet she sense that he was frustrated at never knowing quite what he wanted, never sure enough of himself to make a move. Alex had never been able to read her friends as she could these two. It wasn't part of her skill set until she became a vampire.

She also told them of Velinar and Catalin, although she left out the part about them being divine, but she did say that they seemed to appear out of nowhere. "I was bitten," she said, "and wondered if I'd become a vampire too. But a friend of my grandmother's, Father Zosimos from the Monastery, has proven that I'm alright. See? I wear a cross. Yet, something about me is off kilter," she said. "Stefan said so. And he's right."

"You are different, Missy," said Jaklin with a sheepish smile that betrayed her goth stature. "But it's such a wonderful difference."

"This afternoon, I went into the mountains, and I found a cave in the side of a cliff. It was an entrance to a vampire cavern. That's where I met Emelia and Rutfen. I met others there, too, normal people who claimed to be vampires. They seemed nice and trust-worthy, and yet, something evil is at work there, at work in the world, and its leader is a great vampire called Alucius Kardasian, or Alu Kard for short."

"This world is really getting strange," said Mikhail.

"Well," said Alex, "I'm about to make it even stranger. I had a discussion with my grandmother and learned that I'm also a descendant of the Cantacuzene family."

Both of them moved in closer to Alex. She could feel their breath on her face.

"We're cousins. Distant cousins for real."

As her voice slowly trailed off, the sound merging into the room's shadows, Alex felt a tingle of excitement ripple through her.

"So we really are sensing something. We're kissing cousins."

The faint light from the window glistened off Jaklin's cheeks, and they seemed to glow in the dark. The smell of her breath was like a fine Chablis, Mikhail's, a rich Bordeaux. The three so close together, talking had a mesmerizing affect on her. She remembered kissing each of them two nights before. They edged closer, and their voices became quieter, almost a whisper.

And then it happened.

Alex kissed Mikhail. His lips, the taste of his mouth, produced a longing in her that she'd never before felt. They lingered with their tongues barely touching, savoring the presence of their faces together. When they separated, she turned her head just a little and saw Jaklin, so very close. She kissed her too, and the tips of their tongues again touched as they had two nights before, and she felt her head spin.

Jaklin took Alex's face in her hand and pulled her closer, stuck her tongue deep inside her mouth. At the same time, she felt Mikhail kiss her neck. She pulled away from Jaklin and watched Mikhail kiss her. Alex wedged her face in with theirs and her cheeks touched both. She placed her lips on theirs, and with her tongue, she felt the inside of both their mouths.

Alex moved her body around until her legs touched Jaklin's. Then Jaklin turned on her side, and Alex slid her leg underneath Jaklin's skirt and between her thighs. She was hot and moist. Alex put her hands underneath Jaklin's blouse and unsnapped her bra, then moved her hand around to her breasts, those gorgeous breasts, felt her nipples with her finger tips.

They stopped for a second listening the each other breathe. And then the two girls went to work on Mikhail. Alex felt the taught hardness of his body, the tense muscles, put her hand down his pants, unbuttoned them. The smooth softness of Jaklin's body, the silky sweetness, buttery taste of her skin, the lemon freshness of Mikhail.

"Are you two ready for this?" asked Jaklin. "Yes," answered Alex and Mikhail simultaneously.

And then their clothes were off, and they were in each other's arms. Alex loved everything she tasted, sucked everything she could get into her mouth, relished every crease she could get her tongue into. She felt Mikhail enter her. Her muscles tightened about him, and he groaned.

Alex had never been loved. She was so consumed by the affection, the way her body yielded to them, craved them, that she just let herself go, and it was as if she'd been trained for that one event all her life. She knew what she wanted, how to get it, and instinctively what they needed, craved, and how to send them to elevated heights of ecstasy.

While Alex devoured them, she felt a faint craving for blood, and felt obscurely achy. But this was minuscule compared to her sexual desire. Alex's passion kept propelling higher and higher. Their bodies didn't even seem to belong to themselves but to some communal, genderless corporeality. The soft pliable flesh of a breast, the taught prickliness of a nipple, the pulsing toughness of a phallus. Kissing her, kissing him. Him on top of her, in her. Kissing her while he was in her. Making him groan, her sigh.

Afterward, they talked in the dark.

"I am different than I've ever been," Alex said. "I have more to tell you, but can't just yet. I'm still changing."

"Individually, we're no different from other people," said Jaklin. "But together, we are something quite different, something extraordinary."

Alex remembered what Catalin said about living a myth. "I know," she said. "It's as though together, we have a purpose, and our lives take on a mythical existence. Without both of you, my life is empty, and I don't know who I am. Around you, I become myself, as if living my true life. This is not life as usual."

*

Sometime before sunrise, they kissed her goodbye at the door, and Alex left. "I don't know how this happened," she told them, "but I love you. I love both of you." When she stepped out into the dark street, she saw several people walking about. She could tell who was a vampire and who wasn't, but the vampires passed by her as if they didn't suspect anything.

Alex went back to her grandmother's home and went to bed. She laid on her back staring up at the dark ceiling. The surprise was that what she'd just done didn't seem strange. Thoughts of her lovers brought such tranquility. Even being a vampire seemed normal now. How quickly she'd fit into the role of an immortal being. So close to sleep, she felt and perhaps even saw, another world full of dark strange beings. They seemed to call to her. This was the one aspect of being a vampire that scared her. She fought sleep, clutched her cross close to her breasts and pushed the dark psychic world away.

Strangely, Nălucă, the cat, left her grandmother's bedroom and came to sleep with Alex, which had never happened before and felt unusually comforting. Alex tiptoed down the hall and peeked into her grandmother's room.

She was fast asleep.

17

Bunică

The next morning Nălucă was still sleeping beside Alex, and her grandmother wasn't up. Thinking it unusual, she went to check on her. She never closed her door at night, but Alex knocked on the doorframe and then walked into the room.

"Bunică?"

Alex could see her grandmother's head on the pillow turned away, just as she'd been when Alex had checked on her last night, so she stepped to the far side of the bed, and looked down at her. She seemed to be peacefully sleeping, but Alex didn't notice any movement or sign that she was breathing. She called once again, "Bunicuţă?" But she didn't stir. Alex placed her hand on her grandmother's shoulder and shook her. Still no response. Alex tried to turn her over but could tell that she was already stiff.

At first, it seemed so normal, just a person motionless in bed. Then a strange feeling crept over Alex, and she knew. Her grandmother was dead. The cat. Yes, her grandmother had been dead when she came home last night.

Alex went to the window, pulled back the curtain and tied the sash. Sunlight spilled into the room. She went to her grandmother and shook her again. She felt her throat for a pulse. None. She went back to the window and closed the curtain.

Alex stood facing the wall. She heard birds fussing outside the window, children's laughter in the distance. A dog barked. She'd never felt so utterly alone. She remembered the night she came home after killing a man. She thought she'd felt lonely then. But it was nothing compared to this. She felt for the cross beneath her blouse, squeezed it with her fingers. She pulled it out, and took it to her grandmother, touched it to her forehead.

Alex went to her own bedroom, picked up her cellphone and called her mother. When she answered, Alex said, "Bunică isn't feeling well."

"Is she seeing a doctor?" her mother asked.

"No, Mamă. She's beyond that."

"Don't be silly. If she's sick, she needs a doctor."

"She's not moving, and she's stiff."

"What did you do to her?"

"Mamă, Bunică died during the night."

"Honey, are you sure? Is she breathing? How fast is her pulse?"

"Mamă! She's stiff. She has no pulse. It happened during the night."

Her cellphone clicked dead. Alex walked downstairs and into the kitchen. She didn't know what to do, couldn't think it through. It seemed just a few seconds after her mother hung up on her that she heard someone banging on the door.

It was Father Zosimos, huffing and puffing. "Hurry, child. Where is she?"

Alex led him upstairs to her grandmother's bedroom. He felt of her, then raised his arms in the air and looked toward Heaven. "Why, Father? Why?" Great anguish came from his voice. Then he turned quickly and came to Alex. "Oh, dear child," he said. "I'm so sorry you had to be the one to find her. Come. We must get you downstairs, and find someone to stay with you. A nun is on her way."

"But Father. I don't want to leave her. She should never be alone, particularly in death."

"Oh dear Heavens! What am I to do with you. You're stronger than I am. But then, she was precious to me... beyond words," he stammered. "We've been expecting this for sometime. She was afraid that she wouldn't live long enough to see you again. But she also feared that she'd have a stroke and be a burden to you."

"I would have preferred the stroke, if she could still be here."

Father Zosimos smiled. "Child, you certainly loved her. But this was her final gift to you. A sudden death."

"Tell me what to do," she said. "I feel so useless."

"It's not for you to do. You've been her great pleasure in life. That's something no one else could have been. Your job is through. In death, she's my ward."

"Please, let me do something. May I say the Lord's Prayer?"

"Together. We'll say it together."

They began, "Our father, who art in heaven, hallowed be thy name..." All the while, Alex felt a great calm come to her. The words flowed with a significance she'd not before known. "For thine is the kingdom, and the power, and the glory, for ever and ever. Amen." There. It's done, she thought. At least I helped that much.

Father Zosimos turned to Alex. "May I use your cellphone?" he asked.

She handed it to him.

"If you must do something, get white sheets and cover all the mirrors and pictures. Stop all the clocks."

He pushed the buttons on her cellphone. "Zosimos," he said. "Yes, yes. Listen to me. It's Margareta. She's passed on. Yes. Yes. Immediately." He hung up and turned to Alex. "The officials will be here in just moments. Now do as I've instructed, if you wish." Then he pushed the cellphone buttons once again, and Alex heard him talking to her mother.

Alex went to get Nălucă, and then sat in a chair close to her grandmother. The nun arrived, and since Alex had forgotten, the young woman went about covering the mirrors and pictures. She unplugged the electric clock in the bedroom and stilled the pendulum in the big clock in the living room downstairs.

Alex held Nălucă until the authorities arrived, which was well over an hour. Before they removed her grandmother, Father Zosimos had Alex taken from the bedroom and down into the living room. Alex stood at the large window staring out into the distant mountains and valleys of Sinaia. It wasn't until they closed the door, her grandmother having been taken, that Alex realized she was still in her bathrobe.

Father Zosimos found her wandering through the garden with the hose, trying to water the tomatoes. She'd forgotten to turn on the water. He'd advised the old man and woman caretakers and the maid of their employer's death.

Finally, Alex's father called to say that they'd be there tomorrow morning. He'd called Gavril and Sonya, and they would also be coming the following day.

Alex said, "Okay," and hung up. She seemed to come out of her daze. She called Jaklin. "This is Missy," she said. "I need help." She gave her directions to her grandmother's home.

A couple of minutes later, Jaklin and Mikhail arrived. Alex was out front, still holding Nălucă, when they rode up on mountain bikes.

"What's wrong?" asked Jaklin. "What's happened?"

Alex said nothing, but led them inside where Father Zosimos was taking care of some last minute details. "Good," he said. "Now she'll have company. I must return to the Monastery."

"She won't tell us what happened," said Mikhail.

"She's distracted. Her bunică died. Stay with her as long as you can, and bring her to the Monastery when you have to leave. We'll take care of her tonight." Then he left.

Alex sat on the sofa stroking Nălucă with Jaklin next to her. Mikhail pulled up a chair.

"My name is Alexandra Marie Eidyn," she told them, "but you may call me Missy. I'm an orphan, it seems." But then she shook her head. "No, my parents will be here tomorrow along with my sister's family and my brother. Or maybe they're coming the next day."

Then she fell into Jaklin's arms. Nălucă jumped down and scurried upstairs.

"Bunicuţă has died," she said. "I don't know why, but I can't cry."

Mikhail then set on the other side of Alex, and he held her in his arms and kissed her face. Jaklin held her again for a while, then went into the kitchen and fixed a pot of tea.

Alex took a couple of sips, then rose and said, "I have something to show you."

She led them out the backdoor, across the yard, and into the edge of the forest. She pointed to the remains of a building. "This is where the gazebo stood," she said. She stepped off into the dirt and fallen leaves at the end of the old foundation and said, "This is where I found the body, or at least I thought it was a body. It smelled really bad. It was Velinar. She grabbed me, and we staggered back into the gazebo. Only it wasn't just a foundation then. The gazebo was really here."

She looked at both of them, first one and then the other.

"I swear," she said. "The gazebo was here. And then Velinar bit me. She said, 'Dear Lord, forgive me,' and then bit me." Alex rubbed her neck. "Catalin appeared out of nowhere. He stopped Velinar because she was taking all my blood. Velinar disappeared, and Catalin told me he was sorry. He then disappeared, and I fell here on the ground outside the gazebo, and passed out. Or at least I thought I passed out. Alu Kard, the old vampire I saw a couple of days ago in the cavern, said that I died, but he revived me."

Alex stopped and looked first at Jaklin and then Mikhail. "I swear. It really happened, just like that."

"How did your grandmother die?" asked Mikhail.

"Her heart just stopped, they think," Alex answered. "She had heart trouble. I didn't know."

"We're really sorry," said Jaklin. "You must have been very close."

"I spent a lot of weekends and summers with her. I'm like her. The rest of my family are strangers."

"We'll help in any way we can. Just tell us what you need," said Mikhail.

"Is any of this real?" Alex asked. "The gazebo doesn't exist. Have I lost my mind?"

"The events were real enough," said Mikhail. "I can't answer for what you say has happened to you, but you did save the lives of two people last night. The gazebo... Well, that's another matter."

"Was I really with you last night?" Alex asked.

"Yes," said Jaklin. "You were with us, and you loved us, and we loved you. I'm not sure about the gazebo. But I'd bet everything happened as you told us, just now."

"Am I a vampire?"

"No," said Mikhail. "You're simply a beautiful young woman, whose grandmother just passed away."

Jaklin held one of her hands, and Mikhail held the other. They hugged her.

"You must take me to the Monastery now," Alex said. "I'll not be any more trouble to you today."

"But we'd like to stay with you as long as we can," said Jaklin. She took out her cellphone and turned to Mikhail. "I'm calling work. I'll take off the rest of today and tomorrow."

They went back inside, and Jaklin reheated the tea. They sat on the sofa, and first one held her, then the other. Nălucă came and sat in her lap. Alex said, "This is the little critter that caused all the trouble."

"Spend tonight with us, not at the Monastery," said Jaklin. "You can return in the morning, before your family arrives."

*

During the night, Alex woke in pain. She was sleeping between Jaklin and Mikhail. Her entire body ached as if filled with infection. The problem was her need for blood. However, she felt new affection for her cross. It seemed more than just a symbol she wore to ward off vampires. It seemed to bolster her emotional well-being and fend off bad dreams.

She cuddled up close to Jaklin. She'd discovered that she liked to sleep with her arm around her, but when she nuzzled up close, Alex now had an urge to bite her. She rolled over and cuddled up next to Mikhail. She liked to put her hand on his chest while she slept, but the urge to bite him was also overpowering. She rolled to her back and looked up at the dark ceiling. She felt sick all over.

Alex slipped out of bed, bundled her clothes and shoes in her arms and slipped into the bathroom where she quickly dressed in the dark. She slipped out the door, down the stairs, and walked out into the cold night air.

Alex knew what she had to do, not only to ease her pain and deteriorating physical condition, but also for Jaklin's and Mikhail's safety. She had to do it quickly and return, before they missed her.

Once on the street, in addition to physical discomfort, Alex felt condescension and arrogance, a great desire for violence. She felt a moral authority above civilized behavior.

She had to get a grip.

The main street was still full of tourists going from bar to bar. Coffee shops were still packed. It was the beginning of summer tourist season. She had an idea. This might not be as difficult as she first thought.

Alex ducked into an alley and walked down a back street. She spotted several drunks staggering in and out of pubs. She could easily get blood from any of them, but protecting her identity could be a problem.

One man stumbled down the street and off onto an even darker side street, and she followed. He walked into a residential area and was obviously going home. She followed at a safe distance until he made the turn up a dark walkway into a yard, and she made her move.

Alex came up behind the drunk, grabbed him around the neck from behind and sank her teeth into him in one fluid motion. He was young and struggled against her, but Alex found that she was strong beyond all reckoning. He started to scream, so she put her hand over his mouth. The man's fear, outright panic when she grabbed him from behind, fueled her desire. She tried to suppress the feeling of invincibility that had taken her over. She sucked as long as she dared, and then shoved him away. But just as she thought she had her hand off of his mouth, he bit her. And it hurt.

After this act of violence and physical violation, and with her craving now sated, the reality of her attack hit home. She licked her lips and savored the remaining traces of blood mixing with her saliva. It had been more satisfying than a meal when starving, and for just a moment, she couldn't wait for the craving to return.

Alex tried to retrace her footsteps, but found that she was staggering and weaving a crooked path home. It was the man's blood-alcohol level. She was tipsy.

Quickly, she walked back to the flat, snuck inside the door, removed her clothes, donned her night gown and slipped back into bed between Jaklin and Mikhail. Her finger still hurt, but at least he didn't break the skin. She'd have to be more careful. She could have turned him.

18

The Funeral

The next morning, Alex woke late and with a headache. She roused her two friends, and they hurriedly dressed. Alex helped them choose their clothes.

"Think avocaţi. Lawyers," she said. "Both părinţi."

Jaklin pointed to a small tattoo on her shoulder.

"Cover it," said Alex, but when Jaklin started to remove her eye shadow, she objected. "I do like the goth," she admitted. "Black for a funeral is a good thing. Let's try it on them."

Mikhail said, "When they see us gothed out, they'll hate us and dis-own you."

"Wrong," said Alex. "They are related to me. They'll love you."

Since her grandmother's home was only minutes away by foot, they walked in the fresh cool morning air. Alex was quiet and kept to herself. She was mulling over what she'd done during the night. She'd sucked blood from another human being and had a slight hangover. Yet she was pleased that she'd easily satisfied her first vampire craving.

Once they entered her grandmother's front yard, she put her arms around Jaklin and Mikhail and drew them to her as they walked up to the front door. She'd spotted her father's car, along with those of her brother and her sister's family. She thought her siblings weren't supposed to be there until the next day. She heard kids' voices coming from the backyard. She hoped they didn't trample the garden.

As Alex opened the door and stepped into the entryway, Jaklin and Mikhail dropped back behind her. Her sister Sonya was the first to see her. "Here she is!" she shouted and ran to her, hugged her. "We were beside ourselves with worry," she said.

"Where have you been?" It was her mother scolding from the kitchen. "Father Zosimos has been out looking for you. You were supposed to spend the night at the Monastery."

"I've been with friends," answered Alex. She pulled them forward. "The two best friends in all the world."

"You? With friends? That's not the Alexandra I know." It was a man's voice, not one she recognized at first. Then she saw him. He was her brother, Gavril. It'd been a while.

"This is Jaklin and Mikhail," she said.

What surprised Alex most was the way her family had taken over her grandmother's home. It seemed presumptuous. Yet, it would now belong to Alex's mother. For just a single day, it had almost seemed to belong to Alex, and she felt resentment at having it jerked from her grasp.

The backdoor popped open, and in ran four screaming little girls. It'd been several months since Alex had seen them, and my how they'd grown.

"Tanti Alex!" they screamed. They engulfed her in hugs.

"Shush," said their mother and then turned to Alex. "They were so excited about coming to see you that they hardly understood their mare bunică had passed away."

Alex had all but forgotten that the girls would be there, and now she resented the fact it was so good to see them, that her grief had been put on hold as she hugged these glorious little girl bodies, squeezed them until they squealed.

Alex saw that her father and brother-in-law had commandeered Mikhail and were already questioning him about his family. Alex heard Mikhail say, "My family name is Volsky, and I'm from Saint Petersburg, on the Baltic Sea. I'm the disowned son of a Russian Orthodox priest, who was imprisoned in Siberia for five years by the Communists. My mamă is the minor poet, Sonya Volsky. I am a disciple of Dostoevsky, having graduated this spring from the Russian Academy in Moscow."

"I too am a great admirer of Dostoevsky," said Alex's father, "particularly his *Notes from the Underground.*"

"Ah, an excellent work!" said Mikhail. "The first existentialist novel."

Meanwhile, her mother was pumping Jaklin for information on her background. "Where are you from in Bulgaria?" asked her mother, Madalina.

"I'm a coastal girl from Balchik," she said, "but I've spent the last four years at New Bulgarian University in Sofia studying International Relations. I hope to work for the United Nations. My mamă is Greek from Thessaloniki, and my tată an engineer."

"Do you work?" asked Madalina.

"At Casino Sinaia."

"You work at a gambling house?" Her voice was marked with disapproval.

Alex stepped in, and she was angry. "It's not a casino, Mother. You know that. It's the International Conference Center. She works for the Bulgarian Consulate."

Her mother changed the subject. "And your family name?"

"Dafovska."

The goth didn't seem to matter.

Alex was proud that her friends were so accomplished. One impression startled her. And that was how much Jaklin and Mikhail reminded her of her two siblings. Nothing Freudian in that, she thought.

Alex resented the fact that they already knew more about her friends than did she. Just as they had taken over her grandmother's home, so they now had monopolized her friends. But she consoled herself. They will never know how they feel in bed, she thought, what bliss it is to be cuddled up next to them, to be in their arms. What they taste like. How they groan in the midst of passion. They are mine, she said, stiffening her resolve. They are both mine.

*

Late afternoon, her father went back to Bucharest and his pressing business dealings. Father Zosimos had scheduled the funeral for the next morning at the family cemetery alongside the gazebo. Her father wouldn't be there, but the rest of the family would, and so would Jaklin and Mikhail. They tried to get Alex to spend the night with them again, but Alex's nieces put a stop to any talk of that. Tears flooded their eyes with the first mention of her leaving.

Jaklin and Mikhail left at three o'clock with promises to return early the next morning. Alex saw them outside and hugged and kissed both of them. Jaklin was off to work at the ICC after all and Mikhail to write on his Russian literature blog. Alex felt jealous that they would be alone in bed together.

That night, Alex bedded down with the two smallest of her sister's girls, Karolina five and Anica three, who kept Năluċă beside her. They brought in a mattress from another bedroom, which they placed on the floor for the two larger girls, Monika ten and Maja eight. Alex recited nursery rhymes for the little girls until they dropped off to sleep, and then she and the two older girls whispered ghost stories until the witching hour.

Finally, they all slept, but Alex kept feeling the powerful love she had for her nieces and scooted up closer to them, knowing she could never have her own children. She worried about her grandmother and wondered if she was on her way to Heaven. She remembered her dream of the City of God.

*

They followed the tradition of burying family members in the graveyard next to the gazebo where Alex had been bitten. They all stood around the mound of dirt and casket, with Father Zosimos at one end flanked by two young priests. Although Alex had met some of her grandmother's friends, many more were present than she'd imagined. She even suspected some of being royalty.

Jaklin and Mikhail stood to either side of Alex, each with an arm about her waist. They were both decked out in goth, but no one seemed to notice. Alex herself was dressed in a long full-length black dress her mother had found among her grandmother's wardrobe. It was for a slim, rather tall person and fit her better than could have been expected. It was obviously well made but very old. Mikhail kissed her on the cheek when no one was looking, and Jaklin kept telling her how gorgeous she looked in black while hiding an irrepressible smile. "You were made for black," Jaklin said. "Makes those golden curls glow."

Though blustery, the day was warm with bright sunshine, which caused Alex to go into a daze, and she lapsed into remembering that when her grandfather died, her grandmother spent a month with them in Bucharest. Alex loved having her there. She'd made Alex special dishes, and they'd drunk tea together. Her grandmother did so enjoy a good cup of tea. On weekends, they were off together to visit a museum or an art gallery. Her grandmother was highly educated, and she'd read Alex the novels of Dickens and strange short stories by Kafka. Alex had seemed to be her grandmother's antidote for grief.

Although later she tried to remember the ceremony, Alex could not recover much. She simply recalled that it was a strangely generic ceremony, a lot about the spiritual connections of all mankind and our striving for a closer connection to the divine, of peace and understanding with a few sprinklings of Christian thought. It seemed to be at least partially in the tradition of the Baha'i of which her grandmother had spoken.

Alex did remember Father Zosimos swinging the censer throughout and all holding lighted candles. The service consisted of the "Kontakion of the Departed," Father Zosimos speaking the words as the scroll unfurled, then the final singing of "Memory Eternal." At the end of the service, during the final hymn, all extinguished their candles. Father Zosimos said the "Prayers for the Departure of the Soul." Alex seemed to partially come out of her daze as Father Zosimos ended with the words, "...as it was in the beginning, is now and ever shall be, world without end. Amen."

It wasn't until after Jaklin and Mikhail left, and the family members all gathered in Father Zosimos' office at the Monastery, that Alex's awareness fully returned. Father Zosimos had been in possession of her grandmother's will, he said, for the past few years as her health declined. He put on his glasses in preparation for reading it.

"This may come with some puzzlement," said Father Zosimos.

"What? She's left it all to the Church, hasn't she?" her mother interjected, cold anger at the edge of her tongue.

The biting comment didn't perturb Father Zosimos. "Let's read the will first, and then I'll answer any questions," he said. He put on his glasses and raised what was a smaller stack of papers than one might have expected for a fairly large estate. Then he read the will, legal wording first, then the giving of certain objects of value to each member of the family: Alex's two siblings first and then her mother. The will said nothing of Alex, and Father Zosimos had stopped reading, as if finished. Alex wondered if she'd been left anything at all. Well, what would she have expected anyway? She'd had her grandmother's unconditional love, and that was something she'd always cherish.

And then Father Zosimos came to the very heart of the matter. He continued reading, "...as to my home estate, and the rest of my wealth and acquisitions, I leave it all to my granddaughter Alexandra Marie Eidyn."

Alex felt a great welling up of sadness in her throat. She choked back a sob.

Father Zosimos continued. "Alexandra has been my one true love in life from the day she was born, and she has been more affectionate toward me than anyone I've known. I couldn't forgive myself if I didn't see to her future. I hope the rest of you will understand, for I truly do love you all. It's just that Alexandra has stolen my heart."

With that Father Zosimos put down the paper and removed his glasses. Alex had heard gasps during the reading but was unable to determine from whom they came. She could no longer contain her sadness and gratitude. Her grandmother actually loved her in life and in death had provided for her. She cried uncontrollably.

"Was Mamă in her right mind when she made out the will?" asked Alex's mother. She seemed hurt and a little angry.

"Margareta had all her mental faculties right up to the end," said Father Zosimos, quite plainly. "The will was written in consultation with me fifteen years ago, when she was sixty-five and Alexandra three. Although she's reviewed it with me several times through the years, it has never been altered."

That's the way it stayed. Alex brought her emotions under control, and they left the monastery. They all acted a little cold toward Alex after that, and she wished that her grandmother had been a little more generous with them. She knew that she'd been given more than her fair share.

Gavril left immediately after the reading of the will, didn't even say goodbye. Sonya and her family left late that afternoon, and her mother, after crying all evening left the next morning. She had to get back to her law practice. Alex dropped her at the train station. Once she was gone, Alex felt more lost than ever. She went back home and wandered about the old house trying to get a grip on the fact that she owned it.

Later that afternoon, Father Zosimos called. He inquired about her family, and when Alex told him that they had all left, he asked if he might come over. He had one more bit of business they had to dispense with.

Alex wouldn't have called him happy, but he did take a certain pleasure in what he had to do. He sat on the sofa again, as he had when he tested her for vampirism, and put on his glasses. He had another wooden box that he sat on the coffee table. He opened it, sorted and removed some papers from inside.

"No sense in troubling the others with these mundane money matters," he said.

"Did Bunică have some bills that'll have to come out of the estate?" Alex asked. She wondered if her grandmother had some bad business investments that might liquidate her entire holdings.

"No, young lady, that's not what this is about. Your bunică had a considerable sum of money that she's left you."

"Considerable?"

"I mean that you're now independently wealthy. Basically, it comes in two parts. You have close to three million lei in your bank account. Plus, you have an allowance from a privately administered trust fund that gives you an additional sixty-thousand per year. If you exercise a little restraint, you'll never want for money again. You won't have to work, if you choose not to."

"But where did this come from? Bunic never had much money. Bunică never worked."

"An anonymous donor, over many years. I'm sure she told you of your kinship with Queen Marie. I'm not privy to the information myself, but I suspect she had something to do with it."

They talked for a few minutes more, and Father Zosimos told her that she could always come to him with any advice she might need and that he'd help her get a reputable financial consultant, if she wished. "All this can be worked out in the coming months," he said. "In the meantime, I recommend you tell no one of this. Money begets animosity between friends and attracts all forms of charlatans."

Alex looked up and scanned the living room, looked out over the yard and garden. "I'll not want to touch anything," she said. "I'll feel guilty and that she might not approve."

"You must make her home yours," Father Zosimos said, sternly. "She gave it to you. She'd be disappointed to know that you couldn't come to think of it as your own, as she did. Remember, she was given it also. It came to her by way of her mamă."

"Yes," said Alex. "Queen Marie's illegitimate child."

"Then she told you?"

"A couple of days ago."

"There you have it. She prepared you for it."

Alex took a deep breath. Sighed. Shook her head.

"You're right to feel some skepticism about having all this. It can be a burden and could slip through your fingers like quicksilver."

"That's what I'm worried about. Not living up to her expectations." She wondered what she would have received from her grandmother had she known that her granddaughter, Father Zosimos' testing not withstanding, really was a vampire.

Alex had one last question for Father Zosimos. "I've heard a prophecy concerning a special vampire that is to lead them all to redemption."

"Is this something out of the Roma, again?"

"Possibly," she lied.

"Hogwash!" he said. "Redemption is not possible for the forces of evil. They'll all die out eventually, and history will never remember they were here."

19

The Medical Clinic

The evening following the reading of the will, Alex called Jaklin and had her and Mikhail come for a visit. She'd delayed calling to bask in being in her own home alone. She wished to follow Father Zosimos' advice and make it hers. She and her two friends spent a rather crowded night together in her small bed. Once again, the three intermingled their bodies and took their liberties, but it was a calm, slow process of savoring. It contained little of the urgency that had marked their first night of passion. This was slow and deliberate, a rather sad relishing. They slept, woke and cuddled again, slowly, sleepily. Alex felt a profound love for them. This must be what divine love is like, she thought. She shed a tear to happiness and contentment but still deeply felt the loss of her grandmother.

Sometime toward morning, they could sleep no more, so they slipped on their clothes and went down to the living room where they pulled aside the curtain and looked out over the sleepy little city's sparkling lights still enfolded in darkness. They sipped coffee, held each other and spoke of the play of light on the sparse clouds above, the darting car lights off to Braşov and Bucharest. Alex held Jaklin, and Mikhail put his arms around both young women. Such contentment within grief. Alex felt no urge to bite them, none of the craving or pain, or sickness. She felt normal again, as if her vampirism had all been a bad dream, and as if she were again just a human being, a girl in love, captivated by her lovers' affections. They returned to bed and slept until noon.

And so it was in the coming days. Alex felt normalcy return to her life. She didn't want either of them out of her sight, and complained when Jaklin had to work. Having Mikhail to herself consoled her, and she sat beside him all the time he blogged. He made some futile attempts to teach her Russian. Otherwise, the three were constant companions. They took over the master bedroom, her grandmother's, rearranged the furniture, and made it their own. Alex talked them into giving up their flat, and they moved their few possessions in with hers. They didn't press too hard about what all this meant, how long it would last, the nature of their commitment. They worked the garden on their time off, and it grew as if under professional care. Evenings they spent reading to each other, sometimes a short story and at others some philosophical work.

Mikhail was an obsessive blogger. Alex thought he looked quite studious in his short beard and glasses sitting before the fireplace working on a laptop. He also tried his hand at fiction, and whispered both Solzhenitsyn and Tolstoy under his breath. She and Jaklin would curl up together on the bearskin rug at his feet, each hugging a leg, Alex reading history, Jaklin reveling in a romance, both reading from iPads.

Mikhail was an insomniac as was Alex, and she'd wake at night to find him in a chair by the window staring out at city lights, and she'd go stand beside him, her hand on his shoulder, the two lost in just being together while Jaklin and the rest of the world slept. Of course, Nălucă was always at their feet when they were up at night, and he had developed a particular fondness for Mikhail, the only other male in the house. Mikhail put up with him, although it was obvious he wasn't very fond of cats.

And Jaklin was the one who needed sleep because of her job at the International Conference Center, the ICC she called it. Although part-time, she took her job seriously and frequently had to leave in the middle of the afternoon or evening to put out a "bureaucratic fire" as she termed political crises. She must have been good at her job because they approached her with an offer of a full-time position, but she kept putting them off, unable to reconcile her desire to be with her lovers with that of professional responsibilities. It wasn't as if they needed the money.

They didn't talk of vampires or evil beings. Alex managed to hide her need for blood because her problem seemed to moderate and feeding became a matter of once every couple of weeks. She didn't crave anything but a delicious breakfast, a cup of tea and a pastry from the nearby bakery. She found that she had a newly acquired aversion to meat in any form. She lost her taste for most animal products and went on soymilk. They had candlelight dinners with fresh vegetables from the garden. It was a quiet time, halcyon days of adjustment and living a privileged life.

Alex became more concerned about her dreams. She visited dark places, saw deformed creatures milling about, but generally just felt lost in them. She was like an orphan roaming her own psychic world, unable to find her way.

As the days turned into weeks, Alex came to realize that she'd missed another period, two more in fact. Jaklin asked about it. She smiled. "Could you be pregnant?"

Alex admitted that she wasn't on the pill, but secretly believed it was because she was a vampire. Vampires don't bleed, she reasoned.

Alex could also tell that her abdomen was beginning to swell, and she thought she felt something move, just a little tickle. So she snuck out one day and went to the apothecary where she bought a pregnancy test kit. She took it into the bathroom, held one of the strips in her stream, and felt the blood drain from her face. She had to lower her head to keep from fainting. Her eyes opened wide, and she smiled. She shook her head. Vampires don't get pregnant.

Here was her dilemma. If she told Jaklin and Mikhail, they'd assume the child was Mikhail's. She'd never told them of being raped. Truth was, the father could be either. Alex did a little search on the Internet and learned that paternity could be determined by a noninvasive procedure, something called "fetal cell testing," as early as, depending on testing company claims, the fifth week following conception. They needed a little of the mother's blood, and a DNA sample from the prospective father. She surreptitiously gathered a few strands of Mikhail's hair from his brush and hit the road to the medical clinic. They drew a vial of blood from her arm, accepted the strands of hair, and, requesting a surcharge to expedite, told her they'd have the results in a week or two.

The morning she received the phone call, they wouldn't give her the results over the phone. "The doctor wants to talk to you," the receptionist said.

Alex was in a state of panic. Did they know she was a vampire? She made an excuse to Jaklin and Mikhail, "I'll explain all when I return," she told them, and quickly left for the doctor's office.

When she returned, Jaklin was waiting at the door. "What's wrong, Missy? Why the gloom and doom?"

"Get Mikhail," she said. "I have a confession."

Jaklin called him out of the garden. He'd become obsessed with clearing weeds. "You want to manicure it," is how Jaklin had chided him over his gardening.

When he come in, Alex sat them both down on the sofa. "One thing you should know, and I'm sorry to have kept this from you. I was raped a couple of nights before we slept together the first time."

"Who was the bastard?" asked Mikhail. "I'll take him down myself."

"I'm so sorry," said Jaklin. "Why didn't you tell us? You seemed so serene to have suffered an attack like that."

"Another unexplainable response. I keep telling you that I've changed. That this isn't who I am. But I now have trouble stacked on top of trouble. I'm pregnant."

"How far along are you?" asked Jaklin.

"Just eight weeks. It could only be from being raped, or from being with Mikhail."

"You should get a paternity test," said Jaklin.

"I did. It's not yours," she said, looking at Mikhail. "Sorry. I stole a couple of strands of your hair. It's quite conclusive."

"It's the rapist's?" asked Mikhail. "You should get rid of it."

"Mikhail!" said Jaklin. "Let her speak. Didn't you have a boyfriend in secondary school?"

Alex laughed. "If anyone had put a hand on me, I'd have broken his arm." She laughed again and looked away. "I've considered abortion, but couldn't convinced myself that the baby is an 'it'. Besides, the test wasn't so cut and dried. Something unusual about the results. Something they've not seen before. Still yet, the rapist is the only possibility if it's not Mikhail's, and they tell me it isn't."

"Does this have anything to do with the murder of that serial rapist?" asked Mikhail.

Alex didn't know what to say. Could she come clean about all of it? "I don't want to get into that," she said. "Trust me a while longer."

"Still..." started Mikhail.

Jaklin put her hand on his arm, then said, "Talk of vampires, rapists, and all of it on top of your grandmother dying. Yes, Missy, all the time you need. Whatever you decide, we'll stand by you. Won't we, Mikhail?" She turned to him, but he was noncommittal.

"I'm thinking of going to see Father Zosimos," said Alex.

"You know what he'll say," said Mikhail. "Don't let him dictate. Make the decision yourself. After all, it'll be your responsibility."

"But how?" asked Jaklin, "How could you destroy a child that's half you?"

"Exactly," said Alex. "Give me a few days. I want to get this right."

Alex could tell that Mikhail was drifting from her, but it seemed to draw Jaklin closer. Of course, the big problem was that someday soon she'd have to tell them that she'd killed a man and fed off another. Since then, she also had this string of attacks she'd committed to feed her vampirism. She'd have to come clean about all of it. That's what she planned to do when she went to see Father Zosimos. Her grandmother had said he was wise. She'd have to trust him with this.

20

Visit from Rutfen and Emelia

Later that night, just at bedtime, they heard a knock on the front door. Alex went to answer it, but Mikhail beat her to it. He swung back the door and discovered Rutfen and Emelia looking up at them from the base of the steps like baby birds waiting to be fed by their mother.

"Would you like to come in?" asked Alex.

Rutfen wouldn't, and Emelia came into the entryway but no farther. Jaklin greeted her, but their guest was nervous.

"Would you be free for a couple of minutes?" Emelia asked Alex.

Alex turned to her two friends. "I'll be right back," she said.

"No way," said Jaklin. "You're not going anywhere without us."

"You'll have to chain me to the wall," said Mikhail. "Weren't these two vampires, at one time?"

"I'm concerned for your safety," Alex said. Though worried about both, she was especially uneasy about Jaklin.

"And what about yours?" said Mikhail.

With that, they all stepped out the door into the night air. "Stay behind me," said Alex.

"It's not far," said Rutfen. "We'd like you to meet someone."

They walked to a rundown section of Sinaia, and Alex wondered what she'd gotten herself and her companions into.

"We've leased a home," Rutfen said.

"We now have day jobs," added Emelia. "Just a Laundromat, but we've not been so happy in decades."

"Yes, Lord Rutfen is now a clothes cleaner," said Rutfen.

"You're a Lord?" asked Jaklin.

"Many decades ago," he answered. "Not by the name Rutfen. They turned me two centuries ago in Missolonghi. Perhaps someday I'll returned to merry old England and see if they recognize me."

"I just wish we could have children," said Emelia. "Love to have a couple to take care of."

"Who is this I'm to meet?" asked Alex.

"Someone who doesn't care for the vampire lifestyle," said Lord Rutfen.

They'd already come to the house. It was unlit inside, and Alex felt a little natural fear of the dark. She thought they'd turn on a light, but they didn't. What did their lifestyle have to do with her?

"Not enjoying this," said Mikhail.

"So we're about to see a vampire?" asked Jaklin in a squeaky little voice.

"And... how does this involve me?" asked Alex.

"When did you learn you could do it?" asked Rutfen.

"Do what?"

"Turn back vampires."

"I'm not sure what you mean."

"Turn 'm back. Make a vampire human again."

Alex stopped walking. "I can't do that."

"Of course you can," said Emelia. "You did it for us."

"I did?"

"Yes. That day in the cavern. Once we tasted you, it was immediate, and we had to leave in a hurry."

"So that was what happened to you?"

"And now we have another seeking conversion," said Emelia.

"Where is he?"

"Right in front of you," said Rutfen.

Alex felt Jaklin move up close and put her arm around her. Alex's eyes had adjusted to the dark, but it was pitch black inside. "Couldn't we have just a little light?" she asked.

"He has an acute aversion to it," said Emelia. "That's why he wants to be turned back."

A gruff voice came out of the darkness, uncomfortably close. "Not either. I was a monk. Want my old job back."

And then Alex saw him, a huge vampire, so tall he had to stoop to get into the room. She was greatly afraid of him.

"Turn him," said Rutfen. "Turn him back."

"So he's going to bite me?"

"I don't think so," said Mikhail, and he stepped in front of Alex.

The vampire was already advancing and seemed to have a bad attitude. He pushed Mikhail up against the wall and pulled Alex away from Jaklin and into his massive arms. She could feel his breath on her, and he smelled so bad she wondered if he wasn't rotting. Caught by surprise, Alex panicked. They struggled, she broke free, and as he reached for her arm again, she grabbed his with both her hands and, surprising even herself, threw him up against the wall. She'd never felt such a charge of energy.

"Wow!" said Rutfen. "You are one strong sister."

The vampire was already up and grabbing for her again, but she ducked, grabbed an arm and bent it behind his back while grabbing a handful of hair and pulling his head back. She felt the training her previous victims had provided.

"We'll do this my way or not at all," she said. She bent his neck farther back and brought hers forward to allow his massive mouth to touch her throat. "Just a little," she said, but he'd already broken the skin and was drinking. She shoved him away, and into the corner with a thud. He slumped to the floor.

"Could have made him bathe first," she said. But the truth was, she got a buzz from him feeding off her. She liked his neediness, that she could satisfy it. Good thing she wasn't alone with him.

"Striking!" he said. "Marvelous!" He smacked his lips. "A little disgusting at the end."

"Philosophically, he disagreed with the entire vampire existence," said Rutfen. "Not many want to be human again. He's one of the few. Strangely, he was violent, and uncooperative."

"I had more power in the Church." he said. "Now, instead of feeling guilty myself, I'll make others."

"There's more to turn back, if you can handle it," said Rutfen.

"I shouldn't until I get this figured out," said Alex.

"I'll not have anyone else biting her," said Mikhail. "You've put her through enough."

But Alex had already spotted a female vampire entering the room. She was a cute little thing, gorgeous girl even younger than herself. Alex felt an immediate affection for her, so much so that she felt she would be betraying Jaklin and Mikhail. She wished they hadn't come with her. She was so pretty.

"Maybe just one more," she said.

"Missy," said Jaklin. "Do you think it's wise?"

The girl came forward as Alex went to her. "This'll take just a second," she said.

Alex let the girl bite her, and she held her close and felt the warmth flow back into the young body. She didn't want her to quit feeding, but the girl did, seemingly having lost her taste for blood. Alex then showed her the cross, and the girl took it into her hands and kissed it. She cried. She clung to Alex, and Alex couldn't help but comfort her. She kissed her and had to hold herself off the girl.

Jaklin separated them. "Enough!" she said.

"That was sexual," said Mikhail.

"Really hot," said Jaklin.

"No, you can't take her home with you," said Mikhail. "We better get you out of here before you let them suck you dry."

But Alex had a question before they left. "Does Alu realize I turned you two back?"

"No. We were just visiting the colony. Vampires come and go there. No one questioned our leaving."

"I'd prefer no one know I have this talent."

"Don't worry. No one you've seen tonight will divulge your secret. We'll see to that."

"By the way," said Alex, turning to Emelia, "I thought you said vampires can't have kids."

"That's true."

"But I'm pregnant."

"Then you were pregnant before you became a vampire."

"Will my baby be a vampire?"

"You're not a true vampire. We're not sure what you are. How did you get turned?"

"Special circumstances." Alex knew better than to get into that now.

They left, the three of them together, all very quiet with their own perceptions and reservations of what had just happened. Mikhail whispered incessantly to himself. Jaklin was also quiet but held Alex's hand and put her other arm about her waist. Once home, Mikhail was really excited, over-the-top impressed. He talked about what Alex could do for the world. Alex was afraid to tell him the full story, that she also had to feed.

Jaklin was concerned for her. "The unknown is rarely all good," she said.

Then they tore into each other, all three so filled with passion that sleep was not an issue for a good while.

*

The next evening, Alex heard another knock at the door. It was a young man, the boyfriend of the girl whom she'd turned back the night before, a short timid young man, a little chunky. She took him out into the dark, and let him bite her. She got so turned on herself that she could hardly resist having sex with him right there. While he fed on her, she rubbed his shoulders. When he stopped feeding, she had to pull herself away from him. She then spotted his girlfriend waiting in the shadows. "Hmmm...," she said.

21

Confrontation with Father Zosimos

A couple of weeks later, Alex screwed up her courage, gathered Jaklin and Mikhail, and said, "I'm off to see Father Zosimos and would appreciate you coming."

Her dreams lately had turned increasingly ominous. They were not just dreams. They were a separate reality, as if she'd stepped into an alternate existence, one that paralleled our own. In them she felt frightened and confused. Her cross seemed her only guard against the dreams driving her crazy. She hoped that getting a little support from a priest might make them go away entirely.

"I won't let him bully you," said Mikhail, concern wrinkling his forehead. "These priests... I have a little experience with them."

The monastery was a five-minute walk toward the center of town. Mikhail sauntered quietly alongside Alex. Finally he said, "This is going to be a disaster. Priests are assholes. He'll mess up your life."

"He's always been kind and understanding," said Alex.

"He'll castigate all of us. Have us before some sort of inquisition."

They entered monastery grounds from a tourist parking lot and walked through a roofed entry with two redwood gates that were already swung open, then through a gravel courtyard and up the steps into the new chapel. They found a monk in the far corner inspecting a painting of Carol I. Alex asked if he knew where they might find

Father Zosimos.

"And who may I say wishes to see him?"

"Alexandra Eidyn," she said.

"Oh, yes. We've been told to watch for you. Follow me, please." Alex thought he bore a close resemblance to Father Zosimos. Perhaps it was the attire.

They left the chapel through the back door, crossed Monastery grounds to a row of rooms along the side of the square, past the old chapel. Mikhail pointed it out. He'd researched Sinaia on the Internet. It had been built in 1695 and was the founding structure for both the Monastery and the town of Sinaia, which grew up around it. Alex wondered why he knew more about her hometown than she did.

They stopped outside one of the rooms, and the young monk asked them to wait there. He'd see if Father Zosimos was available.

Alex felt displaced there at the Monastery. This was supposed to be holy ground, and yet, her own gazebo seemed more sacred. She looked at Jaklin and Mikhail. "I feel foolish," she said. "Wish I hadn't come."

But the monk returned just then, and Father Zosimos was with him. "Thank you, Daniel," he said and dismissed him. "My dear young lady," he said. "What a pleasant surprise, and I see you've brought friends?"

"Yes, Father. They are the dearest in all the world. I have something important to discuss with you, and I want them present."

"Then let us find suitable quarters," he said. He led them away from the outside row of rooms and to another chapel. He entered and led them down the isle, footsteps echoing. He seated them in the first row and brought up a chair so that he might face them.

Alex noticed that Christ's cross, large and intimidating, stood in the background behind him. The cathedral was deathly still, quiet. Their every word reverberated.

He motioned for her to speak.

"I've a confession," she started, and looked down at her folded hands. She pulled her cross from within her blouse, so that she might gain courage. "First I must tell you the humiliating news that I am pregnant."

"And who is the father?" he asked, glancing quickly at Mikhail.

"I've had a paternity check, and although it could be Mikhail, it isn't. The other sad news is that several weeks ago, I was raped. It was just before you came to test me for vampirism with the crosses."

"My child, did your grandmother know?"

"No one but me knows what I'm about to tell you. Perhaps you should just let me say it, and then you can do with me as you wish."

"Please proceed."

"We've all heard of the serial rapist that was murdered in the park. Well, it was he who raped me. Since the child does not belong to Mikhail, I can only assume that it must be the rapist's child I carry."

"Oh, Christ in Heaven!" the priest exclaimed. "So unfortunate." He was visibly shaken.

"It was I... who killed him," she confessed.

"But that was a bear. No one of your stature could have mangled him so."

"Trust me on this, Father. The pain and humiliation he put me through triggered such rage that I became something other than Alexandra Eidyn. "

"Oh, child. This is so difficult to believe."

"But you see Father, I am a vampire, and I hunger after blood from time to time. I go out at night, when I can get away from Jaklin and Mikhail without their knowing, and I find someone to feed on. I've done it several times, and I'm afraid that I'm causing much of the hysteria now raging in Sinaia."

She'd heard both her friends gasp at her revelation.

Mikhail interrupted. "This is such a shock. Why did you not confide in us?"

"I simply couldn't. I kept hoping it would go away." She still couldn't look her friends in the eyes.

"But we could have been a comfort to you and helped you weather this storm," said Jaklin.

"Sorry, but this storm is not temporary," Alex said. She felt so disappointed in herself.

Father Zosimos started to speak but then fell silent. Alex could see tears in his eyes. Finally he spoke. "Were you wearing the cross?" he said. "You promised."

"I was. Even when he raped me. Why didn't it protect me?"

"He wasn't a vampire."

"Yes, but he was evil."

"The cross can protect your soul but not your physicality."

"I had such great hopes for it." Alex still felt betrayed.

"Enough! Please!" shouted Father Zosimos. "Perhaps the cross is deficient, as I suspected from its questionable heritage. Such profane things spoken here before our Lord in his own temple. I know these evil beings exist because I've seen them with my own eyes. But never would one enter such holy ground as this. Yet, you have."

"That is the way I differ from normal vampires. I don't fear the cross." She knew this revelation sounded like callousness instead of piety.

He shielded his face in his hands for a moment and then turned to Jaklin. "Have you seen any of this? Do either of you," and he looked a Mikhail, "know this to be true? Is she delusional?"

"She is not delusional," said Jaklin, greatly offended. "Yet she only gives the sorry side of her condition. Just a few nights ago, we witnessed what is all but a miracle performed by Missy."

"Missy? Who is this Missy?"

"That's the name Alex gave to us as her own. We've known her as Missy from the first.

"Go on. The miracle?"

"We, the three of us, were taken to a home where Missy was requested to allow a vampire to bite her. This she did, and her blood cured this thing of vampirism."

"And another also," added Mikhail. "She was a wonder. Even the two people, whose home it was, claim to have been turned back from vampirism by her. She has a gift. But these new revelations of rabid vampirism, and murder. I've heard none of this." He glanced at Alex but immediately averted his eyes, as if repulsed at the very sight of her.

"And this relationship between the three of you, what is the nature of it?"

The room fell silent, none of them wishing to tell their secret.

Finally, Jaklin answered. "Mikhail and I love her," she said. "It's just quite simply true. We love her."

"Is your friendship carnal?" the priest asked.

"Yes, Father," said Alex. "I'm afraid it is."

"Don't be afraid," said Jaklin. "Be proud. Our love is nothing to denigrate."

Father Zosimos rose from his chair and paced a bit in front of the altar. He looked at them, opened his mouth, but no words came out.

Alex spoke. "Yet another plus to this terrible affliction is that those off of whom I feed are inoculated from ever having the vampire's disease, even if bitten. The other man I bit the night I committed the murder, he was bitten again by a feral vampire but has not become one. I am not normal, not even as a vampire. It has to do with Velinar, the woman who bit me, that divine being."

"Okay. That is enough. I get the picture," said Father Zosimos, finally finding his voice. "I have a tendency to be lenient with the human failings of Christ's followers, but this goes beyond anything I have encountered. Yet, this seems an absolute certainty. Your nature and the lifestyle you've chosen say to me that you must give up the cross. That which I gave to you should not bring comfort to one who practices such acts."

"Oh, Father, I do so love this cross. Please don't take it from me."

"Then promise that you will give up these two friends of yours, and that you will no longer feed off the blood of other human beings."

"I cannot give them up. They are a compulsion. And the drinking of blood is not a choice. It's a directive from my physical wellbeing. I have no more control over it than I do breathing."

"These persons you suck on, do they voluntarily give up their blood?"

Alex looked away. "No Father. I take it by force."

"As I thought. And this carnal relationship with your two friends?"

"I love them both so completely that I would give them up no more than I would Christ."

"Is it not lust that drives your need? Is it not the carnal part of the relationship?"

"But the true essence of my feeling for them is the love and compassion they show me. Their great kindness and affection. Their concern. That and their sympathy for all things that live on this Earth and the love of life here."

"Are they practicing Christians? Are you a practicing Christian?"

"No, Father. Not in the sense that we belong and participate in the Church. But the way they live their lives is the true path shown by Christ's life and teachings."

"Yes, well the carnal nature of your relationship would seem to show a different side of that story, wouldn't it? One of your lovers is a woman."

"Perhaps, Father."

"The cross, child. I'll have it back."

"But Father. It's the only protection I have from being consumed by hideous dreams. Giving it up will break my heart and leave me vulnerable."

He reached out his hand.

Sadly, slowly, Alex lifted the golden chain from around her neck and over her head. "You'll have to take it from me," she said, "for I cannot give it up of my own freewill."

With that, he grabbed it, but she would not turn loose.

"I wish I'd left it at home," she said.

They struggled.

"Please, Father."

"Relax your fingers."

She did and felt her cross leave her possession. She cried. Again, she experienced an encroaching darkness of the soul, dark shapes flitting about her.

"Here's my question," she said, tears streaming down her cheeks. "I feel that I should have the child. I don't want to end its little life. It is half me, after all. Yet, how can I have the child of a serial rapist? I lament that Bunică is not here to advise me on this."

Zosimos expression softened. "That would have been a wonderful thing. She was a great believer in the lost and forsaken people of the world." But Zosimos shook his head, and his expression changed, sympathy evaporating from among his deepening wrinkles. "You intend to carry it fullterm?"

"I've weighed both sides of the argument many times," Alex said. "I'm looking to you for guidance."

Alex saw darkness in his eyes and regretted coming to him. He seemed aloof. "To hear that you, an unholy vampire, wish to carry a child of rape and murder full term is a concern. It is not God's child, and to end it would not in itself be murder. It is a child of Satan. I must say that if you do carry this child to full term, you cannot raise it. It should be given to a proper family, unless it's a vampire."

Now that she had his opinion, her own surfaced. The thought of giving up the child was a grief she could not bear. "Oh, no, Father. I already have a great affection for the child. I love her. She is my daughter. Surely that will be my continual act of contrition, to see to her wellbeing always."

"But it is not your comfort and desire that should be considered in this but only the welfare of the child, the best situation for the child, if it is indeed a child. Surely you can see that being raised by a vampire, and particularly one involved in a ménage à trois, is not in her best interest? And if it were a vampire?"

"This child, regardless of the father, will be the only child I'll ever have. I've always wanted children, and regardless of the father, this is my only chance."

Alex broke. Something inside her seemed to crack open and all the grief flowed out. She sobbed. Like gusts of a hurricane, the misery of the soul pounded her. Her very bones ached.

"I came to you for help. I've not suffered any of this by choice." She creaked to her feet and looked directly at him. "Your council has failed me."

With that, she walked away from the priest, and they left the cathedral. Outside, the sun was too bright for Alex. Jaklin held her all the way home and shielded her from the sun with her jacket, but Mikhail was distant, quiet, and kept a pace behind them.

"I can't believe it can be this bad," he said. "You're a vampire. We're in love with you. I'm so messed up with you two that I don't know if I can live without you, either of you."

I'm losing him, Alex thought. He is such a fine young man, and I've lost him.

22

Alucius Then Catalin

That afternoon, Alex sat with Jaklin on the sofa reading. Mikhail was in the library surveying the books Alex's grandmother had collected throughout the decades. Alex had watched him grow restless, more distant, and dissatisfied as the day wore on. He even pushed Nălucă away. Jaklin went in to talk to him, and Alex overheard them arguing.

"My complaint," continued Mikhail, "is that not only did she kill someone, but she immediately turned on another innocent human being and almost killed him. This is like Dostoevsky's *Crime and Punishment* where Raskolnikov kills the old woman and immediately turns on her sister and kills her also. This has really thrown me into intellectual turmoil."

"Sonia is my favorite character in all literature," said Jaklin. "She believed in Roskalnikov."

"But a serial bloodsucker?" asked Mikhail. "She's not giving it up, you know. She didn't confide in us. She stood talking to that bounty hunter, Stefan, at the crime scene with the police investigating it right in broad daylight."

"Sonia, Mikhail. She gave Raskolnikov hope that redemption was possible, even though he'd committed the two brutal murders and one of them her own friend. Alex did this not out of intent but self preservation."

"I do believe in her, Jaklin. It's not that. Sonia knew her course before hand. I have to understand what this means. Missy is no longer human."

"Don't talk like that, Mikhail. That's disgusting."

"I know. I know. Yes, she is human, but not a normal human. Plus she assaults people. She has no control over that. She's taken a life, and I don't even believe in capital punishment."

"She turned four vampires back human, two right in front of us."

"Yes, I know. She was amazing."

"So why can't you just trust her, love her?"

"I do love her. I just need time to work this out. It's not a part of my philosophy."

"But that means you might quit loving her."

"No, it doesn't. Something about the three of us goes beyond even love. I just have to work out my reservations."

"She needs us. Think of her, not yourself."

When they returned to the living room, Alex went to them. "I know what you think of me," she said. "I'm so sorry that I didn't confide in you, but I couldn't stand to lose you. I didn't know what to think of myself. I know you're ashamed of me, Mikhail. I tried to tell you when my bunică died, when I took both of you into the gazebo. I just couldn't believe it of myself."

"I'm torn," said Mikhail. "I want to love you, to console you, but I can't. I just can't imagine you doing such things. I myself couldn't believe what you are, even when we followed you to that house, and you let those vampires bite you. But you were the cure then, not the disease. What bothers me most is that you have to feed. I don't know what to think."

Alex covered her face with her hands.

"The police are going to come for you," said Mikhail. He seemed desperate. "We'll be questioned as accessories to murder. And you've been attacking people on the street at night."

"I wish you wouldn't keep repeating that," said Alex.

"Listen to me, both of you," said Jaklin. "It's too soon to judge this. You've not brought any of this on yourself, Missy." Tears formed in her eyes and her voice cracked. "I for one would accuse you of nothing you did while being raped. A serial rapist, no less. Think of the women you've saved."

"I've always felt as though I was a non-person," said Alex. "I've seen myself as some strange being split into two parts that could never know each other. When we fell in love, it was as if I'd found myself. Without you two, I am a non-person. You are more than lovers. You make me who I am."

"Can you see why that close bond makes this even more critical?" asked Mikhail. "I've found myself in you two also. And I don't know what to think of myself."

"I know," said Alex, overcome by sadness and slumping onto the sofa. "I understand completely."

*

Come evening, Alex felt restless, and quite abruptly got up and went out the backdoor. She walked directly to the gazebo, but instead of Catalin, she found Alu Kard there, standing before it among the trees, his dark shape flitting about like a shadow in the breeze. Alex imagined that he could not actually enter the gazebo because it was in fact sacred ground. Why was he there so much? she wondered. But what really disturbed her was that she no longer felt afraid of Alu. In fact, he seemed a friend. She'd have to hide this change in attitude from him.

Alu was dressed in black, with a cloak that concealed his thin, insect shape. His manner was slow, like a preying mantis. The black cloak seemed to Alex more for stealth than effect. When the wind opened it, she saw a thin red band along the inside at the waist.

Alu started on her without salutation, as if it were a continuation of their discussion in his Throne Room. Alex wondered if thoughts of her had ever left his mind since they parted.

"Our mission is to make the people of Earth immortal," he said. "We have no entry fee into worldly immortality, no confession or repentance, unlike this other so-called spiritual world you so desire. Give up this fear of moral turpitude and join us."

Alex wondered why he was there, and then thought that maybe she held the key to him accomplishing some grand plan. Perhaps she was the one who could make or break his dream. "You shouldn't be here," she said. "I have no desire to talk to you."

"You've abandoned your cross?" he asked with obvious pleasure.

"They've taken it from me," Alex answered, feeling humiliated.

Alu roared with laughter. "The most powerful weapon in the history of the world and in the hands of the only one who can actually wield it, and they take it from you. So typical."

Alex got the irony and almost laughed herself. "I have committed a crime," she countered.

"They've convinced you of that, have they? These imbeciles are not worthy of you. Join forces with us, and little could stand in our way of bringing immortality to the masses. We could create a new race of vampires that can live in sunlight. Remember how you felt in the cavern? Lust! Power! It is your destiny, Miss Eidyn. Join me."

Alex was surprised at how tempting it was to just walk away with him. Everyone either condemned or questioned her actions, but here was the one being who cared not at all about her moral transgressions, and he commanded international legions. Yet, she couldn't bring herself to do it.

"I want a better life, one that can't be attained here on Earth."

He laughed again. "All the divine forces of the Universe, since Adam and Eve, have forever abandoned mortals in time of need, but still they grovel before them. The human race must evolve past this silliness," he said. "Humanity has pursued eternal life for millennia, and it's finally within reach."

She noticed that he seemed to be including her among the humans. "But immortality isn't intended for here on Earth."

Alu was indignant. "How do you know? Just because that's the way it has been? What do you know of eternal existence in the spiritual realm? If it's so great, why do they keep it secret?"

Alex had to think about that one. She remembered Michelangelo's painting of God and Adam on the ceiling of the Sistine Chapel, their fingertips not quite touching. "It's just a matter of not being able to bridge the void between this world and the next, not until death."

"Is it really? You've been there? Perhaps nothing exists beyond death for humans. Besides I received my immortality from a divine being, Prometheus, who wished humans to be immortal here on

Earth."

"I have seen the City of God. I saw it in a dream the night I killed a man. Life is tough here. People suffer. Why should I want to stay forever? Life in God's City was beyond imagining."

Alu scoffed. "You had a dream. And you base your real, actual life on it?"

"More than a dream. Besides, life here isn't easy for vampires."

"We don't suffer. No disease."

"Of course, we suffer. That's why we need blood."

"A triviality. A little human blood now and then." He smirked. "Perhaps we'll solve that deficiency someday. And you believe souls don't suffer in the Afterlife?"

"Perhaps in Purgatory. But it's a place of infinite justice. Once out of Purgatory, if you have to suffer it at all, you live in the one true utopia."

"What about the *Inferno*? Have you not read Dante? Or, perhaps it's a gray world without definition, full of amorphous beings and muted desires and feelings, as the ancient Greeks envisioned. All you know of Paradise is what you've been told. But you do know what life is like on planet Earth. You've experienced it. Here the world is in Technicolor with ambitions and lusts. Why not stay for eternity instead of getting just enough to whet your appetite?"

"You exclude love. What can you offer that provides meaning? Where does immortality in the real world lead?"

She saw a light flicker over the Gazebo behind Alu. He jumped as if hit in the back, and turned to look.

"Love is a torture they inflict on you. Don't let them deceive you," he said in hasty retreat. "Make them give up their secrets. They have no divine plan. Never have."

As Alex walked toward the ruins, he shouted after her. "Eventually, you'll see I'm right. You'll come to me." He disappeared among the trees, taking a wide birth around the gazebo.

Just as Alex stepped into the gazebo, Catalin appeared. "I've witnessed you speaking with Alucius of Kardacia, the original vampire. He's an evil being."

"Yet, he claims his status was a gift from the divine."

"So it was. Not all divine beings are moral creatures. Alucius is the source of Velinar's illness. Velinar thought she had learned his secret, and that she could deal a mortal blow to the entire vampire movement by instilling a little divinity in him. She let him suck a little of her blood. Instead of subduing him, Velinar was subdued herself, and their encounter invigorated Alu. As a result of her failure, the movement has become more powerful and threatens us all. He has amassed considerable power and influence during the three millennia he's been a vampire."

"I feel myself falling under his influence," she admitted. "How has Alu changed?"

"It's a matter of methods, I believe. Our knowledge of your world, his world, is not always transparent to us."

"My sole protection from him was the wooden cross. Father Zosimos took it from me."

"Oh dear Lord. How could this be?" Catalin said. "That cross was meant for you, and you alone. It's no ordinary cross. No telling the trouble that will come from this."

"I feel as though I'm stripped of my soul. It was the one thing that held me together."

"And perhaps you have been. That cross is the reason I've returned. It has an unparalleled lineage. Not only is it from Christ's cross, it is also from the Tree of Life."

"What Tree of Life? Should I know of this?"

"You do. The Tree of Life is in the Garden of Eden. After being evicted from the Garden, Adam had his third son, Seth, ask the Arc Angel Michael to bring him a branch from the Tree of Life, which he did. But by the time Seth returned, his father was dead. Seth planted it on his father's grave, and it grew into a magnificent timber. Solomon cut it down to build his temple, but found that it wouldn't maintain its shape, and he discarded it. Many generations later, the Romans used it for Christ's cross."

"Then what Father Zosimos told of its history is true. But why would it adopt a vampire?"

"Your cross is not an 'it.' A divine being radiates influence through the cross. And you are no ordinary vampire. I keep telling you this, but apparently it doesn't register."

"How could it? How can anyone come to terms with being a bloodsucker? How could I be the bearer of such of a cross? I'm bisexual and involved in a profane relationship."

"Your thirst for blood is not lust. It is a worldly necessity, life sustaining. And this love... Love is what God puts in your heart to work good in the world. If they share this love, then it is one of God's great earthly mysteries and must be honored. Unless, of course, you were to tell me that it's based on power and debasement."

"Never would I wish my will upon them, but only seek their fulfillment and happiness. My greatest pleasure is just being in the same room with them. To have them touch me with kindness is the source of my contentment."

"This then is true love, and the highest form of God's gifts. Not everything carnal is heavenly, and much of it is profane, but to touch with tenderness is divine."

"That's not what Father Zosimos said. He took the cross from me because of it."

"Oh, Marie!" said Catalin, throwing up his arms. "Such strange notions. We care less about carnal acts than the nature of love and compassion. We have our equivalent in the Divine World. Yours is but a metaphor of ours."

"I've already lost Mikhail," Alex said. "He's drifted from me."

"Love has its great moments, but also ebbs and flows. Yes, he may grow distant from you for a time, but if it is the love you've described, he'll return."

Alex thought this sounded like wishful thinking. "But I have killed a man."

"The Wrath of God can be a terrible thing. At times, he expresses it through a mortal. It is a great crime to take the cross from you over this, that which God himself has designated as yours."

"My story has more tragedy that Father Zosimos has levied against me, and it breaks my heart to even say this again." Alex looked down. She couldn't bear to see his reaction and turned her back toward him. "I'm pregnant."

"Heavens!" Catalin shouted. "Glory! An earthly immortal

conceived?"

"I carry the child of the man I murdered." She turned back, expecting an expression of horror, but instead, his face expressed wonder, amazement.

"The rapist is the father? You know this for a fact?"

"It's not my friend's, so it has to be the rapist's."

"The gender, is it a girl?" If she didn't know better, she'd believe she saw fear in his eyes.

"It is. Does it matter?"

His voice was a whisper. "Oh, Marie!"

"Father Zosimos suggests I abort it since it's a child of Satan. Otherwise, it must be put up for adoption."

"This is no child of the Great Evil. Do neither. I'm not allowed to reveal all that I know of this. Perhaps another will come concerning your fate and that of the child. You're beyond my Heavenly Order in so many ways. Just realize that you haven't gone unnoticed, and that your plight is of great concern to all of us."

"All of us?"

"I can't say more."

"Alu said you'd keep secrets. He said to press you. He's a great believer in life here on Earth. Eternal life."

"Alucius knows nothing of life in the Divine World. You cannot depend on his guidance."

"Then tell me, am I destined to live forever here on Earth and never get into Heaven?"

"Nothing on Earth, even Earth itself, is eternal, although it may seem so to Earthlings. Divine life is truly eternal."

"What happens to vampires? What is their ultimate fate?"

"When a human becomes a vampire, the soul loses its tether to Heaven and resides solely on Earth. When a vampire dies, the soul evaporates. Nothing goes to Heaven. Just fades into nonexistence."

"But I've turned some vampires back human."

"Once again, their soul becomes tethered to the Divine World. Such a gift you have, dear girl! Imagine how we admire and thank you for that."

"Yet your Church castigates me."

"Truly regrettable."

"Plus, I no longer have a presence in the Divine World. I'm an outcast."

"Don't try to apply this to yourself. You know that you're not like other vampires."

"Sure as hell not like other humans."

Catalin smiled. "Certainly not. The reason you're now more susceptible to evil is that you've inherited knowledge and immortality. It's the effect of the Tree of Knowledge and the Tree of Life."

"I am still human, then?"

"I cannot answer."

"Can't or won't?"

When he didn't respond, Alex turned from him and left the gazebo.

23

Breakup

When Alex returned from seeing Catalin, she discovered that Jaklin was still there, but crying. "He's gone," she said. "Missy! Mikhail is gone!"

Alex realized that she meant more than just Mikhail, but also what the three of them had together. Their sacred romance had disintegrated. The purpose that had gathered them into one had abandoned them.

Jaklin reached for Alex, and they clung to each other. For Alex, the hurt was growing ever deeper. She'd lost not only her grandmother but now her cross as well, the one thing that had made her condition, this feverish vampirism, tolerable. She was unraveling internally.

"I was so afraid here in the house alone," Jaklin said. "With the three of us, I had such courage. I've always been a coward. But with the three of us together, when we loved and trusted each other, even when I was alone, I had courage. I feel like a child again."

"Yes," said Alex. "You were extraordinary. You must learn to have that now for yourself alone."

"I can't, Missy. Our love had transformed me."

Alex and Jaklin sat before the fire. Alex ran her fingers through Jaklin's thick hair, and then went to get the brush her grandmother had used on her own. She undid the hairpins and let it fall below Jaklin's shoulders, and Alex brushed down in long flowing strokes, feeling the rich softness of the deep chocolate strands. Alex pulled it back over Jaklin's ears and noticed the clear, creamy complexion, the pale translucence that glowed in firelight, the light within the darkness. Jaklin was goth without trying to be. No wonder I was so captivated by this girl's presence that first night in the pub, Alex thought. Jaklin's eyes were crystal clear, the dark brown almost black against the white ceramic-like surface with just a pucker of fluid at the eyelid, the long dark natural lashes.

Jaklin smiled, noticing Alex's attention. "Why do you look at me?" she asked.

"Because you are such a beauty," she answered.

"Let me brush your hair," Jaklin said. "It's like golden silk in my hands, and I crave the feel of it."

Alex touched Jaklin's breast through her blouse and lingered there.

"Don't," said Jaklin. "Get me turned on, and it'll take hours for me to come down. I want to just sit here before the fire and enjoy this quiet time together. My passion goes so deep, it can be a burden."

Alex kept her hands to herself, and let Jaklin brush her hair, felt the firm tug of it pull her head backward.

"You're not real," said Jaklin. "Your hair is too golden and reflects too much light. You're like a walking dream, and when I look at you, I love you so much it hurts."

"Since Velinar bit me, I've grown into myself. Jaklin, I realize now that I've been lost all my life. I know that I'm a vampire, but now I am not the little lost child I've always been. For the first time, I feel as though I'm actually one with the world. I've lost Mikhail. Hopefully, I'll never lose you."

"I'll never quit loving you, regardless."

"I have to learn more about what's going on with the vampires of Sinaia. But I also need to learn more about myself. I have a strange attraction toward their dark world. I feel something wonderful there, and yet I also sense great evil." Alex wouldn't tell Jaklin that she'd talked again with Alu Kard. She was afraid that she might betray her attraction to him. She knew it was dangerous, but she had to find the boundaries of this new life she'd stepped into.

Alex also realized that she'd lost her moral bearing. She felt little, perhaps no, guilt over killing the rapist and attacking the other man. She felt no remorse over feeding off people or her sexual relationship with Jaklin and Mikhail. She wanted to bite Jaklin right then. It seemed the ultimate way to experience her. To literally consume her. Yet she did have some moral weathervane because she did restrain herself.

Jaklin read her silence. "Do you wish to bite me?" asked Jaklin. "You can, you know, if you want."

Alex felt a surge of passion light up her whole body. "No," she said. "I'll love you, but I'll not violate you."

"Do you not desire me?"

Alex smiled. "More than I can say. But love must have its limits. With you, I'd be a cannibal."

Jaklin smiled and seemed more pleased than Alex had ever seen her. "Then you know how I feel about you," she said.

"We do consume each other, don't we? You are an ever-replenishing source of the nectar of life. Love."

"It seems that I could literally live off my love for you."

"But a day may well come when I have to bite you to inoculate you against vampirism."

"Or perhaps, I'll ask you to turn me, so that I'll be with you for all eternity."

"That is a really interesting question. Can I turn someone? And if I can, what kind of vampire would they become?"

"I believe a time may come," said Jaklin, "when both of us will want that question answered. Right now, I'm caught between you and Mikhail."

That night, the two slept together without Mikhail. They held each other and cried. Alex felt a deepening, hard-hurting grief that went beyond even that over her grandmother's death. She tried to sleep but shuffled around and kicked most of the night. The strange dark shapes returned to terrorize her dreams, and she had no cross for protection. Jaklin woke every time Alex moved, and grabbed her again.

The next morning, they awoke to a bleak, dreary day. They were in the kitchen making separate breakfasts, their movements at cross purposes, bumping into each other, when Mikhail called on Jaklin's cellphone. She left the room to talk to him. Alex looked out the kitchen window at the garden, greener and more perfectly managed than she'd ever seen it throughout the years her grandmother cultivated it. This is Mikhail's influence, she thought. He's done the same with me. And now I've lost him.

When Jaklin returned, Alex spoke first. "You should go, Jaklin. He needs you, and you need him. I'm a lost soul."

"I can't leave you."

"We both need to get a grip. I don't even know who I am anymore. I could use a little time alone. Where is he?"

Jaklin's lips moved but no words came out. "Say the word and I'll stay. I love you more than anything or anyone."

"I'm a vampire!" Alex shouted. "You can't trust me. Go to him!" she ordered.

As the door slammed behind Jaklin, Alex fell to her knees, great sobs of grief overcoming her. When her moaning over what she'd just done subsided, Alex closed off the rest of the windows and cracks through which sunlight filtered. It had given her a headache. She sat on the sofa staring at the wall, her mind blank.

That afternoon she called her family, one at a time. After talking to each, she sat staring at the wall before calling the next. First, she called her mother, just to hear her voice. She was distant, still peeved over the will. Alex called her father, told him about her friends dumping her. He didn't know what to say. She called Gavril, but he was too busy to talk, so she called Sonya and talked to her girls. "Are you coming to see us?" they asked. "No, not now," she replied.

When her sister got back on the phone, Sonya said, "You sound so forlorn, Alex. Is something wrong?"

"I've lost my friends."

"You'll find others," she encouraged.

"But they were the first true friends I've ever had."

She hung up the phone and fell asleep with Nălucă in her arms. She dreamt of a great argument between amorphous shapes that flitted about her — quarreling, frightening voices. The dark shapes returned but seemed unconcerned with her and were rushing along a road toward something. Just before she woke, she had a dream of a winged creature leaving the City of God and descending through the firmament. She jolted awake.

She sat on the sofa blinking and felt as though someone from the City of God was actually coming. She thought how silly this sounded while watching the last spark of sun dip behind the mountains and twilight envelop Sinaia. Alex forced herself off the sofa and fed Nălucă. She stepped out of doors barefooted, still dreamy and blurry eyed. She walked to the hearth where she'd burned her clothes and shoes the night she became a vampire. Seemed an eternity ago. She ran her hands through what remained of the ashes and felt as though the remnants of her previous life in Bucharest were sifting through her fingers.

She walked to the gazebo. Perhaps Catalin would come talk to her. He didn't. She'd had such great plans to rebuild it. Now, she didn't know. The Church had turned against her. Mikhail had left her, and she'd driven off Jaklin. She didn't have the strength to even think about rebuilding it.

Alex walked to her grandmother's grave. It was amongst the trees just a few steps from the gazebo, alongside Alex's grandfather's. Alex remembered him, a small man with an easy smile and quiet manner. He had been a mathematician but rarely had work. She used to sit in his lap and he'd read to her, his voice intoning the great poetry of the ages. Alex thought of how her grandmother had encouraged her friendship with Jaklin and Mikhail. It seemed that her urging had come to naught.

She walked through the garden, felt the cold soft earth on the bottoms of her feet. She sat amongst the tomatoes, the ball-sized green fruit knocking against her skull, not caring that the moist earth soiled her bottom, and looked out at the mountains in the direction of the vampire cavern. She felt a pull toward it, and worried that she could easily fall under the influence of Alu Kard. Perhaps she already had more than she knew.

She'd be better off if she no longer existed. It seemed that if she didn't, so much would be put right. Her mother would inherit her grandmother's home and money. Perhaps Jaklin and Mikhail would get married. Vampires can die. I can die, she thought. She wondered what would happen to her soul. Did she have a soul anymore? Was she untethered?

Alex felt a quickening in her abdomen, just a butterfly flutter, the first wrestling of the baby. She ran a hand across the small bulge. It's a little girl, she thought, and for the first time, she started considering names. Should she be named for royalty? Should she give the little girl several names? And perhaps one of them a reference to the rapist? But Catalin has said that he was not the father.

I must deliver the child before I do anything about myself, she thought. This tiny little being must have a chance in the world. Until then, I have to do what I can to make it a better place. Father Zosimos had probably already told Stefan that she was a vampire. Perhaps if she went to him and offered her services, she could join forces with him. Alex didn't see vampires as necessarily evil. She couldn't allow him to kill vampires indiscriminately. And what about Alu? If it came down to killing him, could she do it? Would she? The problem, of course, was that while she'd be helping Stefan, she'd have to sneak off to get a little blood for herself from time to time.

Alex couldn't quit thinking these dark thoughts. She sat in the garden's failing light, evening's darkness creeping in from the forest and invading the tomato and pepper plants. She relished it, the darkness. It matched her heart's mood.

24

Graveyard Conniption

As the days came and went, the failure of Alex's friendship with Jaklin and Mikhail ever plagued her. She became increasingly despondent and couldn't keep from wondering where they were and what they were doing, if they were happy without her. Before knowing them, she'd prized time alone buried in a book, but now reading seemed empty and meaningless. She found a book of Plato's dialogues in her grandmother's library and reread *Symposium*, then ruminated over the purpose and nature of love.

One evening alone before the fireplace, the purr of Nălucă the only sound to break the silence, she thought she heard a faint clink in the backyard. She went to the door, opened it and peered out into the darkness. Nothing. Just as she was about to close it, she heard the noise again along with a dull clank and possibly hushed voices. She saw a dim light moving about in the direction of the gazebo.

At first, Alex felt fear, shuddered and closed the door, vowing to find out what had been going on out there in the morning light. Then she said to herself out-loud, "An immortal vampire with suicidal thoughts afraid of the dark?" She slipped out of her robe and into a pair of dark pants, pulled on Jaklin's black parka she'd left behind, more as a shield than for warmth. It reminded her of Jaklin's courage she'd demonstrated the night they saved Emelia and Rutfen. Alex raised the hood over her head to conceal her blond curls, pulled the drawstring tight about her face, opened the door again, and ventured silently into the gloom.

A wisp of fog had formed among the trees, and Alex walked across the yard into it. The commotion seemed to be coming from the graveyard adjacent the gazebo, where they'd buried her grandmother. As she drew closer, she saw the shapes of two, perhaps more, men shifting about in the dim light of a cellphone wedged in the crook of a tree trunk. She'd not seen an iPhone since she left Bucharest. In the fog, it provided a glowing halo about the workmen.

It'd been a while since Alex had fed. She'd suffered the last couple of days with fatigue and nausea, the initial stages of blood deficiency, but she wouldn't give in as self-punishment. The scent of these sweating men woke the urge, and she imagined that she could smell the blood surging their arteries. Quite the cliché, she thought. But she began to salivate and, since she hadn't had a good meal in days, envisioned herself on all fours devouring a caucus.

Alex recognized two of the men. Stefan Stanescu and Radu Cuza stood over her grandmother's partially uncovered grave that Alex had personally witnessed her grandmother being lowered into only a few weeks before. Two more men were down inside the soft earth, one digging with a shovel. This sent a surge of primal rage through her, the millennia worth of abuse and hatred felt by the race of vampires. She considered killing them all.

Even that explosion of emotion was nothing compared to the betrayal she felt by the fifth person standing over the open grave orchestrating the travesty — Father Zosimos in his dark flowing vestments, the friend of her grandmother and until recently Alex herself. She felt an instant hatred for the man, the priest who had taken her cross.

"Hey!" Alex shouted as she stepped into the light and lowered her hood. "Get out of there. You! Of all people!" she shouted, and as she did so, they turned to see who'd come among them.

"Stay back, Alex," Stefan said. "We're just verifying she's alright, that she hasn't been turned."

"Going to sever her head? You worthless piece of cow dung."

"Alexandra!" Zosimos shouted. "Leave! We have to do this. You lived with her."

"Coming after me next? Or sending the police?" she asked.

"Seize her!" Stefan shouted to the other two men. "Don't let her escape."

Alex had been walking into the scene and didn't even break stride. She felt her body come alive.

Zosimos backed away, but the others stood their ground. "She's no different than other vampires," said Stefan. "We can stake her."

"Alright then," said Alex. "Let's test this immortality thing."

She jumped down into the pit, grabbed the shovel from the frightened workman, and swung it forcefully, hitting him in the side as he lunged away from her. Her actions were smooth, coordinated, as if she'd choreographed them.

Stefan shouted at her. She looked up at him and utter hatred overcame her. But she heard something behind her and two more men jumped into the grave with her, knocking her from her feet and up against the dirt wall of the grave. She lost the shovel with the impact, but turned on her two advisories, cold rage guiding her.

Father Zosimos again shouted at her to stop, but words no longer mattered to Alex. One man grabbed her from behind, both of his arms locked about her waist. Alex struggled but he had her feet off the ground, so she reached up, grabbed him by the hair of his head, pulled it over her shoulder, and sunk her teeth deep into his neck. She didn't hit the jugular, but the flow of fresh blood then fueled the fire of her rage. She tore off a piece of human flesh and spat it out as he screamed in pain, turned her loose and reaching for his injured neck.

Alex turned on him anew. She kicked him full-force in the chest so hard that she propelled him out of the grave just as the other man grabbed her by the hair of her head and slung her in the other direction, up against the far end of the grave. Then he turned to run, but Alex was instantly on him from behind, her arms and legs wrapped around him like a gigantic spider. She clawed at his chest with her nails, tearing through his shirt and into his flesh. Her teeth found his hot, sweaty neck and again she tasted human blood, the rhythm of his heart synced with her own and driving her ever deeper toward seeking his death. The man screamed for some one to get her off him. Alex felt her fingernails penetrate to his rib bones and realized that her strength was so great that she could break open his chest cavity, if she allowed herself. She let him go, and stood in the soft earth now covered in blood looking up at a frightened bounty hunter.

Alex heard a shot rang out. Sounded like a handgun. She felt a tug at her chest, and something seemed to pass through her. She expected to weaken and feel pain, but she felt nothing. If anything she felt even stronger. She took one step and levitated up beside Stefan, who started backtracking. Alex heard another shot and felt a sting at the side of her head, as if being bit by a mosquito. She placed her hand over the spot but felt nothing. She looked at her hand but saw no blood. Three more shots rang out. Alex didn't know why she didn't fall. At lest, she should be in pain. She grabbed Stefan by the throat, and knew she was about to kill him. She could crush his larynx in a heartbeat, rip his throat from his body, but Alex felt something, just a slight fluttering in her abdomen. It was the child. Just that single thought, the child, stopped her cold. But as she did, a tremendous force hit her from behind. It knocked her loose from Stefan and to the ground. She scrambled to look back as would a cat on all fours, ready to pounce on her assailant and realized that the first man she'd bitten had tried to drive a stake through her back and into her heart.

She ran for him, and he lunged forward with the stake again hitting her directly in the chest. She hardly felt it. Instead, she was on him too, sank her teeth into his neck and fell on the ground with him. This time the blood gushed, and she swallowed and would have drained him, if it weren't for words close to her ear.

"Alexandra, please, Alex. For the love of God, don't do this. We'll cover the grave. Please. Stop." It was Father Zosimos.

Alex quit sucking and let the blood drain back onto her victim. She wiped her mouth with her hand and stood to face the priest. Words flowed from her lips without the thought forming first in her mind. "The wrath of God is upon you. Hell fire itself awaits if you ever raise this coffin."

"Yes, yes," he said. "It's a mistake we'll not repeat. But Alexandra. Don't do this. You're injured. Let us get you to the hospital."

"I shot her five times," said one of the men. "She should be dead."

"I'm not hurt," said Alex. "Get out of here before I kill all of you."

And they did. They ran like rabbits from a hound. Only Father Zosimos turned to look back.

Alex shouted after him, "The cross belongs to me. Catalin said so."

They disappeared into the dark of the forest.

Alex didn't have thoughts or feelings about what she'd done. She grabbed a shovel and started filling in her grandmother's grave. Once covered, she kneeled before it, said the Lord's Prayer, and left carrying the shovel over her shoulder. She walked back into the home that now seemed more her grandmother's than it ever had. This pleased Alex greatly. She felt her grandmother's presence, her love and affection. She didn't bother turning on a light because she could see perfectly well in the dark. She ran a bath, poured a little, maybe a lot, of bubble bath and soaked for a long, long time. The baby moved again. Alex hugged her abdomen and felt as content as ever had an Earth-bound immortal creature.

*

The next morning, Alex rose early, dressed, and walked along the edge of the forest, up the cobblestone footpath, and into the Monastery courtyard. She passed the row of offices and walked directly to a little cottage. She knew exactly where she was going. She opened a side door into a small room. There, she found a startled Father Zosimos and Stefan in deep consultation. They jumped to their feet.

"I want to help," she said.

25

Hunting Vampires

Alex had promised herself that she'd not again ask Father Zosimos to return her cross. Seeing his rather large silver one hanging firmly from a chain about his neck made her want to strangle him with it. Even light-haired, freckle-faced Stefan had a little gold one jangling. Standing before the two frightened men there in Zosimos's chamber, rather than admonish them, she simply said, "Let us not mention last night. I wish to help you rid the world of vampires."

"Promise not to attack us," said Father Zosimos.

"Unless provoked."

Father Zosimos stared at her, looked away, but eventually said, "Agreed. We thought a peaceful coexistence had settled in between us and the vampires of Prahova Valley, but lately, even as far away as Bucharest, we've had some rather brutal attacks on our citizens. Do you know of this?"

"The leader of the vampires has recently gained an advantage. Not sure what that means, but the Divine World believes the change is serious." Alex purposely withheld Alu's name, out of distrust.

"You speak to me of the divine? The irony of that is compelling," He shook his head in admonition. "Are you sure these apparitions you see are from Heaven?"

Alex didn't respond immediately. She stared at him. "Are you sure you represent Divine Will?"

Father Zosimos didn't respond, just lowered his head.

Stefan hadn't spoken, but watched her closely, and even now appeared hesitant. "What part do you play in all this? Father Zosimos tells a strange story of you being bitten by some divine vampire. Who are you? Aren't you really just one of them?"

"Apparently, I am a vampire although I'm not allergic to sunlight. I do require blood, but I also have a gift. I can turn vampires back human. Perhaps, I even have the ability to inoculate. Radu Cuza might testify to that."

"Radu has had enough of you, no doubt. But where do vampires hide? Can you take us to them?"

Alex had anticipated this question. "You'll have to prove yourself, your intent. Perhaps we can work together, perhaps not."

"Our intent is to rid the world of vampires. You've already said you wish that."

"But I wish to restore their humanity."

Stefan laughed, snickered and looked at Zosimos. "Humanity for bloodsuckers and murderers?"

"Again with the attitude. My being here seems a mistake."

Neither seemed forthcoming. Father Zosimos spoke. "Go out with them tonight. Learn to work together."

"Can I trust a bounty hunter?" Alex asked.

Stefan laughed out loud. "You don't trust us? You threatened to kill us all."

"I told you not to mention last night," she said, taking a step toward him. "You shot me five times."

Stefan held up both hands. "Peace. No offense."

Alex then bid Stefan leave her alone with Father Zosmios, and after getting assurances from the priest, Stefan left.

"I need to know what you're going to do with my assets," she said. "My ownership of my grandmother's home and my finances are all subject to your influence. Will you try to ruin me?"

"Never will I take such drastic action," he said. "Let us both trust each other," he suggested. "Let's see where all this leads. Perhaps, we'll learn if your condition is permanent, or perhaps temporary as this Catalin suggested at one time."

"I believe he's spoken plainly on that issue," she said, realizing Father Zosimos was no longer being honest. "But I'm pleased to hear you've not totally passed judgment. Perhaps you're right. After all, I am pregnant, and who knows the influence of divine forces on the future."

"Yes. We're both concerned about the child. Perhaps after you deliver, we'll get a clearer picture of the situation."

"You don't give a damn about this child," said Alex, growing more alarmed at his feigned sympathy. "You already told me to get rid of it."

She couldn't take anymore. Alex turned her back on him, walked out of his office and left Monastery grounds.

*

Alex left her home at sundown and walked the short distance down hill to Dimitrie Ghica Park, where over the phone she'd agreed to meet Stefan. They were only to use her skills to identify the vampire and subdue it — hopefully one of the more aggressive ones — and see if Alex could turn it back human. This would confirm to Stefan that her blood was a cure.

These more hostile vampires had recently been seen around Sinaia Casino, which was a block away. Alex was concerned about Jaklin since the ICC was there. Alex could see light from it through the trees and hear faint voices from within. King Carol had built it in 1913. Originally, it had in fact been a casino, but when the communists took over Romania, one of the first things they did was to abolish all gambling houses, most of which had been restored. Now the Romanian government used Casino Sinaia as a meeting place and the ICC staged events there.

As the darkness deepened, Alex felt a chill and wished she'd brought a sweater. Her cellphone rang. It was Stefan.

"We have a live one," he said. "Undead one actually, on the loose a few streets over, outside the park."

Alex left immediately, crossed the main thoroughfare. The sidewalks were full of tourists out for a stroll and an evening meal. A couple of streets over, no streetlights lit her way, and pedestrians were nonexistent. Alex didn't like the looks of it. Out in the open and in a public place, she felt the situation wouldn't get out of hand, but out of sight in a private home? She wasn't so sure what Stefan would do.

At first, Alex saw no one and thought she must have gotten the directions wrong. Then she heard a faint cry from inside a house across the street, and Stefan appeared from behind a tree in the front yard.

"She's inside," he said. "Hurry, we may be too late already."

A female vampire. Alex realized this wouldn't be easy for her if it became violent.

"Who lives here?" she asked.

"An old couple," he answered.

It was a dilapidated, two-story building dwarfed by trees and surrounded by thick bushes. They opened a creaking back gate, walked through the porch and opened a door into the kitchen. Stefan motioned Alex in first, not something she was particularly crazy about. The house was dark, but she could hear the vampire at work upstairs. Probably a bedroom, she thought. "Kill your flashlight," she said. "I can see." She felt his hand on her back as he followed her.

They exited the kitchen into the living room, and Alex saw the stairs off to the right opposite the front door and started up it with Stefan's hand on her back all the way. She heard an old woman's voice raised in protest. Once inside the bedroom, she saw that the feral vampire had already killed the old man, lying on his back and blood drenched, and was on her knees astraddle the old woman working on her neck.

The female vampire was dressed in a black, fluffy blouse and jeans, long stringy hair pulled into a tight bun. She rose from her victim and turned to look at Alex as she entered, blood streaming from the corners of her mouth, fangs glistening in the pale light from the open bedroom window on the left wall.

Alex motioned to the window, and said to Stefan, "Close it." As he made his way toward the window, Alex turned to the vampire.

"Come to me. I can help you."

The vampire shrieked, levitated from the bed, kicked to repel off the far wall, rebounded off the right wall, and was instantly at the door from which they'd just entered, all the time shouting and screaming. The vampire didn't seem to be a woman at all, but a caged mountain lion. Alex thought she'd surely escape, but she seemed strangely transfixed on Alex, her eyes locked like laser beams. Alex felt sorry for her. The fear in her eyes was unimaginable.

As Alex tried to talk to her, she repelled around the room once again, and smashed into Alex so quickly that she was helpless to defend against her. Just as she was about to bite into Alex's neck, Stefan staked her from behind. Alex screamed to stop him, but Stefan was crazy for the kill. The vampire turned away from Alex, jerking the stake out of Stefan's hands and slung it across the room. He'd missed the heart. She then turned back to Alex, but had now become even more agitated. Stefan quickly retrieved his stake, and as Alex screamed, "No!" he drove it through the vampire's chest and this time found her heart, blood gushing, spurting up from the wound. The vampire gnashed its teeth, emitted a great shout, followed by words of poetry streaming from her lips.

Alex ran to her, held her head in her own lap as the woman coughed, sputtered, choked back clotted black blood. She looked up at Alex, grief emanating from her eyes. In a halting voice, she said, "Sorry. So very... sorry," and died. Alex thought that this feral hadn't been turned by choice.

Such a pitiful death. "It didn't have to end this way," Alex said. "I could have saved her."

As Alex rose to her feet, ready to take on Stefan, the old man, whom the vampire had killed, rose up from the dead and made for Alex.

"Back off this time," Alex said to Stefan. "Let me handle this."

Stefan ignored her and went for the old man with his stake anyway. Alex grabbed Stefan from behind just before he reached his target and threw him up against the wall. The old man came for Alex, and she let him take her to the floor, bite her. As Stefan looked on, the old man became confused, rose up from her vomiting blood and stumbled to the far side of the room. He stood against the wall for support as his body started shaking and trembling. It gradually became a full-blown seizure that enveloped his entire body. He fell to the floor screaming as sparks and flames started at his mouth and gradually crept over him. A smoky stench filled the room. Alex looked back at Stefan, but he'd collapsed also.

Alex was confused. What had her blood done to the creature? Why didn't he become human? But then, in what seemed to Alex an unending saga, the old woman, who had also just become a vampire, shouted an oath and rose up off the bed. Alex grabbed her, and let her sink her teeth into her neck. Once again, the vampire became confused, then went into the same trembling-seizure routine that had been the ruin of the old man, followed by sparks and flames. Alex let her fall to the floor. The smoke made Alex dizzy, and she staggered to the window to open it and let in fresh air.

While the air cleared, Alex went into the hall and seeing a door open to another bedroom, she went inside. In addition to a single bed, Alex saw a desk with several sheets of handwritten poetry. A large bookcase against the far wall contained several volumes of verse but also many of philosophy from ancient times to modern. Humm, thought Alex. A scholar. Obviously, she was the daughter of the elderly couple she'd turned. What a tragedy they were feral. None of this was by choice, she realized.

Alex heard the rustle of footsteps and the banging of doors as two of Stefan's crew searched the rest of the house. Alex went back to the parents' bedroom and dragged Stefan's limp form out into the hall. She thought of inoculating him right there, heaven knew she needed the blood, but right then she was so mad at him that she thought it could wait awhile. She stood over him as he revived.

"What happened to me?" he asked.

"The smoke of burning vampires," she said. She helped him to his feet. "Made me a little dizzy too."

Stefan's crew loaded the three bodies, two of them badly charred, into a van.

"We have our own crematorium," said Stefan getting into the drivers seat. "We'll finish the job. Want a ride?"

"No. I want to walk back through Sinaia. Clear my lungs of vampire smoke."

"So tell me, what happened to this turning-back hypothesis of yours?"

Alex stood in the street staring at him through the van's open window. "You were right. These are different. I've turned five vampires back human, but these ferals burst into flame."

"You have holy blood in your veins," said Stefan. "As for you turning vampires back, I'll believe it when I see it."

"I can do it," she responded. "We can save the lives of regular vampires."

"For what? Toast the bastards."

"Murder isn't right."

Stefan scoffed. "They're all alike and should be killed and cremated. This business of turning them back and forgiving their atrocities... No way. This is war."

What a disappointing evening, she thought. And here I reckoned I could save all the world's vampires. What could possibly have gone wrong? But she realized that these were a different type of vampire, much more violent and erratic. Perhaps Stefan was right about her blood. She'd heard that when vampires drank holy water, they went into spontaneous combustion. Her blood seemed to do the same thing to a feral.

Alex watched the van drive away. She hadn't told Stefan, but with the loss of blood, she had to feed, and soon. Already, she felt the fever and body aches. As soon as the van was out of sight, she found a secluded alley, and slipped into the darkness, attacked a young man on his way back to his hotel. While feeding, she thought she saw someone spying on her from behind a trash bin. She released her prey and quickly exited that alley and entered another a block away. And then she saw them following her. It was Stefan and his two associates. She stepped out into the open and called to them.

"You just had to witness it, didn't you?"

"You're a one-hundred and twenty pound mosquito." He drew a weapon from within his trench coat. "All vampires should die," he said. He raised the weapon and fired.

The impact knocked Alex backward. She stumbled and fell flat on the ground.

Stefan was on her immediately. "Look!" he said to his associates. "Everything born will die. Just like all the rest of those bloodsucking maggots. It's the crematorium for her. Quick! She might regain her strength." He handcuffed her.

Alex was so weak that she could barely move, but she managed to say, "Stefan, you fool!" and then passed out momentarily. She started to revive as they dragged her by the feet out to their van. Through her mist-filled consciousness, Alex heard someone shout.

"Stop!" The voice rang out. Then even louder, "Halt! We've called the police." It was just a couple of passersby, a man and a woman.

Alex ripped open the handcuffs and threw them aside.

Stefan and his cronies quickly abandoned the rapidly recovering Alex, and her two saviors were at her side. "Help me up," she said. "This ground is cold."

"We thought they'd killed you," said the middle-aged man.

"I couldn't be so lucky."

"Were they Gypsies?" the woman asked. "I've heard of abductions, but never witnessed one."

"Thanks for you help," said Alex. "But I'm in a horrible hurry." She had to get to the Monastery. Father Zosimos must know what happened.

"The police will be here any minute," the couple called after her.

Alex rapidly recovered and walked quickly to the Monastery. Inside the main gate, she saw what appeared to be Stefan's van. When she neared Father Zosimos' chamber, Alex proceeded more cautiously, went into the bushes and peeked through the window. She saw Stefan talking to the priest. She overheard bits of their conversation.

"We fired an ironwood slug from a sawed-off shotgun straight through her chest," said Stefan. "Firing one through the heart of a vampire has killed them every time."

"But not so our Miss Eidyn," puzzled Father Zosimos. "And she failed to turn the vampires back human. Really disappointing."

Alex had heard enough to realize that Father Zosimos had been complicit in the whole affair. She quietly retreated, tears streaming down her cheeks. She headed home to consider what to do next. She'd gone into a depression, and although she now cared little for her own safety, she cried for her child. How could she bring her little girl into such an unhinged world?

26

Home Invasion

When Alex got home that night, she left the lights off. She felt hunted, and with her night vision, she was on a level playing field with anyone who might try to enter her home, even other vampires. Not to mention that she was proving rather difficult to kill. She stuffed her bed covers to look like she was underneath sleeping and grabbed a dark blanket and pillow from another bedroom and took them downstairs where she curled up in a corner out of the light of the glowing coals of the fireplace.

Alex remembered the nights she'd wake to find Mikhail staring out the window. She'd get out of bed and go stand beside him, look out at the city lights below and listen to night noises. How she'd loved those times. How she missed their quiet hours together with Jaklin soundly asleep nearby.

That night was uneventful. The next morning she called Oxford to inform them that she would have to delay her matriculation one year. They gave her directions on how to accomplish a deferment on their website. She sat before her computer and cried. She didn't realize that she did actually want to go to university. She even missed her friends back in secondary school. The humiliation of being pregnant and unmarried she'd take as a blessing if she could just be a normal human again. She steadied herself and filled out the online form.

Once finished with Oxford, she went down the hill to Sinaia and asked around until she found a store that carried baby clothes. She bought the cutest little jump suit, a couple dozen diapers, some tiny little tops and bottoms, some unbelievably small socks, and a pair of itsy white shoes. She bought bibs, a rattle, a mobile and a couple of stuffed animals: a rabbit and a donkey. An adorable pink baby blanket.

She was beginning to show even under casual observation, and thought this would help her get serious about being a mother. She was going to have the baby regardless of what Father Zosimos thought. And the little girl wasn't going to be a daughter of Satan either.

Once home, she opened all the packages, laid the baby clothes out on the sofa and watched the light from the fireplace flicker on her prized possessions. When she squeezed the donkey it brayed, which made her laugh in spite of her depression.

Alex realized she would have to protect the child from Father Zosimos, that he might even try to make her miscarry. She'd have to stay indoors as much as possible. She could get much of her food from the garden, but she'd need bread and soy milk from the market. She'd go out during the day. Surely they wouldn't attack her in public and in broad daylight.

Alex considered confessing her predicament to her parents. Perhaps they'd understand and protect her. But she couldn't endure the humiliation. They'd never been close; she'd lost what favor she had with her mother by inheriting her fortune. And being a vampire was not one of the things parents ordinarily hoped for in a teenage daughter. Father Zosimos hadn't contacted them. He'd never let it get out that he believed in vampires. Alex thought of going to her sister's, but that would put her girls at risk. Alex didn't even know what she herself might capable of. Those sweet little bodies were so bitable.

Alex went up into her grandmother's attic and retrieved, with some difficulty, a small crib for when the baby arrived. The attic had been something of a family mystery, no one ever having been permitted up there, not even Alex's mother and father. Her grandmother had mentioned something about it containing a family secret that she wanted to share with Alex, something so heart wrenching that she had to gather her courage to do it. She'd not lived long enough.

Alex loved the musty smell of the place and the sense of history in the old objects cast carelessly about. The attic was a large space with unfinished flooring beneath the exposed underside of the roof. Nails stuck through the rough surface, and 2x4 crossbeams on edge reinforced it. It contained odd pieces of furniture, a small desk, and several cardboard boxes packed with old kitchen utensils.

Off in one corner against the wall, stood an iron-barred cage big enough for a large animal. It had been anchored to the house framing with huge bolts and had obviously been brought in piecemeal and welded together there. Inside were a bunk bed mattress and a portable toilet seat. The small door was chained and padlocked. Alex had never seen anything quite like it. Perhaps this was her grandmother's secret.

She also found her grandfather's staff that he'd used later in life. He was a great hiker, even into his seventies. It came to him in the post one day unannounced. She remembered that he'd let her play with it. It was made from extremely heavy wood, straight, and practically indestructible, with a large natural knot at the top and stood to her shoulders. He'd taken to it immediately, but never learned who sent it. He'd also taught Alex how to swing it, confessing he'd been taught a Japanese style of self-defense while on the island of Okinawa during his military service. Alex felt such great affection for it that she set it aside. Perhaps she'd find a use for it.

Two chests, one large and one small, were pushed up against the wall with boxes stacked on top. Alex set the boxes aside and open the larger chest, the more interesting of the two. She brushed off the dust with a rag, coughed, and raised the lid. Inside, she found a cardboard box of old family pictures, even pictures of family members with Queen Marie, definite verification of Alex's grandmother's story of the dark side of royalty. One person stood out, a rather strange woman with black hair and dark sunken eyes. Curious, Alex thought.

Alex kept back the box of pictures, lowered the lid and opened the smaller chest. It contained love letters from her grandfather during their courtship. Interesting, but also private and not a confidentiality she wished to violate.

Next to the smaller chest, Alex noticed a peculiar pattern in the rough wood flooring. The square pattern appeared to be a firm part of the floor, but yet why would it be shaped so? She found an old table knife among the discarded kitchen utensils and inserted it along one edge. She pried but nothing budged. Then she tried along the other edge, and thought she felt movement. She tried the opposite edge, and gradually it gave way.

Alex raised the small section of flooring, and in the space below, found a small wooden box. She raised the lid. Inside was a leather-bound book. Alex removed it, and as she opened it, it cracked and threatened to fall apart. Apparently, it was a diary. She read a page in the middle dated December 22, 1921. She turned to the first pages. It was the property of Catherine Cantacuzene. Catherine was Alex's great grandmother's name. She remembered that Cantacuzene was the family name of Queen Marie's lover, the Hussar, Lieutenant Zizi Cantacuzene. This was her great grandmother's diary. She had used her father's family name.

Alex replaced the floorboard but kept the diary. She also picked up the cardboard box of pictures. She climbed down from the attic to the second floor hall and took the stairs to the living room. She located the biography of Queen Marie that her grandmother had given her and turned to the index. Alex thought she remembered something strange about a family member, and sure enough there it was. Queen Marie had a friend named Manuka Cantacuzene, obviously a relative of Zizi. And here was the peculiarity. Manuka had an aversion to light and crowds. She hardly, if ever, ventured out of doors. The thing was, she only allowed candles for lighting. Her home stayed so dark that guests frequently tripped over furniture. She wondered if Manuka could have been one of the Undead. If so, Alex's family had a connection to the race of vampires going back some ninety years.

Alex looked through the pictures in the cardboard box and again located the picture of the strange dark woman. Was that Manuka? She also found the pictures of Queen Marie, only two, but here was the interesting thing. One of them was taken with a young woman holding a child, which Alex thought had a strong resemblance to her own grandmother. Was this Catherine? Was this a generational picture: Queen, daughter, grandchild?

One other thing about the picture struck Alex. It had been taken out of doors before an open-air structure. Only part of it was visible, but it had to be the gazebo. Queen Marie had it built about the same time. What was so special about the gazebo anyway? Velinar was the source of the apparition that first night, when Alex believed it had been rebuilt, and this added further complexity to the mystery. Had Velinar created the illusion to attract Alex? Was the gazebo a portal to the Divine World? Or built over such a portal?

Then she wondered what Velinar was doing so close to the gazebo when she collapsed. Had she been trying to get to it? Would she have been safe if she had made it inside? But what if Velinar wasn't allowed into the gazebo because she was a vampire? That sounded even more likely. Alu was frightened of it. Alex remembered that when Velinar first grabbed her, she bit her then shoved her into the gazebo while drinking her blood. Perhaps it wasn't just that drinking Alex's blood had saved her, but the fact that her contact with Alex had allowed her to once again enter the gazebo.

Another thing about the name Cantacuzene came to mind. Mikhail had mentioned it. Back in 1695, Prince Mihail Cantacuzino built the Sinaia Monastery after a trip he made to the biblical Mt. Sinai. The entire town of Sinaia grew up around the Monastery. And Alex's biological great great grandfather, Zizi Cantacuzene, was a member of that same family. Somehow, it all was starting to make sense. She wondered if it could have something to do with the disappearance of her great grandmother, Catherine.

That evening, Alex set before the fire petting Nălucă and reading Catherine's journal. Most of it was just personal stuff, things that would interest only the author. Toward the end, the narrative changed and was mostly about Catherine's baby, Alex's grandmother, and her antics as a child. So adorable. But the last few pages concerned an aunt that sometimes came to visit, one from her father's side of the family, and her visits caused great excitement. Catherine would then have been twenty-four years old. Catherine's excitement centered around a mysterious gift, one that would change her life forever, that her aunt would have bestowed on her, if she wished. But the narrative came to an end at that point, and the gift remained a mystery. Alex wondered if the aunt was Manuka, the woman she suspected of being a vampire.

The only thing Alex remembered her grandmother saying about her mother was that she'd disappeared when she was young and never returned. Alex's grandmother was actually raised by relatives, until she was old enough to take custody of her estate. Could Manuka have turned Catherine or have had her turned?

Alex shook her head, closed the biography and the journal, put away the pictures. This was lunacy. Surely someone in the family would have known if Catherine had been a vampire. She'd never figure it all out. Perhaps it didn't matter anyway.

Alex let the fire burn low so that only the glow of coals sent a pale red light about the living room. Again, she cuddled in the corner with her blanket and pillow. The absence of Jaklin and Mikhail descended on her like a disease. Never had she felt the vacuum left by having lost friends. Always she'd been able to walk away from those she knew, even her own family, but Jaklin and Mikhail were closer than family, more than friends. They had taken a piece of her with them, if not taken all of what she had recognized as her new self. She was now a non-person, as she had been before meeting them. She was again Al-Ex, the non-existent person. Alex began wondering why she was staying among humans at all. No one liked her.

Alex longed to enter the cavern again. Vampires were the ones who truly understood. They accepted her. The only reason Alu had kicked her out was that she brought the cross with her. Not a problem now. She remembered how they'd all gathered about her and wanted to touch her. With them, she'd felt special. Yet, here she stayed, toughing it out in the World of the Living, putting her child at risk.

It was more than that. If she were to live for eternity, she wished to be among those who knew about the problems of immortality. They could tell her how to cope with the boredom that would undoubtedly set in after a while. She wondered if immortality had consolations that made seeing all those you knew and loved grow old and die while staying young yourself not seem so bad. She wished to sit amongst the small groups of intellectuals and discuss the great philosophical issues of the time, to hear of their exploits, the origin and lore of the vampire.

And then there were the orgies.

Alex's child would be safe there. It would have no father and be shunned by human society as a child of a vampire, shunned and hunted, ever at risk. Alu already had a plan for the unborn child and believed she could be a great boon to the vampire community. Somewhat of a scary thought, she had to admit.

She'd just dropped off to sleep when something woke her. It wasn't a noise or a light. The baby had moved, just a flutter, but she'd not felt it since the night she'd wanted to kill Stefan at her grandmother's grave.

From her corner of the living room, Alex saw, not shadows, but the sequential eclipsing of distant lights penetrating outside darkness. She heard a faint rustling in the backyard and even a whisper from the front of the house. Had Alu come for her? She felt panic but didn't know where to run. She saw a flash of light from the stairs and realized that someone had entered her bedroom, her grandmother's bedroom. Her panic turned to anger. They'd obviously come up the outdoor stairway to the balcony, perhaps slipped in a window. They'd know by now that she wasn't in bed. She heard more whispering, this time from upstairs.

She raised up, dumping Nălucă from her lap. Somehow, she knew it wasn't vampires. Yet she wondered who it could be: Stefan and his group of bounty hunters? And then she saw the silhouette of someone peeking in through a window in the kitchen, and that of another on the curtains. She could hear them communicating over their wireless radios. Police. She imagined them whispering into their sleeve cuffs or their collars. And then she realized that it was a swat-team, and a wave of foreboding and fear come over her, but quickly turned to rage. They'd violated her sanctity.

Instinctively, Alex moved quickly and quietly into the kitchen and retrieved a large roll of duct tape. Then she scurried up the stairs and into the hall, just in time to see one of the intruders enter her spare bedroom. Silently, she came up behind him in the dark.

As the instant of violence approached, her body seemed a finely honed instrument. When the policeman turned to see who was behind him, possibly thinking it was one of the swat-team, Alex hit him in the solar plexus, knocking the wind from him and doubling him over.

She then threw him up against the wall, taped his mouth, kicked his legs out from under him, and taped both hands together behind his back. She then taped both feet together, pulled his feet up behind to his hands, and strung the tape up to his neck. He could scarcely move, and she'd accomplished it all in a matter of seconds with her vampire agility and quickness. She had the man's automatic weapon in her hands, which she didn't know how to use, but she didn't need to.

As she waited behind the door for the next one, she had to calm herself. The urge to feed was strong, but the desire to kill was even stronger. When the next policeman entered, she hit him in the temple with the butt of the automatic rifle and knocked him out cold as a doorknob. She taped him up also. Then she heard the squawking of more radios.

She had to hurry.

Alex cast aside the weapon, left the bedroom, closed the door and quickly moved into her grandmother's bedroom. The window had been pried open. No one else appeared to be upstairs. She unlocked and jerked open the door to the outside, crossed the balcony and ran down the stairs to the ground below. She saw a uniformed man standing beside a tree, shrouded in darkness. He shouted at her. "Is that you, Jarek?" He raised his weapon, but Alex collided with him as he did, shoving him up against the tree. He was a little man, fat and out of shape, and he wilted like a weed without water. She taped him to the tree.

Alex ran a few yards away from the house, took her cellphone from her pocket, and called the local television station. She gave them her address and said that she'd been attacked by a band of robbers and the police were at the scene. She'd heard gunshots and thought someone was down. Perhaps several had been wounded. Then she dialed 112, the Romanian emergency hotline. She left only her address, said, "Hurry!" and hung up.

Alex then stood back in the shadows and watched while as many as twenty policemen in the swat-team siege her home. When the journalists arrived, Alex stepped out of the shadows into the headlights of their van and waved to them. The woman in the passenger seat rolled down her window

"I called you here," Alex said. "This is my home. I have no idea what they're doing."

"Have you talked to them?" the woman asked.

"No. I'm afraid they might mistake me for a burglar and shoot me. They are out of control."

Following the van, two police cars came up the drive with red lights flashing. The journalists' van started to move on ahead, but Alex stopped it.

"Can I get in?" she asked.

Once inside, she saw two more men in the back with a large video camera and boom microphone. The van continued on, headlights flashing on her home and exposing members of the swat-team. They shielded their eyes from the glare. The van stopped, and the two police cars came up behind them. A police officer stepped out of the lead car and shouted.

"Get out! You have no business here."

Alex knew that she could not run from the police and lead any sort of normal life, and being with this film crew would be the safest way to confront them.

"Start filming," she said. "You're my only hope."

She slid open the van door and stepped outside. The two journalists in the back followed her, camera whining, and the sound boom over her head.

Alex turned to look at the policeman behind them. "I have business here," she said. "This is my home. I called 112."

"There she is!" the policeman shouted to the swat-team.

The woman journalist stepped in front of Alex. "What are you here for?" she asked. "Have you come for..." she looked around at Alex.

"Alex Eidyn. My name is Alex Eidyn. I live here. Nu am făcut nimic greşit."

"What do you want with this young woman?" the journalist asked.

"This is police business, and none of yours," he said.

Alex heard the patter of feet as the swat-team converged on them.

"If you wanted to talk to me, you had but to asked," said Alex.

"I've nothing to hide."

"What has she done?" the female journalist once again asked.

Finally, the policeman said, "She's wanted for questioning in the murder of Petru Balc."

"What?" said the woman. "You send a swat-team to arrest someone for killing a serial rapist? Do you think she's a vampire?"

"Police business," he said. "Get out of here!"

The word "vampire" froze Alex. Now the world knew she was at least suspected of being one. "If you want me, you have but to take me," said Alex holding both hands out in front of her.

Immediately, three men were on her, shoved her to the ground and handcuffed her. Alex restrained herself. She knew she could kill them all, and if that policeman didn't get his knee out of her back, she just might change her mind about going quietly.

27

Jail

The Sinaia jail was a makeshift structure, a commercial business during the communist regime, but converted some years after the '89 Romanian Revolution. All the building's windows were now covered with iron grating to confine prisoners. Alex Eidyn would become their most infamous.

When the police brought Alex through the backdoor of the precinct, all the employees scattered like rodents from a wildcat. Even police officers kept their distance. The police chief, Captain Mariusz, eventually found someone willing to photograph and fingerprint her. Alex acquiesced to a pat-down. They took her cellphone, house keys, and other assorted items from her pockets. When they tried to strip search her, she said, "Try it, if you have no wish to live."

They backed off.

"La ce oră este micul dejun?" she asked.

All the prison cells in the police station were not barred. Some were normal rooms with reinforced doors and iron mesh over the windows, sealed from the outside to prevent escape. But they did have one barred area where they could keep watch over the most violent criminals before they were transferred to Bucharest or perhaps Codlea prison. This is where they put Alex for overnight observation. When she asked them to call, not her parents, but Father Zosimos, they said that she'd be permitted no visitors until morning. The police chief himself came to get a look at her, and with the violent animal, which they'd been told she was, safely behind bars, many of the officers came to get a peek at a vampire, although truth be known, few believed after seeing her that she really was one.

"She's cute and totally wimpish," said a young patrolman. "A good breeze would blow her over."

Her cell had a single cot and a toilette without a door where she could relieve herself in semi-privacy, although someone was always outside trying to get a peek at her in this compromising position.

Later that night, Alex lay down on the cot and tried to get a little sleep. She worried. Not only was she not going to Oxford, now she was a convict. How long would this descent into degradation last? Undoubtedly they had enough evidence from the murder scene to put her away for as long as they wished. What was the penalty for being a vampire? Could they prove it?

She'd just dozed and was again experiencing troubling dreams when two whispering men outside her cell woke her. The lights had been turned off except for a nightlight in the hall, but she still recognized one as the night guard. The other was a policeman with a sidearm, nightstick, and handcuffs on his belt. He was a great brute of man, hairy and muscled like an Olympic weightlifter, and reminded her a little of the vampire she'd turned back that night in Emelia's and Rutfen's home. Curiously, he wanted the night watchman to let him into her cell. This, Alex greatly feared. Though she was strong, this man would not be someone she could manhandle, she thought.

Finally, the guard unlocked her cell door, the brute entered, and the guard locked it behind him.

Alex set up and put her bare feet on the floor. "What are you after?" she asked.

It was obvious what he had come for, and equally obvious that he wasn't used to being refused. He walked up in front of her and unbuttoned his fly.

Alex had felt a certain sense of security behind bars, curiously, and thought that within the control of the police, no attempt on her life would be tolerated. Yet here in the dark, she would be tried again.

She rose and retreated to the corner of the room. The man followed. He came up close to her, put his huge hairy hand on her head and shoved her down to her knees. Alex leaned forward like she was going to accommodate him, reached up with her hand as if to take control of his now-erect phallus, but instead grabbed him by the testicles and squeezed. As he groaned in agony and fell forward over her, Alex slipped between his legs, rose up behind him, and shoved his head into the wall with all her might. With her left hand, she brought his huge phallus down between his legs and pulled it as far up the crack as of his ass as she could. At the same time, she grabbed him by the hair of the head with her right hand and bent it back as far as it would go. She could smell the fresh blood from his forehead, which had split from the impact with the corner of the window frame. She hit him in the back of his knee with her knee, and his legs doubled up. He slumped to the floor.

Alex then sank her teeth into his neck and started sucking. She gorged herself until she felt him weaken, then slump into the corner. She knew he wasn't dead. She had enough experience feeding that she realized this man would live but was in a critically weakened condition. She handcuffed him and removed his handgun, which she slid out under the cell bars into the hall. No sense in keeping it herself and frightening the guard into shooting her. Although it might not actually be that big of a deal.

Alex was glad this had happened, now that it was over. She'd had a chance to feed, and what a banquet this man had been. She'd not have to feed again for weeks. She dragged him to the front of the cell where she left him lying on his side with his hands cuffed behind his back and his deflated penis hanging out his open pants. Alex sat on her cot and waited.

A few minutes later, the nightwatchman came to check, saw the unconscious policeman sprawled on the cell floor and left at a run back down the hall. He returned a few minutes later with reinforcements. "Have you killed him?" he asked

"He'll live," she replied. "But you might want to get him out of here. I'm not very fond of him anymore."

*

Next morning, the Chief of Police, Captain Mariusz, was the first to come see her. Every policeman on the force was with him. He accused Alex of attacking the guard who tried to feed her.

"If you consider raping my mouth feeding me," she replied.

"That's not what happened," Mariusz said.

"You've filmed the entire episode on closed circuit television. You know what happened."

"It was... out of order," he stammered. "You've assaulted one of our officers and will pay for it."

"You knew what he was doing. You sent him to me. You're all ticăloşi."

Alex heard a commotion down the hall, the sea of police officers parted, and she saw Father Zosimos enter.

"What have you done this time?" he asked.

"Yes, well that is the way you'd view it, isn't it," she said. "They invade my home without provocation, drag me in here, and turn loose a monster who wants a little fellatio. What do you expect?"

"But Alex, you assaulted three police officers in your home and almost killed another here in the jail."

"And he's your concern, instead of me? What a dirtbag. I've done him a favor. Now he's inoculated."

"They have your DNA. They know you killed a man. It matched that of the killer of Petru Balc."

"The rapist? That was self-defense, and you know it. So do they. Now get out. You don't want to witness what I'm about to do. I thought I'd get a fair shake in here, but now I know I won't. I'm leaving. If they try to stop me, if they injure the child I'm carrying, I'll kill everyone in this building." Of course, she was bluffing. If they had guns like the one Stefan used on her, they might be able to subdue her and kill her.

"Give me a few minutes. Let me talk to them," said Father Zosimos.

"Five minutes, and then I'm tearing this cell apart, and if anyone gets in my way, I'll shred them like a beef at the butcher."

They all left the room. A few minutes later, Father Zosimos returned with Captain Mariusz. He carried a bag with her personal effects.

"They'll release you into my recognizance, until the inquest," said Father Zosimos. "I've posted a hefty bond. Promise to do what I say."

"Why would anyone not do what a priest asks of her?"

Mariusz opened her cell door, and she and Father Zosimos left by the backdoor.

"I could have helped you. We could have worked together," Alex said.

"You'll be safe at the Monastery until we get this figured out. The murder charge will never stick. The nuns will take care of you, and even deliver your child."

"And take her from me. No thanks, Father."

"What do you mean?"

"I have to get some things first."

On the way, Alex called Jaklin on her cellphone. "Can you meet me at home?" she asked.

When they arrived, Jaklin was already standing on the front steps, tears streaking her cheeks.

"No more tears," said Alex. "This is business."

Alex and Jaklin went upstairs to the bathroom first where she washed her hands to get the smell of the policeman off, then to her bedroom where she packed a small bag. She explained to Jaklin that she was going away but that she'd return to have the baby, if at all possible.

"Where are you going?" Jaklin asked.

"You'll be safer not knowing."

"Oh, Missy. I've missed you so these last few weeks."

"Just a few more months, and maybe we can be together again. I'll need help with the baby."

"That sounds wonderful."

"It would be nice if you and Mikhail would stay here in my home and watch out for it."

"That would solve Mikhail's problem. He's running out of money and was considering returning to live with his parents in Russia."

"You two split up? Please, don't do that. Go with him, Jaklin, if he leaves. By all means, do it. But if you want to stay..."

"We're just not the same without you. I don't want to give up my job."

"Then get him to stay. You two will get through this. Use my assets. That is, if you still want him."

"In the worse way. Mikhail does love you, Missy. But, I mean, vampires. It's just really tough."

"I don't blame him for a second."

Alex showed Jaklin the safe place in her closet where she'd stashed her money, pulled out a clump of bills and stuffed some into her bag.

"I won't need much where I'm going. Use whatever suits you. Tell Mikhail to take what he needs. And don't worry about it, Jaklin. I have more money than you can imagine. Don't starve yourself, and if you need some new clothes... Well, that's what it's for. And use my grandmother's car if you need to. Just don't run over anyone, I care about. Father Zosimos, on the other hand..."

When Alex and Jaklin went back downstairs, Father Zosimos was standing in the middle of the room. He looked downhearted. "You not going with me, are you?"

"Sinaia is no longer safe for me and the child," she answered. "I don't trust you, Father." She plugged her cellphone into her computer and downloaded the rest of the music she'd bought recently.

"Your grandmother would have wanted you to." He seemed sincere. She thought she saw a tear.

Alex turned on him. "Three nights ago, I came to see you when Stefan tried to kill me. I heard him telling you about it. You'd planned that with him."

"Never did I conspire against you. He told me it was an accident, that you got in the line of fire. I would never order your murder." He looked shaken, stammered for words. "I'll talk to him about it. He's a good, God-fearing man trying to rid the world of evil."

"He should be behind bars. Where's your sense of mortality? You've aligned the Church with murderers."

"Perhaps I've not done well with this, or you," he said. "I've been harassed by swarms of angels in my dreams lately."

It was too little, too late. Alex showed Jaklin where she kept Nălucă's food and the litter box. She started to take her grandfather's staff, but thought a sharp stick might not fit in too well where she was going. She hugged Jaklin, kissed her on the lips. Alex had something to say, but she didn't want to. She stiffened her resolve.

"Here's my most fervent wish for you and Mikhail," she said with tears in her eyes. "Don't stay here. Leave. Go to Bulgaria or Russia. Leave immediately and never come back. You are not safe, and the life choices you make here could take you on a path of spiritual catastrophe. Take Mikhail, get married, have kids. Love and be loved. Forget you ever knew me."

Alex left by the backdoor with Father Zosimos following. As she walked off into the woods, he called after her.

"The police, they'll come for you again," he said. "You'll be safe with me."

"Would I be safe from you?" Alex shouted over her shoulder.

"I promised Mariusz. I'll lose the bond money."

28

Millennium Road

On her way up the mountain, Alex stayed off the trail amongst trees and bushes. This was the height of the summer tourist season. Sinaia and its environs were crawling with European men, women and children, all hikers with their daypacks and walking sticks. All to be avoided. She felt like a hunted animal, every few steps looking back over her shoulder, wishing it were the middle of the night to cover her entry into the cavern.

When Alex tapped out the code on the rock wall, she had none of the apprehension or anticipation of her first visit and was in fact eager to get inside. She waited impatiently but nothing happened. She heard no grinding of rock against rock; the stone surfaces didn't part. She heard voices coming up the mountain behind her, so she stepped away from the entrance and quickly moved on up the mountain. Hidden within a dark crevasse, she found another shallow cave and entered.

From her hiding place, she peeked out and immediately went into a rage. It was Stefan, the bounty hunter, and a policeman who carried the shotgun with which they'd subdued her a few nights before. When she saw Father Zosimos trailing along behind, she choked up. She remembered seeing him with her grandmother, how congenial they'd seemed with each other. And now this. She had been abandoned by her parents, double-crossed repeatedly by Father Zosimos, violated by the police. She felt betrayed by humanity.

She crept deeper into the little cavern and found a small opening at the base of the stone wall. Somehow this must lead to the main cavern, she thought. She squeezed through. In complete blackness, she sensed a larger chamber and felt her way along another stone wall, all the while measuring her steps to ensure she didn't fall into a precipice. The draft was cool but fresh. She heard the trickle of water.

Then from behind her, she heard stone grate against stone, and she felt a gush of cold air. Someone had entered the chamber. She suppressed a surge of fear and stood still, then felt the icy hand of a vampire clasp her arm. She was forced through an opening and heard the rocks scrape closed.

"I'm Marie Eidyn," she said.

"We know who you are," said a familiar female voice. "You've been here before." It was Cosmina, the large, rough vampire who had taken her to see Alu.

"I remember you too. How did you know I was here?"

"We have a security force," said Cosmina, her voice strong with disapproval. "We have procedures too, and you've violated them both times. I hope you didn't bring that nasty cross with you."

"I'm better prepared this time."

"We're better prepared for your return, too." Cosmina's voice had become kind, gentle, excited, much different than Alex had remembered. "At least partially prepared."

She led Alex along a winding, descending tunnel, faintly lit from some source in front of them. Gradually, the corridor opened into a chamber Alex recognized as Alu's Throne Room with its massive stone formations. Cosmina took her through the passageway behind the great chair from which, when Alex was here before, Alu had appeared and disappeared. Though dimly lit, Alex saw that this larger chamber was elaborately furnished, great curtains in reds and golds covering the walls and possibly hiding other entryways and exits. Sofas and easy chairs sat in organized groupings.

Alex realized Cosmina had left her. She was alone. But then she noticed a part of the dark wall move. Alu Kard unfolded like a giant erector set from his perch where he slept hanging upside down like a colossal bat.

Seeing him this way was so strange that Alex wondered if she'd made the right choice by returning. Are all these vampires that much like another animal species? She spoke as he approached her. "I've come, as you said I would," she admitted.

"I'm sorry that your first visit within my private chamber found me sleeping. Cosmina should have been more discrete. I frequently hang from my roost. Promotes blood flow to the brain during sleep and improves memory in one my age. Vampirism does have subtle aging effects, even if they're dramatically reduced from that peculiar to humans. A disturbing sight, I'd imagine."

Alex hadn't thought, but of course Alu would be asleep in daytime. She didn't want to insult him since she needed his protection. "Curious," she said.

"That's diplomatic of you. But welcome again to my palace in the Carpathians," he said. "Palace is a bit of an overstatement. I've dwelled within these rock walls for centuries." He seemed formal and aristocratic. Even though he was more congenial than before, she still sensed his tremendous age. His voice seemed to have somewhat of an echo, and it didn't appear to be just because of the cavernous stone walls. She wondered what he would have been like three millennia ago as a young man.

"And walked the streets at night."

"I do work the nocturnal shift," he confirmed with a faint smile.

She heard a commotion in another chamber behind a partition, scuffling. "Just let me see her," said the distressed voice of a woman, and it sounded as if she might be crying. "I just want a quick look."

"One moment please," said Alu. He disappeared behind the curtain, and Alex heard muffled voices receding in the distance, and then Alu returned. "Sorry about that," he said. "Not every vampire is a congenial member of our society. Some we have to exercise a little more control over than we would wish."

Then as if to reassure Alex that everything was okay, he went behind another curtain, and when he returned, he had six people with him, four men and two women. One man and the two women were human.

"These are my companions," Alu said.

"Three are human?"

"You do have amazing powers of perception. We tolerate some of the more enlightened civilians. We value contact with the others, even if they, for the most part, don't approve of us. Some of my closest servants are human."

They were handsome men and women. Young, healthy. Each of the vampires in turn took her hand and bowed. They seemed quite ancient. The last shook his head and said, "You're sure of her vampirism? I wouldn't have guessed it, and her warmth is puzzling."

"I can vouch for it," said Alu. "That's one of the many reasons we're so fortunate to have her join us."

"The humans, they are your blood source?" Alex said, realizing the obvious.

Alu seemed hurt. "Yes. That also. But first and foremost, they're my companions."

"I'll look forward to getting to know each of you," she said to them.

Alex knew she had to get the pregnancy thing over with quickly, but she didn't want to tell him in front of the others. Turning back to Alu, she said, "I need to speak to you alone. I hate to be rude, but it is a private matter."

"Certainly," he said, surprised and a little confused. "Ladies. Gentlemen." He motioned for them to exit and turned back to Alex. "I know you must have reservations about becoming a part of such an ancient order, but let me assure you..."

Alex cut him off. "Not at all. I'm here for protection and can tell that your security concerns are everything I hoped. But I have a condition that you should know about."

"Of course. Take a seat." He motioned to a sofa and chairs.

Once comfortable, Alex said rather dramatically, "I'm five months pregnant."

Alu's immediate response was one of concern and confusion. His eyes immediately went to her midriff. "You're sure? We've not encountered this," he said. He seemed shaken.

"I wear clothing to hide it, but I am showing. I can feel the baby move."

"We'll, that is certainly... surprising. Never in all my years..." Alex thought she could see his mind working a mile a minute to recalculate the situation. "You'll require special care," he said. "Are you in need of any immediate medical attention?"

"No," said Alex. "I seem to be remarkably healthy."

"Pregnant. This changes everything," said Alu, a look of disillusionment settling upon him again. "We should have someone with you at all times to ensure if anything should go wrong that we can provide medical help immediately."

She could feel him trying to close in upon her. This sounded controlling. "I would prefer my solitude, if it's all the same to you."

Then he seemed to regain his footing. He had gone from confusion to understanding in a heartbeat. "Of course." He seemed overly pleased, and as he moved his chair closer, she backed away along the sofa. The look on his face was one of such surprise that she was afraid of him.

"Forgive me," he said. "I've startled you. It's just that — a pregnant vampire! I had imagined you becoming my close companion, but with this set of personal circumstances, perhaps it would be best if we let you find your own place among the Colony. Your future station and relationship to me will be determined in time."

Alex wondered what sort of lewd activity he'd been contemplating. This could have been really scary, she thought, something on the order of the Sinaia detention center.

"I'm different," she confessed. "Not affected by sunlight, at least not drastically, and my body is still warm. Only two degrees below human. Yet I am a vampire. I must have blood every couple of weeks. Plus, I seem to have a difficult-to-make-dead thing going for me. I've been staked and shot with a couple of different weapons, but I don't die, not even when shot through the heart with a wood slug."

"Remarkable. Vampires are so naturally immune to disease, and non-fatal injuries heal so rapidly that healthcare has not been our focus." He thought for a moment. "However, I... we do have a research group, medical professionals. I'll summon our most enlightened, and we'll set up a monitoring protocol. Not only ensure your health but also monitor the baby's physical progress. Perhaps we'll be able to assist you and add to our database."

Alu stopped cold, looked about as if wishing to address a subject but didn't know quite how to approach her.

Alex suddenly realized what it was. "The father," she said. "Yes, well, I would have thought you'd know. All indications are that it's the rapist. The man I killed in the park."

A dark cloud seemed to come over him, and she realized that he hadn't known that she was the perpetrator. She wondered why Cosmina hadn't told him. He tried to disguise his disappointment, but it was projected like a dark beacon.

"That's the reason the police are after me and Father Zosimos has rejected me. I'm a murderer."

"In their eyes," Alu said quickly. He'd partially recovered. "Of course. I knew you'd had a violent encounter. I didn't know the full story. I saw you in its aftermath and went to you. I hope this hasn't tainted your affection for your offspring. It could be an incentive for the vampire community."

"Not in the least. I love my child. That's the reason I'm here. Her protection."

He'd flinched when she said "love." Again, he quickly recovered. "Of course. We'll do everything we can to make this a trouble-free experience."

He smiled broadly, raised his hands in the air and then dropped them. "You've really made an impression. I'm so glad you came to us."

Alu seemed too pleased. She hadn't thought that he might develop plans for a child born into the vampire community. She had a inkling that her child might still be at risk, a different type of risk than that from the human community.

"I'm tired. Rest, that's what I need," Alex said.

"Of course, and I'm delaying you. Cosmina will find a place for you to bed down. I'm afraid your sudden appearance has caught me... us off guard. And now this delightful pregnancy. We'll get a temporary place for you tonight and find permanent quarters tomorrow." He took a deep breath. "Well! Welcome to our home and our society. I hope you'll be as happy staying with us as we are to have you."

Alex was speechless and a little scared. He was so artificial in his complimentary assessment. But perhaps she should get to know him better before passing judgment.

He raised his voice. "Cosmina?" When she appeared, he said, "Provide for Miss Eidyn. She needs a place to sleep. Stay close to her this first night, if you don't mind, and insure she's taken care of. She's quite the surprise. She's pregnant."

Alex wished he'd been more discrete concerning her condition. Now, it was already out there.

"What?" said Cosmina. "That's not even possible." She took a chair along side Alu.

"My initial reaction also," said Alu. "Yet, we can't argue with reality. Perhaps that's the reason for her elevated body temperature."

"The child will be stillborn," said Cosmina.

"The child is alive and well," said Alex. "I can feel it move. I became pregnant before I became a vampire. "

"Why did you come to us with a problem like this?" Cosmina seemed belligerent toward the whole idea. "We have no special facilities."

"Because it isn't a problem," answered Alex, with a nasty tone. "The father was a serial rapist. All the authorities know me to be a vampire, and neither the child nor I are safe among humans. I've come for refuge. I believed we would be welcome, perhaps even safe here, among those like me."

"She'll be a curiosity," Cosmina said. "They'll come from all over the globe." She folded her arms against her chest and stiffened. She look toward Alu and something in the way of communication passed between them.

Alu relaxed, even smiled. "So it is that the evil race of vampires becomes the last refuge for the innocents of the world. You must excuse Cosmina. She's overly pessimistic when it comes to human institutions. I'm pleased you've come to us in your hour of need. It's an unexpected vote of confidence."

Cosmina unfolded her arms and raised her palms to Alex. "I'm sorry," she said. "It's such a shock. Perhaps I'm a little jealous." She almost smiled.

"I'm here for more than refuge. I also need to learn about being a vampire. If I'm going to live for a couple of millennia, I'd appreciate knowing what that life will be like. You have all the answers. Humans are idiots when it comes to vampires."

Alu had a good laugh. "And many other things as well. This is a much different attitude than on your previous visit."

"I need food and a small amount of blood from time to time. I can't linger out of doors because I've been on television, and now I'm recognizable as a vampire by the general population. I'm hunted."

"Perhaps you should not go out at all," said Alu, seizing the opportunity it would seem to voice an unspoken preference. "Your concern and confidence in us is appreciated and will be well rewarded. You'll be safe. We'll see to your basic necessities. Food and blood? Not a problem."

With that, Cosmina took Alex to her own boudoir, a large open space between stalactites with minimal furnishings. It was late morning and most had already bedded down. Alex had slept little the last twenty-four hours and now felt even safer in the cavern than she'd imagined. The fact that she'd not be forced into a personal relationship with Alu was a relief.

"The cavern is larger than I remembered," she told Cosmina. "The air circulation is amazing."

"This part of the cavern, the Cathedral, is just a small part of a much larger system that extends for miles underground. This giant room is closest to the surface, and from here it descends many thousands of feet." Her attitude had changed remarkably from hostile to conciliatory and now to down right helpful. That quick instant of private communication with Alu had dramatically changed her.

Cosmina provided a place for her to sleep near her, two small stalagmites separating them. "We'll find a permanent place for you tomorrow," she said. "Few spend more than a day or two inside the cavern. I spend more time than most, but even I have a permanent residence in Sinaia."

It was not a proper bed and consisted only of a pile of quilts and blankets on a rough rock surface, a thin pillow. Alex curled up amongst them and covered herself. It felt more nest than bed. And it was cold.

The Cathedral was dimly lit and down right spooky. Although she was one of the Undead and felt safe, she sensed a great gulf between herself and these vampires. Her life was caught up in so many ironies. During these first months she'd been a vampire, she'd felt more a part of human society. She'd enjoyed nightlife for the first time, had fallen in love, had a home, and could make her way in the world. Other than the continued assaults from the authorities, her only problem had been troubling dreams since Father Zosimos took her cross. Here amongst vampires, she had nothing.

A single candle lit the great chamber, and once she bedded down, even it was snuffed. Her eyes could no longer adjust to the light because there was none. She wondered why they kept it so dark. Alex got no sense of a great population inside the Cathedral, nothing like the crowd she'd seen before. The place felt dead, as if she'd stumbled into the cavern as an explorer and discovered a nest of mummies. Everyone was in fact dead, their past lives forever lost. She had to resign herself. After all, she was a vampire among vampires.

*

That night, Alex dreamed of a road with an unending stream of vampires coming up from behind and trailing off into the distance. This had been the source of her troubled dreams, and now it was more vivid and heavily populated. It had always seemed small and too dark to make out. The travelers now were still engulfed in darkness but with just a hint, a halo of light surrounding them that dimly illuminated the way forward. Alex was amongst them but near the end of the line, and she didn't know why she was there or where they were going. It was a simple dream, but seemed important, even profound, and apparently continued all the time she slept. Alex had seen someone up ahead of her walking laboriously forward. The young woman said only, "I don't belong here."

The next morning, Alex jolted awake. She thought she was human again and back in her home with Jaklin and Mikhail and that a vampire was loose in the house. Gradually, she realized that she was in the cavern, the Cathedral, and that she was the vampire. She raised up and saw dim candlelight flickering and casting shadows on the stone formations. Cosmina was already milling about.

"Why do they keep it so dark?" Alex asked. She heard voices, and their echoes coupled with the shifting shadows to bring visions of the lives of ancient occupants.

"Vampires are overly sensitive to light. Darkness promotes dreaming, the mainstay of our psychic life. Each morning, the light of a single candle wakes everyone at the same time."

"What do vampires dream?" asked Alex. "I had a strange night. Saw a long train of vampires."

"Ah," Cosmina said. "You've dreamed it, then."

"Dreamed what?"

"Millennium Road."

"Is that what it's called?"

"All have the Millennium Dream. Takes a while for some."

"I've been plagued by it for months. What does it mean?"

"That you are truly a vampire, something I've questioned with your flesh so warm, and being pregnant. It represents the history and direction of the race of vampires. Talk to those traveling with you."

"I tried, but they just said 'This is the journey.'"

"Yes. They would. You haven't been initiated. And here's what's interesting." Cosmina was really excited. "To go forward on the Road, is to go backward in time. Those are the vampires who came first. Going backward on the Road is to go forward in time because they are the ones who've more recently joined the race of vampires."

"I was close to the end of the train but not the very end. I did meet one woman up ahead who said she didn't belong."

"Strange. I've never heard of that."

Alex didn't quite know what to think. "It's a psychic connection between all vampires?"

"And ancient memories, amazingly. The older the memories, the more they are a part of the collective. The meaning of it all? A really good question."

"Why would we have that ability?"

"I believe it's because we are dead. It's possible that humans have this ability once they die. We experience it because we bridge both vampire worlds, the here and the Hereafter."

"Are they the Undead, those still here on Earth? Or are they also the dead Undead?"

"Both. You're there, but you're also here. When, or if, you die, your body decays and turns to dust, but your soul remains on Millennium Road, heading into eternity."

"It's the vampire Afterlife?"

"Of sorts. The human mind dreams all the time, but when awake, reality drowns out that part of the psyche. Vampires are much closer to and more aware of these activities of the soul, which are in large part disconnected from conscious daily life in the real world. The fact that you've had the Millennium Dream means you'll have to be initiated."

"I'm not interested. I just came here for security."

"It's not up to you." She gave Alex a quick smile. "It's in your best interest."

"Perhaps we shouldn't tell Alu."

Cosmina laughed. "He already knows." She walked away.

29

The Pleasure Dome

Alex sat on her bedding considering what Cosmina had just told her about the initiation requirement. This wasn't in her vampire playbook. She'd have to find a way around it.

When Cosmina didn't return right away, Alex went for a short walk to see what other vampires were up to. They pretty much ignored her, so she listened in on some of the philosophical conversations, which were very much over her head. I'll have to educate myself to have any sort of social life here, she thought. All discussions were congenial except one on economics. She heard shouting and two vampires got in each other's face over a couple of things called austerity and stimulus. Their colleagues had to separate them.

Must have been an hour later that Cosmina returned, and she had several female vampires with her.

"Where have you been?" asked Alex.

"Shadowrise," said Cosmina. "We go outside to a hilltop where we can watch the mountain shadows blanket Sinaia. Humans have their sunrise; we have our Shadowrise. It has a deep spiritual significance. Some humans participate. The high priest of the Coven presides. Alu Kard used to officiate, but lately he's been too busy and has relinquished the duty to me. It's a great privilege."

"So what is this initiation you were talking about?" asked Alex.

"You must bathe first," said Cosmina. "The Cleansing Pool and Pleasure Dome are both in an area we call Xanadu."

"Xanadu? Like in the Coleridge poem?"

"Perhaps Coleridge got his poem from our Xanadu."

"How can I get out of it? I came here for sanctuary, not to join an organization."

"This isn't Parliament, and it isn't a B&B either. The initiation is about you and your transformation. Vampirism is a state of being. You're about to become one of us. I thought you wanted to know about vampirism, immortality. This is it."

Alex felt guilty, shook her head and wondered what she was getting herself into. "I thought you would simply teach me. Tell me stuff."

"It doesn't work like that. Vampirism is a state of being. Your relationship with it is determined in large part by your state of commitment." Cosmina still looked a little confused.

"Something's wrong, isn't it?" said Alex.

"Alu didn't know you'd had the Millennium Dream. Strange. But he will officiate for your initiation. That's quite the honor."

The women walked Alex through the dark down a descending, twisting stone staircase to an underground pool where they all bathed. Light from an unseen source lit the surface that rippled, shimmied like liquid gold, and cast a glow on their naked bodies. Deep darkness surrounded the little radiant oasis. The water was cold, and Alex shivered, but the other women only felt it comfortably cool.

"You use no soap?"

"It would contaminate the Alph. A tributary of its continuous stream of fresh water feeds the pool here, which is simply an intermediate stop for water on its way to the lower chambers."

Four men, vampires obviously, came to the edge of the pool, and they also took off their clothes. Then out of the darkness stepped Alu Kard, solemn, his actions of undressing coordinated, ritualized. He looked even taller and thinner unclothed, a near skeleton, dark skin stretched over bone. He splashed water on himself, his actions slow, methodical, precise. He took no notice of Alex.

"Men and women bathe together here?" Alex asked quietly,

trying to find a body orientation that revealed the least to their eyes. She couldn't keep hers from drifting toward them, and they seemed intrigued by her baby bump and oblivious to the exposure of their own nakedness.

"Only for ritual cleansing. This is a sacred stream and not for common use."

After a quick sprinkling, Alex and the others anointed themselves with a thin film of olive oil. She felt an outsider to all this, the community bathing ritual seeming foreign and strangely perverse in mixed company.

"This ritual I'm destined to experience, it's not some capricious liturgy, is it?" Alex said.

Without looking up, Alu said, "No more talking. Only sacred utterances from here on."

Cosmina whispered in her ear, "If you'd not be so obstinate, perhaps it'd not seem such an ordeal."

Alex kept her mouth shut but sulked. She realized she'd have to be more accommodating if she expected them to accept her and provide the sanctuary she and her child needed so desperately. They all donned black bathrobes and disappeared into the shadows. Alex could barely make them out.

"On to the Pleasure Dome reciting the oration," said Alu.

Just as I thought, said Alex to herself. Some messed up ceremony to embarrass me.

He led them along a winding path with Alex forced to take up the position behind him and the four men and four women, including Cosmina, trailing behind. They chanted in Latin with a rhythm that matched their steps and made it seem a march. Alex had studied a little Latin in secondary school, but this seemed a more ancient form.

Down they went to even lower-levels, wet stone walls leaning into them, and the stream, the Alph Cosmina had called it, now a torrential flow among rocks and along the water-chiseled chasm. The rushing river seemed enchanted, music coming from the wailing water gushing along its stony banks. The flume flung up ghostly, water-created wraiths that called to her with their warbling sprite-voices.

Through a narrow tunnel, they entered another domed chamber, and Alex's internal reference shifted. She experienced a strong sense of déjà vu. She heard music that sounded ancient and came from a single instrument, a dulcimer, plucked by a damsel sitting on a mushroom-shaped formation above the stone floor. She hummed the wordless melody like some daemon lover's lament. Stalactites wept water into a pool, all lit by bioluminescent. She took a deep breath, and the air seemed alcoholic. It smelled like a sweet perfume and reminded her of the pneuma she'd read about that gave the prophetic trance to the Oracle in ancient Delphi. She felt drugged, dazed, stumbled and almost fell. Cosmina and another woman caught her by the arms. Alex couldn't get over the feeling that she'd been there before.

They removed their robes, and Cosmina indicated that Alex should do likewise. Naked again. Cosmina stepped aside, and the dark shape of Alu Kard extended his hand. It felt cold and bony, just loose skin over skeleton. They began to sing, and Alex realized that this was a practiced chorus and in fact a sacred group among the most ancient of vampires.

Alu led her out into the middle of the pool, which was much deeper than she thought, coming to her breasts. The others followed and formed a ring, a halo, alternating woman-man-woman-man about Alex and Alu. As they slowly circled, the water rippled around them creating a swirling luminescence, a multitude of tiny suspended stars. Alex's emotions resonated with the music from the dulcimer, and its tune orchestrated them so that they danced. She seemed slave to the melody so completely that she was unable to resist its harmony of feelings.

Alu turned toward Alex and for the first time looked directly at her. He said, "You have lived, died, and wandered in the civilization of the living, and now you must descend into the Underworld, where you'll find your home and establish your relationship with your immortality. That which is born must also die. Death by violence, rebirth by blood, sustained by the community of vampires. Now begins your journey into Eternity. Your existence is being rewritten in the Book of Life. We will mark your soul with the knowledge and wisdom of the Undead. You will now take the Oath of Cheiron."

That was exactly what Alex didn't want. She felt her former self slipping away, and as Alu looked directly into her eyes, she caught her breath. Alu's words seemed to touch her to the depth of Millennium Road. She saw flashes of it, the gathering of spirits close to her, the closeness of common souls.

"Repeat after me. *I swear to obey the laws of my oath, to believe in Darkness, be loyal to the immortal Undead, and speak only truth to them and of them in public and private. I swear to protect planet Earth, for it is the one true sustaining element of the Immortals. I will forsake all friendships and worldly possessions prior to my death and resurrection.*"

At first, Alex thought this was unacceptable, but then she remembered that she'd become a vampire before she consummated her relationship with Jaklin and Mikhail. Plus, her grandmother's home had come to her after she became a vampire. She'd already given up her adolescent friends when she came to Sinaia. Her grandmother had passed on. Her family had always felt like a group of strangers. Even her cross, which she hoped to get back someday, had also come to her after being bitten by Velinar. It was as if it had all been planned.

Alu's words had resonated within her, and now she repeated them, slowly, precisely.

"Vampires also share a Covenant," said Alu. But if broken, no retribution is taken. You will repeat the Covenant: *To be true to those of the Colony, to report misbehavior of any vampire, to have the best interest of both vampires and humans at all times, to strive to reduce our suffering, to take blood from humans only when offered, to solicit blood only under the most dire circumstances, to never harm a human being, to never steal human blood, to never kill a human, to serve the twin sisters Darkness and Light.*"

This, she could not only live with but believed in herself, although she had violated portions of it already. She repeated his words.

"Welcome to the Pleasure Dome," Alu said, then started chanting in archaic Latin.

Respice, quaesumus, Domine
Super Maria, tua humilis servus.
In hora infirmitate
Animam refove, quam conversum

Ut potest confortatus
Per Dominus Cheironum
Qui regnat et semper.
Amen

In one swift motion, he scooped Alex into his arms. He whispered, "Relax," which she did as best she could. As he lowered her horizontally into the water, Alex felt it touch her bottom first and then start to envelop the rest of her body. Alu's touch was much colder than the water. Gradually, it covered her legs abdomen and breasts. She took a breath and her head and face went under, and he held her there. She started to panic when she felt his arms release her, but realized that she was floating in the glowing liquid. She could still hear Alu's chanting overlaying the hymnal. Alex relaxed and floated free.

"Close your eyes," he said.

She did. Those circling about them created a slow strobing of light and shadow that seemed to hypnotize her.

"What do you see?"

Once again she was on Millennium Road traveling with another group of vampires, nine in number, four women and five men, none of whom did she recognize. These vampires of the dream world were much different than any she'd seen. Their skin was metallic, a mixture of gold and silver, and shimmered with their movement. They led her off the dark road into a dimly glowing edifice.

Alex followed them inside, and the four women came in close, caressed her each in turn, and laid her on a silk covered circular bed where they anointed her with a warm, sensuous oil and exotic perfume. The men joined hands and formed a revolving five-pointed star about the women. They hummed an ancient melody. Something told Alex that these were not beings of the real world. They were the dead Undead, ancient vampires from the time of Alu's first millennium, back even before Abraham.

The women anointed her with the sweetest smelling oil. Each of the women caressed her, their hair softly falling about her body. Then one of the men broke from the revolving male halo, while the others continued to circle and sing. The women raised her knees. At first

Alex objected, "No," she said, but her body was so tuned to the music that it pulsed with every beat, and her mind went blank, and even later she could not recall what actually happened, just that it seemed a sacred act of communal intercourse. Still yet, she felt trapped in an atrocity wrapped in a sexual liturgy. Soon this man relaxed, released her and resumed his place in the circling, singing halo of men. The women and men again circled singing.

Another male vampire stepped from among the halo, and once again the women spread Alex's thighs. Again the chanting of the voices drove home the act. So it was with all five male vampires. Then the men circled, and the women again caressed her. The four women rose up from her and joined the men in the circling formation about the small circular bed. Their chants turned to wordless humming that gradually escalated to a screech of unbearable volume.

A group of dark, vile, unclothed creatures entered the edifice. They are both animal and human but nasty, stinking brutes, humped, cankerous, warted. While the vampires sang a dirge, these corrupt creatures fed on Alex. They sucked and ate her body, consuming her in great gulps, burping grossly and passing great flatulence. Once sated, they backed off from her but were consumed by violent shaking and burst into flame, then suddenly turned to ash.

Alex woke in the Pleasure Dome, the voices of the men and women vampires lofting as they raised their eyes to the ceiling where now Alex saw a circling pentagram of fire, perfectly synced with their motion. Alex was still submerged in the pool and once again in Alu's arms. She raised her head up out of the water. He carried her to the bank where the women wrapped her in a soft cotton robe. The woman playing the dulcimer then raised her voice, and they all joined in the chorus. Although Alex didn't know when, she'd joined the singing. They turned her so that she faced into the deep darkness of the cavern, and then she saw the outline of a symbol, faint at first but then flowing in flame. It was another pentagon, and within it was the nude figure of a woman, her four extremities and head forming the five corners. The perfect female vampire.

But Alex felt compromised, damaged. The initiation had been a horror and cultivated unsavory feelings. She felt assaulted, tortured, and didn't understand why the creatures who fed off her had then sparked, then flamed. What the hell? Sparked? This was the same as the feral vampires who'd tasted her.

Alu said, "You must now discover your new self. You have been born again and in some ways are a different person. You are merely clay remolded by destiny and given new aptitudes. Your initiation in this pool has bound you to your myth. You now have a destiny. What you have experienced is your private undertaking that provides clues to who you are and how you relate to the world. We do not know, and you are under no obligation, to tell anyone what happened. You must find your path, the mythic life element."

His words were not comforting but disturbing, and not just the part about the abuse being clues to her new identity, which by the way reminded her of being raped by Petru Balc. Alex had always thought that by becoming a vampire, she'd escaped death. But now it dawned on her, coming as a churlish epiphany, that she really was dead. Her death wasn't an illusion but a stark reality. She realized that her problem had been trying to live in the world of humans since Velinar bit her. She had not embraced her own death, not acknowledged it, never grieved it. Alu's words during the Oath of Cheiron had triggered this realization. She was groggy, and felt that she just woke from a dream that had lasted since Velinar bit her. Her previous life flashed past in quick episodes. Her stupor vanished. She was fully awake. And she was undead.

The glowing image of the perfect vampire superimposed on the pentagon extinguished, the music stopped, and the damsel with the dulcimer vanished. She'd been an apparition all along.

30

Conversations with the Undead

While dreaming the first night after her initiation, Alex discovered that Millennium Road had changed. It wasn't quite so dark and everything was more vivid. She noticed something she'd not seen before: a flaming pentagon in the distance, toward which they were all traveling.

"I saw that in my initiation," she said. "Or at least another manifestation of it."

Cosmina was pleased to hear this. "Not everyone can see it," she said. Alex took the symbol to imply that movement along the Road was toward perfecting the race of vampires. Cosmina had been correct about Alex's relationship with her fellow travelers. They could now talk to her and seemed coherent. She also felt more awake while there in this vampire psychic space. Her dreamscape now seemed almost as real as her waking state.

Alex also saw something else that had not been there before: a glow far in the distance to the right off Millennium Road. Vampire activity off-Road had been to the left, as was the edifice where she'd been initiated, and the area to the right had been barren, deserted, and had an ominous feel to it. She mentioned the glow to Cosmina, but she didn't know what Alex was talking about, nor did she know anything about the area to the right of the road. Alex didn't press it. She'd have to investigate alone once she became more acquainted with vampire psychic space.

Alex was still reflecting on what had happened to her during the initiation. She realized that nothing had happened in the real world, but she was still bothered by the female tenderness and male serial ravishing and could not fathom why she felt so guiltless about allowing it, if not all-out embracing it. But the violation had made her feel that she belonged to the race of vampires. She'd forfeited any remaining innocence. She wondered if the ritual had originated in prehistoric human civilization. But the ghastly creatures... She didn't think she'd ever be able to come to terms with being consumed by them.

Cosmina set up Alex with her own living space that would serve her special needs. She now occupied a recess in the Cathedral wall but outside the main activity. Her biggest problem was that she was perpetually cold. Vampires didn't need much warmth, but Alex was an exception. She reasoned that being pregnant caused her to be different. Her compartment had no amenities, and she had to scrounge for herself what fixtures and storage facilities she needed.

Few vampires lived in the cavern, most having jobs and lives outside the vampire circle, so they placed little value on having their own space. Practically all vampires who did put up permanent residence inside were involved in some sort of administrative function serving Alu. When told this, Alex smiled, realizing that even the society of immortals had need of order and direction, and she wondered if it involved paperwork. Cosmina had a good laugh.

Alex heard rumors of a lower chamber to the cavern, one beyond Xanadu, but Alu permitted no one down there. Legend had it that a vampire got lost there in the deepest of all darkness, and could not find his way out. He had neither nourishment nor blood, and was lost for a hundred years, suffering the agonies only a vampire could suffer.

Several times, and by several vampires, Alex had been invited to Shadowrise. But she declined. Her face had been on television. She was the only one who would not venture outside. Left to her own devices, she set about learning why others spent time there in the Cathedral. Some locals came for the intellectual stimulation, and some came from far away to meet friends who lived in other parts of the world and at times passed through Sinaia. Others came from all over the world to attend vampire conferences. They told of colonies in far off places, other countries. Many sought advice and spent hours in consultation with Alu or another of the ancient vampires. A few came to recruit for their clan from the more recent inductees.

Alex listened in on the philosophical discussions and learned that some of the younger-appearing vampires were in fact among the oldest. Looks in the vampire world could be particularly deceiving because vampires didn't mature physically beyond their conversion age, and that created a curious phenomenon where some of the youngest, but the longest lived, were the more wise, and some of the oldest but more recently turned were the most naive. Every permutation was represented: young-old, old-young, young-young, and old-old, and all shades between, each grouping with predictable characteristics and multitudes of exceptions.

In spite of the categories, they all had great affection for one another and valued the diversity, although each group would laugh at the weaknesses and idiosyncrasies of the others. Cosmina it turned out was a millennium old although she would never admit it. At first the quiet got to Alex, but after being there a while, she seemed to hear the thoughts swirling in vampire minds, like milk in a butter churn.

After familiarizing herself with the cavern and its social strata, Alex waited for a time when she could investigate the mysterious glow off to the right of Millennium Road. She'd talked to no one concerning it since she'd mentioned it to Cosmina. She waited until she was particularly satisfied with her living situation, and then one night, she went to bed early.

Once on Millennium Road, she stepped off to the right and turned toward the glow. The uneasy feeling she had about the terrain returned, and she saw a scorched landscape where previous dwellings had been decimated and left in ruins. It used to be an old battlefield and now possibly a demilitarized zone. Off to the right and in the distance, she saw the dim outline of a ravaged mountain that must have previously been much larger. Some explosion ripped it apart. Now all that remained was a jagged hill of obsidian with an even darker depression in the middle that extended to the ground, obviously an entrance to an underground chamber now blocked by debris. All had not gone well in vampire psychic space sometime in the past. She experienced great fear of the place and walked on toward the light in the distance.

Although Alex walked for what seemed an eternity, the glow got no closer, but then, rather abruptly, it rose up before her, a small opening in the firmament above the horizon. At the center, she saw the framework of a structure under construction and a flurry of activity on the ground and in the glow above it. As she approached, she realized that all the shapes performing the activities were winged. They came close and fluttered about her like human-sized butterflies, or perhaps seraphim with three pairs of wings. They had soft pastel coloring with some light green, others of pale pink. They bowed to her, and seemed to solicit her opinion of what they were doing. Such a structure out in the middle of nowhere made no sense. Telepathically she got the idea that it was called the Chateau. She tired of watching, and, believing it had nothing to do with her, she left.

One night, Alex startled awake. She'd not fed in a couple of weeks, and after feasting on the policeman she was not yet close to the time when she would have to, but she knew the time would come in perhaps another week. She talked to Cosmina about this. Cosmina said it wouldn't be a problem, that she'd bring someone to her when the time came, but Alex realized that when she fed off that person, the donor would be immune. The person could not know this but should have no plans to become a vampire. She had to keep it from Cosmina. Alex thought that this might also be best for the baby, so Alex asked Cosmina to find someone for her who had never been tasted.

A week later, Cosmina brought Alex a local girl, heavyset with short black hair. She spent a couple of days with Alex, the two of them talking continuously. Those who knew of such things had screened her, and the girl had been sworn to secrecy and paid a substantial sum. The girl, whose name was Gail, was a little spooked over the whole thing, when it came right down to it, having never been bitten. Alex hadn't been that close to a human since she'd come to the cavern, and immediately her craving ignited. She restrained herself.

Gail presented a severe disposition at first, a false goth front similar to that donned by Jaklin when they first met, but Alex could tell she was quite pleasant underneath. Gail's grandparents were both very old, and she lived with and took care of them. This kept her too busy for a full-time job, but she could be away for hours and certainly needed the money. Alex promised her more, if she'd save her blood for her exclusively. "Plus, you'll get a little non-monetary compensation that I'll tell you about after I have the baby."

When the time came for Alex to bite her, Alex learned that it was customary to bite a donor on the wrist. She took Gail's arm and was amazed at how warm she was, positively hot, and though her blood was sweetly satisfying, it came slowly from the wrist, and Alex longed to take the girl into her arms and sink her teeth into her throat. With her bulk, she must have enough of it, and nothing like great gulps from the jugular quenched a vampire's thirst. But Alex restrained herself, and a bond formed between the vampire and the human. Gail even liked to snuggle while Alex fed off her, which was not surprising because vampire saliva was an aphrodisiac.

*

In the months to come, Alex spent her time alone, except for Gail and vampire women who had an interest in her pregnancy. She received all sorts of advice from those who'd had a child or two before they'd been turned, but so little of it applied to a pregnant vampire. They were surprised that her body was so warm. Themselves, they were only a few degrees above room temperature. They wished to feel the baby move and would place a palm on her abdomen, rub it and smile.

Regardless of popular mythology, vampires do have a heartbeat, and they do breathe, although both are reduced considerably because of superior metabolic efficiency. They are faster, stronger, and have greater endurance. They heal faster, can endure more pain, and suffer no use injuries. They don't have to workout to maintain physical conditioning. Alex learned, as she suspected, that the need for blood was not as food. "It is more like the need for water, a life necessity without nourishment. It allays the flu-like symptoms and excruciating pain," said Cosmina, who seemed to have an answer for every question. The symptoms, though they could be severe when first turned, tended to mellow through the years, and one could learned to manage blood intake and the agony of deprivation.

True to his word, Alu set up a monitoring program for hers and the baby's health. Daily blood pressure checks turned out to be a nuisance, and security guards shadowed her twenty-four hours a day, something that made Alex nervous and irritable. Alu seemed to be overreacting. And Alex wasn't convinced that it was all to ensure her health and safety. She also wondered about the angry voice she'd heard when she had first been in Alu's chamber, the voice of what he'd called a disturbed woman. The more she thought about it, Alex believed that the woman had wanted to see her. Why, she couldn't imagine.

Alex pushed back on all the medical attention. She and the baby were healthy and did not need it. A technician brought in a portable 3D ultrasound machine, which Alex permitted once. She saw her little girl sucking her thumb and felt that it was a violation of her baby's privacy, which she would not allow again. That night Alex had trouble sleeping with images of her little angel crowding it out. She couldn't quit smiling.

Once a week they drew blood, something Alex resisted at first but eventually allowed. They made a big deal of her having only one set of DNA, the same thing the Sinaia medical clinic told her. They asked if she'd ever heard of parthenogenesis. When she said no, they told her it was a form of asexual reproduction where the embryo develops from an unfertilized egg. This pleased her greatly because that meant her child may not have a father, at least not in this world. But Alex also felt that their interest in her child was excessive and quit letting them take blood.

Herself, Alex felt fine. She suffered no morning sickness, and her ever-enlarging abdomen felt a comfort. Her biggest problem was getting the right food in sufficient quantities. She was concerned about vitamin D for the baby. Cosmina helped with this by making frequent trips to the market. But mostly, Alex wished to be left alone, "alone with my baby," as she put it. At times the Cathedral was so quiet she could hear her own heartbeat. During the vampire night, when the Undead seemed like the dead, she'd listen for the baby's heartbeat and tuned herself to it. It was a rapid, steady ping going off inside her.

She'd listen to it for hours and took special pleasure in any movement. At first, these felt like simple flutters, but as the months passed, Alex learned the difference between tiny arm and leg movements, and a shift in body position. Sometimes she felt a hiccup. Her bond with the baby became an obsession, and when she thought of Father Zosimos planning to take her baby from her, she'd feel a flash of rage and the baby would quake.

Among the permanent residents of the cavern, Alex met two children from America, a black boy, six, named William and a white girl, eight, named Jessica, who were both turned recently. They had the same mother but different fathers. They'd been in an orphanage when forcefully turned. After their caretaker got staked, they'd been brought to Romania and the cavern for safety's sake. They came to see Alex frequently, and she loved to talk to them.

Alex's one excursion outside the Cathedral came at Christmas. She knew her mother would worry, so she stepped out of the darkness and into the cold wind to use her cellphone. It was snowing, and although overcast, she was blinded by the sunlight. Across Prohova River Valley, she saw the white shape of snow-laden mountains. She'd never realized their beauty until now. How she missed the outside world.

Alex explained that she wouldn't make it home for Christmas, but assured her mother that everything was alright. She just had too much going on to break away. Her mother had been concerned. She'd tried to call but got no answer. Her voicemails had not been returned. Alex explained that her cellphone was malfunctioning and that she'd missed other calls also. Frequently, she was outside the service range. She could tell that her mother didn't believe her.

Alex thought of calling Jaklin. She got so far as calling up her cell number, but just couldn't push the button. If they were gone, she'd cry at their absence and worry about her home. If they were still in Sinaia, she'd worry about their safety. She turned off her cell phone and reluctantly squeezed back inside the cavern.

It was when returning that she accidentally came upon Cosmina in conversation with another vampire, the strangest Alex had ever seen. Alex hadn't meant to eavesdrop, but the whispering voices startled her, and she stayed back out of sight to honor their obvious desire to not be overheard. Alex's enhanced hearing still latched onto the raspy voices, and her mind couldn't help trying to make sense of what they were saying. Something about a scythe and problems on Millennium Road and a heated discussion of Alu's recent activities. Much of it she couldn't make out because it seemed to be in a foreign language. Suddenly, the whispering stopped, and Alex realized that they'd sensed her presence. She walked toward them, but the strange vampire seemed to flicker, then vanish into the darkness, as if she were an apparition.

"Alex? What are you doing here?" asked Cosmina, her voice still a whisper.

"Who was that?"

"You don't want to know. Were you eavesdropping?"

"No! Not intentionally. I've been outside calling my mother," she answered. It was the truth, but still, she felt guilty.

"What did you hear? Tell me. How much?"

"Little, really," she said. "Something about a scythe, but I could tell it was a private conversation and tried not to listen."

"Say nothing of what you did hear. And say nothing of the person I was talking to. I trust you, Alex. Believe me, you don't want to get involved."

"Then let's not mention it further," said Alex.

And they didn't mention it again, either of them, but Alex's mind wouldn't leave it alone, picking at the memory of the disjointed details of the conversation and extrapolating, collating. Even the foreign words seemed to linger in her memory for later translation. The dim, strobing image of the strange vampire wouldn't disappear either, and the longer it remained in her mind's eye, the more vivid it became. It seemed that a secret group of wayward vampires with unusual skills roamed the Earth correcting Alu's wrongs. This was her first confirmation that everything Alu was involved in may not be for the good of all. And the strange looking vampire was a female, short-cropped black hair and large flashing eyes. Ephemerally beautiful. She shimmered in the pale light and seemed transparent. It was obvious that Cosmina was not the unquestioning follower of Alu she'd seemed. Alex remembered how confused Cosmina had been over Alu not knowing that Alex had dreamed of Millennium Road. Cosmina's secrecy was a shock, as was her seeming trust of Alex to not divulge what she'd seen and heard. This simple act of faith brought with it amplified respect and new admiration. But perhaps it's biggest impact on Alex was the confidence it gave to her own questioning of the world Alu had created. Now she realized that she should take nothing she saw on faith.

*

During the later months of her pregnancy, Alex sat in on many philosophical conversations, one on the physical manifestations of quantum mechanics and the implications on paranormal activity. She was amazed at how much smarter she'd become, and how easily her mind absorbed information. She realized that her new intimate connection with her psyche allowed her to gain insight into any subject quickly. She'd gained access to some sort of communal knowledge and intellectual dexterity. It was much like being on the Internet. She longed to attend Oxford to see how this would enable her.

Alex then migrated to discussions of major historical events of which some had witnessed firsthand. Alu occasionally sat in on these, and with them all gathered in a circle around a single candle, he told of witnessing and participating in the Trojan War, how he'd never heard of Achilles and that retrieving Helen was an afterthought. She'd almost been left behind once the Greeks had burned Troy. He'd known Oedipus and his sons, and saw the famous battle of what is now known as Seven Against Thebes, and then a generation later, the burning of the ancient Kadmia. He'd known Teiresias, the great Greek seer who'd lived 140 years, which wasn't so impressive to a vampire. In the flickering light of the tiny flame, Alu told of witnessing the Crucifixion, although he wouldn't talk about it further. Alex questioned some of the elders later and learned that Alu had actually tasted the blood of Christ, and that it was a huge mistake. It had caused the vampire's fear of the cross and all the afflictions that come with just simply viewing it: the lashes, excruciating pain in the hands and feet, consuming tiredness, even disillusionment.

Humm..., thought Alex. All the afflictions I didn't inherit, except possibly the disillusionment.

Alu did talk extensively about WWI, in which he'd also fought. He spoke fondly of Queen Marie, how she'd given hope to the Romanian troops in their most desolate hours and the tragedy during the later years of her life, when her own cowardly son turned on her. Though his comments seemed targeted to get Alex to speak up, she remained quiet, not wishing her own heritage exposed to the public.

Alu thought the fifty years under communism particularly abhorrent. The suffering of the people reflected in a degradation of their blood and made it little more appetizing than that of an animal's. "Let us never forget," he said, "that our wellbeing depends directly on that of humans. We are inexorably linked."

Alex marveled at how these ancient beings were still alive in the world. Outside, humans had written history. But within the vampire community, they had actual memories of historic events and personal experiences to season the tales of yore. She felt that somehow the Cathedral was ancient and yet timeless. In a sense, time stopped there. It went on outside, but within the vampire world, time had little meaning. Since they were eternal, they had every wish to maintain the world as it was and only sought to reduce suffering in both communities.

Everyone was glad to see Alu come among them again, even though he was fidgety and cranky. After one such symposium, another vampire from within Alu's inner circle told Alex that Alu had been different of late. At first, they'd thought it was because of her presence, but they'd come to realize that it was more than that. For some time, he'd been more distant, less interested in the intellectual side of vampirism, and less concerned with each individual. He'd been distracted, as if preoccupied with some weighty concern about which he wouldn't talk. He was gone much of the time.

Alex related this to the whispered conversation she'd overheard between Cosmina and the ephemeral vampire. Something was going on beneath the surface of normal vampire life not only in the Sinaia colony but also internationally.

Alu did have one personal contact with Alex. He came with two armed vampires that were obviously from the Cathedral's security forces. Alu explained to her the special need for protection during the later stages of her pregnancy. "Word has spread throughout the vampire world that a pregnant vampire has come among us. Some unaffiliated groups may try to kidnap you. I offer this higher-level protection. Both of them will stay out of sight but respond if you should need them."

Alex let it go at that. She did however suspect there was more to his security precaution than he let on. And indeed, that turned out to be the case. The two men started giving her orders and tried to control her movement. She developed means of evading their control to their consternation.

Alex was a favorite of those who'd been young when turned. She talked with them for hours, and some she spoke to in private. They'd come to confess their sins. These isolated, one-on-one conversations were highly emotional, and many tears fell. Through youth, they'd developed a great arrogance and come to know regret. Some had used war as an excuse to drain and kill indiscriminately. They corrupted themselves through their love of carnage. Alex could relate to that. At times, she'd felt a pull toward butchery herself. Memory of the wild frenzied killing of Petru Balc, the thrill of it and the unbridled rage, still haunted her. Of course, she frequently ruminated over her assault in the graveyard when Father Zosimos and his henchmen tried to uncover her grandmother's coffin. At times, she felt regret over not sucking a couple of them dry.

But one vampire, named Braxton, a small, smelly vampire with a short greasy beard who had newly come to the Cathedral, told her of the crimes he committed before becoming a vampire. He had been a child molester, and was still, self-confessedly, on the prowl. He was proud of his abuse of children and seemed to be bragging instead of owning up to his sins. Alex thought of William and Jessica. The baby kicked the wall of her womb all the time Braxton talked to her. She saw this vampire's remarks as a challenge and silently vowed to accept it. Her blood boiled.

Alex learned that vampires have an active social life on Millennium Road, and during their waking hours, they talked of their experiences on it. Millennium Road seemed to be the source of new intellectual strength and a way to absorb others' wisdom. Some dreams they viewed as prophecy and tried to relate to coming events in the real world. She heard from them that Millennium Road had become disturbed of late. They had visions of a coming war, and realized that something had recently changed. Many were afraid. Alex's own dreams, visions of Millennium Road, pointed to a great evil coming upon the world. They foretold of the Vampire Wars, a cosmic conflict among different races of vampires. She questioned them about other types of vampires, but they knew of only one, and that composed of all human races. No one had ever heard of feral vampires.

Alex asked Cosmina, "If my child is born a vampire, will it always be a baby?"

"Children who become vampires age until they go through puberty. From late teens on, they no longer age. Your child won't be a vampire. It takes more than contact with a vampire's blood."

"So William and Jessica do age?"

"Of course. And will until they become fully adult. It's the age-related disintegration process that's suspended. Not growing up."

She learned that the two children were forever sad that they'd become vampires. They had no other companions to play with and wished they had a mother and father instead of the being raised by communal effort. Alex thought about the situation and that she just might be able to solve their predicament, but she'd have to wait until the time was right.

Alex heard that a great woman called Kate had come amongst them. She was visiting Alu, and such was the fuss her presence created that Alex hoped to at least catch sight of her before she left. She was not supposed to be of great age, but never the less had become an important person among the vampires of Sinaia because she was originally from there. Kate had returned to Sinaia because her daughter had recently passed away.

And then one morning while Alex was enjoying her splash bath along with other men and women, this woman showed up with Alu. Alex was just patting herself dry when the famous vampire entered the pool, acknowledged Alex with but a nod and didn't speak, remaining at a distance. At first, Alex didn't believe it could possibly be she who had created such a stir. Kate was rather small and quiet, subdued actually, but she had the golden hair Alex had heard so much about. They shared that attribute. She seemed quite bashful. Alex thought there was something familiar about the woman, and then she realized what it was. It was the woman on Millennium Road who'd said that she didn't belong there. Alex looked at her again, this time in recognition, but Kate was also looking back and shook her head no. Alex said nothing and looked away. What could that mean? Who was that strange woman?

Alex lingered at the edge of candlelight hoping to get a chance to speak with her, but she and Alu were in and out of the pool quickly and on their way.

"How did her daughter die?" Alex asked Cosmina.

"Old age," she replied.

Alex thought a moment. Kate had looked so young. "Oh," she said. "I get it." Obviously, Kate had the child before she became a vampire and hadn't physically aged since becoming one. Her daughter had.

Generally, vampires took little notice of their own past lives, but Kate had been unable to completely give up her past. Although she'd been on an international assignment of great importance, she'd returned over Alu's objection.

"Why is she such a great woman?" asked Alex. "What has she done to have such acclaim?"

"She's a lawyer, involved in international law. She advises all the countries of the world."

Lawyer, huh? thought Alex. The word "lawyer" always made someone commonplace in her mind. Kate's big bubble popped, at least for Alex.

One thing Alex experienced that she would have never anticipated. She loved the Cathedral. She'd grown attached to the tight-nit community and the ever-present sense of purpose. But she also like the way her body felt, the intense passion. She was physically more functional, even being pregnant. She enjoyed feeding, the flow of warm blood from a human being into her body, the awakening and sense of gratification, the intimacy. In short, she loved being a vampire.

*

Out of curiosity, Alex while dreaming again trekked off to the right of Millennium Road to the glow above the horizon. This time the structure had a golden bridge across a fast-flowing river and leading away from it to a locked gate in the heavens. She continued to puzzle over it.

Alex was forever curious about Millennium Road, and frequently investigated its possibilities. She learned that one could navigate forward and backward on it while undead in the real world, but once totally dead, the soul became locked in position. She found that she was unusually adept at navigating its pathways. The rumblings that Alu had changed recently and quit officiating at initiations made her curious enough to go farther on Millennium Road to see if he was actually there, as reported. He should be the very first in the train. At least, she could see how far she could go.

She found that the farther forward she moved in the train, the more difficult it became. The first night, she seemed to make little progress, but curiously the next she entered at the same forward spot. She simply had to recharge her nocturnal traveling batteries with a little wake-time and then try again. Several nights later, she notice that the appearance of the vampires had changed. The skin of those that far forward was more metallic than those farther back, a mixture of gold and silver that shimmered as they moved, as had those who initiated her. A few nights later she came upon both the men and women of her initiation, who were greatly surprised and not a little perturbed that she was there. "No one from your time is allowed this far forward," they said. She quickly retreated, flying at great speed along the Road back to her proper place.

But Alex had seen what she'd come for. She just didn't know what to make of it. In the front, the very first being on Millennium Road, she'd seen the Centaur, Cheiron himself. Wow! What a sight! A being part-horse and part-human. But Alucius Kardasian, who should have been the first follower of the Centaur, wasn't there, and all those who would have been close behind him were confused and in disarray.

This created another concern for Alex. Millennium Road had a backward end, one not far from where she belonged because she'd been so recently turned. Alex wanted to go there and witness the newest vampires entering the Road. She couldn't remember her own emergence and wondered how it happened. This would be much easier because she only had a few months to travel backward instead of the few millennia going forward.

The next night, Alex entered Millennium Road and backtracked, passing vampires that appeared less sure of themselves and some even scared, bolting when she came among them. She reassured them and hurried on. When she reached the end of the train, she could see only darkness past the last vampire. Nothing else. Nothing. Just as she started to leave, she saw a small spec of dim light, which started to grow. It rapidly changed, becoming brilliant white as someone broke through. A newly turned vampire. Then all was black again. Alex helped her. She was glassy eyed, and seemed to have little brain function. Alex realized that this was how she must have been when she was first turned and before she'd dreamed the Millennium Dream. She remembered all the nightmares she'd had, the dark shapes, confusion, and realized that she'd been experiencing Millennium Road all that time. She felt sympathy for this new vampire, but realized she could do little until the girl was initiated. Her physical body could be anywhere in the world.

Before she left for her proper place along the Road, Alex looked once again into the darkness from where the next vampire would emerge. She wondered if one could go backward through the wall when a vampire wasn't coming through. She had to force herself to remember that this was psychic space, and that it existed only in the collective unconscious, something all vampires shared. They were always there, once turned, but Millennium Road didn't come into consciousness through a dream until they were with a group of vampires. Once they were with a colony, the dreams of Millennium Road started, and they were ready to be initiated.

The next morning, Alex woke with a start. She'd slept long beyond her normal waking hour. The flicker of candlelight already broke the darkness. She heard vampires in conversation and the normal shuffle of people moving about in the early hours after waking. But this morning was different for her, and it would have been for them also, if they'd known what she knew. She now realized that vampires were being created much less frequently than they had in the past. This coupled with the fact that Alu was no longer in the lead on Millennium Road, and that it was in disarray, told her something was bad wrong in vampire psychic space, and possibly in the real world too. This was one bit of knowledge she could share with no one. Cosmina has her secrets, and now I have mine, Alex thought.

31

The Ichor Dome

Alex had come to view darkness as her friend. It wasn't just that she could see so well in it. She enjoyed the way it heightened the rest of her senses. She could smell better, hear better, and use sound to judge distance. These new talents enabled her to distinguish the smooth gait of a vampire from that of a human more easily. Vampires were agile, quick, fluid. They had music in their step and a bearing that went beyond confidence to a sense of perfect existence.

Some things seemed to come to Alex by instinct. She'd had some furniture brought into her recess in the side of the Cathedral, her own little grotto. She'd had Cosmina pickup some clothes for her, maternity clothes, and she kept them in a cedar chest. One day, she broke off one corner of the backboard, a piece a half meter long. She used a sharp rock to whittle one end to a point. She started carrying it with her under her clothes. Sharp sticks were not a popular item in a nest of vampires.

Braxton was ever on Alex's mind, and one day when Cosmina mentioned that William and Jessica turned up missing, as they were apt to, she decided to go looking for them herself, down past Xanadu, where of course everyone had been warned not to go. Some unnamed danger was supposed to lurk there, but she knew the two little immortals had little sense of danger, even less than mortal children, and an exaggerated fondness for adventure. Cosmina wanted Alex to go with her to Shadowrise services, but Alex begged off again. She was more concerned about Will and Jess than she let on.

First Alex had to get rid of Alu's two security guards who shadowed her every movement. This was an easy thing for her because she'd groomed them for some future escape by sneaking out of sight for a short time and then magically reappearing just when they became concerned. She kept extending this period of vanishment until they became comfortable with her not always being around.

This was the situation when Will and Jess disappeared.

Light beyond Xanadu was nonexistent, so Alex stopped at the pond in the Pleasure Dome and gathered a little bioluminescent water in a phial to light her way. She didn't call out to Will and Jess because she knew they'd hide from her, them being in a forbidden area, if they were actually there. She was eight and one-half months pregnant now and quite large in the abdomen, but moved remarkably well. She found them a ways on, a little flickering candle that illuminated their playroom, a small flat area to the right of the path among the stalactites and stalagmites. Those in charge of the two children generally dressed the little renegades in light clothing, the better to see and find them.

Alex hid her own light in a fold of her clothing and approached quietly, but then heard another voice among them, a more mature, smooth and slimy voice that she recognized as that of Braxton. The baby jumped and her own heart raced as she stopped to determine her next move. She felt for the stake within the fold of her skirt. Sure enough, still there.

Having found him with the children, Alex knew she was going to kill him, the only question was how without the children knowing. Braxton was dressed in black, and probably didn't realize yet that she knew he was present.

She called out, "Will, Jess. Are you there?"

They went silent.

"Don't make me come get you. You know it's difficult for me now."

She heard them whispering, and then Jessica spoke up.

"Do we have ta?"

"You know this area is off limits. You'll be grounded."

Alex saw Braxton's shadow disappear off to the left, as the children started toward her.

"Go on ahead," she said. "I'm slow and need to take my time, but I'll be following. Cosmina has been looking for you. Hurry along."

When they were a safe distance, she entered their playground. "Come on out, Braxton, I know you're here."

He didn't. He was a slick maneuverer, but Alex heard him just in time. He'd come around behind her somehow, and she dropped to her knees, as a swish of some object he'd just swung at her whizzed over her head.

Then in spite of the baby, she sprang off the ground, clutched a stalactite high above them, and looked down upon him. She caught a faint glimmer as he moved to block her exit from the off-path chamber. He'd decided to take her on, which pleased Alex greatly. She dropped from her perch to stand a few yards from him.

"Let's do this," she said. "We both knew it was coming."

"I'll kill the child."

"You'll never make it back to them," she said.

"Not Will or Jess," he said. "Your child."

This stopped Alex for a just an instant, but somehow she knew he'd underestimated her. She walked toward him. He came for her.

Quick as a fluttering bat, he sprang from side to side using the hanging formations to push off. He seemed different. He'd changed, seemed more violent. He could have run from her and escaped with her being pregnant. But he didn't. He seemed attracted.

The world seemed to shift to Alex, seemed to go into slow motion, yet her movement was quick as ever. She caught him in mid flight, grabbed him by the arm and threw him crashing through stalagmites to the wall of the cave. She was on him before he could come to his feet.

Though she'd pinned his arms, he lunged at her with his head, busted her lip, and licked the blood. She saw him instantly undergo a change.

"Oh!" he said. "A hidden attribute." He laughed. "A vampire with sweet blood."

She felt for her wood stake and brought it out of hiding. "There are more things in my body and soul, Braxton, than are dreamt of in your philosophy." In one swift motion, she drove it at his heart.

But Braxton brushed it aside. The taste of her blood had somehow excited him, and he found a new quickness and strength. He pinned her arms and sunk his fangs into her neck, sucked great gulps of blood. But it then turned on him. He sputtered and her blood belched from his mouth. His whole body trembled, lips quivered. He released her.

"Don't try to speak," she said. "Child molesters don't get last words."

His body started to glow. She smelled smoke coming from it, saw dim sparks arching along the skin as it sizzled like steak on an open flame, sizzled and then went out. A dark cloud of stench filled the cavern momentarily but was swept on down to the lower depths by air currents. Alex remembered the feral vampires that had bitten her that night out with Stefan. She realized that Braxton must have been feral and would have had to achieve that status rather recently. She felt dizzy and staggered against a large stalagmite. Breathing the smoke seemed a narcotic.

Alex knew she couldn't leave the partially burnt corpse there. Even though it was forbidden territory, someone would eventually stumble onto it. She pulled him out to the path. She retrieved her phial of glowing water and dragged him into forbidden territory. If a precipice did exist farther down, as they'd all been told, she'd throw him off it.

But the path didn't end. She did encounter a sharp drop, but it was negotiable, and she pushed Braxton off and climbed down herself and dragged him farther on. She detected a draft from what might be a branching cavern off to the right. No path led to it, but trusting her instinct, she dragged Braxton among loose rocks and stalagmites, weaving a trail for a ways, but then saw what appeared to be an ancient path covered with rocks and other cavern debris. Farther on, the path cleared and she dragged his body with her, now clearly in full exploration mode, through a small opening into a larger cave that she thought would be a excellent place to leave him.

Alex felt no guilt over the murder. She'd thought this through over the past few weeks, and now all she felt was relief that he was no longer a threat to the children of the world. The farther she went into this cave, the more she realized that at one time it had been occupied. It was a small tunnel actually, one artificially cut through sandstone. She noticed an obstruction up ahead, and when she got there, found it to be a gate, or more accurately an iron fence with a door, now standing open and hanging by a hinge. She dragged Braxton inside and looked around.

She discovered some ancient structures, small buildings and cages where at first she believed they'd kept animals, but upon closer examination, she realized it contained human skeletons and mummified remains. Farther on, she located another chamber with an ancient throne that obviously belonged to someone of Alu's stature, and adjacent to it, another incarceration facility and beyond this, a torture chamber with stacks of skeletons. The room was a virtual museum of pain-inflicting devices. On one wall, scratched with a spike, were the Romanian words *Casa de Durere*, House of Pain.

This had at one time been a prison and not one predisposed to rehabilitation. It was all made of stone and iron, and not of high-quality metal at that. Alex dragged Braxton's charred body into a far corner and stacked rocks and other debris on him. She left using her phial to illuminate the way. Back along the tunnel, she hurried, but when she reached the main pathway, she heard voices and quickly slipped back inside the tunnel, hid her light within a crack in the wall and slid a rock after it into the crevice to extinguish all its light. What she'd just seen in the torture chamber had spooked her, and she didn't want anyone to know she'd been there.

In the distance, back at the main path, she saw a light. Two vampires were coming up from even farther down below, where no one should be. They carried a flashlight, something she'd not seen anywhere in the cavern before. She heard them talking.

"I tell you, Mitchum, I did smell something."

"Must be someone roasting a little meat, Cletis, in spite of the edict against any form of fire other than candles."

"You may be right, but I tell you, I've smelled a combusting vampire before. Someone's been drinking holy water."

"We've come two kilometers up the trail, and haven't found anything," said Mitchum. "I smelled it too, but I'm not so sure what it was. It's gone now. We need to get back. You know how Alu hates any of us coming this far toward Xanadu."

Alex waited in the darkness for a while longer, their voices trailing off into the cavern below, and then all was silent. But Alex didn't wait until the glow of their light completely extinguished. She retrieved her phial, slipped out of hiding, and instead of returning to the Cathedral, silently scurried after them. Something about these vampires intrigued her. They were different, as Braxton had been different. Their gait wasn't smooth and coordinated. They were jerky and unpredictable. Vampires, but somehow not vampires. These were the characteristics of a feral.

Alex had fallen so far behind that she could no longer hear them or see the glow of their flashlight. She heard the quiet rush of an underground river, and realized that it was the Alph that fed their bathing pool and also the Pleasure Dome. She continued endlessly on, hoping to eventually learn where Mitchum and Cletis had come from, but the path became more difficult to follow, being covered with loose rocks and winding continuously among stalagmites and stalactites. She finally gave up and turned to go back, took a few steps and halted.

She'd heard a noise.

It could have been nothing, but she'd come a long way to leave without learning anything. She couldn't imagine how far she was below ground. She'd descended for what seemed hours. She peered off into the black depths and heard a reeking sigh leach toward her, just a faint but ominous sound that somehow stirred her soul. Down she descended again. And then she saw it: a faint glow far ahead on the ceiling above the plummeting cavern floor.

She scrambled down an unruly rock formation, and as she got closer, the glow grew but strangely. The light was all on the ceiling of some giant cavern, the floor of which was not yet visible. The baby quaked, and Alex stopped dead in her tracks. She'd learned that that movement meant trouble. She backed up, saw a break in the path, and realized that she'd almost stepped into a bottomless chasm.

Off to right, she saw a bridge and standing on it, the two guards she'd been following, Mitchum and Cletis. She heard them talking and, listening closely, heard them call the place the "Ichor Dome."

Concerned that they might see her, Alex scrambled off to the left across a rock field and soon found an outcropping that had broken off the low ceiling and fallen over the chasm. Its sharp edge was up, but Alex felt sure that she could negotiate it to get to the other side, if she were careful. While traversing it, she heard the roar of a waterfall, and realized that the Alph dumped into the chasm.

Once on the other side, she crept through the stalactites and stalagmites until the floor dropped away exposing a gigantic cavern below and the source of the glow on the ceiling. The Ichor Dome. A hundred candles twinkled along paths and at the entrances to buildings. A distant groan and cry issued up toward her. The cavern's floor, if you could call it that, was not level but sloped downward and contained much cavern debris, and what surprised her most, actual habitable structures. The closer she looked, the more detail she could make out, and she finally realized that they were not dwellings at all, but prisons for human captives. Vampires were everywhere, ants along the maze of trails like streets of a small city. But these were not normal vampires. Their gaits were jerky, not agile, not coordinated. She could distinguish the smooth quick gait of a vampire from that of a human, "the dance of the vampire," she called it. Though she was a good distance away, she could see humans in chains, and vampires feeding on them.

And then she realized that the din she heard coming up from below was the groan and cries of human suffering. Vampires fed off them indiscriminately. A vampire would suck on one a while and then move to another. She saw humans being led in and others being dragged out. The vampires moved rapidly, gigantic black spiders pouncing from one victim to another. She saw a sparkle of silver light threading along the floor of the Ichor Dome and realized that the Alph had surfaced again.

Alex heard a commotion and saw the vampires separate, move to the side off the main street as another vampire, a special one, entered. He had a different stature, tall, proud, erect. He looked about as if viewing his realm. She knew this vampire. She couldn't believe it. It was Alucius Kardasian, and this was his kingdom of feral vampires, the über-coven of the Ichor Dome. Her heart just gave way.

But then yet another enormous vampire entered following Alu. He was a giant, some mythological beast, and not thin like Alu, but broad shouldered and heavily muscled. Pale as death. Alex heard the name "Pagomas" shouted among the crowd that formed about him. He looked a little like a cave troll. The ground seemed to shake with his step, and Alex felt as though she could feel a chill emanating from him. He carried an enormous axe.

The baby fluttered again. Alex had seen enough.

She scurried back to the chasm, scrambled across the jagged rock over the gorge, and worked her way back to the main trail, the image of Pagomas seared into her brain. She heard something from behind and saw a shape coming up toward her. She'd been seen.

Quickly along the trail she went, at first using the remaining glow from the great cavern behind her to illuminate the way, but soon it became very dark, and she had to once again break out her little phial of glow water. She began to tire. The child had become a burden. On she went although she could hear at times a small sound that told her she was still being followed. She struggled up the face of the cliff, shuffled quickly past the secret cave where she'd hidden Braxton's body, the Casa de Durere, and finally made it to Xanadu. She'd not heard anyone following her in a while. She'd shaken her pursuer.

She was overcome with sadness. Alu was indeed evil, and she'd fallen under his influence, just as Catalin had warned. She felt sick and realized that she needed blood and food. She was weak from the hours of walking. She'd committed another murder, this one premeditated. Perhaps she felt more guilt than she realized.

Alex's heart pounded and ears rang. What kind of colony had she joined? What form of creature had she become? Were these vampires really destined to be the end result of humanity? An immortal race of feral vampires? The revelation was more than she could bear. It affected her physically, and as she approached the Cathedral along the cold stone trail, she fell ill.

It all made sense. By biting Velinar, Alu had developed the ability to turn someone into a vampire by simply sucking their blood until they died. The victim was passive, did not have to wish to be turned. This was the advantage he'd gained. Everyone a feral bit would also became a vampire. But they wouldn't be ordinary vampires. They were feral, conscienceless daemons without a soul and thus would not show up on Millennium Road. Everyone said that Alu had changed. Little did they know how much.

Alu had kept his new talent secret even from his own followers, which meant that he was planning something. The really scary part of all this was the prophecy coming from the vampire community that a war, wars actually, were imminent, something called the Vampire Wars.

Just before she reached the Cathedral, a pain hit her across the abdomen, a sharp biting spasm that knocked her to her knees. The agony was so intense; it brought tears to her eyes. And then it quit. She rose up and continued on but heard a noise behind her just as another excruciating contraction gripped her abdomen. "Oh no, not now," she said. Again, she fell to her knees. And then from behind, she felt something grab her arm. The cold hand of a vampire.

32

A Birth

Alex opened her eyes to the dim light and saw the mysterious female vampire, Kate, peering down at her. "Come with me," the woman said. "You're in danger."

"I can't," replied Alex. "I'm in labor."

"You must," said Kate. "Your life and that of the child depend on it."

"Was that you following me?"

"Yes, and others are following me."

The darkness seemed to deepen, and struggle though she might, Alex still could not move, so Kate took her hand in hers, held it, and though cold, was a great comfort. The contraction finally eased, and Alex struggled to her feet.

"How long have you been in labor?"

"It just started."

"How far apart are the contractions?"

"Ten minutes," said Alex.

"I know a place. You'll be safe."

The woman led Alex along a maze of passageways, stopping once while Alex had another contraction. Finally, Kate located a small hole in the wall, and they squeezed through. It opened up into a space large enough for them to move about. Alex heard the faint echo of dripping water.

"This'll have to do."

"You're Kate, aren't you?" said Alex.

"Catherine, but among the Colony, they do call me Kate." She was small, almost frail, and young. Yet her high-pitched voice made her seem even younger.

Catherine? Alex wondered where she'd heard that name recently. "My name is Marie," she said.

"I know who you are," said Kate. "All about you, but we can talk later. I need to get a few items. You'll have the baby soon."

"You've midwifed before?"

"No, but I had a baby once, years ago. Hang on. I won't be long."

Alex was afraid for her to leave and stopped her as she stepped into the exit. "Are you sure I'm in danger?"

"Alu knows you've seen his band of ferals. He knows better than to trust you with that secret."

"What he's up to is unconscionable."

"I know. I just recently found out myself. He's not pleased that I'm here, and particularly not that I found his Ichor Dome. I knew something was wrong with him when I first saw him. I tracked him."

"Why did you come back to Sinaia?"

"To visit my only child's grave. She passed away not long ago. Alu forbade it."

"I've heard that he's become angry recently. He doesn't mingle with the Colony as he once did. So they say."

"He's all wrapped up in the Ichor Dome. This new breed of vampire experiences passion without love, violence without regret, and hate without restraint. Everyone a feral vampire bites can became a vampire. What's more, Alu is himself feral."

"So I've learned. That's the reason he's no longer on Millennium Road," said Alex.

"You know that for a fact?"

"I've been to the front."

"Wow! You are something special. I've tried but never made it that far."

"He's not there. He should be right behind the Centaur, but isn't."

"It's even worse than I imagined. I'm pleased I found you. I thought I'd never get away from this new über-coven. Alu has plans for your child, and if he found out that you've delivering early, he'd take you into custody."

"He's always been overly interested in my baby," said Alex. "Seemed to resent me being pregnant, too."

"Of course. He wanted to make you feral. He was afraid if he bit you, you'd lose the child. Trust me on this. He wants to create a new kingdom of feral vampires. I've heard him tell others that with you and your child, he will rule the world."

"I just can't imagine why he's gone rogue."

"He says there's more to it than the Ichor Dome. I tried to get him to tell me more, but he's really secretive about it. He wouldn't tell me more until I let him turn me feral, he said."

"You wouldn't go along?"

"Lie still. I'll be right back."

"My grotto. Baby clothes and other items in the cedar chest. Ask Cosmina."

Kate squeezed through the opening and was gone.

As Kate's footsteps faded, Alex felt another contraction grab her, its gripping force strong and persistent. She writhed in pain and felt a wetness between her thighs. Her water had broken. The contraction finally turned loose of her.

Alex was immensely tired and felt as if she'd been drugged. The cavern was so quiet that her eyelids drooped, and she dozed. She dreamed of Millennium Road but immediately left it and headed toward the glow in the distance as if drawn by gravity. Alex could now see that the Chateau — she was surprised she remembered what they called it — through its splendid bridge, adjoined a door in a wall that surrounded a magnificent city, one she recognized from her dream the night Velinar bit her. The Chateau was now finished, and a beautiful pale-blue seraph stood before it beckoning, wings all aflutter. When Alex approached her, she offered a golden key, which Alex took, then the angel disappeared. The Chateau was a magnificent structure formed of pentagonal sections, sort of a flat, multi-sided sphere. The frame of the Chateau was formed of adamantine, and its

walls overlaid with pure silver trimmed in gold. Alex recognized the
geometric shape from her geometry class. It was one of the Platonic
solids, a dodecahedron. She used the key to unlock the door and went
inside.

The Chateau was one room and sparsely furnished, no kitchen
appliances, no bedrooms since it was in psychic space, she reasoned,
just a couple of sofas and easy chairs along with gold throw-rugs
strategically placed about the floor. One pentagonal section opened
onto the bridge, which led to a gate in the wall of the greatest of all
cities, the City of God. The see-through pane of the pentagon was a
door made of one enormous flat-cut diamond. She tried to open it, but
found that it could only be opened from the outside.

Alex looked around, and hearing voices behind her, turned to see
two children, a boy and a girl, walking along the bridge, enter through
the diamond door, and come into the Chateau with her. "We've come
to play," they said.

They taught her a game for three and made her sing and dance.
She'd never been so happy.

Podul de piatră s-a dărâmat
A venit apa și l-a luat
Vom face altul pe riu, în jos
Altul mai trainic și mai frumos!
Vom face altul pe riu, în jos
Altul mai trainic și mai frumos!

"Bring your friends here," they told her. Sing and dance to that song
only in the Chateau, only with friends." Then they turned to leave.

"What friends?" she asked.

"You'll know when the time comes."

Once outside the Chateau again, she was able to see the gate into
the City clearer. It was made of pure pearl.

Kate's return startled Alex awake at the same time another
contraction threatened to squeeze her in two. Kate had brought an
aluminum chair with a reclining back, on which she spread a thick
blanket. She helped Alex onto it and left her legs hanging off the end.

The contraction was brutal, and when Alex started to scream, Kate shoved a rag into her mouth.

"Bite down," she said. "You can't allow yourself to voice the pain. Keep it inside."

Alex bit down and wrestled angrily with the contraction. Finally it let up, and Alex relaxed. She started to ask Kate a question, but then came the next one. When it eased, Kate checked Alex's uterus.

"You're fully dilated. It's baby time!" she said.

As if triggered by Kate's enthusiasm, a mighty contraction grabbed Alex and would not let go. Alex growled into the pain, pushed with all her might, and felt it give.

"I can't believe this is so quick, but here it comes," said Kate.

Alex kept pushing, but all at once, it got easier. She saw Kate pull the baby from within her, as if she'd performed a party trick, and then Alex heard a squeak, a cry.

"It's a girl," Kate said, dipping a rag in water, dabbing and rubbing the baby. It kept crying, more loudly now.

"Yes," said Alex. "I've known for some time."

"You didn't deserve such an easy delivery. You're supposed to have more pain and heartache before you get such a beautiful child."

Alex wasn't sure Kate was going to give up the baby. She was suddenly afraid that taking charge of her delivery had been a trick to steal the child. "Can I see her?" she asked, panic in her voice.

"Oh! Sorry. I'm really excited myself. I won't say why just yet, but let me tell you. This little girl is very special to me too." She set her in Alex's arms.

Alex couldn't imagine what Kate was talking about, and the thought evaporated with her first view of her daughter.

"Hold still now," said Kate. I've got to remove the afterbirth."

Now that the mad rush for safety and delivery were over, Kate seemed to sink back inside herself. She held the baby while Alex cleaned up, and put on the clothes Kate had brought from her cedar chest.

"You have to get out of the cavern now that you've delivered," said Kate.

"This business of being immortal is still strange. I've only been one a few months. Even with you as young as you appear, your child died of old age?"

"Yes." Kate considered something for a moment and didn't speak. Finally she asked, "Why did you become a vampire?"

"Not by choice," said Alex. "I was bitten in the woods near my grandmother's home. I fainted, or I guess died, and when I woke, I had started to change."

"So you didn't want to become one either?"

"It was thrust upon me by special circumstances. I've been pissed off ever since. Cost me two loves."

"I had a husband who lived with me here in Sinaia. He fought in WWI, survived it but died a few years later from a wound he suffered. Since I'm on Millennium Road, I can never be with him in Paradise." Kate grew quiet. "Or with my daughter," she added, sadly.

In the dim light cast by her glow bottle that was gradually losing its luminescence, Alex could see that this bothered Kate greatly. Alex thought that possibly she could help with Kate's problem.

"Have you named the baby yet?" asked Kate.

"Since I'm not going to be able to live openly in the world, I've given her my name, Alexandra Marie Eidyn." She held the baby close and longed to have her in brighter light, so she could get a better look at her.

"That's a really interesting name."

"My grandmother gave it to me. I'll call this lovely little lady Andra."

"Alex-Andra? That's really cleaver."

"And Ra. The Egyptian sun god. She's already lit up my life greater than any sun. I've never liked any of my names for myself. Maybe they've always been meant for her."

Little Andra made a small sucking noise. She had her tiny fist in her mouth.

"Give her a nipple," said Kate. "She'll need the antibodies in the colostrum. If she gains the immunity of a vampire, she'll certainly be healthy." She put her cold hand on Alex's arm. "You're still warm. Such an amazing thing." She sat close to Alex, and gazed down at the child. "She's so active for a newborn."

Alex pulled open the front of her blouse, and put Andra's little lips up against her nipple. Andra smacked then took it. A powerful sensation of warmth and great love came over Alex. She saw Kate's eyes fill with tears.

"I have something to tell you, Marie. They tell me you're called Marie here. Is that what you prefer?"

"No. I gave them that, but I go by Alex."

"Your grandmother called you Alex, didn't she?"

"What do you know of my grandmother?"

"My name is actually Catherine. I was born here in Sinaia. So was my daughter. She passed away the same day, the same instant, your grandmother passed away."

Alex's mind went into a whirr. Catherine. Where had she heard that name recently? The cave seemed to darken for an instant, and then she realized. Catherine was her own great grandmother's name. "You can't be," she said.

"Yes, the child you hold to your breast is my great great grandchild. Your grandmother was my daughter."

"But you're so young." Alex tried to to fit it all together. She remembered her grandmother's words and the journal she found in her grandmother's attic. "You are the illegitimate daughter of Queen Marie. You're a Cantacuzene."

"Yes. That's why Alu wants us both. We're royalty."

33

Court and Spark

Alex could feel her muscles tighten and her joints sliding back into place. Her body was like a machine that had performed one function and was now gearing up for another. The soreness she felt immediately after delivering was slowly dissolving, her body regrouping. It sensed danger. She was a vampire, a daemon protecting her own, an animal with physical resources she'd never tried.

With the child there at her breast, Alex wondered what sort of mother she could be. She'd made a certain peace with being a vampire, but now little Andra changed everything. The more she learned about Millennium Road, the more she worried about her own fate. She'd never been one to focus on what happened after death. Yes, she'd been christened at birth, and she'd gone to Sunday school as a child, but her parents were not regular goers, only occasionally stepping inside a church. Hers was the modern, big-city religiosity — recognized but ignored. She felt pushed up against a wall, and this immortality thing, along with the apparitions at the gazebo, forced her to take a more serious look at the situation. For a vampire, Millennium Road was a dream world that became the only reality after death. Quite possibly, life after death was more important than she'd realized.

"We'll have to make our move after sundown," said Catherine. "When I left you, I spoke to a couple in the Colony. They'd heard rumors of feral vampires coming up from down below. I could sense the panic."

They heard an echo of voices off in the distance. Catherine went to the opening and peered outside. "We're in trouble. They're coming."

"I'm ready now. Let's get out of here."

"But it's still light out. We'll fry."

"I'm different," said Alex. "Sunlight doesn't bother me."

"You sure?" Her disbelief was obvious.

"I spent months out of doors before coming here. It's another reason Alu wants me."

"I can go only as far as the exit. You'll be on your own once in daylight. You and the child."

"Not a problem. What will happen to you? They could turn you feral also."

"I'll have to take my chances. I've eluded them so far."

Alex didn't like it. While she fitted the baby pack, she tried to conceive a scenario where Catherine could escape with them. "How long to Shadowrise?" she asked.

"An hour or so, but you're right. We can't wait. You and the baby wouldn't be safe even outside. This mountain will swirl with ferals after sundown. If you can take the sunlight, we must move now."

They took only their clothes, Andra and her blanket. Alex remembered one last item. Her stake. They also took Alex's little phial. It was dim now, but still helped.

"Just outside this chamber, we'll go left," said Catherine. "A hundred yards or so, we'll make a hard right down another tunnel that opens into a small cavern. It looks like a dead end, but I know a way out. Stay close, and if you have any problems, speak up. Ready?"

"Go for it."

They slipped through the small opening. Quickly Catherine turned left and started running with Alex right behind, the pale glow from the phial lighting their way. Alex heard shouting and rapid footsteps back toward the cavern. They'd been seen.

"Faster," Alex said. "I can keep up."

Catherine went at a full run with Alex still right on her tail. Alex had the baby in the pouch up against her bosom. She could feel the heat from its little body, feel and smell its breath, hear its squeals, cries and laughter as they moved forward. Andra was definitely more active than a normal newborn. Alex wondered how she could be so alert just a few minutes after being born. It must be the vampire colostrum, she thought.

Alex could hear quick footsteps coming up behind, but when they made the turn, they ran smack into two vampires guarding the tunnel. They were Alex's security guards. Catherine stopped so quickly that Alex ran into her.

"Out of our way," said Catherine. "We're on orders from Alu Kard."

"Fraid not," said the big vampire. "Alu told us to hold both of you for him."

"Perhaps we could negotiate." Catherine started to turn back. "I'm not good at the violence thing," she whispered.

"I am," Alex whispered in her ear. "Normal vampires. Not a threat."

Catherine went forward as if resigned to being taken into custody, but then dodged and darted past the first one. He let Catherine go, focused on Alex and the child. Alex spun around, kicked his legs out from under him, and drove her stake through his heart, all in one fluid motion. He spit blood, gurgled and died.

Seeing what just happened, the other vampire turned to run, but Catherine grabbed his arm, held him back. Then he turned on her, shoved her up against the wall, and would have broken her neck, but Alex kicked him in the side and knocked him to the ground. Instantly she was on him and again drove her stake through the heart. She waited to make sure he was dead. "Some security force," she said. She hated killing these normal vampires, but they'd chosen sides and soon would have been made feral.

"Wow!" said Catherine. "You are good, aren't you?" She looked into the large chamber, and they started forward. But as they entered, three more vampires, ferals this time, blocked their way.

Alex loosened her pack straps, and handed little Andra to Catherine. "Carry her," Alex said. "I can take these guys, too."

"They're feral, Alex. They'll turn you."

"You're going to have to trust me on this," said Alex.

Catherine took Andra and cowered in the background.

Alex stepped forward. "Come on guys. Let's do this."

The female feral stepped forward. "We're going to eat you like a kosher sausage," she said. "From both ends and the middle."

Alex walked into them. The female grabbed Alex's arm, and Alex threw her off to the side crashing among the stalagmites. But the two male vampires were on her immediately, and their aim was her neck. Alex didn't struggle as the first bit into her, and while she allowed him to suck the other held her still, not realizing that Alex had just driven her stake through his heart. He slumped to the ground dead. The other feral stopped sucking, started choking and stumbled backward. His skin started scintillating, as had Braxton's, and he screamed as his flesh turned to cinders on his bones and he too crumpled to the ground, dead.

"What did you do to him?" asked Catherine, astonished. "Who are you?"

"Someone special turned me," said Alex.

They heard more ferals enter the chamber.

"Quickly," said Catherine, handing Andra back to Alex and leading the way forward. They zigzagged through the stalagmites to a wall with a seam that they squeezed through. They were out of sight for now, but heard the chamber quickly fill with ferals.

Alex peeked back inside and saw a huge bat-like shadow flitting along the walls of the cavern. They heard voices.

"Who is it?" asked Catherine.

"Alu Kard. I should have killed the female. She knows where we are."

They ran another twenty yards to the exit. The light before them was blinding.

"This is as far as I can go," said Catherine. "You're on your own."

"They'll be here any second," said Alex. "Alu will kill you."

"Maybe not. We have a history. He'll take pity."

"He's feral, you won't live two seconds."

"I won't last much longer in sunlight."

Alex knew what she had to do. "I know another way, one where you can walk out with us."

"What are you talking about?"

"Do you want to remain a vampire?"

"I don't know. What would I be, if not a vampire?"

"Human again," said Alex.

"I don't follow you."

"Do you trust me? Can you trust me, Catherine?"

"Well, yes. I believe so."

"Then bite me."

"What? Your blood just torched a vampire."

"He was feral. Listen!" She heard voices back in the cavern. "They just found this tunnel. Alu's coming. Suck my blood, Catherine. If you want to live, bite me."

Catherine hesitated.

"Quick! Do it now."

Catherine leaned over the baby and put her mouth to Alex's throat. "This seems so... well, incestuous."

"Just do it."

Alex felt Catherine's teeth break her skin and the blood flow. Catherine made soft gurgling noises, and then stopped. Her eyes opened wide, and she caught her breath. "Oh my God!" she said. "Oh! My! God!" She had tears in her eyes.

Alex said, "I can resurrect the Undead. That is my gift."

Together, Alex and Catherine stepped out into blinding sunlight. They heard a screech that shook the mountainside and turned to look back. Standing in the cave entrance and unable to step outside stood Alu Kard.

34

Death at Shadowrise

Alex and Catherine ran a good ways down the mountainside and stopped. The sunlight was blinding, and Alex squinted and shaded her eyes with her hand. She'd been inside the cavern for months, but Catherine had not been in sunlight in ninety years and was now human. She had to keep her eyes closed, and Alex led her like a blind person down the mountainside using shadows whenever possible. "I'm freezing and feel bad," Catherine said. Alex kept a blanket over little Andra's eyes, but it became increasingly obvious that she wasn't a vampire. Still, she was hyperactive for just being born.

As soon as they were out of sight of the grotto, Alex called Jaklin on her cellphone. Her heart raced, and she said to herself, "Please be gone. Please be gone."

Jaklin answered at the first ring. "Missy!" she screamed.

"Tell me you're in Bulgaria," Alex said.

"Of course not. We're here waiting for you. Both of us."

Alex choked up, couldn't get her words out. Finally she asked, "Are you home?"

"Yes. Well, no. Not actually home," said Jaklin. "I'm a ways up the hill in the forest."

"You sound scared. What's happening?"

"Stefan mobilized some of the towns people, and they are about to attack a vampire ceremony. Mikhail has gone to stop them. Oh Alex!" she cried. "He could be killed."

Alex realized that it could be worse than that. "Where are you?"

"Not far from Peleş Castle."

"Come back toward home. I'll meet you halfway."

Alex turned back to Catherine. "Hurry! Lives are at stake. Why does everything have to happen at once?"

"I can't walk fast," said Catherine. "I'm so weak. I feel less alive now than when undead."

Alex kept encouraging her forward. Once they got home, Alex located the spare key she'd hidden in a stump, and unlocked the backdoor. What a great place for the baby, she thought. Nălucă came to her whining for food. He looked as if he'd gained a pound or two. That'd be softhearted Jaklin's doing. She went upstairs and brought down the bassinet. Catherine was still suffering from becoming human again, but Alex needed her to care for Andra. Can I trust her? she wondered. I have to, but she's my baby, and only an hour old. Yet, if something bad did happen to Mikhail, I'd never forgive myself.

"Can you care for Andra?" she asked. Alex still hadn't fed, needed blood badly and couldn't take her eyes off Catherine's throat.

"Of course," said Catherine, but seemed distracted. "I didn't realize. This is my home. You live here?"

Alex felt alarm that Catherine would still view this as her home. Alex started to say that it belonged to her now but bit her tongue. She was losing precious time. She located her grandfather's staff she'd found in the attic. She'd need it.

"I haven't seen that in a while," said Catherine.

"It was my grandfather's," Alex said.

"Yes, I sent it to him. It's black ironwood from southern Mexico."

"You can't imagine how much getting it pleased him. He was rarely without it."

"That's gratifying. Such a small gift."

"That brought so much pleasure."

Alex changed clothes, slipping into a pair of Levi's and a T-shirt. Amazingly her pre-pregnancy clothes fit. If anything, she'd lost an inch or two, except in the bust. The rest of her vampire body was trim and ready for whatever.

Alex stood for a second over little Andra staring down at her asleep in the bassinet. She couldn't drag herself away. "Lock the door after me," she said. "Admit no one." She kissed Andra on the cheek. "I'll be back," she whispered as she grabbed her staff.

"Alex!" Catherine shouted. She looked terrified. She came to Alex and took both her hands. "Be careful. I couldn't stand to lose you."

What's this? Alex wondered. She hardly knows me. She turned from her great grandmother and was out the door.

Alex ran toward Peleş Castle through trees avoiding streets. Halfway there, she spotted Jaklin running toward her although in a skirt and heels. They collided into each other's arms, hugged for a second, and were then off to find Mikhail.

"He's changed, Missy," Jaklin said. "He has vampire friends now and feels so badly about the way he treated you. You should hear him. He believes you're an angel sent to save the world."

And then she stopped dead cold. "You've had the baby. Missy! What happened?"

"I gave birth an hour ago," she said as she kept walking. "The baby's fine." Alex's need for blood again returned. The look and smell of Jaklin were almost more than she could bear.

"How about you? An hour?"

"Vampire resilience." She had to look away from Jaklin to keep from biting her. So professional, dark-blue skirt, white blouse and black pumps.

"Where's the baby?"

Alex looked back to talk because Jaklin kept falling behind. "I left her with a friend. Tell me about this group of vampires. Where will they be?"

"On a hilltop," said Jaklin. They go there at twilight to see Sinaia in the sun's last rays."

"I've heard of these people," said Alex. "It's a ritual that goes back a thousand years. They tried to get me to attend, but I was afraid of being recognized. They go there to watch the shadow crawl up the eastern mountains of Prahova Valley. It's the Mystery of the Rising Shadow. They call it Shadowrise. These vampires are good people.

It'd be a crime to harm them."

"That's what Mikhail said. Oh, Alex, you know him. When he believes in something, he'll give his life for it."

"We mustn't let that happen." But Alex wondered if that were true. He certainly hadn't given his life for her.

Alex saw the service taking place on a bald, low-lying hill surrounded by pines. She ran on ahead of Jaklin. As she approached, she counted maybe twenty people and five of them humans. Cosmina stood at the apex of the knoll, her back to the valley and the others gathered in front of her like a choir. They started singing. The sun had gone behind the mountain no more than ten minutes before. Alex looked east and saw the shadow now at the river and slowly climbing the mountain on the far side of Prahova Valley. The choir went from singing to humming, and Cosmina started her prayer, or poem it was most probably. Alex thought she looked quite beautiful.

"*Shadowrise. Forces of the deep, bring on your darkness. Bring forth the night so the hidden things of the world might find life among the living. Rise up, oh Shadow, claim your prominence over the brilliance that denies the subtle powers that bind us even to ourselves. Give us the gray havens, the demarcation that brings clarity to the World of Light. Without Shadow, even enlightenment has no form.*"

Alex heard a shout from behind the chorus, and a man entered the clearing. He was dressed in gray, had dark hair, a bit of beard and wore glasses. Of course, it was Mikhail. "Scatter! Run for it," he yelled, just as a gunshot blast went off and echoed out in the valley. A member of the chorus fell, and the others started to scatter. Cosmina, still focused on her poem, took longer to recognize the danger. She fell into confusion and froze.

Alex was at a full run now, and to her left, up from below, came the source of the gunshot. She recognized the redheaded man carrying the shotgun: Stefan leading a group of shouting town folk. Complete chaos erupted, with people and vampires running in every which direction. Stefan pointed the shotgun at Cosmina. Alex screamed, but she was too late. Mikhail stepped in front of Cosmina just as Stefan fired again. Mikhail fell and Cosmina ran for the trees, but Stefan cut her down with another blast. Alex started to run to her, but she jumped off the ground and made it into the forest. Alex knew that he'd missed her heart.

Alex had forgotten about her staff, but when Stefan fired at her, she turned on him, knocked the shotgun from his arms, clubbed him in the ribs and knocked him cold with a blow to the head. She was pleased at how much she remembered of what her grandfather had taught her about using the staff. She thought about jumping on Stefan and sucking his blood, but she heard more screaming as a new group entered the scene and at the head of them was another man dressed in black and swept round by a cape. It was Alu Kard, and he turned his group of feral vampires lose on the lot. It was a screaming, crying, crawling mess.

Alex knew what she had to do. Ferals had no place in this world, no place in this fight, and could do neither humans nor vampires any service. She knew Mikhail was down, but they'd all be dead or turned feral if she didn't do something quick. Ferals were all around her. She clubbed some, kicked others, and then she drove her staff through one's heart. He fell to the ground.

Alex went crazy. She spun, kicked, thrust and the ferals ran. She'd downed three more when she heard another blast from the shotgun and felt a thud at her chest. Stefan was up off the ground and had just fire his shotgun at her again. She ignored him and continued killing ferals. She felt another blow from Stefan's shotgun, but saw a feral feeding off a human and ran to his aid. The feral would have taken most of his blood to turn him, but he never got that far before Alex drove her staff through his heart from behind. Then she turned on anyone present. All the regular vampires were already gone, and it was just ferals and humans. She clubbed the humans and staked the ferals.

Alex had never forgotten Mikhail. She knew that the only way she could save him, if he was still alive, was to clear the area, but now standing over Mikhail was a dark, loathsome shape, and instantly she knew real hatred. The black shadow of Alu Kard fell over Mikhail, but someone attacked him from behind. It was Jaklin, who jumped upon his back, legs clamped about his waist and clawing at his eyes. Her skirt slipped up her legs to her hips and she pulled off a heel and pounded him on the head with it. Alu threw her off down the mountainside as if she were a rag doll. Alex was instantly upon him. She lunged to drive her staff through his heart, but he deflected it with a brush of his hand, unaccountably sending the shaft flying off away from her.

"Stop, Eidyn! It doesn't have to be this way," he said.

Alex saw her movement once again go to lightening speed. She hit him in the ribs with a left, and drove her right fist splat into his face. He fell backwards but was instantly on his feet and grabbed her, spun her around, and pinned her arms behind her. Alex fell forward, rolled and slung him down the slope. She pounced on him, and when he rose up, kicked him in the chest sending him careening into a tree. He came at her again. They collided and he took hold of her head with both hands, tried to snap her neck, but she spun her whole body to face him. She was within his arms, and she had hers around him. He lunged forward to bite her but stopped. And then she stopped too. She released him. He was afraid to bite her.

"Why, Eidyn? Why?" he said.

"I've seen your Ichor Dome," she said.

"You don't understand. They don't all turn out like that. They are the mistakes."

"How about your House of Pain?"

"You shouldn't be down that far," he said. "It's forbidden."

"And now I know why."

Alu turned and fled. Alex wondered why, and then she saw Stefan running after him firing his shotgun.

Alex turned back to Mikhail and saw Jaklin bent over him crying. Alex ran to them.

"He's dying," said Jaklin.

Alex sank to her knees. The smell of blood was everywhere, overwhelming even her concern for him.

"I'm so sorry I abandoned you, Missy," he said."

"That's all past," said Alex.

"Please forgive me."

"We need to get you to a hospital."

"No time. It's up to you."

"What?"

"Turn me. You need to turn me."

The smell of blood coming from Mikhail was so strong she could taste it on her tongue. "No, Mikhail. You're one step from Paradise. Just a few breaths away. You don't understand about the soul."

"I don't care. My love in this life or the next is invested in you two. We three belong together."

"I can't Mikhail. I just can't."

"We are the only things in this world or the next of value to me. I see angels hovering about me. Still, I know this. I've questioned more than either of you. I found the answer. You transcend all things, Heaven and Earth. Turn me, Missy. Don't let me pass from this world."

He'd lost all his strength, and was perhaps even now beyond her reach. She realized that he was dying from internal injuries and not because of the loss of blood.

"Don't doom me to a death without you."

"Aieee!" Alex sent her heartbreaking shriek to the heavens, hoping for guidance. She looked at Jaklin. Tears streamed down both her cheeks. "What am I to do?" she asked. Saliva was forming so fast that she was about to choke. Yet, she just couldn't bite him. She'd never forgive herself.

Jaklin looked unsure, a blank gaze hewn of uncertainty that suddenly changed into unmitigated conviction. "Turn him!" she shouted. "Do it, and don't look back."

Alex realized that ultimately it was her own choice. Could she live with what she was about to do? With a deep sigh, she flopped down on him, placed her mouth on his throat, chewed into him and felt the sweet nectar of his life flow into her. Her thirst was so strong that she had difficulty pulling herself off him, even when she felt his body go limp, delirious as she was with the taste of him. She felt a change come over her own body, felt a flush, a glow that she'd never felt from anyone she'd ever bitten.

"Let him go," said Jaklin. "He's dead already."

Quickly, Alex raised Mikhail's mouth to her throat, and he bit into her. Alex cried while he sucked her. She looked down into his face, his eyes rolled up until only the whites showed, then came down again as a pale light glowed within them and then flashed so brilliant that it momentarily blinded her. She pushed him off.

Mikhail sat on the ground blinking like a night owl. He started to cry. Alex expected him to go crazy violent as did she when she was turned. He didn't. Instead, his eyes filled with tears.

"Mikhail, can you hear me?" she asked

Jaklin knelt beside them. "Speak to me, Mikhail," she said.

Yet he was still confused, didn't seem to know where he was or even who he was. He put his forearms over his face and shook with great sobs.

"We need to get him home," said Alex, but saw that his wounds were already rapidly healing. She wondered at the grief. Was he already sorry she'd turned him? Watching him cry broke her heart. Alex heard a movement behind her and turned from Mikhail to face Stefan, who'd just returned from chasing Alu.

"Who was that bastard in black?" he asked. "He's even more elusive than you."

Alex ran to him, jerked the shotgun from him, threw it off into the bushes, and shoved him up against a tree.

"You listen to me, you stupid, cheap little sonofabitch. You even so much as point that shotgun and any of us again, I'll kill you so quick you'll not remember that you were ever alive."

From down below, five policemen came running up the hill. Captain Mariusz led them.

"You!" he said, seeing Alex. "Zosimos said you'd left Romania. And now here you are again, right in the middle of all the trouble."

"Where is Zosimos?" asked Alex. "If he's a part of this, I'll stake him, even if he is human."

"Zosimos is no more," said Stefan.

"You mean he's dead?" Grief gripped her.

"Might as well be. He mumbles into his beard, and stays in seclusion. He hasn't just lost his faith, he's also lost his wits."

Alex relaxed, realizing she cared more for the old priest than she thought.

A gorilla of a policeman came down the hill from where he'd chased the vampires. "She tried to stop it," he said pointing at Alex.

"If it wasn't for her, many would have died. She may have clubbed the humans, but she killed several vampires." He turned away and wouldn't look her in the eyes.

Alex thought he looked familiar, and then realized who he was. This was the man who wanted a little fellatio while she was in jail. "So we meet again under somewhat different circumstances," she said. He had a welt on his neck where she'd clubbed him during the fracas.

Mariusz looked at her questioningly and then also realized the situation. "So," he said, somewhat embarrassed himself. "It's as Zosimos said. You are not the evil being we thought."

"Father Zosimos said something good about me?"

"I told you. He's lost his mind," said Stefan.

Mariusz looked Stefan off, turned back to Alex. "He believes you would help with this vampire infestation, if we'd give you a chance. Is that true?"

"For the past months since you first tried to incarcerate me, I've been living with a colony of vampires. Many more live here in Sinaia than you realize. Most are decent people and actually a benefit to society, not a pestilence. But just within the last year, a new form of vampire has come on the scene. I'll not go into how this came about, but that is what's happening. The two factions of vampires are at war. You need to stay out of it. Let me handle it."

"How can I afford to sit by and wait for you to do something? I have to protect the community."

"You have no choice. You'll make the problem worse. Trust me on this."

"How about that man there?" He pointed at Mikhail. "Does he need medical attention?"

"It was stupid Stefan." She glared at him. "Stefan shot him, but he's okay now. I've taken care of him."

"Whatever that means. Well, he's your friend, your problem."

"And Stefan here is your problem," said Alex. "Keep him and his band of vigilantes out of this, or he will show up in the morgue."

"You heard her, Stefan," Mariusz said shoving him back a step. "I'll give you some time, Miss Eidyn, but if we have another attack, I'm coming for you first."

With that, the police went back down the hill, and Alex ran to Mikhail and Jaklin. Stefan went with her. Jaklin was talking to Mikhail who was still disoriented. He could remember little of who or where he was even though his wounds were mostly healed.

Alex turned on Stefan. "Listen to me, you stupid red-headed, freckle-faced bastard. I've put up with your crap for the last time. I will kill you, if you hurt anyone else close to me. And that's not a threat. It's a promise."

But Stefan only smiled and backed away from her down the hill.

35

Begging for It

Alex and Jaklin walked Mikhail back home as darkness encroached. He'd stopped crying and seemed to become more aware. They encouraged him to talk. At first, he thought he was back in Moscow, but gradually began to remember Romania and Sinaia. Jaklin, he recognized right away, but it took until they almost reached the Estate before he remembered Alex.

Alex had Mikhail's arm around her neck to support him, and it felt so unbelievable good to be with him again. She kept reaching across and touching Jaklin. She couldn't quit smiling, but the catastrophe at Shadowrise lingered in the background. Still, she was with her friends, her lovers, and Mikhail was now immortal. She'd not have to face eternity alone after all. Jaklin looked worried, and Alex wondered at her concern.

As they approached the front of her home, Alex saw an ominous bank of clouds hanging over the mountain. Lightning lashed its flanks. A major thunderstorm was on its way. Mikhail flinched at each rumble. The inside of their home was lit up like a jack-o-lantern. A wave of cold rain swept over them. Alex banged on the door and shouted for Catherine. They heard her working the latch.

"Who is this Catherine person," asked Jaklin, but Alex didn't answer.

The door swung open, and Catherine grabbed Alex and hugged her. "I was so worried about you." She held her at arm's length. "You didn't get hurt, did you?" She finally let her go. "Don't leave me alone again. I've seen vampires lurking about outside, and thought Alu might have come for me." And then she laughed. "I sound so human. Afraid of the dark, again. I felt so vulnerable."

"These are my two friends, Jaklin and Mikhail. And this is..." She indicated Catherine, "...is my... Faery Godmother."

Jaklin wrinkled her forehead. "What?"

"Let it go," she said. "Everything in due course."

"What's wrong with him?" asked Catherine, looking at Mikhail. "He's not well. And covered in blood."

"Mikhail was wounded at Shadowrise and would have died. I turned him. He became disoriented afterward."

Catherine put her hand on his shoulder. "Then he did die. And now he's undead. He may not fully recover until he's initiated."

Alex realized she was right. Mikhail did die. She felt a wave of guilt but brushed it away and leaned over the bassinet. She just couldn't deal with all of it. "How is my little girl?"

"She's been whimpering," said Catherine. "I was so nervous and restless waiting for you that I gave her a sponge bath. She's amazingly healthy and as active as a six-month old."

Alex scooped her up out of the bassinet, held her close and felt that she'd never let go of her baby again. "My little angel." Andra was nestled inside her pink blanket fast asleep. Alex hadn't had time to even get a good look at her. She had more hair than Alex initially thought, blond fluff over the back and fuzz across the top. Alex could see her pulse in her soft spot. She pulled open the baby blanket.

"Oh! You dressed her."

"I found the little one-piece bodysuit in the baby bed upstairs. You sure have a lot of disposable diapers."

Alex had wondered how she'd look in that little white garment with "te iubesc" in red letters across the front. "Such tiny hands and feet." Alex felt like a woman for the first time, so motherly.

They all gathered around the tiny infant, Mikhail crowding in to get a better look.

Alex handed her to Jaklin. "You must hold her," she said.

"How about me?" said Mikhail.

"Not until you've cleaned up," said Catherine.

Mikhail picked up Nălucă, something he would have never done before. Nălucă licked the blood soaked into his shirt.

"A group of bounty hunters attacked Shadowrise. They shot him. He's not his normal self. Perhaps I did it wrong," said Alex. "I had no experience. I was desperate. I expected him to become violent."

"There is no wrong way," assured Catherine. "Either he is or he isn't. Initially, they adopt the attitude they were in when turned. Perhaps it's also because you are not a normal vampire. Give him time."

"He was in full guilt mode when Stefan shot him," said Jaklin, "and full of regret at the way he'd treated Alex before she left."

"That'll take some time to come to terms with," said Catherine. "Go easy on him."

Alex wanted the lights off so Andra could sleep. Jaklin relit the fireplace. Catherine stood before it warming herself. Mikhail seemed to have an aversion to light, not severe, but noteworthy. His wounds had healed but scars remained.

"How did you come to terms with vampirism, Mikhail?" Alex asked. "You were so disillusioned when last I saw you."

"It was the gazebo," he said. "I fixed it up a little, Missy, at least what I could. Uncovered the edges of the foundation. Found some of the stone furniture. Then I kept seeing lights flicker in it at night, but when I went to investigate, no one was there."

"After that, I could still go inside," said Jaklin, "but Mikhail couldn't."

"When I tried," said Mikhail, "such great fear came over me that I'd run back in the house. Then one evening, I went out to investigate a blinking light. An apparition leaving the gazebo confronted me, chastised me and said to quit trying to enter, that I was a scourge and would not be allowed inside. I realized that everything you'd told us about the gazebo was true, that a divine being had actually bitten you and you had seen Catalin there. I'm convinced the gazebo is a portal to the Divine World."

"He started preaching your virtues," said Jaklin. "I couldn't shut him up. But that's enough talk for now. I'm taking him upstairs for a bath and change of clothes. He must have fallen in a pile of bear dung." She took him by the arm.

Mikhail was still carrying Nălucă and won't let go of him. Nălucă was purring loud enough to wake the neighbors.

"Really. Who are those two?" asked Catherine. "Why would you turn him?"

"Just friends," Alex said and paused for a second but realized that she could never hide the truth. "And lovers."

"Oh!" Catherine blushed, then smiled. "Both... lovers?"

"Both."

"A ménage? Not so unusual in the vampire community."

Alex looked away. After Father Zosimos' castigation, she felt ashamed.

"We'll fix a room for you," Alex said. "You can stay here with us."

"My home... This is where you all stay."

"Live. Where we live. It's mine now, Catherine," said Alex. "Given to me by your daughter, my grandmother, before she passed away. But you are welcome here, will always be."

Catherine looked disappointed, perhaps even sad. "My daughter. You'll have to tell me about her. I've not been allowed in Sinaia the last ninety years. Alu convinced me, and perhaps rightly so, that my presence here would be a danger to both me and my daughter. But then I heard that she'd passed away and that you, my great granddaughter, had also been turned. I cried for days about both of you. I had wanted so badly to see her before she passed away."

"That's a long time to be in exile."

"And it was an exile. I must say, the old place looks remarkably well kept."

"Bunică employed a couple of servants to help after Grandfather died. I came here every summer the last few years. We worked setting it in order. She'd put off things, so we could work together. I grew fond of the place long before she left it to me. It's not been a year since she passed on."

"How I would have loved to have been in your shoes, to have

spent time with her, helping her with her home. While away, I never spent a day that I didn't wonder about her. What a tragedy for a mother not to be able to raise her own child. I'd love to meet your mother."

Alex wondered how that'd go over. "You look so young. Hard to believe you're my great grandmother. I'm sorry I had to push you into allowing me to turn you back."

"If you only knew how much I've wanted this. I was married for four years. When my husband died, my mother, Queen Marie, attended him on his deathbed. She had little belief in Romanian Orthodoxy, unlike me. I've always been a Christian. While a vampire, I couldn't even look at a cross. My vampire aunt tricked me into it. But she, amazingly, was turned back human, and I was left alone. I was never much for Millennium Road. But one lives the life one has, not the one they wish they had. Immortality here on Earth seemed such a burden."

"So that answers the question. I've read your diary. I came to feel that I knew you."

"My diary! You found it? God, I'd love to see it."

"Who turned back your aunt? That is a rare gift."

"Not been heard of before or sense, until you came along, that is. It was a strange creature, Alex. Perhaps a heavenly being. I've recently heard that she's returned, but had some disastrous encounter with Alu."

"This is starting to make some sense. Was the divine being called Velinar."

"Why, yes. I believe she was. How did you know?"

"She was the one who turned me. She came into this world, took on mortal form and had Alu bite her, thinking she might turn him back human, but instead it made her undead."

"That's not the full story. Is it?"

"What do you mean."

"She had to drink his blood also to become a vampire. It's doubtful he forced her. Something strange about that scenario."

Alex looked up from the baby and thought about what Catherine had just said. Catalin's story of Velinar had always seemed a bit off.

"She was stuck here until she drank my blood. It cured her, and now she's back in Heaven. At my expense, I might add. I have taken on her vampirism." She'd have to question Catalin about this.

Jaklin returned with Mikhail, who now looked remarkably refreshed. He even smiled at Alex. "So... we're both now creatures of the night," he said.

"We'll have to wait until morning to see if you can handle sunlight. Perhaps you'll be like me."

"I can't wait for sunrise," said Catherine. "No more Shadowrise for me."

Catherine and Jaklin were feeling cold, so they threw a log on the fire, pushed back the sofa, and all gathered around on the floor before it to discuss the situation. Alex held little Andra. She wouldn't let her out of her sight. Andra was so tiny and Alex cuddled her close and kissed her, rubbed their cheeks together. What delicious warm skin. So soft. She craved some time alone with her baby. Just an hour or two to get acquainted.

"All this is well and good," said Jaklin. "But we have one thing that can wait no longer."

"And what might that be?" asked Alex.

"I'm not going to live a mortal life, grow old and die with two immortal vampires perpetually in the flower of youth." She stared daggers at Alex. "You're immortal. I want to be too."

"No," said Alex. "You can't ask this of me, Jaklin. You're not injured. You aren't dying."

"Ever since I learned that you are a vamp, I've wanted to be turned. Mikhail didn't. I was caught between you two, so I never asked. Now, I'm begging you."

"With Mikhail, I got caught off guard. And my need to feed also clouded my judgment. I'm not going to make another mistake with you."

"Wouldn't it be great though? The three of us for eternity. We've sworn to live our lives together. You can't doom me to a mortal existence. You need me. I want to fight alongside you. With this mortal body, I'll be a liability."

Alex couldn't deny the excitement she felt thinking of Jaklin as an immortal. She looked at Mikhail, and heard Jaklin whisper "forever." She was right. The possibilities were irresistible. "But what about your job with the Bulgarian Consulate?"

"I'll ask for the nightshift. You're not going to talk me out of this."

"You have such a bright future."

"Look," said Jaklin. "The entire area is now infested with feral vampires. What if one of them gets me? I'd be feral and you'd have to kill me yourself. What a future. I wouldn't even have a soul."

"Not going to happen. I'm not leaving you two."

"I could inoculate you."

"And why haven't you done that? You know as well as I do that you've avoided inoculation simply because you really do want to turn us."

Alex looked away. She knew Jaklin was right. "What do you think, Catherine?" she asked. "What should I do with her?"

"The life of a vampire is no picnic. What happens to the soul is horrible. Millennium Road is only three thousand years old, still changing and trying to find its truth and purpose. Human psychic space has been around for a couple hundred thousand years, and its connection to the Divine World, which has been around since the beginning of the Universe, is evolving too. But Millennium Road is going somewhere and a big change is about to occur. It has to do with the pentagon they are headed toward. It still hasn't come of age. Once they reach their destination they will understand what the race of vampires is all about. I have always been a Christian; therefore, as for turning Jaklin, I say no. But you are different from other vampires."

"I can wear a cross," said Alex.

"But you don't," countered Catherine.

"I had mine taken from me, and I plan to get it back."

"That may signify a huge difference in someone you turn. We know Mikhail is different, but we don't know the full extent. Sometimes things are just meant to be. This you must decide for yourselves."

"I turned Mikhail without knowing what I was doing."

"Initiating the transformation is simple," said Catherine. "The internal process is complex. A vampire must drink the blood of the person they are going to turn first so it can reconfigure its own blood.

The human's blood only changes the vampire's for a few moments. Once the vampire's blood has undergone the transformation peculiar to that particular human, then the human can drink of the vampire, and its blood will do the trick. If they don't bite the vampire immediately, they won't turn. All traces of the person's blood are then erased as the vampire's liver and kidneys process the vampire's blood. The human must be practically empty before they ingests vampire blood."

"Why does this conversion happen at all?" asked Jaklin. "How can vampire blood be that different?"

"The vampire community has done a lot of research on this. The blood of a vampire isn't just for circulation, carrying oxygen and nutrients to replenish the body and disposing of waste. It supercharges the system. When a vampire drinks blood, it doesn't just enter the digestive track. Part of it is absorbed into the tissue where it forms bonds not possible in humans. It changes metabolism and allows the body to operate more efficiently. "

"Is that the only difference?" asked Jaklin.

"Over time, the new blood upgrades the flesh also. Vampire saliva is an aphrodisiac, and addicting. Once they have kissed a vampire, they are sexually supercharged. It's similar to alcohol but even more directed toward sexuality. Sex for a vampire has been liberated from reproduction and is much more about the caring and craving people have for each other."

"That explains the first night we met," said Mikhail. "It was as if you put a spell on us. Seems you have a certain responsibility."

"I didn't know," said Alex. "I was just as entranced by you."

"If you turn Jaklin, you simply drain her. But you must stop before she completely loses consciousness, or she might not be able to bite you. Even if you do, you can still open a vein. The blood of a vampire is absorbed through the mouth lining, awakening even the dead like a shot of adrenalin."

"That's it?" said Alex.

"Yes." Catherine smiled. "Except it's like the best sex you've ever had." She blushed.

"So you've actually turned someone?" asked Alex.

"I'm very tired and going to bed now. Talk it over amongst

yourselves. When you turn someone, you should sleep with them that night and look for them on Millennium Road. A friend can easily awaken them to the vampire psychic world. They wander and become lost until they have the Millennium Dream. May be Mikhail's problem."

"What's this... Millennium Dream?" asked Mikhail.

"It's vampire psychic space," answered Catherine. "You dream of Millennium Road. It's analogous to the ancient mysteries. The soul is no longer a sieve with life just passing through it. It becomes closed off so everything is retained and important. Instead of it being wrapped up in the trivialities of everyday life, the vampire is aware of its destiny. Life makes sense where to many it didn't before."

"But what about Heaven?" asked Jaklin. "Does a vampire ever get to Heaven?"

"Millennium Road is vampire Heaven. They've bridged the void between life and death. They no longer have to wait until their life here is over and then be judged to start living their true life, as do humans. The vampire is never judged, but always accepted into eternal life here on Earth. The Undead live in dual worlds of consciousness: the real world and the psychic world — the world of the soul."

"Don't vampires have normal dreams?" asked Jaklin.

"Yes. But most human dreams are ephemeral and come from a remote psyche. Vampires have a much closer relationship with their psychic life on Millennium Road and their dreams. After all, they're dead. Or undead."

"What happens when the Undead die?" asked Jaklin.

"It loses existence in the real world and has only the world of the soul left. Death is a real loss for the vampire. It loses the real part of its eternal existence but remains on Millennium Road."

Jaklin became lost in thought.

Catherine then went on up to bed, and with her gone, the three lovers sat looking into the fire. Alex held baby Andra close for a while, then put her in the bassinet, and returned again to stare into the coals. Jaklin was in the middle, the three holding hands.

Jaklin shook herself out of her thoughtful trance and looked at Alex. "Mikhail's hand is cold," she said. "Make mine cold too."

Alex sighed deeply. "Help me, Mikhail. Help me with her."

Mikhail took Jaklin into his arms, laid her back and kissed her on the lips. Then Alex kissed her, lifted her hair off her neck and kissed her again on the throat.

"Going to hurt a little at first," Alex said. And then she did what she'd been dying to do ever since she first met Jaklin. She bit her. The warm gush of fresh blood sent a charge of sexual desire stronger than anything she'd ever felt. Jaklin leaned into her, and Alex devoured her. It was as if she'd suck Jaklin into her own body, not just her blood, but her entire being seemed to flow into Alex, more delicious, more precious than sex had ever been. She pulled her from Mikhail, and squeezed her within her own arms.

"Stop, Missy," said Mikhail.

Alex pulled away and put Jaklin's mouth up against her throat, but she was lifeless. She'd quit breathing.

Mikhail had hold of Jaklin's wrist. "You've killed her. Her heart has stopped."

"You're right. She's unresponsive. I've gone too far." Alex then took the kitchen knife, slit the edge of her palm and squeezed her fist until a stream of fresh blood poured into Jaklin's mouth and down her tongue into her throat. Mikhail held her mouth open.

Nothing happened.

"She's not coming back, Mikhail. I've done it wrong," said Alex. She'd killed her sweetheart by her own lust for every drop of her blood. Alex started crying.

Mikhail sobbed. "Quick, Missy. Do something," he said.

Alex grabbed the knife again and made a deep cut along the side of her own throat. She pulled Jaklin's limp body to her, took her head in her own hands and shoved her open mouth down on her. Still nothing. She laid Jaklin's head back on the pillow and laid her throat down on hop of Jaklin. She felt her blood pouring into her. Still nothing.

Then Jaklin coughed, sputtered, and like a ferocious beast her teeth sank into Alex. Her arms came alive and locked around Alex. Alex could feel the suction drawing the blood from her. Then quite suddenly, Jaklin went lifeless. She fell away.

"What have I done?" said Alex, tears streaming down her cheeks. "She's not coming back, Mikhail."

"Here," said Mikhail, and he took Jaklin from Alex into his own arms. He bit her, sucked a little of her blood and then put her mouth up against his throat.

Instantly Jaklin came alive, sinking her teeth into Mikhail and sucking ferociously. Alex saw Jaklin's eyes open wide, emit a pale light that brightened and flashed so brilliant that it momentarily lit the entire room. Then quite as abruptly as she'd started drinking, she stopped, pulled away from him and looked around. Blood streamed down her chin and over her breasts. She looked at her friends with a strange frightened expression, as if she didn't recognize them. She jumped to her feet and ran, bumped into the door, fell on her back, jumped to her feet and ran into the kitchen. Alex and Mikhail went after her. She backed against the wall, screamed and showed her teeth like a wild animal.

"Don't push her," said Alex. "Just contain her."

"It's okay," said Mikhail. "You're with friends."

Jaklin grabbed the large chopping knife from the wood block. She held it in front of her and moved it threateningly, as if she'd used one before in self-defense.

"I think she'd gone feral," said Alex. "What a catastrophe."

"Never," said Mikhail. "She'll calm. We'll just have to give her a little space until she gets her bearings."

As suddenly as she'd jumped up from the sofa, Jaklin collapsed like a marionette. The knife fell from her hand onto the floor.

"She died again, Mikhail."

He bent over her and raised her head with his arm. "Her heart's beating. She's alive. Or undead, at least."

Alex fell to her knees at Jaklin's side. She put Jaklin's mouth to her throat. Again, and again she drank. Slowly, Jaklin regained consciousness. She smacked her lips, looked up at Alex, grabbed her and kissed her, a hard ferocious kiss. She kissed Mikhail like she could eat him. She rose up, taking them both in.

"Finally!" she said. "Eternity."

36

Reconciliation

At sunrise, Jaklin and Mikhail, fully healed, were still too wired to go to bed. Jaklin kept asking about side effects and wanting to find someone to bite. They had to see what their relationship with the sun would be. They'd already tested for cross aversion, and found themselves immune. Then they stepped out onto the front porch and waited for the sun to break the mountaintop, leaving the door open so they could make a fast retreat. Helios flashed his rays, and Jaklin and Mikhail ducked for cover.

"I don't remember it being so bright," said Jaklin.

Mikhail hid his face at first but then peaked out from between his fingers. "I definitely prefer a dark room, but it appears that I can tolerate it. What happens to normal vampires?"

"The skin blisters almost immediately and starts to smoke. If they don't seek shelter, they burst into flame," said Catherine.

"I suffered a little from bright sunlight at first but built up a tolerance," said Alex.

Finally, Jaklin stepped out into direct sunlight. Nothing happened. "Guess I get to keep my day job," she said. "And here I was hoping to go on disability."

They still watched Jaklin closely. Although she appeared to be alright, she was erratic, her arms flailing at times for no apparent reason, and she laughed excessively and at the strangest things. When she did so, they'd stare at her, and she'd laugh again. They kept her away from the kitchen knives.

Alex said she needed to talk to Father Zosimos, and they immediately volunteered to go with her. Catherine, who'd been up before sunrise, flinched at the name Zosimos.

"My late husband was a Zosimos," she said. "Perhaps the priest is a relative."

"You should come," said Alex. "I want him to baptize Andra. Even at one day old, I want this behind me."

They left on foot walking downhill, Jaklin and Mikhail feeling a surge of energy, and Catherine wanting a daylight look at the Sinaia she'd once loved.

Jaklin called the ICC and told them she would have to take a couple of days sick leave. "They are not pleased," she said. "Ten-nation conference going on right now. Lots of dignitaries."

"What position do you have at the ICC?" asked Catherine.

"I represent the Bulgarian Consulate. Logistics, passports, visas. I'm a notary."

"We'll have to talk sometime. I'm a professor of international law. Used to teach at the University of Edinburgh."

Alex looked discouraged. "Lawyers. Seems it's a family tradition."

They entered the monastery through the wood gate, which had just been unlocked and swung inside, and walked on to Zosimos' residence. After knocking and getting no response, Alex worked the door latch and, finding it unlocked, entered, the other three right behind her.

"Stay here," she said, turning Andra over to Catherine. "I've heard he's not well. Let me see if I can rouse him."

Alex walked through an archway into a short hall that led to a bedroom. She saw no one inside. She entered the small chamber. It was cluttered with books left open and lying on chairs, shelves, the unmade bed, and a writing desk, which had several sheets of unfinished writing Alex recognized as Latin. She heard a whimpering from the closet, went to it, and pulled the sliding door aside. There was Father Zosimos cowering against a corner among stacks of both fresh clothes and dirty laundry. He shrunk away from her, hiding his eyes from the light. She wondered if he'd been turned.

"Father?" She wasn't even sure it was him. "Why are you crying?"

Finally, he opened his eyes and looked up at her. "Thank the Lord it's you," he said. "I was afraid they'd killed you. I've been accosted by a flock of angels, come to admonish me over my crimes. My dreams are torture. Forgive me, Alexandra. Call off the angels. Please!"

Alex helped him to his feet and into the desk chair. He sat holding his head in his hands. "I've come for my cross," she said. "I won't take no for an answer."

"I've been hoping for an opportunity to return it." With that he limped to the cupboard, slid open a drawer, and retrieved her cross still on its chain. "You wouldn't believe the burden this has put me under. I've been chased by visions during the day and hounded by unholy demons in my dreams."

"You brought this calamity on yourself," she said. "I'm sorry it's come between us."

"Not you and me. Heaven and me. Kneel, child, and quit lecturing."

She dropped to her knees.

Father Zosimos cupping the cross within both his hands like the precious object that it was, and with tears streaming down his face said, his voice cracking, "It is with great pride and humble awareness that I present this cross to you, child, in the Name of the One Who fell to it, our own Lord Jesus." He took a deep breath and a great sense of relief came over him. "In the name of Jesus Christ, the Child All Mighty, I do hereby grant you possession of this cross for eternity. Whomsoever shall attempt to relieve you of it shall be cursed until death." He slipped the chain over her head and let it fall to her chest.

Alex rose to her feet. "I've brought three others with me, actually four. I have a task for you," she said.

They left his chamber and walked back into the receiving room.

"You know my friends Jaklin and Mikhail. I'm sorry to have to tell you this, Father, but I have turned both. I'm not proud of it, but it seems that is the way it is meant to be."

He raised his eyes to the heavens, and then threw up his hands in resignation. "I'll not question your actions, but accept these two young people as they now are." Still, he was overcome with emotion. He looked up. "Father in Heaven! What has become of the world? Do none of the old teachings hold?"

"I turned them myself, one through necessity, the other by choice," said Alex. "And they seem to also have a touch of the divine."

He closed his eyes and steadied himself. "So be it," said Father Zosimos. "Hopefully someday the Lord will reveal the nature of this new world to me." He took another breath and motioned toward Catherine. "And pray tell who..." he seemed to want to say what monstrosity but restrained himself, "...is this?"

"This young woman, Catherine..." Alex paused searching for a characterization, "...is a relative of mine."

"And human, so it would seem?" he said, greatly relieved.

"Yes, very much so," said Catherine.

Alex took the child from her. "And this is my daughter, Andra. Although less than one day old, I wish her baptized." She paused for a second. "And in case you're wondering, she's healthy, human, and not a child of Satan."

He did seem to be leery of the child, taking a step back as if afraid they'd ask him to hold her. "I'm sorry I questioned her virtuous and noble state of being."

They heard running footsteps outside, and a young man burst into the room. He was rather tall, gangly, with unruly black hair.

"You're up, and seeing people," he panted. "What's happened?"

"The cause of all my concern has returned alive," said Father Zosimos. "Or at least present in this world. You're just in time to help with a little officiating." He turned to the others. "This is my grandson, Daniel Zosimos," he said.

"But how did you recover so quickly?" asked Daniel.

"Heaven has chased off the Hounds of Hell," he replied. "At least for now."

A squeak came out of Catherine. "Oh," she murmured and collapsed like rag doll. Alex and Jaklin were on her in an instant. Catherine tried to struggle to her feet but didn't make it.

"Sit for a moment. Regain your strength," said Alex. "What

happened?"

Father Zosimos retrieved a bottle from a cupboard behind the desk, opened and poured it into a glass. "Holy water," he said. He offered it to Catherine, obviously wishing to test her.

Catherine seemed afraid of it at first, then drank a little. She rose partially and slumped on the sofa. She was crying. "My late husband was named Daniel Zosimos," she said. "He was from Sinaia. But it's not so much the name as his appearance. I would swear that he's my husband come back from the grave."

"This is not possible," said Father Zosimos, obviously relieved that he'd finally found something he could comfortably be contrary about. "I would know of another Zosimos living here. My grandson was named for a granduncle of mine who died at the age of thirty."

"That would have been him," said Catherine. And then she told them her strange story of being turned by her aunt ninety years ago. She ended her story with Alex turning her back human. She then said, "I am the illegitimate daughter of Queen Marie. I was born in eighteen ninety-seven. I am the great great grandmother of Alex's little girl."

Mikhail seemed to wake from his trance. "This is a strange world I live in," he said. "Last evening I was killed and resurrected as a vampire, and yet here I am in a room with two priests and a woman who is one hundred and fifteen years old, and yet looks to be no more than twenty. And she was once a vampire but now human, again."

"I have been a priest but a year, and I'm confronted with... with... this," said Daniel. "Grandfather! Tell me what to make of it."

Father Zosimos shook his head but restrained himself. "All in due course. Accept the situation as it is for now, and we'll try to come to terms with it together another time."

"And this child I hold in my arms," said Alex, "is the first human born to a vampire in three millennia."

Father Zosimos had them each grab a chair, and form a circle. He shut his eyes, hummed quietly, and when he finally had control of himself, spoke. "These are indeed profound times. I've been tried and broken, but I can tell now that the good Lord has brought us all together for a reason, the extent of which, none of us yet realize. Let us have faith in one another as we have in our Lord Jesus that we might accomplish these profound tasks sent by Divine Will."

And they all joined hands in the center of their circle, and Zosimos placed his left at the bottom of theirs and the right at the top while he said, "Let us form a covenant of trust with one another and work to fulfill Divine Will." Then he said a prayer for them, and they all said, "Amen."

"Please. I need you to baptize my child," said Alex.

"So it will be then," said Father Zosimos but then hesitated. "However, Jaklin and Mikhail can't witness the ceremony."

"But they have to," said Alex. "It wouldn't be right to exclude them."

"Alright then," Father Zosimos said. "But they'll each have to wear a cross to prove they're not totally hostile to the Church."

"Not a problem," said Mikhail.

"Which would you prefer, a new shiny one or something old?"

"Ancient," said Mikhail. "Something orphaned by an unbeliever."

"And you, my child," said Zosimos turning to Jaklin.

"The smallest you have, to remind me that I have so little faith."

"And for you, Catherine?"

"I'd have the one I wore ninety years ago, taken from me when I was ostracized."

"Take this for now," he said. "We'll have to look into our stack of repossessed ones later."

They all walked to the baptismal chamber in the Old Monastery, where Daniel filled the ancient stone font with holy water while his grandfather put on his robes. They gathered about the font. Father Zosimos said, "Ordinarily we'd hear from the child's godparents at this time."

"I would like to be her godmother," said Catherine. "I cannot imagine another."

"I would like to be her godfather," said Daniel. "I am so taken with these young people and this child that I would like to play a role in her life."

"Let it be so," said Alex.

Father Zosimos, who now appeared to have overcome his fear of the infant, took the sleeping child from its blankets, submerged her three times within the holy water while saying the words, "In the name of the Father, the Son, and the Holy Spirit." Little Andra shivered and cried at the first dunking but remained quiet at the following two. He placed a tiny cross about her neck.

After the christening, Alex requested that Father Zosimos help her make out a Last Will and Testament, wherein, if anything should happen to her, she could leave everything she had, the Estate and money, to Andra, and Andra would be in Catherine's charge until the age of eighteen.

When all was complete, the four started to leave the monastery, but Daniel requested that Catherine stay a while. "To see if we can locate your cross," he said.

And so she did.

Father Zosimos seemed relieved to see the vampires leave.

*

Jaklin, Mikhail, and Alex with little Andra safely tucked away inside a blanket in her arms, returned home. Once there, the three vampires gathered in the kitchen where Jaklin and Mikhail prepared lunch while Alex nursed Andra sitting in a chair next to the table. When she opened her blouse, she saw her own little wood cross against her cleavage and smiled, sensing the calm that had come over her since regaining it. This was their first meal together as immortals. And then as vampires are apt, they went upstairs to their bedroom and slept together while, in the city below, humans went about their business in full light of day.

Alex dreamt of Millennium Road. It was the first time she'd slept since giving birth, and now those occupying the Road were more vivid, even more humanlike than following her initiation. Slight tinges of color marked their features. They also had more interest in her and showed affection for her.

She'd been on the Road for some time when she remembered Jaklin and Mikhail. She rushed back to the beginning of the Road, but didn't find them. Perhaps three together wouldn't be enough. She looked off to the left of the Road, and there she found a lost wandering vampire who could hardly stand. At first she didn't recognize him, but then realized that he was just a shadow of himself, with hardly a shape at all, a patch of darkness moving along the ground. He could barely stand. It was Mikhail. She helped him to his feet and tried to talk to him, but he didn't seem to hear her. Quite suddenly his awareness came into focus. "Alex," he said. "I'm glad you found me. I was lost and alone in this God forsaken wilderness. I was as afraid as a child."

"I'm with you now, Mikhail. Hold to me, and I'll help you back to the Road."

They struggled back and started looking for Jaklin. Alex wondered if she might have already come across, or perhaps she was feral and wouldn't appear at all. They saw a sudden flash of light in the pitch-black at the beginning of Millennium Road, and another male vampire burst through, confused and disoriented. They helped him to find a place on the Road behind those who came before, and then returned to look for Jaklin. They waited for what seemed an eternity. Still nothing. Alex was afraid she'd wake without finding her. Then she saw another dark shape wandering about. Alex knew immediately that it was Jaklin. She took one arm and Mikhail the other, and they helped her onto the Road. The three huddled together standing, arms around each other.

"Where am I?" Jaklin asked.

"You're on Millennium Road with Mikhail and me," said Alex.

Once Jaklin had regained partial awareness, Alex took both off the Road to the right and asked them to look into the distance. "Do you see the light?" she asked. "It's a glow along the horizon." But no, neither could see the Chateau though she continued to describe and point in its direction.

*

They woke late in the afternoon, groggy but refreshed from their first experience together in vampire psychic space. Alex again breastfed little Andra, cuddled and kissed her, that tiny warm and precious being. "Who are you?" Alex asked of her. "Do you have a father?" She thought she managed to get a smile out of the tiny infant.

They took the liberty of going downtown to a jewelry store. Mikhail said, "We become immortal vampires with obvious aspirations of saving the world, and the first thing we do is go shopping?" They bought three identical eternity rings of tarnished silver with pentagonal lapis lazuli insets containing pyrite flakes that sparkled like stars in a deep-blue firmament, what the ancients knew as the "stone of heaven." They each wore it on the third finger of the right hand. They joined hands and said, "Forever and ever, throughout eternity."

Once back at the Estate, Alex breastfed Andra again. She was perpetually hungry and always fell asleep while feeding. Just as Andra finished nursing, Catherine returned from the Monastery. Daniel had accompanied her to the door. They were obviously taken with each other, and Catherine had found what she believed had been her old cross.

"I'm infatuated with Daniel," she said. "And overcome by how much he reminds me of my late husband. He's like a reincarnation. What am I to do but fall in love?"

Alex had been anxiously anticipating Catherine's return because Shadowrise was upon them. "I want us all to go out to the gazebo," she said. "You must meet someone, or at least I want someone to meet you." Alex had wondered if anyone besides herself could see Catalin, and this was as good an opportunity as any to find out.

While nursing little Andra, Alex had noticed that her own skin felt cool compared to her baby's. She checked her body temperature and found it to be ninety-two. She'd started to cool and realized that if she kept it up, she'd soon be room temperature. Catherine bundled up especially warm in Alex's heavy coat with its fur lining and collar and put the baby inside next to her breasts where she'd be warm as toast.

They all walked out to the gazebo to watch Shadowrise.

37

Reckoning

As they walked through the grass in the backyard, Nălucă followed along after Mikhail, and once he saw the cat, he picked it up and carried it cuddled in his arms. Alex was pleased to see the work Mikhail, with a little help from Jaklin, had accomplished on the gazebo. He'd located much of its stone furniture.

"It wasn't easy, Missy," said Jaklin.

Mikhail had dug between the trees around the gazebo to locate the missing pieces. He'd stumbled upon the pentagonal tabletop mostly buried nearby, and while digging it up, located the large pedestal upon which it sat. He'd found two of the arched chairs submerged in soil just beyond the family graveyard and located one more in the tool shed. One had been in use as a surface for minor blacksmithing and the other in the coop as roosts for chickens. All this he had cleaned, dragged into the gazebo, and properly positioned. It brought the gazebo back to life, and Alex was thrilled beyond words, as was Catherine. They'd have to consider rebuilding the external structure.

"Setting up the stone furniture somehow seemed to activate it, Missy," said Mikhail. "We sensed something immediately, even in daytime, but the real change came at night."

"Missy?" said Catherine. "I've been meaning to ask about that. Missy was my mother's, Queen Marie's, endearment."

"I assumed it after reading her biography," said Alex. "At least it's what I asked these two to call me. I couldn't resist. Your daughter used to call me Missy at times."

Jaklin was still thinking about the gazebo. "It, or a portion of it, often glowed," she said. "Some heavenly light emanated."

As the sun set, Alex and Catherine walked beyond the gazebo to the family cemetery. The graveyard had an even more ancient history.

"Initially it was supposed to have been a Roman burial site," said Catherine. The most ancient marked grave was that of the Sibyl." She pointed to a tombstone in a remote part of the site that was now nothing more than a weather-beaten slab of granite. "Several nuns are also supposed to be buried here." She paused before an unmarked tombstone and shook her head. "This is my own grave, but was just to keep neighbors and local officials from inquiring into my disappearance. It's empty, of course," she added with a laugh. "Alu Kard has a long history with the site. He used to visit the Sibyl. But, and this was a source of both confusion and anger, he couldn't enter the gazebo. The Divine would not tolerate his presence, and it made him bitter."

Alex showed Catherine her daughter's grave. Catherine knelt before the tombstone and said a prayer. Alex told her of her grandmother passing in her sleep, the most peaceful death imaginable. She told her that her grandmother had been the most loving person she'd known, and how they spent weeks together every year, how she'd guided her life, and provided a sense of true joy to all aspects of living. Then she left Catherine and Andra alone at the grave and walked back to the gazebo.

Alex, Jaklin and Mikhail sat quietly at the table holding hands across its rough stone surface, just being vampires together. Nălucă was cuddled up in Mikhail's lap. Alex saw the small tree that she'd planted the night Velinar bit her. It seemed to have never lost its leaves.

"I guess my tree made it through the winter cold."

"It didn't bear fruit last fall," said Jaklin.

"Why are we waiting here?" asked Mikhail.

"Catalin," said Alex.

Catherine returned shortly, a tear in her eye and little Andra sound asleep against her bosom. She joined them at the table, and they gave her a round of hugs. She looked at Alex. "I'm going to steal your baby," she said. "She reminds me so much of mine many years ago. She left this world as yours entered. Life is full of its little coincidences."

Alex forced a smile in response, but the thought of losing her baby sent a chill through her. She retrieved little Andra hiding her sense of panic and held her with a death grip.

Catherine was enthralled with the gazebo and had a little history to tell them. "It was originally built over a secret Roman temple to the goddess Diana," she said, spreading her arms and looking heavenward. "The original temple was destroyed after the fall of the Roman Empire and a home for the Sibyl built in its place by Christians about a thousand years ago. When an earthquake destroyed it, locals built a small chapel to the Virgin Mary to accompany the building of the Monastery, just down the road. It was never sanctioned by the Church, which had it destroyed out of the belief that it would promote the worship of Mary to the detriment of faith in Christ. When Queen Marie became pregnant with me, she knew a nun who had a vision of the temple rebuilt as a nonagon in the faith of the Baha'i. The Queen had it built with a home alongside it for me. The gazebo became a place of intense scrutiny when reports of visions at the site created suspicion. Although it never had electricity, several people saw the gazebo glow in the dark, and apparitions came and went within its luminescence."

"As have we," said Mikhail. "After we put the table and chairs back inside, it came to life."

They then quizzed Catherine concerning Alu and his feral vampires.

"I spent weeks imprisoned in a private chamber in the Cathedral and finally the Ichor Dome," she said, "while Alu tried to talk me into becoming feral. I resisted. He could have turned me feral without my permission, but that wasn't his way, or so he said. I feigned interest but was horrified. He told me that the Ichor Dome was just the incubation chamber and that he'd show me the final product if I'd let him 'extend' me, as he put it. I was planning my escape when I saw

Alex at the entrance to the Ichor Dome. I followed her back to Xanadu where she went into labor."

"What is Xanadu?" asked Mikhail.

"You'll learn soon enough," said Alex. For the first time, she worried about their initiations. She realized that theirs would be different from hers, but she was still concerned about them and what sort of abuse they might suffer. She didn't feel inclined to discuss hers or to warn them. They'd just worry about the inevitable.

"Where did you spend all those years you were away from Sinaia?" asked Alex.

"Many places," Catherine said. "All over the world really, advising government officials on international law. Much of the time I spent with Alu who roamed from place to place mostly teaching but also turning people from time to time. I was surprised at how non-violent he was, never turning anyone who didn't wish to become one. He's highly discriminatory. Though I'd not wanted to be a vampire myself, I realized that they weren't the evil beings imagined by the civilian population. Of course, most of the phobia is caused by vampires' need to feed, and many abuse their physical and intellectual superiority, not to mention, their millennia of experience solving this problem."

"Which reminds me," said Michael, "Jaklin and I will have to feed soon. I'm noticing a compulsion to bite someone now."

"I want to get one thing straight," said Alex. "None of us will ever feed off Catherine. The need for blood is a problem solvable without resorting to those closest you. Tomorrow when I take you into the cavern to be initiated, we'll find an agreeable source."

The gazebo had grown dark, and Alex noticed something out the corner of her eye and turned to see someone standing in the shadows observing them. "I don't want to frighten you," she said. "But Catalin has joined us."

Mikhail was the only one who rose. When he did, Năluċă jumped down and went to stand before a tombstone in the graveyard and stare back at them. Jaklin was the only one to cower at the image of Catalin, who stepped forward to the edge of the table. Michael reached out to touch him, but his hand passed right through Catalin. "It's an apparition," he said. "Is this that being you encountered when you became a vampire?"

"Yes," Catalin said. "I was with Velinar when it happened. But be seated, young Mikhail Volsky. I have something to say. First of all, I'm surprised to see Catherine once again human. What a marvelous feat you've accomplished, Marie. A servant of God returned to the flock is always an occasion to rejoice."

"I've had my child too," said Alex. She took Andra from Catherine and walked to Catalin to show him.

"Your child you thought was from the rape?"

"Yes." said Alex.

"This child's soul is different and of a purity that I've not seen. The rapist is not the father. I told you this once before."

"I've been told that she is a product of parthenogenesis."

But Catalin had already turned from her. "Now I must address all of you," he said, "for you have come together by virtue of Divine Will. I cannot tell and do not know the extent of your mission on Earth, for much is hidden from me as it is you. But the four of you, perhaps five, have fallen into one of the great rivers of existence, and that divine stream has swept you up and will carry you into dangerous and normally forbidden territory. You cannot escape it, nor will you want to. The only advice I can give is to be ever alert to evil and trust your intuition toward your actions as events unfold. Troubled times are ahead for the mortal world, but also for the divine. Have faith that the good forces of the Universe are on your side and will aid you in any way possible. But you must realize that a great gulf separates the divine and mortal worlds. You bridge that divide. Those of us in the Divine World don't relate well to yours. Not all our advice will make sense to you. Since you live in the natural world, your intuition will frequently be better than ours. I wish you well."

"What is this that's coming?" asked Mikhail.

"I can say no more," said Catalin. "You must leave now, for I have such little time and much to say to Marie alone."

Once they'd cleared the Gazebo, Catalin said to Alex, "Your soul has darkened. You've become partially evil."

"I had to live with vampires for a while," she answered. "Your Church was so hostile to me and my pregnancy that I couldn't trust it or anyone associated with it. Alu Kard offered sanctuary under the condition that I be initiated."

"So you've become evil."

"A certain amount of darkness is involved, but I witnessed no more evil than I have seen in your Church, which participates in evil on Earth all the time."

Catalin open his mouth to say something, but nothing came out. Finally he said, "I'll have to tell Velinar of this."

"Run to mommy. Tattle-tale on the bad vampire."

"You are so insolent. I don't deserve that." He looked at the ground, obviously disappointed in her. "I see you're wearing your cross again."

"Father Zosimos returned it."

"I was told he would, or else. Him taking it from you created quite a stir in the Divine World." But then Catalin frowned and with a stern voice said, "I also see that your two companions are now vampires."

"I turned them," said Alex. "I turned Mikhail because if I hadn't he would have died. I had no time to make a calculated decision."

"Turning Mikhail Volsky, I can forgive. But Jaklin Dafovska is a different story, isn't she?"

"I turned her because she wanted to be turned. She begged me, and Mikhail and I couldn't live without her."

"Couldn't or didn't want to?"

"I questioned it too, but in the end, I weakened. I couldn't bear to be without her." She thought for a second. "You know, it was really more than that. She's committed herself to us being together and dealing with this feral vampire menace. If I hadn't turned her, another vampire could have made her feral. You have to realize the practicality of what I did."

"She could have made a different choice, said no, so I can't forgive turning her. You could have inoculated her. That act is a transgression that will stain your soul forever. What's done cannot be undone. That act was premeditated and has consequences that have already started to unfold."

"Like what? Am I being punished?"

"I wouldn't look at it as a punishment. It's the way existence works, the physics of the problem, you might say."

"That's a distinction without a difference. What is this to be? Some crippling deformity?"

"It's the child. I believe she has already found her new mother."

Alex was devastated. How could she not raise her own child? "You can't do this to me. You are a compassionate, divine being."

"As I said, I'm not doing this to you. You did it to yourself. I'm no more to blame than the cat who led you to Velinar."

"But how about divine love, forgiveness?"

"Even forgiveness wouldn't change the consequences. Again, it's the physics."

Alex felt her anger rise. Catalin seemed some agent of Satan come into the gazebo. "Then who controls this 'physics'? I want to speak to him. My predicament isn't acceptable. None of this was my doing. It was Velinar, and you. In failing her, you failed me."

He changed the subject. "I've noticed an unusual tree just outside the gazebo. There," he pointed. "What is its origin?"

"I don't know," she said. "After Velinar bit me, I collapsed there. Died, so I've been told. When I woke the next morning, I had a single seed in my mouth. I pushed it into the soil, and from it grew that tree."

"And a rare tree it is, a pomegranate, the most sacred of all trees, and judging from the shape of leaf, a variety that no longer exists on Earth. Only one other ever existed, and it in the Garden of Eden, the same source as your cross."

"You're sure of this?"

"Yes. Your cross is made from wood taken from the Tree of Life. That sapling sprung from the fruit of the Tree of Life. That being who visited while you were unconscious, did he feed it to you?"

"It would seem so, although everything that happened that night comes as a vague recollection. Alu said he tried to turn me but failed."

"You're different from other vampires. Your cross proves that. Alu certainly played a part because you needed blood, but one far beyond my knowledge resurrected you. Guard well the fruit of that tree. It's a divine gift."

"Yes, well, I'd prefer my own choice of gifts. Such a tree is of no use to me."

"I wouldn't be so sure of that. But you do have one additional gift. Although you can never go to Heaven, you will have contact with it. In your dreams, you've seen the Chateau. It's a place of refuge."

"Millennium Road is more interesting than that glowing little structure off in the distance. I want my other life back. I want to be able to go to Heaven."

"What's this Millennium Road?"

"Vampire psychic space. We go there every night when we dream. The Chateau is there, but off in the distance."

"Vampires are dead. Millennium Road?"

"We travel and suffer hardships along the way. We're headed somewhere, but I haven't learned where or why yet."

"Sounds like a pilgrimage. Surely vampires aren't headed to a holy site."

"All I can say is that I've seen a glowing pentagon off in the distance, and we're headed toward it."

Catalin looked puzzled. "The pentagon is a symbol for the use in the Divine World and was kept secret on Earth until Pythagoras discovered it for the ancient Greeks. Caused some consternation in Heaven. Even your Chateau is formed of twelve such surfaces. But I've been told nothing of this Millennium Road and see no significance to it."

"It's the common purpose that binds all vampires."

"Still, unimportant if it's for the Undead. As for your fate, events realign the fabric of the Divine World and also impact mortal psychic space. I'm sorry. That's just the way it is, not because I choose or decide it to be that way. I usually don't interfere in the lives of humans, but I've been assigned this task because I was present when it happened. My failures have had consequences as well, and now I've been given more than just overseeing the Carpathians. I'm your advisor."

"This problem was caused by the Divine World, and I'm tired of dealing with you, Catalin. Send someone with the authority to do something about it."

"Don't be flippant with me. I'm not some bank clerk arguing over a ledger. I'm a divine being, and we're arguing questions of immortality."

"And I'm a creature of the real world. I'm not being flippant. This business of mistakes and forgiveness goes both ways. Turning me was unforgivable. So I guess we're even. I'm beyond tired of being criticized and kept in the dark about my eternal existence here on Earth. I'm officially pissed off. I don't care what you think anymore. Next time, send someone with the authority to rectify this. I'm tired of your secrecy and forbidden knowledge. And by the way, Velinar had to bite Alucius Kardasian to become a vampire. It's an exchange of blood. She hasn't told you the truth about how she was turned."

"I... well... you... don't understand."

"I know the vampire world better than you know the Divine World. My situation is intolerable, and it's her fault. I have a child. Send the divine being who fed me the fruit from the Tree of Life. I want this reversed."

And then she turned her back to Catalin, walked out of the gazebo away from him and into the dark.

38

Silent Scythe

A deep moonless gloom had settled over her home when Alex returned. She entered and went straight to the kitchen but wouldn't say what had happened between her and Catalin. They congregated around her but where silent.

"First vampires, now spooks," said Mikhail.

No one laughed.

Alex felt their eyes on her. "I have to get a breast pump," she said. "I'm still lactating, but I'll have to heat the milk before I can feed Andra. My body is now room temperature." Her mood darkened with the failing light coming through the windows.

She took Andra from Catherine and clutched her close, kissed her and rocked her back and forth as she took a seat at the table. Little Andra whimpered, so Alex held her up in the air. Andra smiled sleepily down at her. She pulled her close and kissed her again. She smelled of baby powder and lotion. Alex did goochy-coo with her finger under her chin. Andra whined, rubbed her nose with her fist. Alex returned her to Catherine.

"She gets a chill when I hold her. My cheeks are cold, lips and fingers like icebergs."

She looked at Catherine with Andra cuddled contentedly to her bosom. She didn't want to repeat what Catalin had told her, that

Catherine would be Andra's mother. She looked at Jaklin and finally grasped the cost of turning her. She looked at Mikhail in the corner of the dark room leaning against the cabinet eating pastrami on rye. He was also partly the reason for her punishment. She'd created the complete catastrophe. Her own friends and family had been her undoing, always had. For just an instant, she allowed herself to hate them all.

She left the kitchen and went into the living room to sit before the fireplace. The flames had gone out, but the glow of the coals felt hot, uncomfortably so. She hung her head in her hands and cried.

Jaklin came to her, put her arms around her.

"I'm no good for my baby," Alex said. "I've lost her."

"You'll work it out, Missy. It'll be okay."

Alex didn't want to hear it. The others drifted into the living room and stood around her. She dried her eyes and looked up. "You and Mikhail need to be initiated for your psychic wellbeing. With the danger we're about to face, you need full control. I found you both on Millennium Road, but you still haven't found your bearings there."

"You're right," said Catherine. "We're all in danger. Alu's ready to move on his feral vampire stratagem, whatever it is. I'm surprised he hasn't already executed. No telling what has happened in the Cathedral. He could have turned all of them feral by now. I'm surprised he hasn't invaded our home."

The thought of Alu and his ferals crashing through her doors sent a chill through Alex. "I'm a mother," she said. "I don't want this vampire life or the responsibility for all those lost souls. I just want to take care of my baby and go about my life. Bite someone now and then."

Catherine put Andra in her bassinet and came between Alex and the fireplace. She dropped to her knees and looked up at Alex. "You have to take a broader perspective, dear. We are the only ones who know about Alu, where he is and what he's up to. We have to act."

"But why me? I'm just a kid."

Catherine took Alex into her arms. "You're a vampire, an immortal, and that comes with new responsibilities. And what is most unbelievable is that you have direct contact with the Divine World."

She leaned back, took Alex's face in her hands. "You have a destiny. The entire world needs you."

Alex clung to her great grandmother, that warm human body. This young woman, so beautiful and bright. She felt the love flow into her, that which her own mother had denied her. Alex wanted to cuddle up in Catherine's arms and sleep like a baby. She realized that in many ways she'd inherited her great grandmother's responsibilities in the vampire world, and now Catherine had been assigned those in the human world that she could no longer fulfill. Perhaps she'd been wrong about being punished. Catherine was just the person she and the baby needed.

They heard a rustling out back, quick footsteps followed by a light knock on the door. They all turned to look, but the drapes were pulled to and could see nothing. No one moved. The darkness seemed to deepen, and the dim glow from the coals of the fireplace cast their own animated shadows on the walls like augured apparitions.

Alex felt the depression lift and all her senses quicken. Her vampire nature rose up inside her. "Alu?" she asked.

Catherine rose to her feet and went to the bassinet. "He wouldn't have knocked."

"Who is it?" shouted Mikhail.

They heard muffled conversation. "It's me," said a rather shaky voice.

"Cosmina," said Alex, walking toward the door.

"I hear several, Missy" said Jaklin.

"I'll let her in," said Alex.

"What if she's feral?" asked Mikhail.

"No," said Catherine. "She left the cavern as soon as I told her about the ferals."

Alex looked toward the bassinet. "Catherine," she whispered, "take Andra upstairs and hide in a closet." Once Catherine and the baby were at the top of the stairs, Alex unlatched the door, but before opening it, she hesitated. "Are you alone?"

"No," Cosmina answered.

"How many?"

"Just a few. I brought Silent Scythe."

"What does that mean?" She started to relock the door, but before she could trip the latch, it was forced open, shoving her back. A flood of ghosts invaded her home, people actually, but dressed in dark camouflage that made them barely seeable.

Mikhail blocked the stairs.

"Katsumi!" shouted one and pointed at Alex. Katsumi then started toward Alex.

"One more move!" Jaklin shouted. "You're a pile of disconnected body parts."

As the intruders scurried about the room, Jaklin and Mikhail sprang into action. Mikhail blocked one's path, and slung him up against the wall.

"Mikhail!" said Alex. "No violence."

A young black woman shoved Jaklin back a couple of steps. She appeared formidable despite her short, slim stature. Ignoring Alex's order, Jaklin went into action.

"No!" shouted Alex, but she was too late.

Jaklin slung aside the black girl and tripped a larger one as he also headed for the stairs. She shoved him to the floor and put him in a headlock that had him struggling to breathe. Her instinctive battle skills were blazing fast and powerful.

"How many in here?" demanded Katsumi. Her voice was gruff, angry, worried. She had metal bars on her shoulders. Obviously a commander. She still keyed on Alex. She had slim wood rods as protection for each arm, held in place and gripped by a perpendicular knob. The back end of each shaft was pointed, an obvious vampire death instrument. As she made a move for Alex, Cosmina stepped through the entryway with a shout.

"Stop it! We're all friends here."

Alex was on the verge of panic. "What's the meaning of this?"

"Don't resist," Cosmina warned. "We're Silent Scythe and here to help. You're in danger."

With her came the rest of Silent Scythe like a gust of wind blowing though the open door. They were phantoms in military uniform unlike anything Alex had ever seen, except maybe on the big screen, a type of spiderman outfit, sleek, clinging.

Katsumi made another lunge at her, and Alex again felt the vampire rise up inside her. She stepped back at Katsumi's advance and her hand felt her grandfather's staff. Instinctively, she brought it forward to block the first blow.

"Bo no match for tonfa," said Katsumi swinging into action.

Alex didn't know what she was talking about, but when she swung the staff, Katsumi easily blocked it and dealt a nasty bonk with one of the tonfa to the side of Alex's head. A flurry of blows by each were blocked as the knock-knock of wood-against-wood rang off the walls.

Alex noticed a marked reduction at her own physical ability and realized that she was no match for this young woman in skill or speed, but when a blow from her staff shattered one of the tonfa, Alex dropped to the floor, stuck the staff between Katsumi's legs tripping her. She used the staff to pin the remaining tonfa and shoved it up against Katsumi's throat.

"Stop it, I said!" again shouted Cosmina. She was dressed in street clothes and strode to the center of the room barking orders and with sweeps of both arms, motioned for Silent Scythe to take up positions around the room. Alex counted ten, fifteen, maybe twenty phantoms. Their uniforms were pale and shimmered. When they stood in one place, it was as if their coloring changed and they melted into the woodwork like chameleons. They were armed but not in the sense of rifles and handguns. One carried a long bow, another a crossbow, yet another, an axe. They were vampire killers.

"These three are okay. I know them," Cosmina said. "That one there." She pointed at Mikhail. "He died for me. Anyone touch him, I'll tear you limb from limb." And then she turned on Katsumi, "I tried to tell you, you decomposed piece of brain tissue." She looked back at Alex. "Military. Humph. I can see that they've encountered a few skills they didn't anticipate."

Alex was furious. "You said just a few."

"Sorry. Only two were supposed to enter with me, but they pushed me aside as you opened the door. Katsumi!" Cosmina shouted and pointed upstairs.

They heard a scuffle and shouting and Katsumi broke for the steps along with three others. Mikhail tried to block them, but instantly they were around him and flew up to the landing.

"No!" shouted Alex. "That's my daughter." She heard a scuffle, loud shouting and made for the stairs herself. "That's my baby!" Again, she noticed a reduction in both speed and power. What has happened to me? she wondered. How could I not move fast enough to save my own daughter?

The scuffle ended as quickly as it began, and she saw a Silent Scythe holding Andra. Catherine was behind them with three more Silent Scythe.

"We got 'em," said Katsumi from the balcony.

"We had to kill the two normals," said another of the Silent Scythe.

"Too bad," said Cosmina. "The feral?"

They shoved him forward.

"Get him down here."

Alex realized that she'd sent Catherine and Andra into the hands of a feral vampire. Silent Scythe had saved them.

"How did you know they were here?" asked Alex

"We followed them. They entered your upstairs. Had to make sure you hadn't been turned feral before we could trust you."

Catherine and the baby followed the Silent Scythe downstairs but stayed away from the feral. Once the feral came close to Alex, he became more agitated, struggled against his captors.

"You'll have to restrain him," Alex said. "They're attracted to me, uncontrollably."

On the other hand, he ignored Jaklin and Mikhail. "Stand back," said Alex. "Apparently ferals are not attracted to either of you, but no need to take a chance."

Alex got a roll of duct tape from the kitchen and they bound him, hand and foot, to a chair.

"Now that he's subdued, I want to know what's going on. Who is Silent Scythe?"

"But we need to interrogate him first," said Cosmina. "Time is of the essence."

"If you don't explain who these people are and why they're here, we'll take you apart. And trust me on this, we can do the job."

Cosmina was startled. She looked at Katsumi and then back at Alex. "Okay. I can see you're upset. Perhaps reasonably so."

Jaklin had gone to the front window. "There's more outside, Missy," she said. "Not happy about that."

Alex stared daggers at Cosmina.

"Yes," she said. "Your house is surrounded."

"What?" shouted Mikhail. "Get them the hell out of here!"

"For your protection, as well as our own."

"Fat chance," said Mikhail. "We'll not tolerate this. What right do they have barging in like this?"

"None. But we do take certain liberties when deemed necessary. You're vulnerable if ferals come for you."

"Not liking this," said Jaklin.

"And we're supposed to trust you?" asked Alex

"You know me. I cared for you during your months of pregnancy. How about a little trust?"

"Alu cared for me too. But this... invasion?"

"We need to sort out Alu's plans, and what counter-action we need to take. If what we've heard is true, it's not just the vampire colony. Sinaia's entire civilian population is at risk. Silent Scythe will be here all night. With your permission."

At that point Catherine, who'd been occupied with quieting the baby stepped forward. "I know Silent Scythe," she said. "As vampires go, they don't come any better. You should trust them."

"Where are they from?" asked Mikhail. "Who are they?"

Cosmina didn't give Catherine a chance to respond. She acknowledged Mikhail but focused on Alex. "We have a problem with the Ichor Dome," said Cosmina. "I'd suspected something was not right with Alu for some time. When I saw him at Shadowrise, I knew he'd changed. I made a call and got them here overnight."

"Once we got here, we realized that the problem was not a renegade vampire faction," said Katsumi. "Much more serious."

"But to barge in like this..."

"I know," said Cosmina. "But in our defense, we couldn't be sure but what Alu had already invaded your home, turned you feral, and taken it over."

"But who are you?" asked Mikhail, again.

Cosmina continued to focus on Alex. "You have to realize. You've not seen all the legions of vampires, not even all those at the cavern. The World of Vampires is full of secret societies. It has many layers. We only divulge what new members need to know."

Alex had seen nothing quite like them, at least that was her first thought. Then she remembered what had happened at Christmas when she'd gone outside the cavern to call her mother. While returning, she'd stumbled onto Cosmina talking to a strange vampire that had disappeared quickly once she realized that Alex was nearby, and Cosmina had warned Alex to say nothing of the incident. These Silent Scythe wore the same camouflage uniforms.

"So who are you, Cosmina? I thought you were Alu's most trusted servant. And this Katsumi," Alex pointed at her, "I've seen her before."

"Yes, and almost uncovered our secret society. As for Alu, I've been within his inner circle for hundreds of years. But for the last few decades, I've been a double agent. A mole. Alu trusted me implicitly because he'd known me so long, but I've been a plant by my father who'd come to hate Alu because of Alu's seduction of his wife, my mother."

"And who are Silent Scythe?"

Catherine couldn't stay out of it any longer. "They are a security force," she said. "I had them looking out for my daughter, my granddaughter, and you, Alex, ever since you were born."

Cosmina cut in. "It's a mostly all-female military force within the race of vampires. They are young women who without their consent have been made vampires and stripped of their normal lives. Some were discontents who didn't know what they were getting into before being turned. Once inducted into Silent Scythe, they have all been trained not only in self-defense but also the fine art of killing vampires."

"You fight and kill vampires?"

"They? Yes. Me? Not so much. I'm both one of them and yet not. They were all young when turned, but some have been vampires for millennia. They clean up messes made by Alu and other vampires within his community. More autonomous groups exist and have leaders, but Alu, being the first vampire, is the most powerful and respected. I'm a member of Silent Scythe, but I don't fit the mold, and that's why I'm their mole."

Mikhail was still confused. "But that doesn't explain how you got so many here so quickly. Where do they stay?"

"All over. Members are not always in uniform. Most of the time, they are incognito and mix with other vampires, and only through an alert system are they activated. When they decide that they must take action, they determine what form it should take. If it requires force, they don their military garb, grab their weapons and form ranks. They are like fairies, characteristically young, agile, here today, gone tomorrow. In combat against renegade vampires, they are without peer."

"So that's it then?" asked Mikhail.

"No. Not nearly the full story," said Cosmina. "How much more time do you want to take with the entire world at risk?"

"I think you should tell them the full story of Silent Scythe," said Catherine. "It's a story worth telling."

A general rumbling came from all the Silent Scythe to hear the story of their origin. "Me too," said Katsumi. "And tell us more about this Alexandra Eidyn we're here to save." She looked directly at Alex. "She's the biggest mystery of all. No normal vampire can take me down the way she did."

Cosmina took a deep breath. "Okay. I'm getting the message. Perhaps we'll solicit some help in telling Alex's story, but I can definitely broaden your knowledge of Silent Scythe. Keep in mind that what I'm about to tell you is not a part of firsthand memory but simply what I've been told throughout the centuries and what I've pieced together on my own. So gather round, and I'll tell you a little story about the Carpathian vampire."

39

Mary

Vampires are not particularly fond of fire, but they do need a little light, so they left the two humans, Catherine and Andra, on the sofa before the fireplace along with Alex who'd suddenly developed an aversion to it but would brave the heat to be near Andra, and they formed a circle behind it in the center of the room where the soft glow of coals lit their pale cheeks. Jaklin and Mikhail sat on the back of the sofa close to Alex. Some sat off in the dark in chairs, such as were available, some on their knees, and others stood behind them, occasionally shifting for those farther back to see as Cosmina, who sat on a cushion in the center, wove her tattered tale. Vampires are always aware of their surroundings, and although they were indoors, each could feel the mountains and forest close about the Cottage and the presence of the dozen or so Silent Scythe in the woods and dark shadows close by.

"A small, young vampire founded Silent Scythe," began Cosmina. "She never matured past fifteen for some reason. Yet she has been undead for two millennia. She was at the Crucifixion. When Alu tasted the blood of Christ and inherited all his pain and suffering, he went into a fit of rage. He fell upon many of Christ's disciples and sucked them dry. He turned none of them, except one. Her name was Mary, not Jesus' mother or Mary Magdalen — so many were named Mary at that time — but the prostitute who the Church claimed was Mary Magdalen, but in fact wasn't. This Mary was the first Alu killed after tasting Christ's blood. She was standing there watching Alu perform the sacrilegious act and was the first he saw when he look up from tasting Christ's blood and realized what he'd done — that he had in fact acquired all Christ's suffering. He still had some on his lips. Along with the pain, a rage came upon him, and Alu sucked Mary dry and left her for dead.

But Mary had a little life left. She also became distempered and bit him back for molesting her. Thus, unwittingly, she became a vampire. Alu hadn't wanted to turn Mary and tried to stake her afterward, but she eluded him. Eluded but followed him, and he hated her for it. She became a great irritation and shadowed him for hundreds of years."

"But Silent Scythe are different from other vampires. How did we come to be different?"

"Ah, yes. Thank you, Katsumi. That essential element is easy to overlook. Mary found that she had a gift that she could bestow upon those Alu turned, provided Mary found them worthy. During the years following Alu's fateful encounter with Christ's blood, he was particularly hard on Christians. Mary kept him from preying on the Apostles, whom she warned of Alu's presence. She was ever a thorn in his side. So pure at heart was this girl, even after her turning, that she never lost faith in the Savior, although she realized that she could never be in Heaven with him. When Alu turned one of Christ's followers, Mary made an assessment, and if she deemed them worthy, she gave them her gift, which came to her through Christ's blood that Alu still had on his lips when he bit her. She had them bite her, and they became enlightened. They remained vampires, yes, but they were enlightened and set apart somewhat from the rest of the race of vampires. These enlightened ones have been the great philosophers among us through the centuries. However, many have died because of various encounters with the ways that we can be undone, and only a few remain undead."

Katsumi interrupted. "Any vampire who bites Mary becomes enlightened? Even today? Are all Silent Scythe enlightened?"

"Regrettably, no, as demonstrated by some of our actions this evening." She looked pointedly at Katsumi. "Let me finish my story. You need to hear it at this depth to realize the philosophical significance and indelible imprint becoming a Silent Scythe has on a vampire. Mary lost this gift as the years came and went, so we have heard, but she came to realize that she had a similar one that concerned vampire psychic space."

"Our initiations are different from that of normal vampires," said Katsumi.

"That's right, but secretly so. I won't go into the details that make it unique. It's voluntary but only revealed during initiation while in vampire psychic space, and then only if initiated by Silent Scythe. Silent Scythe comes between Alu and his unwilling victims. And this is what is so disturbing about the current situation with the Ichor Dome. We've been derelict in our duties. In the first centuries following the Crucifixion, Alu was even more violent and degenerate. Silent Scythe staked many of the vampires he turned. Not only did they correct some of Alu's worst mistakes, the vampires they redirected had an influence on Alu although he never recognized that this influence came from Silent Scythe. Alu mellowed. The stigmata, he was particularly upset about. He'd been a vampire for over a thousand years and had become used to the Curse of Cheiron, but what he inherited from Christ was new and particularly painful, and he cursed these new afflictions. Gradually, Alu calmed down about the stigmata too, and Silent Scythe nudged him in better directions. He came to appreciate their influence, but they never made peace with him. They always eluded him, stayed at a distance, formed their own community and tried to work good in the world. In that way, we've failed with the Ichor Dome."

"I've not seen this Mary," said Katsumi. "Where is she? Why doesn't she show herself? Is she still alive?"

"We've all seen her on the battlefield, although most of us probably didn't know. Mary rarely comes amongst the Undead anymore. Generally, she's out amongst the people of the world, doing good where she can, practicing Christ's teachings, but never feeding off her human friends who do not guess that she is a vampire. They only see her at night. She is totally ignored by the Divine World. They don't even know she exists, since her soul is on Millennium Road and no longer tethered to Heaven. This bothered her greatly at first, but she is so good at heart that she doesn't care if her works are never recognized. It's enough to know that she is making a difference, that Christ's word is of value and his disciples are protected. The act is the reward."

"How would I ever meet her?" asked Alex. "If I'm to tell my story, I would want her to hear it."

Cosmina thought a moment. "You won't have to tell her. She already knows." She rose and went to the door. The eyes of the many members of Silent Scythe that had gathered inside Alex's home followed her and whispers spread throughout the group. Were they to finally meet their founder? Cosmina went on outside, closed the door behind her, and was gone so long they began to wonder if she'd return at all. Then they heard muffled voices. The door opened, and a murmur passed from outside to inside, and the vampires inside the house parted with many hurried whispers and great excitement, and then a young girl, almost a child, stepped out of the darkness into the dimly lit room.

The girl entered just ahead of Cosmina. Two vampires fainted, crumpled to the floor like unstrung marionettes. This thorn in the side of Alu was unbelievably young appearing and unassuming, the essence of purity. She walked slowly and a light seemed to follow her. The glowing coals from the fireplace glistened off her cheeks and seemed to make light from her fill the room. Although dressed in camosilk darker than that of the others, she seemed to glow, yet it was a dark glow, a shadow of light, as if light had a shadow, and she had captured it. Alex felt both Jaklin's and Mikhail's hands clasp hers, realizing that they were in the presence of greatness.

Mary was a bit of a teenage girl at first, giggling when stopping to acknowledge friends she hadn't seen in a while. Alex was taken aback. Something familiar about this girl worried her. She stepped to the side to try to recover a memory. When Mary came to Mikhail, she was more somber and paid enough attention to him to make Jaklin jealous. "I thought she didn't like men," she said, but when Jaklin spoke, Mary turned to her, gave her a hug, thanked her for wanting to become a vampire, and told her that she had quite a future if she wished to be a member of Silent Scythe. Jaklin was breathless, and Alex was jealous.

Mary turned toward Alex, and she got to see her face full-on for the first time, which immediately turned from a warm smile to somber, a little sad. Alex was intimidated at Mary's beauty, but she still couldn't understand why this girl looked so familiar. Alex took both her hands. They were small, like a child's hands, and trembling. The truth be known, Mary also felt she was in the presence of greatness.

Mary spoke. "Yes, it's me, dear child. Your little Ariel."

And then Alex finally recognized her. Tears welled up, and she got a lump in her throat. It was her mysterious childhood playmate she'd seen so many times in the woods outback of her grandmother's home. Mary had tears in her eyes also.

"I must first apologize, for we had been protecting you all those years, and your first night back in Sinaia this last time, we failed you." She brought Alex's hands close, folded them in hers, and held them to her bosom. "We couldn't protect you from the vampire that bit you because we cannot enter the gazebo. Even in its proximity, we suffer greatly."

"You were nearby? I thought I was alone in the world."

"You have never been alone, dear girl. But we were not the only ones there that night. Alu intended to turn you as soon as he could get his hands on you. We had been on guard against him, but he eluded us. Luck it was, if one can describe a travesty by such a term, that Velinar got to you first. She fed but didn't turn you. You died, and Alu stepped in to seize the opportunity. He tried, but something scared him off. Could have been just the pain of being so close to the gazebo that made him leave. It seems you were a hot commodity that night because something strange and marvelous happened. Someone else came. Something we've never seen before. It finished your conversion with methods unknown to any of us."

"But Catalin said I wasn't a vampire. He said that I'd have to kill someone to become one."

"I don't know this Catalin, but your case is different from anyone who has ever become a vampire. I don't believe anyone, from this or the Divine World, fully understands who or what you are."

Alex remembered the dark figure of her dream as she laid outside the gazebo, undoubtedly Alu, and then the benevolent light that brought a feeling of love. "You saw it? I thought I remembered someone besides Alu. Can you tell me about it?"

"I don't even know if it was male or female. Some genderless spirit, I assume. Even to gaze upon it was a great agony for any vampire. We don't know what it did to you. Afterward, we continued to look out for you and would have protected you from the rapist, but you were wearing your cross. We lost track of you, and you fell into his clutches. We couldn't get to you. From then on, you were immortal and on your own, since you always carried the cross, something the rest of us can't tolerate. We didn't know what to think of you, and left you to your own devices."

"But the priest took it from me."

"Which rendered you defenseless, and you reentered the Cathedral. We knew you'd be in good hands with Cosmina. Just know this," said Mary. "You've never left my thoughts for an instant."

"I never wanted to be a part of such a violent world."

"Nor did any of us in Silent Scythe. But you are now a part of the vampire world, and it is a violent one. From what we've witnessed, you've learned to deal with it."

"I always relied on my cross for psychic protection. It seemed to suppress bad dreams in the beginning. Since I retrieved it, I've not been so dependent on it."

"That would be because of your initiation," said Mary. It seemed she wanted to say something else but was a little embarrassed. Finally, she released Alex's hands and stepped back from her. She swallowed and then spoke again. "You've not said anything about it, but even now you carry a cross. Actually, all three of you do."

"Sorry," said Alex. "We were invaded, or perhaps we'd have been more insensitive."

"The presence of a cross even without it being visible is an irritant, but we don't wish you to remove them. It's a comfort for me to know that such a vampire, three now, exists for I do love the cross."

"I wish I could show it to you. I've been told that the wood has a lineage back to Christ's cross and even to the Tree of Life."

Mary's eyes welled up. "That would certainly be a sight to behold because I was at the Crucifixion. Alas! It can never be. Just be aware that we are sensitive to them and ensure that they stayed hidden. I for one am thrilled just to know that I am in the presence of yours."

Alex wondered what it must be like to have a memory that goes back two thousand years. Her own childhood seemed such a distant thing, and she was only nineteen. She'd have to talk to Mary about the ramifications of longevity, but this certainly wasn't the time.

Cosmina, who'd been lurking in the background, stepped forward. "I hate to break up your little reunion, but we have business to take care of."

"Of course," said Mary. "And unpleasant business it is. We must hear from Catherine." She turned to pick her out of the crowd.

Catherine came forward carrying Andra wrapped in a blanket.

"Is this your child?" asked Mary.

"My little Andra," said Alex.

"The only born of a vampire. And the father?"

"I've been told I became pregnant by way of parthenogenesis."

"A virgin birth. Oh dear! A miracle child! When did you conceive?"

"I'm not sure. Could have been the night Velinar bit me."

"It could have been that divine being who turned you. Wouldn't be the first time it's happened. Not only that, they take their pleasure with anyone they wish and don't leave a trace of what they've done."

Alex went quiet. Had she been ravished by a divine being while unconscious? Could this be the answer to the paternity puzzle? Another assault from the Divine World? Or even more curious, could Andra be a divine child?

"Enough now," said Cosmina. "To the business of war."

"I keep getting distracted," said Mary.

"Alex has seen the Ichor Dome, and Catherine has spent some time there as well," said Cosmina. "Tell what you saw, Alex. What is Alu up to?"

Alex quickly recovered from the shock of having to reassess Andra's origins. "I got only a glimpse of it from a distance, but it was a horror. Humans chained in makeshift cages, and a great hoard of feral vampires feeding on them. I can't give an account with any great detail. Catherine has seen more."

Catherine returned Andra to the bassinet, came around to the back of the sofa, and sat on it beside Alex, Jaklin and Mikhail. "Not as much as I now wish," she said. "And Alu didn't intend for me to see any of it. I was never supposed to return to Sinaia but did against his order to visit my daughter's grave. He caught me and kept me under guard all the time. 'Alu, let me see your special project,' I'd ask, but he would say, 'Not until you commit.' I wouldn't."

"I don't blame you," said Mary.

"I eluded his security. He thought I'd left the cavern, but I had heard him arguing with one of his ferals and thought it must be about his special project, so one night I followed him by car into the mountains just after Shadowrise. I discovered his secret entrance to the Ichor Dome. There I witnessed his little project without his knowledge. I kept on the outskirts of Ichor Village, and he has more than one but very close together, trying to see what was going on. I became trapped there and was afraid he would find me and realize that I'd learned his secret. I made my way around it so as to know its extent. I was horrified. I was afraid of him after that, but I didn't know how to get back to the Cathedral. The entrance I came in by was being watched. Then I saw Alex, just a fleeting glimpse of her peering down from the ledge above the Ichor Dome. Somehow, it was the sight of her that gave me courage to escape. She saved me."

"Is the Ichor Dome really as bad as all that?" asked Katsumi.

"Worse than you can imagine. I've only known Alu for ninety years, but I wouldn't have expected this of him. I've not seen or heard anything like it. Humans chained in cages where vampires can feed at will. They go from person to person sampling blood. Men, women and children crying out for help. When it was quiet, it was eerily quiet, but at times, the captives would start screaming, and the entire cavern would erupt in a cacophony of misery. He and his ferals were oblivious of it. It's like a wine tasting room and animal research center combined, except that the specimens, and that's what he calls them, are human."

"He's turning not only vampires but also humans feral?" asked Katsumi.

"Yes, but I viewed another chamber farther down where he has an even more secret project brewing, something called Ichor Haven. This I didn't get to see in its entirety, but I could tell that he was creating a superior form of feral there, or perhaps they aren't even ferals, but surely some supervamp. With these, I believe he was sharing his blood or doing something else. I heard a lot about a magic potion. Really strange stuff. Normally he only bites one to create a feral. But these, he allows to taste him. He sleeps with them too. Might have something to do with Millennium Road. This helps clean up their act, evidently. But it would seem just a Band-Aid fix to a colossal catastrophe."

"When I fought Alu at Shadowrise two days ago," said Alex, "he told me that the ferals were just the mistakes. He is definitely creating another form of vampire. But the sharing-his-blood thing bothers me. After Velinar bit me and then abandoned me for dead, he tried to turn me by opening a vein and filling my mouth. Yet, I'm not feral, and I'm on Millennium Road."

Alex didn't say it, but now she did have a further concern. She had a raging temper. She remembered how she turned on the rapist and attacked Radu Cuza shortly thereafter. And then there was the conniption she threw when she saw Father Zosimos trying to uncover her grandmother's grave. Was she a little feral herself?

Mary spoke up. "Perhaps you would have been feral, Alex, if the divine being hadn't stepped in and finished turning you. No telling what he did to and for you."

Catherine continued. "But here's the crucial thing that has been unknown until recently. Alu told me that he didn't just open a vein. He placed his wrist over your mouth, made contact with your lips, and what is more important, you drooled, and he absorbed your saliva. Now we all realize what saliva from a vampire does to a human, but the contact of your saliva with his own bloodstream did something strange to the first vampire. If Velinar's blood had given him a new talent that allowed him to create feral vampires, this new talent brought by your saliva, Alex, provided a jolt to his system that pleased him more than anything that's happened since he became a vampire over three thousand years ago. He won't tell what it is, but he now has plans more ambitious than anything he has attempted. He wants to take vampirism mainstream. We believe that he has the capability to create feral vampires that don't fear the cross and have no aversion to sunlight. If this is true, the entire planet is at risk."

"We believe Alu has lost his soul," said Alex. "He's no longer on Millennium Road. He's soulless and totally ruthless. And, Catherine now tells us, without a conscience."

"I tried to get farther in to see what was going on at Ichor Haven," said Catherine. "But that chamber was more heavily guarded, and someone saw me. I eluded capture, but it wouldn't have been for long. Just as I was about to give myself up, I saw Alex standing on the cliff overlooking the Ichor Dome. I knew she'd been seen and decided to make my escape with her since she obviously had a light and knew where she was going. I didn't realize it, but the cavern where the Ichor Dome resides is a part of the same system that contains the Cathedral, just much farther down. Alex made her way back to Xanadu, where I caught up with her, just as she went into labor. I hid her while she had the child, and then we escaped."

"That is enough," said Cosmina. "Let's question the feral. Perhaps he knows what Alu is up to."

"She's right," said Mary. "We can wait no longer. "

40

Interrogation

They all turned to the back of the room where their feral was still taped to a chair and gathered about him.

"What's your name?" demanded Cosmina.

"Jašić," he said, eyes darting about the room.

"Who sent you?" asked Cosmina. "Was it Alu?"

"No talk," he said.

"I know of no torture that will work on a vampire," said Cosmina looking at Mary. "Particularly a feral. Waterboarding the Undead is a waste of time. Thumbscrews? The wrack? They experience pain but aren't afraid of it."

Alex stepped closer. He struggled against his restraints and growled. She put her hand up where he could smell her. "How would you like to bite into my flesh? Just a few answers, and perhaps I will allow a little blood."

Jašić went crazy struggling to get to her.

"Wow!" said Cosmina. "I've not seen that reaction out of any of them."

"How long have you known Alu?" Alex asked. "If you'll answer, I'll let you taste me. Promise."

Jašić calmed. His speech slowed. "Turned twenty years ago. Just a bite now, please."

"Not until you've told all," said Alex. "If you're really cooperative, I'll let you drink your fill. No matter the cost to me."

"Much pain. Bring girl closer," he said. "Jašić tell. Don't like to remember though. Much pain." He started crying. "Poor Ismana. Lost the wife. Hear the kids screaming. Yes, Alu turned me. As a blessing. Kids screaming. Died in pain. Brought partial forgetfulness to Jašić. No troubled sleep now. No dreams. No sleep at all. Secret, that Alu. Always withholding. Can't stop the kids from screaming. Alu so disappointed when turned me. Many curses. Almost staked. Had to run. Some prize ones though. Won't let us see. Stop the kids from screaming, Mirna. Stop the kids from screaming. Need blood from nice vampire. Bring her close. Jašić knows more. Yes he does. Bring good vampire."

"He sounds like Gollum," said Jaklin.

"Minus the schizophrenia," added Mikhail.

"You'll get the good vampire once you've told us everything," said Cosmina.

"I won't let them kill you, if you tell all," said Alex.

"You can't promise that," said Katsumi.

"Yes, I can. And I did. Stand back or you'll be in more trouble than he is."

"Don't push it, Katsumi," said Cosmina. "We have to trust each other."

"That's the way they all are," said Catherine. "Since they're no longer on Millennium Road, they have been psychically destroyed and are in constant emotional pain. They have no reference and are obsessed with the ruin of their lives. Blood only relieves it for a short while."

Gradually, Alex got it out of him. He had lived in Romania all his life. He wanted to be turned after his wife and kids died in the revolution that swept Romanian in the early nineties. He was away from home fighting when they were killed. Then he came home. Normally, Alu wouldn't turn someone who was bitter and resentful, but Alu had paid the man for his and his family's blood for years. Jašić still couldn't get over the death of his wife and children, and Alu thought that this new change might be good for him. To create a feral,

Alu has a normal vampire bite him. It only takes a little blood.

And then Jašić came out with something unexpected. "Sometimes, don't become feral. Doesn't know how, but sometimes, vamp goes see Alu, doesn't come out. Does he die? Maybe not. Perhaps something else. Rumors of supervamp. No one sees new vampire. Very secret. Only Alu turn supervamp."

Jašić became restless again, flopped and jiggled about, his elbows flailing but his arms restrained at the wrists. "Not good for Alu. So disappointed in me. 'Away!' he shouted, 'Get that piece of trash out of here,' Alu said. Later he come back. Had a use for me after all. He'd given up on his great woman, the one who'd change everything. Had his own path now. Found answer without girl."

Their questioning continued on into the night. It was obvious that Alu had created some sort of super-violent vampire, a new breed that could spread this new form of vampirism throughout the world. He may have achieved vampirism without the Centaur's pain or the stigmata. Perhaps they could even go out into sunlight. It seemed they still had the terrible violent streak of a feral. Jašić wondered if they even required blood to maintain their immortality. The one thing that really puzzled them was that he'd heard Alu mention Peleş Castle, but Jašić didn't know within what context. Further questioning became futile. Finally, they were through with him. He'd become more and more enraged at not being fed.

"We should kill him," said Katsumi.

"No," said Alex. "I promised him a taste of me, and I'll be true to my word."

"No telling what a bite from a feral will do to you. We can't take the chance. You could turn on us."

"I've seen it. It's something to behold," said Catherine. "Trust her."

"You should all see this anyway," said Alex. "It's both the power I have over them and the way I dispose of them. Turn him loose."

The Silent Scythe backed to the dark corners of the room.

"He'll get away," said Katsumi. "He's very quick."

"Won't be a problem, " said Alex. "You might want to open the door though."

They started cutting the tape that bound him, and he ripped off the rest. Jašić lunged at Alex. Cosmina and Katsumi started to come to her aid, but it was too late. Alex had deliberately exposed her neck, and he pounced on it. She put her arms around him like a lover and held his head to her throat.

"It'll only take a second." She sounded sad. "Take all you want, Jašić. I won't let them hurt you."

The feral had already stopped sucking. He released Alex and stepped back, no longer ferocious but startled, confused. Smoke started rising up from his body.

"You might want to get him outside. He'll stink up the house. Quickly!"

Sparks appeared around his mouth and spread over his face. By the time they got him to the door, he was on fire. They shoved him out back.

Alex went to open the front door to let a breeze blow through. "Shouldn't breathe the smoke. It'll make you dizzy."

The Silent Scythe stepped back from Alex.

"What is this?" asked Cosmina. "You've been bitten before by vampires. As a matter of fact, I saw two vampires bite you, Rutfen and Emelia, and this didn't happen."

"Only ferals," said Alex.

"But she also has a special talent with regular vampires," said Catherine.

"Let's not get into that right now," said Alex, looking at Catherine and shaking her head no.

"What's this? Secrets? We tell you ours, but you won't level with us?" said Katsumi.

"Please!" said Alex. "Give me a little time on this one. I don't mind telling you, but it should come at the proper place and time. Perhaps later on."

That seemed to satisfy most, but some still grumbled.

"This is what I don't understand about your escape, Catherine," said Cosmina. "It was still light out. No vampire could step outside that cavern entrance in broad daylight."

"That's just it. I couldn't have, if it hadn't been for Alex. She turned me back, and we stepped out into the sunlight."

"Turned you back?"

"Back human. I'm human, again."

Alex heard a gasp come from Mary.

"I was turned by a divine creature. I'm able to turn vampires back human. This I did for Catherine just two days ago."

Mary was quiet a long time, then tried to speak but couldn't find the words. Alex could tell that this revelation had touched her at a personal level. Alex remembered that Mary had been turned against her will, also. All of Silent Scythe had. A hush fell over the room, then whispers. A murmur went through Silent Scythe.

"It's true," said Catherine. "She can bring the Undead back alive."

"Yes. From undead to alive. That is my gift."

Mary continued to struggle but finally found her voice. "For some that could be a godsend. But let us not speak more of it now. We have pressing problems." Still, she seemed lost in thought. Slowly she managed, "We must stop him. Alu, that is."

Alex said, "Even though I'm not as against his whole immortality-for-the-living thing as is the Divine World, I will help end the misery I saw in the Ichor Dome. I can't bear to think that it's going on right now."

"We have the forces to stop him, but we'll need your help to prevent escape out the daylight tunnel through which Catherine entered. Will you help us with this?"

"I was afraid I was going to have to attempt this on my own, with help from those in the Cathedral, of course, but they aren't even used to violence. I suspect we'll experience heavy resistance. Fighting ferals is not like fighting normal vampires. It's kill or be killed."

"As we found out upstairs," said Katsumi. "We had to take out the two normals quickly, so we could concentrate on the feral. We had orders to capture not kill."

Mary said, "I view it as a matter of concern anytime we end the life of a vampire and doom them to Millennium Road."

"You don't have to worry about ferals," said Alex. "When they became feral, their souls have dissolved back into the ether. They are soulless."

"You know this for a fact?"

"Where could they be? They are no longer on Millennium Road. Being soulless makes them ruthless."

"Besides," said Catherine, "it's not as if they can get to Heaven someday from Millennium Road."

"Heaven knows nothing of Millennium Road," said Alex. "Catalin said so."

"Not true," said Mary. "Velinar knows. She was there while a vampire. She disappeared and Alex emerged within a heartbeat, a vampire's heartbeat anyway."

"You saw her there?" asked Alex.

"Yes. Velinar knows about Millennium Road but clearly isn't telling anyone in the Divine World."

"She also came to Earth, took on human form and tried to turn Alu back human, without telling Catalin," said Alex. "After letting him bite her, she had to bite him back, otherwise she wouldn't have become a vampire. Yet, she's telling Catalin none of this. What is going on in the Divine World?"

*

Long into the early hours of morning Alex and Silent Scythe planned the first battle of the war against Alu. They would have to kill all of them, at least they would have to be prepared to do it. Still, no one could put their finger on the essence of Alu's plan.

And then Jaklin stepped forward; her bearing had suddenly turned professional. "I've been thinking since Jašić mentioned Peleş Castle," she said, walking into the middle of the room as if she were about to make a presentation. "Perhaps the nature of Sinaia itself, as a center for international traffic, has something to do with it. Dignitaries from all over the world are here right now. A major conference is about to end. I work at Casino Sinaia, the International Conference Center. We have been planning a big celebration that's to be held nearby at Peleş Castle in the State Protocol Building."

"Ferals can turn people by just biting them," said Catherine. "No consent required. Perhaps, Alu has been hiding these elite vampires and controlling them as best he can, so he can release them on people who really matter."

"These Masters of the Universe up at Peleş Castle," added Mikhail.

"And all just before they return home," said Jaklin. "When they get there, they'll seed the entire planet with ferals, and at the highest levels of government and society."

"It really is the entire world," said Alex. "At Shadowrise, Alu told me that this was much bigger than anything I could imagine."

Mary finally came to a conclusion. "Our one chance to stamp out the feral threat is to exterminate them right here in Sinaia. If even one gets loose, it would spread the threat again, but this time it wouldn't be under Alu's control and guidance."

When it came to the matter of what to do about Alu himself, Mary balked. "I've weighed killing Alu for two millennia," she said. "Perhaps you can convince me otherwise, but I've not been able to bring myself to execute the first vampire."

"I've wondered what I would do myself," said Alex. "I had my first chance two days ago at Shadowrise. I let it pass. He has done much good for both the World of Vampires and mankind."

"We can't know the final outcome of this battle before it begins," said Mary. "But news of this conference makes immediate action imperative."

"When does the conference end?" asked Alex.

"Day after tomorrow," said Jaklin. "They've been at facilities scattered all over Romania, but tomorrow evening they'll congregate at Peleş Castle. They've closed it to the public. It's all over the news. Everyone who's anyone will be there, including all the heads of the Romanian government. Not to mention a continuous stream of royalty."

"Just think," said Alex, "after infecting dignitaries, Alu could turn them loose on all the tourists descending on Sinaia. When they returned home, they'd spread it farther. Alu Kard could take vampirism mainstream."

"Shouldn't you warn the ICC?" asked Mikhail.

"As if they'd believe us," said Jaklin. "Despite the panic, no one will admit that vampires exist. I've questioned my colleagues. They're naive beyond belief."

"Worse yet," said Catherine, "if word gets back to Alu that we're on to his plan, he'll scatter his ferals. They're all in one place now."

"Trap 'em in the Ichor Dome. Exterminate 'em," said Jaklin.

"Let's get you two initiated first," said Alex. "If you're anything like me, finding your way to violence won't be a problem."

"Want me to come with you?" asked Catherine.

"Stay with Andra," said Alex. "You'll need protection though."

"Silent Scythe will provide that," said Mary. "The least we can do considering."

Alex continued staring at Catherine. "And I have one more thing to do for you."

"What might that be?"

"When you bit me, you turned back human. But you could still be made a vampire again. You need to be inoculated."

"Never heard of such a thing."

"You wouldn't. It's not in the vampire playbook. I have to bite you. It's my saliva. This is another thing you'll have to trust me about."

Mikhail suddenly raised his arms and shouted to the heavens, "Oh God!"

"What's wrong?" His outburst had panicked Alex.

"We're bloodsuckers! When will I wake from this nightmare?"

Mary smiled and looked them top to bottom, gave a little chuckle. "What a handsome ménage."

Alex smiled. Did she know? Had Mary intended something even more lascivious?

Alex was also worried about herself, having noticed that she had changed in the last couple of days. She felt more compassion than before turning her friends. She'd felt it for the feral they'd interrogated. She felt it for Mary and the millennia she'd suffered with a life she'd not wanted. Most of all, she felt compassion for Mikhail. He too had struggled with what it meant to be a vampire but had chosen to become one to be with her. This new compassion was disconcerting. It was as if she'd actually absorbed a little of Mikhail's. She felt softened, weaker, more thoughtful. Plus, she seemed to have lost her fighting edge after turning Jaklin. Did she now have the stomach and skill to wage a war against feral vampires?

41

Bloody Initiation

Before sunrise, they left the Estate and went back into the Cathedral. A squadron of Silent Scythe accompanied them in the pre-dawn light, but if Alex hadn't known, she would never have guessed, so camouflaged and secret were their movements. Once inside, Alex found that the cavern had lost its mystery and now seemed like home. Still, she was rather proud.

Jaklin and Mikhail were wide-eyed and distracted by the exotic setting.

"So this is where you hid from us?" asked Jaklin.

"You were safer not knowing," countered Alex.

Mikhail knew something of caverns, and he called out names of geological structures and stopped to examine unusual formations. "Gypsum crystals. Makes me want to see the Orda Cave in the Urals again."

Alex thought maybe he was a little apprehensive of being initiated and was biding his time.

"Keep moving, Ruski," said Jaklin. "You're not a tourist."

"Anxious to see him with his clothes off, are you?" said Alex. She'd described the ritual cleansing to them.

"Missy! As if I've never."

Alex's friends were quite the curiosity but also provoked a little fear when they heard that these two new vampires could also handle sunlight and wear a cross. No one wanted to experience the pain and agony should a cross suddenly come into their field of view. Alex took them to her little grotto, where she'd spent so many months, and there they all parted with their crosses, Alex feeling particularly naked and vulnerable without hers.

Word had also spread of Alex's other special status, her unusual gift of being able to turn vampires back human. No one had known of her talent all the months she'd been with them. Interestingly, this endeared her to a few vampires, but some saw her as a threat and kept their distance. They thought it was a blow against the creed to be able to leave vampire society and return to human life. Still, dark faces from around stalactites and stalagmites spied on them everywhere they went.

The first order of business was blood. Conveniently enough, Gail had also entered the Cathedral, so Alex coaxed her into letting Jaklin sample a little. Gail was surprised to learn that, from the first time she'd let Alex bite her, she'd been inoculated. After she fed Jaklin, Alex gave Gail directions to her home, and asked her to come by sometime. She'd like to properly pay for her services. They found another donor for Mikhail.

The select group of Silent Scythe assembled for the ceremony and walked down the winding stone staircase to the shimmering golden pond where they performed their ritual cleansing. Michael seemed a little bashful, but Jakin was completely at home in the nude.

"So that's why you were so anxious to get here," said Alex. "You little exhibitionist."

That brought a big smile from Jaklin. "And you thought my degree got me my job at the ICC."

Mary asked if they wanted to be initiated into Silent Scythe also. If so, they'd experience another aspect of initiation. All three said they would, although Alex was apprehensive.

"It'll not be unpleasant," said Mary. "Painful to watch, perhaps, but not degrading."

"Mikhail and I were turned by choice," said Jaklin. "You should realize that."

"But Alex was turned against her will," said Mary. "If she hadn't been turned, would either of you wished to become vampires."

"Never," answered Mikhail.

"Then it's not a problem. You come as a package."

They rubbed each other with olive oil until their bodies glistened in the pale light, and they looked for all the world as if they were made of gold. They donned the black ritual bathrobes and were off to Xanadu reciting the oration, Mikhail's deep voice booming as he gained confidence in the ceremony. The long train of vampires descended the cascading stone steps into the cavern's dark depths. This time, the intoxicating mist did not affect Alex, but it did seem to heighten her senses. Jaklin and Mikhail were obviously impaired and found it difficult to stand. The damsel appeared on the dome above them and started plucking and strummed the strings of the dulcimer while humming a wordless tune.

Mary told Alex, "Since you've already been initiated, you'll not have to take the oath. You'll go to Millennium Road with us, but only experience the Silent Scythe portion of the ceremony. Then you're on your own in psychic space."

Mikhail looked at Alex. "You said nothing of an oath."

A host of Silent Scythe surrounded the three initiates, and all remove their robes and were again naked. They entered the bioluminescent pool together, the Silent Scythe forming a ring about them. When they took the oath while standing waist deep in the glowing water, Jaklin repeated quickly and precisely, eagerly reciting the words with emphasis demonstrating true belief, but Mikhail stopped, stuttered and questioned the meaning of some passages, particularly "to believe in Darkness." Just as Alex thought the whole thing would fall apart, he nodded yes and repeated his vows with conviction. He still gave her a dirty look when it was over.

"You wanted this. Remember?" she said.

They all leaned back into the water and floated on its surface, including the Silent Scythe. Alex was struck by how different this was from her initiation. They were to all enter Millennium Road together. Alex could see their shadows projected on the ceiling of the Pleasure Dome by the glow of the pool, ten Silent Scythe shadows in a ring about the three.

Mary started humming loudly. "Haayyaa... Hummm... Ooommm..." The sounds reverberated in Alex's ears and seemed to numb her brain. Finally, the fumes of the Pleasure Dome once again put Alex in an altered psychic state. She began to sing with the rest.

Once they'd all found each other on Millennium Road, Silent Scythe took them to a circular structure similar to an amphitheatre, a theatre in the round. Someone called it the Tableau. Once seated, it seemed to spin about the three of them, and they were transported back in time to the Crucifixion. They heard thunder and saw lightning so close that it frightened them. Jaklin and Mikhail clung to Alex. They looked up at Christ on the cross. Alex was shocked at his agony and heard him speak. "My God, my God. Why have you forsaken me?"

Mikhail nudged Alex and pointed to the base of the cross. There on the ground was a man reaching to touch Christ's foot that was covered in blood. But he withdrew his hand, leaned forward and touched his mouth to Christ's foot. A lighting bolt flashed and propelled the man backward. When he got to his feet, Alex saw his face and caught her breath. It was a much younger Alucius Kardasian. Vampires do age, she thought. It just takes millennia.

Alex started to call to him, but just then he was accosted by a young girl with a white veil pulled back to expose her face. The girl slapped Alucius so hard that it rang out. Alucius was startled, but his surprise turned to rage. He lunged for the girl but was immediately consumed with pain and agony. He let out a howl of pain and flew to the girl who had turned to run. She struggled, but he had turned into a ferocious beast. He pinned her arms and plunged his teeth into her neck. She struggled to get him off but went limp, and he cast her aside and howled anew into the heavens, not realizing that the girl was not yet dead.

She came up behind him and tore into him with such anger that it scared Alex just seeing her in that state. She attached herself to him and chewed into him. Alucius fell over backward, and they rolled on the ground like two wild animals in mortal combat. The girl rose up from Alucius and screamed into the heavens. Her eyes flashed so brightly that it momentarily blinded Alex. The girl then disappeared with Alucius in hot pursuit.

But then a strange thing happened. The girl returned and stood before the three initiates. She came to Alex first, and pointed to her throat where Alu had bitten her. It had a ring of glowing red blood, obviously Christ's, circling the wound. The girl was Mary, and she pulled Alex's down to where her lips touched the ring of blood. Then Mary did the same to Jaklin and Mikhail.

Something happened to Alex that she could never explain. She'd later question Jaklin and Mikhail, but they were as confused about the experience as was she. A vague background seemed to open up within her, one so profound that it was beyond human understanding, and although they would discuss it repeatedly, no one could ever put their finger on just what had changed.

Then they were back in the Tableau, still in psychic space with the group of Silent Scythe breaking up. Jaklin and Mikhail had left her side and were being led off to their initiations, as had Alex months before. Silent Scythe disappeared, and Alex thought she was alone on Millennium Road but then sensed someone at her side. She turned to see Cosmina.

"Hurry," Cosmina said. "We haven't much time."

"Where are we going?"

"To find the Centaur. And Alu, if he's still on Millennium Road."

42

Cheiron, Beyond Acheron

They moved forward through darkness more swiftly than Alex could have imagined. They were no longer running but flying above the long train of vampires. Although she had just introduced Alex to flying, Cosmina started to lag, and Alex grabbed her hand to help, but by the time they reached the front, Cosmina was too tired to continue. They stopped at the edge of a dark lake. It seemed to Alex to have been a long while since she'd been to the front, a lapse of years instead of weeks. The lead vampires, elders, had camped out on the lake's shore after arriving. Neither Alu nor Cheiron were among them. Cosmina talked to some of the elders, and they told her that Cheiron, with Alu on his back, had crossed.

"What lake is this?" asked Alex.

"Don't know. Alu wouldn't say."

"We must find them," said Cosmina. "Perhaps here in psychic space, we can learn the truth about Alu."

"Why haven't you crossed?" Alex asked the elders.

"The cold. No soul would survive the swim.

"Why haven't you built a boat?" asked Cosmina.

"Alu did. But one made of material from Millennium Road wouldn't float. Cheiron told us to wait here. He's more rugged, but even he was afraid. It's been a long while, and we became bored, so we started building a city. We call it Vampire Purgatory."

"Alexandra and I don't have the luxury of waiting. We must cross now," said Cosmina.

"A small boat rests at water's edge," he said. "Made for one, but might accommodate two."

"It floats? Where did it come from? Why haven't you taken it?" asked Cosmina.

"After Alu crossed the first time with Cheiron, he returned by the boat. He told us not to use it because he knew a better way. Then he went north. Not only that, he said that if it all worked out, he had a big surprise for us."

"What's on the other side?" asked Alex.

"Alu wouldn't say. He did say it wasn't safe for us as yet."

After locating the boat, Alex and Cosmina each took an oar, and they rowed forward on a glassy surface without a ripple. Alex accidentally splashed a little water on her arm, and it was so cold that it penetrated to the bone. She shivered all over. Cosmina was still tired, and Alex took over both oars. Once across, they coasted onto the sand beach to avoid stepping in the icy water. They saw a cliff rising up and disappearing in darkness. Cosmina was too weak to stand. Alex supported her.

"Cheiron's grotto," said Cosmina, pointing to a cave at the base of the cliff.

They stood before the cave where a campfire smoldered, a stack of boulders to the left of the entrance. To the right stood a stone structure of Doric columns. "Temple of Apollo," said Cosmina. Before the temple sat a slaughter stone, black blood coating the surface of the rock and the ground around it. Next to it another fireplace smoldered. Off to the side of the temple stood a holding pen separated into two parts, one for sheep, the other for goats.

"Are you sure we're still in psychic space?" asked Alex. "This feels real."

"I know what you mean. Looks as if it's been here forever."

They heard a commotion within the cave, a grumbling, growly voice, and the Centaur emerged, the clop of his hooves against stone a warning that he was coming, but he appeared with such suddenness that they stepped back a couple of paces for Cheiron was huge, much larger than Alex anticipated. The horse portion of his body stood as tall as a man, the largest horse she'd ever seen, and the man portion, the trunk of which replaced the horse's neck, was much larger than any man's, with well-muscled arms, broad shoulders, and a neck as thick as most men's waists. The head was the size of a cauldron, with thick curly hair falling past his shoulders in golden ringlets.

Alex's first inclination was to run. But she forced herself to stand her ground. Cosmina was still week, but Alex barely had the strength to support her.

Cosmina straightened herself and spoke to the ancient beast. "We've just crossed the lake and don't know where we've landed. Perhaps you could enlighten us."

"You're from Millennium Road?" Cheiron asked, his voice echoing inside his chest.

"Yes. We're looking for the first vampire."

The Centaur's hooves stamped impatiently as they told him who they were and why they'd come. Cheiron had a cavernous chest from which his voice originated and was then modulated by his vocal chords and further articulated by tongue and lips. He had a full beard, a much darker shade of hair that glistened in the firelight.

"Wish me to divulge the activities of one Alucius of Kardasia? Well, let me fix a place for you to sit. I'm pretty much a night creature myself now. We'll share some meat, break a little bread, perhaps share a cup of wine."

Alex whispered in Cosmina's ear, "We don't have time for this. Alu could return any minute."

"Be patient. He's an ancient creature, and his ways are much different than ours."

"What lake is that?" asked Cosmina.

"Acheron, named the same as the river supplying it," said Cheiron.

Cosmina looked at Alex. "Separates the real world from the Underworld."

"Is that Hell or Heaven?" asked Alex.

"That's beyond my knowledge," answered Cosmina.

Cheiron sat to work, first bringing out fresh dough molded into four loaves and put them inside the oven that was fired from below. Then he went to the pen, bending over it rather than opening the gate, and grabbed a young goat by the leg. He brought it to the altar, flopped it on the slaughter stone, picked up the knife leaning against it, and while slitting the goat's throat, shouted a prayer to Apollo. Cheiron's voice was filled with music as he sang, signifying both love for the god and the many times through the millennia he'd sent forth prayers into the Divine World. His words seem to take on physical form and loft into the dark heavens. Their echo sent gladness and hope into Alex's heart.

"God of prophecy and enlightenment, grant us the gift of wisdom that we might understand these terrible gifts you send us mortals. Help us bridge the gulf that forever separates our worlds. Bring forth the fellowship and understanding that creates our retched civilization, so that we may reach yours. For these gifts, we'll forever burn fat and glistening shanks for your divine repast."

The goat quivered and died as the last drops of blood fell from the cruel throat wound. Cheiron then skinned and quartered the goat, stripped it of the largest pieces of glistening flesh, which he placed on a large rack before the roasting fire. The skin, fat and bone he placed in the divine fire, which roared up searing all he placed on it.

But Cheiron's prayer had a lasting impact on Alex. She felt a closeness to something divine, and it instilled in her a powerful desire to explore the darkness beyond Cheiron's grotto.

Cheiron removed the fat brown loves of bread from the oven and sat them on the table to cool while he roasted the goat flesh over the open flame. The table had chairs around three sides of the stone square. Cheiron stood before the fourth side where he'd obviously stood many times as evidenced by the ground packed by his hooves.

"You might think I've hosted many visitors by the looks of the place," he said. "But Alucius is the only soul to sit at this table until now."

"Where is he?" asked Cosmina.

"Alu went on ahead," the Centaur said, his voice deep from within his chest seeming an echo from the depths, as if he'd spoken the words millennia ago, and they'd traveled through time to reach them that evening as they sat before him sopping bread in rich gravies. "I could go no farther, although I could not tell you why. Perhaps some divine edict."

"How did Alu get through?"

"Because he had tasted the blood of Christ. At least that's what he'd been told."

If that were true, Alex knew she could never make it through either. Then she remembered her Silent Scythe initiation. This just might be doable. Cosmina and Cheiron continued to talk but Alex realized that this could go on forever.

"We should go," said Alex.

"I can't. I'm still too tired. Go on, if you can. Find out what happened to him."

Alex left Cheiron's cove and moved forward scrambling over huge black boulders, the dim pentagon in the heavens becoming obscured by a pale light in the distance. She entered a ravine that went off to the right, a pass between vertical cliffs with barely enough space to wedge through. She encountered an impenetrable wall and had turned back when she found a path off to the left that skirted the cliff. It led to a tunnel that was so pitch-black she had to inch her way forward feeling the sides until she stepped out into fresh air and realized that she was at the edge of a deep dark forest. The longer she stood before it, the more it became visible. She sensed a great calm and serenity. This would be the place to live out eternity, she thought.

She stepped into the forest and walked along a path following the dim light in the distance. Just as she was about to break out into a clearing, she saw a man coming toward her. She stepped back behind a tree and let him pass. Sure enough, it was Alu, and he was carrying something. What, she couldn't tell. She considered confronting him, but realized if she did, he'd spook and turn loose his ferals in the real world. She also wanted to warn Cosmina but realized that this was psychic space and that Cosmina would be safe there with Cheiron in any case. She had to find out where Alu had been.

Alex crept on through the trees and into the meadow. The light she had been following came from a building at the far edge. Alex didn't want to be discovered. What sort of being she would encounter in vampire psychic space she didn't know and wanted to find out before she let them see her. She walked between trees until she reached the building and realized that it was a gazebo, a nonagon, much the same as the one in ruins at the edge of her grandmother's graveyard. When she got closer, she saw two people inside talking. She stayed back out of sight and tried to overhear what they were saying. They were speaking in a language unknown to her. She crept closer through the trees at the edge of the gazebo and peeked around a tree.

The woman seemed greatly distressed, and the man was obviously angry. He was pleading with her, and she was crying and shaking her head no. The man turned his back on the woman and walked to the far side of the gazebo. Alex moved back behind the tree. Somehow she knew this was forbidden territory. She peeked around the tree again and caught her breath. She could see them more clearly now and recognized both. It was Catalin and Velinar. Alex knew she'd be discovered if she didn't leave, so she made her way back through the trees wondering what sort of place this could be.

Once away from them, she turned to look back one last time. She marveled again at how similar this gazebo was to that apparition of one she'd seen the night Velinar had bitten her there in her grandmother's backyard. She saw something she hadn't noticed before. Growing near the gazebo were two trees, both bearing fruit. One seemed to be an apple, but the other was less familiar. Then she realized that it was a pomegranate, the same variety that had sprouted up from the seed she'd pushed into the ground the night Velinar bit her. She caught her breath.

Alex hurried back along the path, felt her way through the tunnel into the dark ravine with its close vertical cliffs but stopped before she reached Cheiron's cave. She was both elated and frightened and now realized why Cheiron couldn't go on ahead with Alu. He had been forbidden to reenter that place back when he gained his immortality.

Alex worked her way forward to Cheiron's grotto. And then she saw the unthinkable. Alu was at the edge of Lake Acheron getting into the boat and with him, seemingly of her own volition, was Cosmina. He shoved off from shore, and neither looked back. Alex stood there alone, stranded. Were they all working together? Was this all a snare for her in psychic space? And the other big question hung in the air. What had Alu taken from the Garden?

Alex realized she was now trapped between the Garden of Eden and the lake fed by Acheron, known as the River of Pain, in a psychic space that was beginning to make a lot more sense.

*

Alex, along with Jaklin and Mikhail, returned from Xanadu back to the Cathedral. The two were shocked and amazed at what they had experienced during their initiations.

"Later. Put a lid on it," Alex said. She couldn't handle more tales of atrocities in psychic space such as she'd experienced. Plus, she was still in a daze from her psychic trip beyond Acheron. The feeling left by witnessing the Garden hadn't dissipated when she'd woke into the real world.

"And by the way, Missy," added Jaklin, "we can now see the glow off in the distance, the Chateau to the right of Millennium Road you'd mentioned."

Alex smiled but said nothing. She'd noticed something new about them that greatly disappointed her. She'd seen it a little when she'd turned each of them, particularly Jaklin, but now it had intensified. A loss of innocence. That fresh human quality that had so attracted her had now turned into the confidence of hardened vampires.

Alex realized that she'd also experienced this maturity in herself, but as a strange new capability she'd not understood. Now, she longed for that psychologically wounded little girl she'd been when she came to Sinaia last summer. She'd been fresh from secondary school, full of childhood friendships, shopping, and the eternal quest for boys, something from which she'd always felt remote, but still, she'd lived in and related, if naively, to that world. Now she was a seasoned vampire, and Jaklin and Mikhail had also made the transformation. They'd gone beyond being adults into eternal beings with a confidence that belied their years. Alex realized that this was the effect of Millennium Road. They now had the psychic maturity of three millennia strengthening their psychic makeup.

Another change had happened that Alex hadn't expected, and perhaps this had to do with the Silent Scythe ceremony. They drew attention everywhere they went. Vampires fogged around them, thank and encouraged them, and when Cosmina called for an assembly in the Cathedral, they received an ovation from the hundreds gathered there. Silent Scythe had established a new line of defense below Xanadu to guard against individual ferals or a full attack coming up from the Ichor Dome. Alex looked out over the cheering crowd and wondered if they could possibly live up to their expectations.

Alex took Cosmina aside. "What happened with Alu at Lake Acheron? Why did you leave with him?"

"I had to, Alex," she answered without missing a beat. "I knew you'd be concerned, but I couldn't let him know you'd come with me. I had to get him across Acheron before he talked to Cheiron and found out what we were up to."

"What did he bring back with him?"

"He wouldn't say. Except that it was just a decoration for his throne room. I talked to Mary about it. Neither of us is concerned. What did you find beyond Cheiron's grotto?"

"Just a pile of black rocks and an insurmountable cliff. You don't think that little decoration had anything to do with those super-vamps he's creating?"

"He was closed mouthed about it, but I don't believe he was hiding anything important, particularly since you say that you didn't find anything beyond the grotto."

Alex trusted Cosmina but not enough now to tell her all of it. She still thought she was hiding something. Besides, she wanted to learn more about what she'd seen before trusting anyone with this.

43

The Arsenal

While Silent Scythe recruited an army from those in the Cathedral for an assault on the Ichor Dome, Alex, Jaklin and Mikhail returned to the Estate. They stopped off at the vampire sacred hill designated for Shadowrise and viewed part of the ceremony although they didn't have time to participate or even watch it all.

Catherine was waiting and called them upstairs. She had little Andra wrapped in a pink baby blanket clutched tightly to her bosom. "Silent Scythe is armed with battle gear that they've been using against rogue vampires for centuries. You three, however, have skills they don't, and I might have some things to assist you in the coming battle."

Alex had missed Andra terribly and took her from Catherine as they entered the upstairs. She watched Mikhail pull a chord that hung from the ceiling, and a section of it swing down and unfold into stairs. This was the entryway into the attic that Alex had explored months before when she'd found Catherine's journal.

Catherine shined a flashlight, and once they had all negotiated the stairs, Alex stood aside playing with her baby who seemed to miss her mother as well. For the first time in days, Andra laughed when Alex made a face and didn't cry to be put down. Alex felt as if her batteries were being recharged.

Catherine took them farther into the room flashing the light on the walls for them all to see. She stopped before the cage Alex had wondered about when she was in the attic before.

"After I became a vampire," said Catherine, "my caretakers became obsessed with treating me and killing my kind. I was locked away for months in this cage while they looked for a cure. I had all form of doctors, witchdoctors and priests visit. Although many professed such a talent, none could change me back. All the while, Alu tried to spring me from my one-woman prison. Many battles were fought outside and in the rooms of this house in the months that followed. He and my vampire aunt eventually freed me, and we were all to escape the area, but something extraordinary happened to my aunt. At the time, I didn't know what. Alu and I fled along the Danube into the Black Sea and on to Istanbul without her. Since returning to Sinaia, I learned that Velinar, ninety years earlier, had turned my aunt back human, much to the consternation of Alucius. He eventually returned to Sinaia, but forbid me to return even to the cavern, so afraid was he for my safety. Or at least, so he said. Now I realize that he's always been afraid that I'd get turned back because I wished for such a miracle." She smiled and looked at Alex. "Something my great granddaughter did shortly after I escaped the Ichor Dome."

Catherine had Jaklin and Mikhail pull a cupboard away from the wall. Then she fidgeted with a loose board, tripped a latch, and swung wide a hidden door. She shined the flashlight into a small room filled with strange devices.

"This is the arsenal my family used to kill vampires. The weapons should be of as much use today as they were ninety years ago."

The arsenal was not large, but what it lacked in quantity it made up for in quality. The weapons were all in excellent condition and made of silver, the one element other than wood and holy water that can kill a vampire.

"If they're made of silver, why haven't they tarnished?" asked Jaklin.

"I'm not sure," said Catherine.

"Because they're coated with rhodium," answered Mikhail. "It's a metal from the Ural Mountains in Russia and naturally alloyed with silver."

"Their use on vampires was devastating," said Catherine. "Alu greatly fear them." Her flashlight lit up the small room.

Jaklin was ecstatic. "Look!" she said. "All the weapons shown me during my initiation." Most weapons were stacked on the floor or standing in corners, but one was mounted on the wall. Jaklin ran to it and stood staring, mesmerized. "Was this yours, Catherine?"

"None belonged to me. I've never fought. Alex can attest. I'm no good at it."

Jaklin turned to Alex. "It must be yours. I was told during my initiation of such an instrument. Achilles wielded it when he slew Penthesilea, the Amazon. Following Achilles death at Troy, the weapon vanished into the mists of time. And here it shows up on the wall in your attic. It has to be yours, Missy, the souls of ancient Amazons told me that one day I would meet a great warrior who could wield it. You are the greatest among us. It must be yours." She took it from the wall, felt its heft and balance. "Perfection incarnate," she said, and handed it to Alex.

Alex took it, and although an incredible weapon, somehow it felt foreign. "I'm not so sure."

"You're not in a fight, Missy. When the time comes, you'll warm to it."

"It wouldn't be Achilles' actual sword," said Catherine. "These weapons were all made in the last century. It's probably a replica of a replica of a replica."

"Still," said Jaklin, beaming.

They picked through the arsenal, setting aside those items they thought might be useful against the ferals. Among all this were several items of body armor, which were also quickly snatched up by Jaklin.

"These are brand new, as if never worn," Jaklin said, strapping them on.

"You and Mikhail take them," said Alex. "They don't feel right for me. Besides, the experiences I've had tell me that I'm not physically vulnerable. The only thing I really need is my cross. Alu once told me that it was the most powerful weapon devised by man, and that only I could wield it. Somehow, I think I haven't learned to use it properly."

"Wow!" said Jaklin, looking at herself in a faded, full-length mirror leaning against the wall. "I have to say, I'm a steely-eyed warrior woman. Much hotter than wearing a miniskirt and sporting cleavage."

Mikhail raised an eyebrow and looked at Alex, who nodded in agreement.

Jaklin insisted that Alex take the sword. She'd already named it Achilles, and reluctantly, Alex accepted it. Still, she felt more comfortable with her grandfather's walking stick. Mikhail settled on a crossbow but would have to grease the loading mechanism that had deteriorated through years of disuse and restring it. "I'll augment this with a simple stake." But before leaving, he also selected a silver sword. "A rhodium keepsake from the Urals," he said.

They left the arsenal, taking only the weapons they felt they'd need, closed the door, turned the latch, and pushed the cupboard back in place.

"You need to trash those high heels," said Alex.

"Hey! They look great."

"Where we're going, you'll need to do more than strike a post. You've got some low-heel boots."

"I get the message." Jaklin looked concerned that she'd been so naive.

*

They had to wait until the hours before dawn, and the downtime gave Alex a chance to worry. She was not as concerned about Mikhail's safety as she was Jaklin's. Even she herself had not actually been tested in combat, but Jaklin was such a diminutive female, a girl's girl, that Alex couldn't envision her in a battle.

Alex expressed this concern to Jaklin when they had some time alone together waiting for the hour they'd leave by car for the mountain entrance discovered by Catherine.

Jaklin smiled, took Alex by the hand as if she were a child and sat her down on the sofa. She kneeled before Alex and looked up with her deep dark eyes glistening. "I've not told you of my initiation," she said. "While in the bioluminescent pool in the Pleasure Dome, a group of women came for me, some of the oldest of the dead Undead among those on the Road. They were from my own Bulgaria but back in a time when it was populated by a band of ancient Amazons straight out of Greek mythology. Chief among them was Penthesilea, the famous warrior woman killed by none other than Achilles himself during the Trojan War. They led me into a cathedral off to the left of Millennium Road and taught me the ways of warrior women. I wasn't there for just a few minutes or hours. I spent what seemed a lifetime with them acquiring slayage skills. I listened, learned, and practiced hand-to-hand combat, the art of killing. I'll not be useless in battle, nor will I be afraid."

After talking to Jaklin, Alex went to Mikhail and expressed her concern. "I'm afraid for her. She thinks she's invincible," she said.

"And she's obsessed with killing," said Mikhail. "But I also worry about you. I've seen how strong and fast you are, but this propensity toward violence disturbs me. It seems to have a place in our world, and now that I'm a vampire, I sense it more clearly. When I was initiated, I didn't go off to the left of Millennium Road as did you and Jaklin. I went to the right, and although I didn't as yet see the glow in the distance of which you spoke and of which I came to see later, I walked for an eternity in the wilderness. Then two men came toward me out of the desert. Upon seeing me, they finished their conversation, or terminated it possibly, and one man walked away. The other man said, 'So you've finally come to me.' We sat there on the ground in the desert facing one another with our legs crossed, and I told him my troubles. I said that I was afraid I'd lost my soul. He told me that I hadn't because I was there with him. Still I said, 'I am in trouble.' He said, 'I can see that you are. And it's good that you've come to me.'

"I don't know who he was," said Mikhail, "but we talked a long time. Most of it I don't remember. What I got from him was a feeling of great calm and peace. Plus a lingering hope that all is not lost. I'm in for trouble, no doubt. But we must maintain our humanity. I'm glad I've chosen the path of a vampire, at least this kind of vampire, whatever that is, but I don't want to get lost in a world without morality."

"Nor do I," said Alex. "I'm glad you've told me of this meeting. I've also been worried about vampirism. If you realized what happened to me when I was initiated, you'd be horrified."

"Why can't you tell me?" asked Mikhail. "Perhaps it would help."

"Maybe later. Right now, I just can't. But I can tell how much I need you. I'm beginning to believe that the three of us can succeed where one, or even two of us alone, would fail. I'm not sure about this struggle we've taken on, other than it's one of tremendous importance, not only for our own souls, but also for humanity for all time to come."

"I want to be part of this, but I'm not sure how much good I'll be. It goes against everything I believe in."

"Then I'll have to trust you'll find your own way forward," said Alex. "We must have faith in each other, and yes, watch out for Jaklin. At times she still has the helpless-little-girl quality that I love so much, but I worry that she could be killed trying to be something she's not."

Alex could tell that their initiations had told them who they were, which made her more confused than ever about her own initiation, so abusive and humiliating.

They both turned quiet as Jaklin joined them.

"What's up, guys?" she asked. "Keeping secrets?"

"As a matter of fact, I have something to tell both of you," said Alex. "You must promise to keep it to yourself and mention it to no one. Not even Silent Scythe."

"And Cosmina, Mary?" asked Jaklin.

"No one."

"This must be serious," said Mikhail.

"I've had a revealing and yet disturbing experience in vampire psychic space."

"You mean Millennium Road?" asked Jaklin.

"Well... beyond Millennium Road. During your initiations, Cosmina and I went off on our own and traveled to the very front of Millennium Road. It ended before a lake called Acheron."

"Freud's psychological underworld," offered Mikhail.

"Trust me," said Alex. "Freud never visited these shores. Here's the thing. Cosmina and I crossed Acheron and met with Cheiron, the Centaur who created the mess we're all in. This vampirism."

"Not a problem here," said Jaklin with a smirk.

"Yes, well, we'll see about that. We expected to find Alu there, but he'd gone on beyond where Cheiron now lives in a cave. I tried to track him down while Cosmina stayed with the Centaur. I found a way through the cliffs to a forest and a meadow beyond."

"Does this have anything to do with the battle we're about to face?" asked Jaklin with growing impatience.

Alex gave her a stern look and then continued. "On my way through the cliffs, I saw Alu returning. He didn't see me, but I saw that he carried a box containing something he obtained in that meadow, I assume."

Jaklin came awake at mention of the box, and Mikhail looked puzzled. "What was in the meadow? Do you think the box has something to do with the feral vampires?"

"Exactly," said Alex, glad to see they were getting the message. "What's happening in psychic space is just as important, perhaps more important than what's happening here in the real world. Inside the meadow, I saw another gazebo, one that greatly resembled the one at the Estate, at least the one before it was torn down."

"Do you believe there's a connection?" asked Jaklin.

"Has to be," said Alex. "Plus, and get this, Catalin and Velinar were inside the gazebo, arguing. About what, I couldn't tell. I didn't want them to know I saw them. It's just that they must have seen Alu. I'm wondering what they're up to."

"And here I was really impressed with Catalin," said Mikhail.

Alex took a deep breath. "Another disappointment. When I got back from the Garden, I saw Alu cross Acheron, and get this, Cosmina voluntarily went back with him." She shook her head. "I talked to her about it, but she just blew me off. Says it's nothing. Anyway, I'm not as trusting of her as I've been in the past. The only people I trust on Earth or in psychic space right now are you two."

"Tell us how to get to the front of Millennium Road. We'll help you," said Jaklin.

"Believe me, I appreciate the offer. But even I could only do it with Cosmina's help. Remember, she's been on Millennium Road a thousand years. Here's the other thing, and this is what I want you to know in case I do get into trouble. I saw a path on the other side of the meadow, one leading away from the gazebo and up the mountainside.

I'm going back there and take that path."

"But you could encounter anything," said Mikhail. "No telling what would happen if you ran into real danger. Surely there must be a way we could join you."

"Again, it's not possible and even if it were, I wouldn't risk you two on such a mission."

"If it's that dangerous, you shouldn't be doing it either," said Jaklin. She looked dejected. "If we lose you, what good are any of us?"

Alex looked at her with sympathy. "I know. I couldn't go on without either of you. But I have to follow my intuition. It tells me that the answers we've been looking for may be at some place beyond Catalin and Velinar."

"We'll have to talk more of those two," said Jaklin.

Alex looked at her. "Catalin didn't like me turning you, but it was inevitable, perhaps even divinely planned. I see that now. I'm beginning to wonder why Catalin said otherwise. I don't know where Catalin is coming from, but somehow it seems that a power far above him is pushing us forward without his knowledge. I just hope its coming from Heaven and... well, not some other place."

"I was always taught that the answers to life on Earth reside with those of the Divine World," said Mikhail. "I'm not so sure they understand us at all."

"Strange thing is, they don't have the answer to this vampire thing either. They've seen it all before when the first vampires were created and couldn't stop them. Stopping these ferals is the task we've been assigned. In that, I have no doubt. Somehow, in our world, divine beings are out of their depth."

"We'll just have to succeed where everyone in the history of the civilized world has failed," said Jaklin.

44

Battle of Ichor Dome

As they prepared to leave for the mountains, Alex still had one last chance to worry. She looked at Jaklin and Mikhail. "Oh," she said. "Here's one. Pagomas. The giant feral. You might want to avoid him."

"How will we know him?" asked Jaklin.

"You see him, you'll know."

Catherine was standing nearby and heard what Alex had just said. "Pagomas is quite a story," she added. "He was always much larger than anyone in his community but a weakling. Some glandular ailment, I imagine. His size was no advantage, and he was quiet, easygoing, always depressed over his anemic condition. His father died before he was born, but he had a very strong mother. He was a mama's boy. Alu recruited him for years before he consented to being turned. Of course, with vampire robustness he became enormously powerful. Dabbled in American basketball. Arrogance and belligerence followed. And now he's feral. Still, it's a shame."

They all realized that if one word of this military operation got out, the ferals would scatter. They were to fight during daylight hours to keep the ferals from escaping. They decided that Silent Scythe would attack from within the cavern, taking the same inside path Alex had trudged down to the bridge after killing Braxton. Alex, Jaklin and Mikhail would enter the cavern from the remote external portal that only Catherine knew about. Since it was well hidden, she would go with them in the hours before dawn but would return in daylight, which wasn't a problem since she was now human and sunlight was her thing. Alex wasn't about to leave Andra alone with a vampire of any caliber, not even one from Silent Scythe, so Daniel and two nuns came to care for the infant while Catherine was gone.

Alex became more fully aware that she had lost her physical quickness to Jaklin and her intellectual capability and decisiveness to Mikhail. Perhaps some of her confidence had been lost when she gave birth. She felt a deep responsibility toward Andra and wanted desperately to be around to fulfill it, something her own mother didn't take seriously. Andra certainly wasn't a normal child either. She was too active and didn't sleep like a baby only a few days old. She was physically normal but too alert, too aware of her surroundings. She saw too well and seemed to understand too much. When she got a little older, she'd be a pill, and would need someone who could understand and not try to break her spirit. Alex felt that she had to live over this battle, for Andra.

All the time Catherine was driving them from south Sinaia along DN71 into the mountains, headlights illuminating the way, Alex was having these disturbing thoughts and also difficulty staying awake. She kept lapsing into vampire psychic space beyond Millennium Road. Catherine was behind the wheel of what had been her daughter's car and jabbering on and on about returning during daytime and having never driven in sunlight.

"Watch the road," Mikhail kept saying as he fiddled with the crossbow mechanism. "Your not in Scotland. We drive on the right here in Romania."

Alex was in the backseat with Jaklin, and Jaklin kept trying to wake her and asking what was wrong. "You're just weird, Missy," she said. "Can't you feel the excitement?"

Alex was struggling. Millennium Road seemed to be flooding into her consciousness, and the darkness before dawn made it worse. Her cross no longer helped. Finally, Jaklin quit pestering her, and she lapsed into a deep sleep.

Alex found that she'd left Cheiron's grotto and was headed back toward the Garden. She again negotiated the dark ravine, passed through the tunnel, and out into the forest. She skirted the meadow and the gazebo, working her way through the dense forest to the far side and stepped out onto the path leading up the mountain that she'd seen before. She looked both ways and, with no one coming in either direction, started up the incline.

The strange thing was that the path and forest looked familiar. She turned to look back over the meadow. And then she realized the cause of the familiarity. The Garden was similar to her grandmother's Estate, without the house and other assorted structures, of course. Only the gazebo was apart of this setting and in the same location as her grandmother's. This was not a copy of her grandmother's property. This was the original. Everything about it seemed perfect, but not perfect in the earthly sense. Perfection, in the divine sense.

Alex turned back up the trail with renewed urgency. She knew what she was going to see before it came into view, so she turned to look back down the mountain again, to verify her revelation. Sure enough, there on the other side of the Garden, farther down the mountain, was a church made entirely of glass and laced with silver and gold, not one of stone and tiles like the Sinaia Monastery, but one of unmistakable similarity. Alex turned back, ran on up the hill to the top, and there it was, a sight even more astonishing than she could have imagined. And then quite suddenly, it all fell into place. She recognized this castle. Actually, it was a temple. Peleş was similar in style but didn't approach the magnificence.

Jaklin shouting jolted Alex awake. "Missy! Wake up! We're here. I thought you were in a coma. What's wrong with you?"

Catherine had just pulled to the side of the road at a nondescript section of interstate. She cut the headlights. They all got out of the car in the dark that was slowly turning to shadows as the orange glow of the sun to the east now provided a pale light. Catherine led the way off the road and down the hill through towering pines and thick brush. They approached what appeared to be the old mossy roof of a structure built into the mountainside. Catherine followed a path around to the front where they saw a normal front door flanked on each side by small windows grown up with shrubs but lit from the inside by candlelight.

"Looks like something out of a fairytale," said Jaklin.

"This is where I'll leave you," Catherine said. "You're not going to find Goldilocks inside but a couple of feral guards is a good bet. I talked my way past them, but I'm sure you'll encounter resistance."

"Hurry home," said Alex. "Lock the doors and windows and let no one inside until I return. Not even a human being. No one."

Catherine wished them luck, hugged them, and with a tear in her eye, clasped Alex's hands one more time, kissed her. "The worries of a great grandmother are many," she said. "Protect yourself. Don't be stupid." She took a couple of steps and then looked back. "One thing I've learned being in the world for over one hundred years is that failure is always an option and never as bleak as it seems. If it gets too tough, run for it." She hurried back up the mountain to the car.

"That's not what I needed to hear," said Mikhail.

"Don't worry, Ruski," said Jaklin. "I'll keep your courage up."

They then turned their attention to the door. Alex tried it and found it locked. They peeked through the windows, and sure enough, four vampires. Alex knocked, but no one answered. "Come on," she said. "We know you're in there."

"Go away," said a voice. "No visitors."

"We're not visitors. We're vampires. The sun is about up. Have a little consideration."

"Find some shade."

"That's rude," said Jaklin.

They looked at each other, and all three put a shoulder into the door at the same time. The frame exploded and the door fell into the living room with a crash, splinters and dust flying everywhere, but the ferals were ready for them.

Jaklin wedged through the entrance in front of Alex and took on the feral guards as if she could do the job by herself. Alex's heart stopped. But Mikhail and Jaklin dispatched the first two, Jaklin with a decapitation and Mikhail a thrust with a wood stake. Alex took on a third and ended the brief struggle with a thrust from her grandfather's walking stick, but the fourth got her from behind and bit her. Too bad for the feral because it instantly burst into flame. They shoved him out the door at Alex's insistence, and they were all a little dizzy from the fumes.

Jaklin had just killed her first vampire. Mikhail had killed his first also, but it didn't seem to affect him. Jaklin, on the other hand, was excited to a point of rapture. "Wow!" she said. "What a rush."

"Calm down," suggested Alex. "It won't all be this easy."

"We just killed four people," said Mikhail. "Have a little remorse."

"Still," said Jaklin. "The thrill of us working together. I mean, this is war." She kept eyeing Alex's sword, Achilles, which Alex had strapped to her back and had as yet to put into action. "Use it or lose it," Jaklin said, as if she were ready to jerk it away.

The rest of the rooms were empty. They'd still have to protect this entrance from escape because the western hillside was still in shadow and would be for a couple of hours after sunrise. Alex checked the time on her cellphone. They were running late. Catherine had told them of a back room with a false partition. They searched all the walls, pounded them but couldn't find the false panel that would indicate an entrance to the Ichor Dome. They stood staring at each other.

"We're going to miss all the fun," said Jaklin.

Just as she spoke, the entire far wall started to move to the side, two ferals pushing as it gradually revealed the dark entrance of a tunnel.

Jaklin and Michael sprung into action with Alex right behind. Jaklin cut down the first one, and then helped Alex and Mikhail take care of the second. Immediately, Jaklin was off through the tunnel, with Alex following and Mikhail bringing up the rear. They felt the humidity increase and encountered a foul stench that did not bode well for what they'd find up ahead. The tunnel was not natural but chiseled out of the mountainside, deep and dark and quite small, but heavily used, the floor swept clean of debris and paved. They crouched low and moved forward quickly. It was much longer than they anticipated, but soon they heard voices echoing in a large chamber ahead. They slowed. They could tell that Silent Scythe had yet to arrive even though they were behind schedule. They saw a dim light and then the end of the tunnel came into view. As they approached the outlet, they saw shadowy figures moving about frantically. Although the battle hadn't started, obviously the ferals knew something was coming down from the Cathedral.

All the ferals' attention had been directed toward the bridge where only a few days before Alex had seen Cletis and Mitchum standing guard. It appeared that a ruckus had broken out just this side of it, but Alex couldn't determine the cause. The disturbance spread like a gust of wind through the crowd of ferals that had rushed there. Then Alex realized what it was — Silent Scythe. They were invisible in the dim cavern light, and they came like a tornado tearing through the legion of ferals.

Their job was to protect this west exit from any ferals escaping, and Alex stayed in the gaping entrance while Jaklin and Mikhail attacked nearby ferals from the rear, lopping heads and running them through with silver swords. Alex hung back but was blindsided herself, bitten, and thus she smoked another feral. Mikhail, seeing Alex under siege, came back to help. Another attacked her, tried to run her through, but Alex seemed to maintain her invulnerability, and it was a good thing too because she no longer had the skill or temperament for the task. Mikhail dispatched him with an arrow from the crossbow. Alex saw Pagomas on the far side of the Ichor Dome wreaking devastation on Silent Scythe.

Alex was distracted and again bothered by vampire psychic space, unbearably drowsy. Why is this sleeping sickness upon me now? she wondered. She had strapped Achilles to her back and carried her grandfather's walking stick, but now she unsheathed it. Perhaps it would add a little zest to her effort. The feral that came toward her, she intimidated by slashing back and forth and twirling Achilles, but the sword felt heavy and unwieldy, her motions encumbered by its primary purpose as far as fighting vampires were concerned: decapitation. She abandoned it, and took the vampire out with her walking stick. She slipped Achilles back in its sheath.

Mikhail shadowed Alex, watching her back. It was as if he had a sixth sense, always knowing her position and able to protect her as she fought. Jaklin was the buzz saw. She knew all the moves, and was quicker than Alex. Jaklin cut her way to the front and fought alongside Mary. They are perfect together, one's moves synced to augment the other's.

Even though the ferals were greatly outnumbered, all was not going well. Pagomas had stopped the flow across the bridge, Silent Scythe avoiding him and the normals cowering before the giant. The huge vampire turned and lumbered toward Alex, his pale presence seemingly lighting the Ichor Dome. The rest of Silent Scythe and the normals streamed across the bridge.

Alex delayed taking on Pagomas herself, perhaps because Catherine had mentioned his mother. But something was not right. The really frightening realization was that so far they had not seen Alu. It was a sad business they were in now, and Alex felt the tragedy of the human lives Alu had destroyed and was eager to see him reap his punishment. She and Mikhail fought together, he always at her back fending off ferals, first with a crossbow, but his quiver of arrows was limited, and once he'd expended his stash, he drew his small sword and beat them off, occasionally driving its pointed end through the heart of one who got too close.

Gradually Alex forced herself out of what seemed an encroaching coma. She came alive and went to work with her grandfather's walking stick. Where Jaklin lopped limbs and heads, Alex clubbed and stabbed. The battle waged on, and finally Alex made it to the street where she'd seen the huts and cages where the humans had been imprisoned. She ran along the paths looking inside the makeshift dwellings. All empty. Turned feral, she thought. She stepped inside many but they were all vacant. She darted along the backstreets still checking.

Nothing.

They pushed the ferals to the far end of the Ichor Dome, but Pagomas finally muscled his way to Alex. Mikhail sprang to her defense, but the giant tossed him aside as if he were a child. Alex drew and tried to wield her sword, but one swipe of the mace sent her crashing into a structure and stunned her, her weapon sent clattering among the rocks. The giant loomed over her to send her permanently to Millennium Road. She struggled to her feet but was dealt another crushing blow that sent her up against the stone wall. She could not defeat this vampire. How did she believe she could accomplish this?

While on the ground, her weapon flung far from her, out the corner of her eye, Alex saw Jaklin pickup Achilles. She stepped forward. "I was wrong about you," Jaklin said, giving it twirl. "That great warrior woman Penthesilea said I'd see? I saw her in the mirror there in the arsenal. Pagomas? He's mine." Jaklin picked up a stone and hurled it at the giant's head, stunning him momentarily, and he turned from Alex and took a step toward Jaklin.

"No! Jaklin, no!" shouted Alex.

But Jaklin flew into him. Alex had thought her own moves before her weakening had been fast, but Jaklin was a marvel. It wasn't so much her strength, and she had considerable, but her lightning quickness. Alex never saw her take a blow. She circled her adversary, dodging the swings of his mace, spinning to avoid a thrust of the sword in his other hand, until she drove her own sword into his midriff. The blow would never kill a vampire, but the pain of his entrails hanging from a stomach wound was enough to slow him, and with that advantage she eluded another blow, ducked behind him and with one swift swing of that shinny silver sword, decapitated him. Blood spurted from the severed neck, a fountain of fell fluid the fog of which lofted into the breeze that always blew in the cavern and lent a stench to the entire Ichor Dome. The mama's boy who had never known his father was no more.

An unrepentant Jaklin stood, arms outstretched, eyes focused on the Dome's ceiling and let out a screech like a gigantic bird of prey, victorious in her first one-on-one against a formidable opponent.

Alex heard a shout. Farther down the cavern another firefight had broken out. This evidently had been only the ferals' first line of defense, and now Silent Scythe was in a tough battle for another chamber. Perhaps Alu is there, she thought. Jaklin and Mikhail ran to help, but Alex heard an unusual noise, a call for help and looked inside a small hut. There she saw three young girls.

"Help us," one said. "We're still human." They were chained to a wall. "They're all gone," the oldest said. "None of the important ones are here."

"Where did they go?"

"No idea."

"Have you see Alucius Kardasian?"

"Alucius who?"

"Alu Kard."

"Oh. You mean Old Rat Neck? The bloodsucker. That's what the ferals call him behind his back."

"That would be him."

"Don't know. It happened suddenly, and those left behind, which were most, were not pleased."

Alex broke their chains, pointed them in the direction of the escape tunnel. "Once outside, go up the mountain to the highway. From there you can flag down a car. Someone will help. When you make it to Sinaia," she said, "go to the Monastery and ask for Father Zosimos. Tell him that Alexandra Eidyn sent you. Tell him what you've seen here." She hated to leave them to their own devices, but she had other business and was beginning to believe it wasn't there in the cavern.

While watching the girls disappear inside the tunnel, Alex was tackled by a feral, and the two fell among the debris as he sunk his teeth into her. Instantly he started to smoke and sparkle, and she struggled to get loose as the fumes caused an unavoidable drowsiness. She rose to her feet but slowly crumbled back among the dead. Sleep overcame her, and she was again in vampire psychic space on the hill up from the Garden viewing the heavenly version of Peleş Castle. But even that structure wasn't what impressed her most. Hovering above it, she saw angels, one or two at first and then more. As she got closer, she saw a multitude of heavenly creatures, not just angels but real people, or the souls of real people. It was such a glorious sight that at first she'd missed something. All was not well. The people didn't seem to realize it, but the angels were in a panic and apparently could do nothing to remedy the situation. Alex tried to enter the complex but security guards, in the form of the butterfly like creatures who'd built her Chateau, came forward and would not let her pass.

She now understood the problem that caused the angels so much concern and realized that she couldn't solve it there. She turned and ran back down the mountainside. Perhaps if she could get back to Millennium Road and the Chateau, she could make a difference, but she also knew that the real battle could only be fought in the real world. Alu was launching a battle not only against the people of Earth but against Heaven itself.

Alex woke and was once again in the Ichor Dome. In her comatose state, she had been surrounded by ferals like a swarm of mosquitos. But once her blood was in their system, they stopped feeding, became confused and wandered off a few steps where they internally combusted. Jaklin and Mikhail had been in a panic looking for her. They scattered the ferals with the help of Mary and Silent Scythe and then roused her.

"Did you see me?" asked a smiling Jaklin. "Did you see me take out that giant? Wasn't I amazing?"

"You were amazing before you took out Pagomas. And that was stupid taking him on by yourself."

"You and Mikhail would have helped me if I'd gotten into trouble. Mary keeps telling me I'm green. But wasn't I amazing?"

"Where's Alu?" asked Alex.

"Well, yeah. There's that. The action has slowed," said Jaklin. "This thing is over. All but the cleanup work. We'll find Alu. He's back there somewhere, hiding."

Alex started to tell them that the rest of the ferals and Alu were somewhere else when they heard a loud shout, and Silent Scythe rushed to another chamber farther down. Loud screaming and a cry of "Ichor Haven!" split the air along with the thud and clang of a short battle, but by the time they got there, it was over.

They entered a dark chamber with more sophisticated housing arrangements. This was not the horror that was the Ichor Done but a plush chamber with expensive sofas, tall mirrors, a dining area with five tables, each set with ten chairs and thrones at the ends. The entire chamber had been swept clean of rocks and other debris and carpeted. The walls had been carved into intricate statues of vampire royalty obviously going back centuries. How had Alu kept it secret? But the strangest part was that, other than a couple of guards and servants, Ichor Haven was empty. Alu was not there, nor were those who would have occupied the seats at the tables.

They heard another shout from the end of Ichor Haven. "Another chamber! We found yet another part of the cavern." It was Katsumi.

They rushed forward to where Katsumi and two other members

of Silent Scythe had pulled down a partition to reveal a small opening into a large chamber that looked hardly used. The problem was, once inside, they discovered that it had four different trails leading off into more dark caverns. The pathways could go on forever.

Mary stood at the crossroads and shook her head. "We have no way of knowing which track they took."

Alex stepped up beside her. "We've been duped," she said. "This isn't where the action is at all. I found a few survivors. They said that Alu and all the really important vampires left some time ago."

"Where would they have gone?" asked Mary.

"Where we knew they were headed all along. Peleş Castle."

"We're too late," said Jaklin. "Alu has already attacked."

"You don't know that," said Mikhail.

"We have until Shadowrise," said Alex. "I'm not sure we can get there in time."

"We can. We have to," said Mikhail.

Mary pulled down the top of her camosilk suit exposing a mass of golden hair. "All this for nothing," she said.

"No. Not for nothing," said Alex. "We'd have had to clean up Alu's mess here regardless. We just have more work to do."

"But how do you know they've gone to Peleş?"

"I've had an unusual experience in vampire psychic space. Have you seen Cosmina? She's not here. Is she?"

"She disappeared just before we were to make our run down the cavern path to come here. We left without her."

"Did she talk to you about coming back from Lake Acheron with Alu?"

"What? Acheron? That's what separates us from Heaven. Alu and Cosmina have been there? Together?"

"Cosmina has defected," said Alex.

"How do you know?"

"During the initiation, Cosmina and I traveled up Millennium Road to find Alu and the Centaur. We found something beyond Millennium Road and beyond Acheron. I don't have time to explain, but if we have any chance of stopping Alu we must leave now. We can't wait for Shadowrise. Jaklin, Mikhail and I are going back."

"I'll go with you. Wait here while I get Katsumi to take command."

She was gone but a brief moment and then returned, her face full of concern. "If I do go, I'll have to stay outside until Shadowrise. I'll miss it all."

"Listen, Mary. You could go out with us."

"What do you mean?"

Alex stepped closer to Mary and lowered her voice. "I could do for you what I did for Catherine. Turn you back human. I saw the look on your face when you heard what I had done for her. Look. Your business here is finished, and I don't mean just this battle. You've fought the good fight for two millennia. Now you should get back to the mortal life you once had and leave this for others. Do you want that?"

"Of course. At least, I've always thought so." Mary looked terribly confused.

"Yes. Bigger decision than you thought. I get that. Also, you'll lose strength and not be able to join the battle once we get to Peleş, but you'd be human again."

Mary took a deep breath, shook her hair out. "Let me think about it. So much to consider. Why don't I just wait until later? You can always turn me back."

"I don't know if that's true. I'm losing strength and agility by the minute. My intuition tells me that something big is going to happen at Peleş. I don't know for sure, but it could be the end of me."

"Whoa!" said Jaklin. "What are you talking about?" She looked really startled.

"Later. On the way, Jaklin," said Alex. She turned back to Mary. "You wait too long, if the window closes, you'll never forgive yourself. I can't promise that you'll have this opportunity much longer."

"I'll go with you and make the decision before we exit the cavern. How long does the transition take?"

"Practically instantaneous."

"If I decide to remain a vampire, I'll stay inside the cavern. If not..." Mary took another deep breath. "Lead the way."

All four were off at a dead run.

45

Rush to Save Heaven and Earth

Alex, Jaklin and Mikhail ran along the cavern floor, echoes of their fellow warriors slowly fading behind them, and the sounds of their own footfalls and voices reflecting from the stone walls gave the eerie feeling that they were not alone, of ghosts lurking in the darkness up ahead. Mary kept dropping behind, and they frequently slowed their pace and turned around to ensure she was still with them. She was lost in thought, mumbling to herself, and obviously had not yet come to terms with Alex's offer. The small beams of flashlights marked their way through pale stalactites and stalagmites standing like statues on another world, and they ran past delicate helictites reminiscent of curly fries and globs of white worms.

They stopped to catch their breaths at what represented for Alex a familiar juncture. She shined her flashlight off to the left exposing a dark portion of cavern wall. "Alu's House of Pain is through that tunnel," she said.

"That was one of Alu's worst periods of cruelty," said Mary. "We searched for decades before finding it and putting a stop to it. I scratched the name into the wall myself. That was eight hundred years ago." She looked at Alex. "Who's going to continue my work if I no longer can? What will happen to Silent Scythe? Perhaps you could take over."

"Katsumi. She seems to like command."

Mary laughed. "For all the wrong reasons."

"I killed Braxton, a pedophile vampire, and hid his body there," said Alex, still pointing to the tunnel.

"You would be so good with Silent Scythe. All three of you, four of us. The things we could do together."

Jaklin laughed. "What we wouldn't do together."

They all four laughed.

"You were going to tell me what you meant about that 'end of me' thing," said Jaklin. "Now's the time."

"It has to do with what happened to me during my initiation. Don't ask me to humiliate myself by describing it."

"I won't. But why does that mean your demise?"

"I'm been having flashbacks." She shook her head. "It is... I'm not sure. Just a feeling."

Jaklin hugged her. "Sorry. I can see the pain. I'll not press you further. I'm here if you need me. If it's within my power, I'll not let anything or anyone hurt you."

Then they were on the run again, scrambling up the cliff off of which Alex had dropped Braxton's body, past the pale light to the right from Xanadu, and on to the Cathedral, where they stopped briefly to tell those who'd chosen not to fight news of the battle, that they were probably safe but nothing was certain. They didn't tell them of their failure to find Alu or his secret band of feral vampires. They could trust no one to know of their current mission.

Instead of going out the main entrance, through which Alex had entered and exited the Cathedral the first time, they chose the one where Catherine had taken her following the birth of Andra, passing over the bodies of the four she'd killed there.

"You really are a terror, aren't you?" said Mary.

Jaklin smiled. "She's a murdering mother," she said.

"Jaklin!" said Alex.

"Well. Just saying."

They squeezed through the tight crevice, entered the final tunnel, and stopped when they could see pale light on the cave walls ahead.

"Time's up," said Alex. "It's now or never."

"I can't make up my mind," said Mary. "I'm not sure I'll be wanted in Heaven, when my time comes."

"Have a little faith," chided Jaklin.

"Two thousand years of violence. I've made some mistakes."

"There is no right choice," said Mikhail. "But you can make it right by what you do afterward."

Alex went to her, took Mary's hands, placed them on her own shoulders, and then put her hand to her throat. "Here is the mark of mortality. But forget all that. Bite me, just because you want to bite me."

Mary lunged into Alex and her teeth clamped down. She sucked and chewed.

"Oh, isn't that sweet," chided Jaklin.

Mary didn't stop at the first few gulps, not as the others had. Perhaps it was the two millennia of vampirism that required it, but gulp after gulp, she didn't lose her taste for Alex's blood. And Alex loved having Mary so close, feeling the flow of her life-giving nectar gush into the playmate she'd known so many years. For Alex, it was the consummation of a friendship.

Mary finally stopped, released Alex and stepped back, her eyes wide with excitement. She broke down crying, fell to her knees. "Oh dear Lord in Heaven, make this the right choice." Tears streamed down her cheeks.

"You'll feel weak for a while," said Alex, sinking to her knees before her. "It'll be an adjustment."

"Oh, no! No acclimation required." She rose to her feet.

"You feel fine?" said Alex, also rising.

"Fine? Not fine. Glorious! I... I'm alive! Who would have thought during all those summers we played together, when I was protecting you, that you'd end up being my savior?"

"So it was the right choice?"

"I'd never have been able to do it, if you hadn't tempted me."

They wiggled through the small opening and were outside in the bright sunlight running along the footpath down the mountain through the pines with Mary in the lead. She seemed to have boundless energy and was so excited at being outside during daytime that she couldn't contain herself. "Whee!" shouted Mary as she ran down hill weaving from side to side with her arms out like wings, as if she could fly.

Alex, on the other hand, was feeling a little anemic.

Since they no longer had Silent Scythe to carry the brunt of the battle, they would need all the community help they could get: police, Stefan, and Father Zosimos.

As they ran, Alex once again got flashes of her initiation — the men and women circling her, the psychic ravishing, rape. She still couldn't imagine what those humiliating images meant, if anything. Yet, here they were, haunting her again. She was afraid she was leading them all to catastrophe.

But her biggest problem was an overwhelming urge to feed. Several ferals had fed off her in the Ichor Dome, and then she'd given up a lot to turn back Mary. Alex had to have more human blood. Shadowrise was only a couple of hours away.

"I'm going to get the police and then to see Stefan," she said. "Go to the Monastery. Tell Zosimos what we're up against. I'll meet you there."

Mikhail stopped in his tracks. "Stefan killed me."

"I need something from him."

Alex split from them and was on her way toward town, cutting through private property and alleyways. She surprised a man in a backyard working in his garden, but before he could get a good look at her, she was upon him, biting and sucking a little blood. She hadn't planned to do it; it just happened, and then she was on her way down the mountain. She ran onto a young couple in an alley very much into each other, their blood boiling. She took a little from each of them, giving them something else to think about. She was a menace and knew it but couldn't stop herself.

Stefan's home was a couple of streets south of the Monastery. It was a large brick building with a staircase outside similar to her grandmother's Estate. Stefan was working on it with hammer and nails. Alex came up behind him, but he heard her and jumped to run. She was upon him in an instant. In spite of his screams and flailing around with the hammer, she bent his head over and buried her teeth into him. She could have sucked him dry out of hunger and rage, but she controlled her urges and shoved him up against the side of the house.

He turned his head away, refusing to look at her, shut his eyes.

"Listen to me, you tall, skinny shit," she said with the uncharacteristic potty-mouth he always seemed to bring out in her. "I've just inoculated you. Do you understand?" She didn't wait for an answer. "We have an infestation of feral vampires at Peleş Castle. I need your help to exterminate them. Are you with me?"

Stefan's eyes were wild with being bitten for the first time and still in the control of a vampire. He couldn't find his voice. He was hysterical. "You're feral. I know you're feral. I'm changing. I can feel it."

"Listen to me!" she screamed and pushed him up against the side of the house again. "All Sinaia is in trouble, possibly the entire world." She hoped this didn't sound too hyperbolic, but she needed to get across the urgency of the situation.

"Stefan, who's the girl?" It was a young woman's voice from the corner of the house.

"Stay away, Raluca," said Stefan. "Run!"

But Alex was upon her immediately. She was remarkably beautiful, flaming red hair, peaches-and-cream complexion, and pale-blue eyes to stop the heart. She could give Jaklin a run for her money. Alex grabbed her about the waist, and when she flinched and leaned back, Alex sunk her teeth into her throat. Sweet nectar of the gods! What glorious flavored blood! She had to force herself to stop.

Raluca smiled and staggered backward. "A vampire, Stefan? You're cavorting with vampires?"

Alex got control of herself, and turned on Stefan again. "Are you with us? I'm getting the police to help. We need everyone."

Still he didn't answer.

"I've immunized both you and your wife."

"Sister," Raluca said. "I'm not married to that idiotule."

Alex looked back at Stefan. "You're both safe now, but I need you to help fight feral vampires. Do you understand? Stefan! Ferals!"

Finally, Stefan came to his senses. "Yes. I think so. Where?"

"Peleş Castle, but we'll muster forces at the Monastery. Soon as you can get there. Bring everyone who'll fight and all your vampire killing equipment. If you turn on me or my friends... Well, I've explained that before."

"Count me in."

With that, Alex was off again, this time toward downtown. At the police station, she barged in and raced down the corridor, policemen and staff scattering like rats, to Mariusz office. She forced open the glass door, and watched as Mariusz back-stepped to the corner of the room. "Stay away!" he shouted. "Talk from a distance."

Alex knew what she had to do. "It'll just take a second. You'll be inoculated." She started walking toward him. "Calm down. It only hurts a little and not for long."

She was up against him now, and he hid his eyes behind his hands. Policeman's blood turned out a little thicker than most. She started to gag, stepped away from him.

He peeked from between his fingers.

"At least you won't have to worry if you get bitten," she said. "I need your help. Feral vampires in Peleş Castle. We attack in half an hour. We could save the world. Are you with me?"

"Feral? You mean like a cat?"

"A new kind of vampire. Really nasty. If we don't exterminate them now, we'll not have another chance."

"Peleş Castle?"

"Right now. We're mustering forces outside the Monastery front gate. If word gets out we're coming, they'll scatter, and it'll all be over." She'd started to leave but looked back. "Remember, keep it quiet. Bring only those you trust." Trust? She wondered how she could say that when she'd invited Stefan.

Alex went out the back way, eyeballs peeking at her from cracked doors. The sun was precariously close to the top of the mountains in the west. Almost Shadowrise. She'd have to hurry. The flashes of her initiation were more frequent and lasting longer. She felt Millennium Road overtaking her conscious mind once again.

Back at the Estate, Alex couldn't wait to see little Andra, but first she had to deal with a terrified Catherine, who grabbed Alex and wouldn't let her go. "I couldn't bear it if anything happened to you," she said. Then she pushed her away. "Where are Jaklin and Mikhail? They aren't..."

Daniel and the two nuns came out of the kitchen braced for bad news.

"No, no. They're fine. But our job isn't finished. They went to the Monastery."

She picked up her little girl, and held her close, kissed her even if she did try to turn away. Alex was going into battle, and this could be the last time she'd ever hold her. Alex raised Andra up in the air. She was so cute, her eyes sparkling. At first Alex thought they were just the bright eyes of a child, but then she felt herself under their spell, as if she were hypnotized. She could not move. Time stopped.

Suddenly, Alex was back in vampire psychic space standing before Acheron wondering how she was to cross. Alu and Cosmina had taken the rowboat. I would hate to swim it, she thought. It's known as the Lake of Pain. Cheiron's fires had burned down to glowing embers, and his grotto looked deserted. She walked to the entrance and peered inside. A single candle burned in a far corner, but she saw no sign of the Centaur. She entered, walked a few paces into the sparsely lit chamber. To the right was a small bookcase with a Bible on top opened to the red lettering of the New Testament. Everything was placed on shelves carved up high into the ancient stone walls, as one might expect for a man with a horse's body. It would be difficult to stoop.

To the left, a partition blocked her view. She stepped farther into the grotto to peer behind it and saw a bed of thick straw. Sure enough, the body of a horse was stretched out on it. At the near end, a quilt was thrown across the upper body of a man. Just as she realized that this was Cheiron, his head rose up, and he shouted. "Ho! We have an intruder." Quickly the horse body rolled from its side and the torso and head of a huge man rose as if levitated by some magic mechanism. He was obviously pissed off.

Alex turned to run, but the Centaur was much quicker. He grabbed her in his gigantic arms and lofted her from the ground. She dangled from his hands like a marionette, feet kicking in thin air.

"A thief!" he shouted "Come to steal our gold and jewels."

"No, no, Cheiron," Alex cried. "It's me Alexandra. I came here with Cosmina but a short while ago."

Cheiron held her out at arm's length, scrutinized her. His eyes widened in recognition, and a smile eased her fears that he might dismember her on the spot. He put her back down on her feet.

"So here's the little sneakabout. Did you find what you were looking for beyond the cliff?" He still looked accusing.

"Yes. Well, maybe. It's much different than I expected."

Cheiron seemed to get a hold of himself. "Forgive me, young lady. I'm too disagreeable for this Afterlife. Tell me, what brings you back to my grotto?"

"A while ago, I saw Cosmina go back across Acheron with Alucius Kardasian."

"Yes. She wasn't agreeable to it at first, but Alucius convinced her."

"Do you know why she went?"

"No. They talked on the beach beyond earshot. I just saw her being thoroughly disagreeable at first, then calmed and got into the boat with him."

"He didn't force her?"

"She seemed quite willing after he showed her something in a box. Excited even."

"They took the rowboat, and that leaves me with no way across but to swim."

"No, no. No one swims Acheron."

"I was wondering if you could take me, since I hear that you brought Alucius across on your back."

"Oh no! Don't ask that of me. I did cross to this side by swimming the ice waters of Acheron, but the pain, Miss Alexandra, the pain. Water here in the Afterlife doesn't freeze regardless of the temperature. I'd not do it again for anyone. I'd have to swim it even once more to get back here."

"How will I cross? I too do not wish to suffer its agony."

"Your soul would never survive. You must stay. Unless, you can find another way."

"Unless? Cheiron, is there another way?"

"Perhaps you'd have better luck than Alucius and I. You may remember that ancient mythology tells of a ferryman named Charon who carries the souls of the dead across Acheron to the Underworld. He resides far north of here. Acheron is quite large, and what you see outside my grotto is only the southern tip. Charon, he might not take you. He ferries souls only one way. He won't even allow a single soul of the Undead aboard his ferry for any reason. Before we first crossed Acheron from Millennium Road, we went north to have Charon take us with the rest of the souls into the Underworld. But he said that souls of the Undead aren't allowed entry into the City of God, which is easily accessible from the Underworld. We'd forfeited that right when we became undead. We returned and I swum across with Alucius on my back."

"Where did he get the rowboat?"

"The City of God. He found a path from here. The first time Alucius went there, he stole it. This was after I swam across with him."

"Perhaps I could get a boat from there also."

"Not likely. They are much more concerned with security since the first theft."

"You didn't go to the City of God?"

"I'd been forbidden back in the beginning of time from ever receiving that reward. It's not possible for me to walk much beyond my grotto. It's like a wall built against me."

"So Alucius went to the City of God and returned with a boat that he used to cross Acheron to get back to Millennium Road. And yet he didn't take the boat the next time he crossed?"

"Alucius' soul had been changed by something else he stole from the City of God, in addition to the boat. He was so happy. He returned to Millennium Road and went north to try Charon once again. He fooled Charon into thinking his soul wasn't of the Undead. After crossing with Charon, he went back to the City of God, stole more of the precious commodity that had changed his soul. He had planned to go north to get Charon to take him back across Acheron to Millennium Road, but he was exceedingly pleased to see that Cosmina had come across with the boat, giving him a way back without Charon knowing."

"Yes, I saw him carrying something on his way back when I went there. Did Alucius know that I'd crossed Acheron with her?"

"Not to my knowledge."

"Thank you, Cheiron. But how am I to find Charon?"

"Follow the shoreline north. Don't under any circumstance tell him I sent you."

Alex was suddenly back home staring into little Andra's eyes, as she seemed to have released her hold on her mother. Alex shook her head to clear the fog, kissed Andra one more time, put her back in the bassinet and started to leave. Catherine had noticed nothing, as if time had simply stopped. Daniel and the nuns also seemed to know nothing of what had happened.

"Talk to me, Alex," Daniel said. "What happened at the Ichor Dome?"

"I can't take time," said Alex. "We did well, but it's not over." She headed for the door. "Lock the doors and windows. Keep all the crosses and icons close about you. Admit no one."

"Be careful," shouted Catherine. "Failure is an option."

Alex was off to the Monastery.

46

Battle of Peleș Castle

Alex found the police already there along with Father Zosimos. She wondered where Stefan was, and thought that he'd probably turned chicken, but then saw him drive up in his minivan. Radu Cuza, the man she bit after she'd killed the rapist, was with him as well as his two companions the night he shot her with the sawed off shotgun. Alex realized what a chance she was taking by including these morons.

Jaklin and Mikhail came running through the gates from where they'd been inside the Monastery. Mary trailed sheepishly behind.

"I want to stay here," she said slowly. "I'm sorry, but I don't want to commit or even witness anymore violence. This seems like home. I feel like a little girl again."

"Oh Missy, you should have seen her. Father Zosimos gave her a cross," said Mikhail.

"She stood before the altar staring up at Christ on the cross," said Jaklin. "She couldn't quit crying."

"Don't feel bad," Alex told her. "You've done more than your share of good for this world. It's time the rest of us shouldered that responsibility."

Mary returned to the Monastery without looking back.

Alex took a deep breath and turned to the officials clustered about her. She would have to clue them in. "We know that a band of feral vampires are in the Castle and that they plan to turn as many dignitaries as they can. Exactly where they will have congregated, I don't know. We'll have to search the place."

"I know where," said Father Zosimos. "The Castle was built over a pagan temple with a little-used underground chamber chiseled out of stone. It has two access portals, one from inside and the other outside. If Alu is really doing this, he'll stage his raid from there."

Alex turned to the police chief. "Once we get to the portal, you and your men start the evacuation of the dignitaries and staff, then enter the underground chamber from the inside portal. Father Zosimos will take us in from the outside."

With that, they all piled into vans and SUVs and were off to Peleș. Father Zosimos had performed religious functions frequently at Peleș, and he was able to get them on the grounds without a ruckus. Jaklin with her position with the Bulgarian Consulate vouched for the others. Of course, the police were the police. Alu would obviously want to provide the freedom for his ferals to roam the area without worrying about sunlight, but they had to work fast. Shadowrise was minutes, if not seconds, away.

Once inside they exited the van, and the first thing Alex did was bite a servant girl and then the young man caretaking the grounds who tried to pull Alex off her.

"What the hell?" said Jaklin.

"For some reason my body's storing blood," Alex said. "I want to bite every one I see."

Mikhail scoffed. "All this oath stuff about not scarfing without permission, and you're feasting on anyone with a heartbeat."

"I know," Alex said. "Can't stop."

"A likely story," he said.

"I bit Stefan," Alex added.

Jaklin nodded. "Okay, we get it."

Alex said nothing more of the continuing flashes of her psychic ravishing. Off in the distance, she observed royalty entering up a flight of steps and through the front door. She and her friends had to enter from the back and go underground. They come to negotiate the important issues of the day and celebrate civilization, she thought. We come to kill.

Father Zosimos took them around back to the storage facility, which, he said, had fallen into disrepair and was no longer used, except as a short-term cache for grounds-keeping equipment. The little stone structure was locked tight, but he found a crowbar, with which he pried loose the latches, and since the door itself was locked with a deadbolt, he had to pry it open also. Inside, Alex saw lawnmowers, rakes, shovels, shears, all rusted and in varying states of disrepair.

Father Zosimos walked straight to a trap door in the floor of the shack, which he raised to reveal a stone staircase descending into the mountain. A soft glow emanated from within. He removed his cross from a pocket of his robe and holding it before him started down the steps. Alex followed with Jaklin and Mikhail descending after her. Stefan and his bounty hunters trailed behind. Father Zosimos stepped from the bottom of the stairs out into a spacious enclosure with a low stone ceiling and stopped. Alex touched the cold, sweaty walls with her fingertips and stopped behind him.

The chamber had been excavated from the mountain with pillars of the original stone left standing to support the ceiling, or floor actually, of a room in the Peleş Castle complex. They looked like a forest of stone spires, but what took Alex's breath and frightened her no end was the hoard of ferals milling about. She and her cohorts had not yet been seen by those congregated for what reminded Alex of bal de liceu, a high school prom, something Alex never attended.

The vampires were dressed in the richest of garments and seemed entranced. All the men were in white shirts, black ties, black pants, and red cummerbunds. All striking and uncommonly handsome. The women were in white full-length gowns, black sashes but cloaked in dark red, and irresistibly beautiful. These were not like the ferals Alex had witnessed in the Ichor Dome. Quick and arrhythmic, but somehow still beautiful in motion, they were perhaps a hundred in number and gathered about something, someone in their center.

As Father Zosimos and the others stepped forward, the ferals turned in unison, as if telepathically connected, to see who had entered. These were vampire royalty, pure and virginal, a glorious gaggle of immortals. Somehow Alu had used that box from the Garden of Eden inside vampire psychic space to transform them from ferals into an exalted form of vampire worthy of mixing with the royalty of Europe.

Alex stepped around Father Zosimos, who had frozen in his tracks. She regretted what she was about to do. They were so regal, so androgynously beautiful. She remembered that Catalin had told her everyone in the Divine World was bisexual and wondered if these were angels. Had Alu trapped a band of wild angels, who had descended, as had Velinar, and turned them?

She wished she'd joined Alu and become one of this prized group of royal vampires. She wondered if the world would be better off in the hands of these immortal beings. They seemed so pure, such innocents. She felt that not only was she susceptible to evil, but that now she had become pure evil. Evil itself. Was it still too late to stop the killing? Did she have the courage? She felt so far from home and out of her depth.

The hoard of vampires parted, and Alex saw Alu standing at the foot of the stairs leading up into the Castle. They had caught them just in time. He looked princely himself in a white cape and black pants and shirt. He was magnificent.

Father Zosimos stepped forward thrusting his cross before him to no avail, for these vampires were beyond all that. Somehow they were cured of Christ's stigmata.

Alex heard pounding on the door at the top of the stairs above the angel vampires, and everyone turned to see what was happening. In what seemed to Alex an explosion, the doorframe splintered, and the door fell onto the stairs. The police burst through.

Out of nowhere, Stefan's shotgun fired and a vampire dropped. Jaklin darted around Alex, and started hacking mercilessly, severing limbs until she could get a clear swing for a decapitation. Alex, having no stomach for it, dropped her walking stick and walked among them. A couple of vampires dragged her away from Mikhail. As one vampire bit into her neck, then another, she couldn't resist. They only drew a little blood then released her, wandered away a few steps, and quite suddenly went into convulsions and their clothing burst into flames exposing the scintillation of their skin like sparklers at a celebration.

Mikhail came to her rescue, beating off two more ferals, but Alex had gone into an altered state. She watched Jaklin fighting, and it seemed that time had slowed for her. She'd become an unstoppable fabled creature, folkloric. Her motion seemed a choreography of archetypal gestures seen in mythical time. Jaklin was the Millennial Woman.

Alex realized it was to be another slaughter. Since Alu's vampires had no weapons, it would be like killing children in a schoolyard. But then she saw Alu throw open a door to another chamber and usher those around him into it. One of them was Cosmina. The sign on the door said "Pivniţă de Vinuri," Wine Cellar. Alex negotiated the mayhem as more ferals poured through the door, realizing she had to enter too, but alone. Anyone who entered with her would also perish. She needed to solicit just one more donation, a topping of the tank, Mikhail would have said. Father Zosimos, the perfect donor, was up against the stone wall panting, perhaps gathering his strength before reentering the fight, his blood churning within his veins and arteries. She went to him, fangs exposed telegraphing her intent.

"No, Alex!" he shouted. "Not me!" He swooned.

"You've owed me a long time," she said and bit into him with a vengeance. Like a spider, she coiled her arms and legs about him, shoved her face into his flesh, the flow close to the surface and immediate. She took two long drafts of holy blood before releasing him. "Debt paid in full," she said, smacking her lips and stepped away. It was faith she gained from him, his blood, faith in what she was about to do and the conviction to do it. Yet, she knew it was evil, that someone or something was set to enjoy the atrocity she was to commit. She had become Evil's scullion.

Alex reached the door, knowing that if the others entered with her — Jaklin and Mikhail, Stefan and his band of bounty hunters, police, Father Zosimos — they'd all die.

47

Battle of Pivniță de Vinuri

Alex was afraid to enter alone, to be by herself with wild ravenous vampires. She was afraid to die, mostly because she'd never again see little Andra. Alex realized that what she was about to do was the reason the divine shape had come to her after Velinar bit her, the reason it created her. He gave undead existence to Alex for this one task. She had been a plant all along, a Trojan Horse. Even her initiation now made sense. This was her destiny. She felt depressed and reflected back on the evening at home, her first night alone after Jaklin and Mikhail left, about wanting to die. Now, her baby had been born, and she knew that not only would Catherine take good care of her, but that little Andra now belonged to her. Alex knew nothing about right and wrong. She had to give herself up to exterminating the angel vampires, knowing she would be doing wrong.

Just as she was about to enter, Jaklin and Mikhail came running.

"No," Alex said. "This is my task. I now realize that it's the reason I've been feeding. You both know what I'm taking about. My initiation."

"You turned us. We have to go with you. It's not just your destiny. We're in this together."

"My initiation and yours tell me otherwise." She turned to enter, but they crowded up against her.

She faced them again, braced herself and removed her chain and cross, handed them to Jaklin. "Give this to Mary," she said. "In vampire psychic space, I've been beyond the Garden of Eden. I saw a castle that must be a heavenly version of Peleş. I know what this is about. Alu isn't just attacking the people of Earth. This is an assault on Heaven itself."

"You have to take this with you," said Jaklin, trying to give back the cross. "Remember? It's the most powerful weapon the world has ever seen."

"I don't need a weapon but the powers of seduction. This is... I must be naked. I am the way, the only way to stop him."

When they both protested, Alex pushed them back, closed and locked the door, and descended more stone stairs. With the violence stopped, the angel vampires calmed in her presence, entranced. The chamber was small and lit by candles along recesses in the walls. They were a glorious, beautifully dressed group of royal vampires. What a tragedy.

Not only were the angel vampires attracted to her, but she was attracted to them. Her hands trembled. She had to give them everything. She wanted them, needed them to feed on her. She had locked the door to keep Jaklin and Mikhail out for their own good but also because she didn't want to share these angel vampires with anyone. She wanted them all to herself.

Alu stood among them, regal and sophisticated, a king among royalty. "Don't do this, Alexandra," he pleaded. This was the first time he had used her full first name. He sounded so respectful, kind, even thoughtful. He looked handsome in his new outfit.

She stopped.

"This is what we did together, you and I," said Alu. "Your saliva did this to me. We created these angel vampires, the culmination of three millennia of vampirism. We are so much more than human. Even more than divine. Just a little more time, and we can offer it to the world."

Alex walked on down the stairs, and they gathered to her, both men and women, feeling of her, slow and methodical now that any threat from outside was gone. Alex remembered when she'd first entered the cavern over a year ago, how the normals had clustered about her, touched her. She'd not known it until now, but she'd felt not only accepted, but loved, loved sexually, but loved. She felt that now, but it went even deeper, a cascading, lustful longing. A cold heat emanated from them, a carnal craving. They kissed her, clung to her, licked her, undressed her. They lay her on the narrow tasting table in the center of the wine cellar and gathered about her, their fangs protruding in feeding fashion.

The stone surface was chill next to her bare skin. Alex had never felt such cold hard burning desire, not even in bed with Jaklin and Mikhail. She felt them kissing and groaned with passion and anticipation. Everywhere, she felt mouths and hands.

And then Alu knelt over her. She felt his long dark fingers along the curves of her body, felt the fingers of one hand enter her, the fingers of the other hand on her breasts, lips, into her mouth, along her tongue. His dark face bent over hers, so close that his long black hair covered her face, and then he sank his teeth into her neck.

The smell of her blood instantly filled the chamber, that rich cinnamon aroma with a touch of oriental spice, frankincense and myrrh. Alex wanted him badly, but that was not to be. At his first taste, Alu swallowed and rose from her. Something had happened. He'd changed. He backed away, staggered and vanished into the darkness.

Alex was intoxicated by the affection, the touch of vampires, and it was just starting. The smell of her blood awoke their ravenous nature, and the kisses became bites. Alex's blood was like a drug, an addiction. Those first few gulps were worth the world to a feral.

Alex then saw one she didn't wish to destroy. "Leave, Cosmina. Please don't do this to yourself. Live!"

"I can't. I must have you. You're my one desire." She bit into Alex's throat, sucked, and Alex noticed a tear form. She removed her mouth and stepped away. Yes, her one desire had been her bane. She stepped back and burst into flame.

Alex looked away. The emotional torture of having the weight of the world on her shoulders was now relieved by the physical pain of giving up her body. From head to foot the ferals sank their teeth into Alex and sucked her blood. But no one sucked for long. Just a couple of mouthfuls, and they rose up from her sated, and wandered off, as had Alu. Another took its place. The ferals committed all forms of corruption upon her body, using her blood and all her orifices for unspeakable acts.

Alex saw a flash of light, smelled smoke, and realized that the first vampire after Alu who had drunk of her blood had just sparked, then crashed into a heap of ashes and charred bone. Still the rest were ravenous for her. She felt her body being rolled about, all forms of obscenity committed against it, delicious bites, delicious pain. Her body glowed with arousal, and the fangs dug deeper into her flesh. No part of her body was without penetration. They bit and sucked, then sparked to their deaths even as another took their place, unable to resist the temptation.

Alex got that calm, tranquilized feeling she always had when a vampire's saliva entered her blood stream, but with so many feeding off her, it was an immense, sublime feeling of wellbeing. She lapsed into it, just as had they, knowing that this was her undoing. She felt her life force wane. Alex welcomed the encroaching darkness that multiplied with each new vampire. They left her corpse limp on the tabletop used up of all life and utility. This was her time.

And darkness did come. It came in great clouds of emptiness. She felt her consciousness hover as if at the edge of a cliff and then plunge into the abyss. It felt as if she would fall forever, but she felt a slight tug at first and then a strong steady force stop her, like the pull of a bungee stopping someone who'd jumped from a bridge into a deep gorge. Her thoughts lingered, then turned to stone. Like a tiny flame in immense darkness, her consciousness flickered and extinguished without even a remnant of a glowing coal.

*

Jaklin stood aside the door through which Alex had disappeared while Zosimos used his crowbar to pop the latch and pry it open. Jaklin shot inside, followed the steps down. Her stomach retched. Something, someone was nude and stretched out along the length of the table in the center of a small room. Siting in chairs crowded about it so close that they could hardly move were vampires feeding off the corpse. Like a pride of lions devouring their fresh kill, a small community gnawed a carcass. She saw the ferals feeding on Missy. Jaklin screamed. She felt faint, yet the glow of the smoke cloud was something special, a divine light. She saw silver angels and ashen daemons hovering in it.

Jaklin felt Mikhail grab her arm, pull her back up the stairs. "We can't leave her," said Jaklin, shaking his arm loose.

"We have to," said Mikhail. "This is her moment. She told me of this, and it's as she and I feared. It's her destiny."

"Back!" shouted Zosimos. "We'll all be killed by these fetid fumes."

Jaklin stumbled and felt Mikhail pull her back up the stairs, and out through the door. Zosimos slammed it to, bolted it. The room seemed to rumble, the ground tremble, and then a tremendous explosion blew the door out, off its hinges, and catapulted them to the far side of the chamber. Jaklin stumbled about trying to regain her footing. Mikhail had collapsed to his knees and was consumed in a fit of coughing.

"What was that?" asked Jaklin.

"Spontaneous combustion," Mikhail said.

Once the smoke cleared, they reentered the chamber. They found desolation and death. Nothing alive. Broken bottles and wine splashed the walls and puddled on the cement floor, a deep crimson, like blood.

*

It had been a long journey along the coast of Acheron from Cheiron's grotto, but finally Alex saw something other than dark sand and black lake. At first it was no more than a glow on the northern horizon, but now she saw bright lights off to the left of the lake that exposed a craggy shoreline. Out on the waters of Acheron, Alex saw a barge propelled and guided by the movement of a large oar that also acted as the rudder, which a short stubby man pushed back and forth at his leisure. Alex arrived at the wood dock, which extended out into the lake, ahead of the ferry, walked the ancient planks and waited for it to dock.

The passengers looked dazed and confused but were focused on the lights of the magnificent inland city of tall buildings and spires extending into the cloudless heavens. Still, something seemed not right about them although she couldn't put her finger on what.

Alex approached the ferryman, who threw the ropes for anchorage to a shore workman. "Sir. Might I trouble you for passage to the far shore of Acheron?" The ferryman had to be Charon because his cargo was the souls of the dead.

"This is a one-way passage, urchin. No one returns to the other shore but as a gift from God himself. Be on your way back to where you belong, content on the better banks of Acheron." His eyes were like coals of fire, and Alex could tell she had already exhausted his patience. He was busy lowering a drawbridge.

"But, sir, I belong on the other side and came here of my own freewill. Others have commandeered my boat, and you have the only other passage. I'm on a desperate mission to save life on Earth."

"I see that you are dead," Charon said. "The dead cannot return to the shore of the living."

"Look closer," said Alex. "I'm one of the Undead."

Charon was startled, and looked afraid. "Unholy thing! My charter is to ferry only those who've given up life due to natural causes. The walking dead are a forbidden cargo."

All the time he was arguing with Alex, he was working at releasing the forward gate so his passengers could disembark. He was about to pull it aside, when Alex realized what was wrong with his cargo. She recognized one, who tried to hide her face — Cosmina. These were the souls of the angel vampires she'd just exterminated.

"Charon! Close the gate!" Alex shouted. "These are also souls of the Undead. You've been fooled." As Charon turned to look at his cargo, she stepped aboard the ferry and shoved back two vampires who were already on the drawbridge."

"Whoa!" shouted Charon. "I provide no passage for undead souls. Those on the other side can deal with you." He shoved off without bothering to retract the gangway.

One of the souls tripped and fell into Acheron's icy waters, screamed, and the soul dissolved in a piercing shriek.

Alex pushed her way through the throng of hostile vampires until she located Cosmina, who tried to hide her face.

"Where is Alu?" Alex asked.

"You fool! Do you really think you could stop the original

vampire? You're a traitor to your own kind. Humanity had this one last chance for immortality in both worlds, to be immortal on Earth with the soul in Heaven. You have committed an atrocity against the future of all mankind."

"I know what you say is true, and I feel that what I've done is wrong. But I've given up my own understanding to a higher enlightenment of which I have no knowledge but trust to exist."

Cosmina cowered before Alex and would have no more to do with her. Yet, the souls of the other angel vampires gathered about and tried to shove her into the dark waters, but they didn't have the strength to overcome her. Alex stood at the edge of the ferry and peered into darkness. The trip seemed to take forever with no sign of progress.

The shore was upon them abruptly out of the darkness, and they hit the dock with a thud. Alex stepped off, but the others refused to leave, and Charon unveiled a whip with which he made them pay for their intransigence. Alex tried to escape the others, but her movement was labored. She had become suddenly weak, and they took command of her, forcing her to march with them back to Millennium Road.

When she reached the newly built city where Alu had told the souls of the Undead to wait, all was in disarray. She wanted to ask what was wrong, but those with her shoved forward and would let her address no one.

Alex tried to leave her companions and head toward the light of the Chateau in the distance, but the closer she got, the more confused she became. She was feeble and trembled. They turned away from the Chateau and headed south. They grabbed her arms and forced her along with them into a deeper darkness, which she greatly feared. She was powerless to escape their grasp and became desperate when they came to a charred mountain that had been the victim of a great conflict.

Out of nowhere, a group of dark, vile, unclothed creatures descended upon her. They had no interest in any of the others, just Alex. They were both animal and human but nasty, stinking brutes, humped, cankerous, warted. She felt an ominous pull into the darkness, and they entered a cavern scorched into the mountain. She realized that feral vampires did have a soul and that this was where they all ended up. The tunnel they traveled became steeper and steeper, the uncouth creatures pushing her along until she could no longer control her steps and started falling forward into a red light and unbearable heat. And then she plunged off a sharp ledge and tumbled into the Depths of Despair.

48

Another Funeral

They held Alex's service five days later. All that time, Jaklin and Mikhail waited for her to wake up, but she remained lifeless. Alex's body had been charred from the explosion, her skin a dark cinder, and her multitude of wounds never healed. Mikhail's complaint was that although her joints were stiff, rigor mortis never fully settled in. Her flesh remained soft and pliable.

The police were satisfied that the public menace was over and went back to fighting crime. The dignitaries who'd been inside Peleș Castle were told the building had suffered a fire in the wine cellar that was successfully extinguished. Everyone went back to their normal duties. The remains of the vampire bodies were introduced to Stefan's crematorium.

When Father Zosimos called them, Alex's family returned to Sinaia, as they had when the family matriarch died. The adults shed no tears, but Sonya's four girls screamed and wailed. The littlest, Anica, fell to the floor and kicked in a prolonged grief tantrum.

Catherine was anxious to see her granddaughter, Madalina, Alex's mother. She introduced herself as a distant relative. "I'm a lawyer also," she said, hoping to bond with this middle-aged woman. Madalina gave her the once-over but was distracted and didn't respond.

Father Zosimos produced Alex's last will and testament, in which she left her estate to little Andra and designated Catherine Cantacuzene as her guardian with complete control over her life and finances until the age of eighteen. Alex's father was dumbfounded and said nothing. Her mother shouted at Father Zosimos for not notifying them that she was pregnant. He pleaded extraordinary circumstances but would not delineate. She would not believe he didn't know the father and looked daggers at Mikhail. She tried to enlist Mikhail's help, to get him to admit that he was the father and own up to his responsibilities.

Mikhail turned away. "I am not the father," he said. "I wish I were."

Again and again she probed Father Zosimos concerning the events surrounding her daughter's death.

"I don't know," he lied, looking off to the side as he did. "We found her in the forest burned with a uniform coating of ashes and naked, except for the lapis lazuli ring upon the third finger of her right hand. Perhaps it was a bolt of lightning."

"I want to see the corpse."

Once at the mausoleum, her mother stood silent before the charred remains. "Okay. That's Alexandra, no doubt. But why all the bite marks?"

"Forest animals tried to eat her," said Father Zosimos. "Probably rats."

"Cremate the body," she said. "Finish the process left so cruelly incomplete."

Mikhail flew into a rage. "Never!" he shouted. "I'll defend this corpse until the end of my days."

They put her in a casket.

Alex's mother looked blankly at Catherine but addressed Father Zosimos. "I want her Cantacuzene genealogy investigated. What legal right does she have to Andra? And the execution of the estate? That belonged to my mother."

Father Zosimos lied again. "I've known her personally all her life and can vouch for her as part of the family." He produced a picture of Alex's grandmother with her mother, handed it to Madalina.

"Yes. The resemblance to both is remarkable. Photoshopped no doubt. I'll file a lawsuit. Something I, as a lawyer, am certainly capable of executing."

"Oh, Mother," said Gavril. "What would you do with another child? You never paid any attention to the three you raised."

"You've already demonstrated your mothering skills with Alex," said Sonya. "The way you failed to raise her."

"Humph," said their mother.

Finally, they began the funeral at the family graveyard. All was solemn and more grief stricken than at Alex's grandmother's, with no one crying except Jaklin and Sonya's girls, of course, who wailed incessantly. Mikhail was rather stoic, as if trapped in a perpetual state of disbelief. Even as they lowered the casket into the grave, Mikhail said, "This is not right."

They all left the family cemetery, except for Mikhail, and the groundsmen shoveled dirt in upon the coffin. Mikhail waited among the tombstones, at times leaning against a tree, at others sitting in the grass among leaves, as if he were waiting for someone. He would not eat. Jaklin came to visit and stared at the grave with him. From time to time, she brought Catherine and little Andra. No one came to violate Alex's grave, and no one rose up from it. And yet Mikhail waited. He had the time. He was an immortal vampire and getting on with his life was not a priority.

"I'll wait a thousand years if I have to," he said.

Jaklin and Mikhail could no longer locate Alex on Millennium Road. She had died not only on Earth but had also vanished in vampire psychic space, as if she had been feral.

Catherine had the gazebo rebuilt from architectural plans she found in the attic. All the while, Mikhail sat leaning against Alex's tombstone watching the workmen and would not budge. Then for days on end at Shadowrise, Mikhail would stand in the finished gazebo shouting first at Velinar and then Catalin, neither of which once showed their divine faces.

They receive a call from the medical clinic asking about the baby and wanting another DNA sample. Catherine, Jaklin and Mikhail were unanimous that they should never again respond to a request from the clinic.

One morning before sunup, Jaklin went to visit Mikhail at the gravesite where he'd again spent the night and found that he'd dug up her coffin.

"Are you going to take her corpse into the house and put it in bed with us? Are you, Mikhail? Speak to me!"

"Perhaps." He stood staring down at Alex in the open coffin. "I think she looks a little better. I just can't leave her in the ground. I'm convinced that she's not quite dead yet."

"Vampires die all the time, Mikhail." Then Jaklin broke down. "I can't believe it either," she wailed. "She can't be dead. She just can't be."

He opened one of his own veins and dripped blood into her mouth. Nothing. He cut Jaklin's palm over her protests and dripped her blood. Still nothing.

"Perhaps Andra's blood," he said.

Jaklin shook her head no. She'd not permit it. "Missy's immortality on Earth has ended." She dried her tears. "We'll have to find a way to accept it."

"Just a drop," said Catherine, who had appeared with the baby from behind them. She too couldn't believe it. Still, nothing.

"But Millennium Road," said Mikhail. "She's trapped there somewhere. I'm convinced of it."

"She's dead, alright." It was a deep shaky voice from behind.

They turned to see Alu step from behind a tree. He had a woman with him, beautiful, ethereal, one of the angel vampires. She too had an ashen look about her. Somehow, they'd both escaped.

Alu was humbled. He sat and talked with them just as would any other human being. He shed tears over the loss of his angel vampires and also for his Ms Alexandra. "I know you think I'm a heartless monster. But I love life here on Earth and simply wish to prolong it for all those sympathetic. Sylphia here is the lone representative of what could have been. I can no longer turn them. She can't tolerate the sun, but she has neither the Curse of Cheiron nor the Stigmata. Nor can she propagate. Yet, she is immortal, an earthly immortal. She'll remain a living symbol of what could have been."

"Perhaps, if you'd been more open," suggested Mikhail.

Alu smiled, looked at the ground. "Perhaps, if she'd been more trusting."

"But the Ichor Dome."

Alu shook his head. "I was horrified too. When the transformation worked, the results were beyond imagining. And when it didn't, it was too horrible to believe. But hideousness did happen, and still, I couldn't stop. Just one glimpse of Sylphia, my first success, and I had to try again."

Just before the sun poked over the mountains in the east, Alu took one last look at Alex, shook his head. "What could have been." Then he and Sylphia walked away.

"You'll stay away from here, if you know what's good for you," said Jaklin. "You got the most precious person who's ever been on Earth killed."

Alu looked back. "The monsters from the Divine World, they used her. She was their instrument. But they didn't completely destroy us, you know. That's an act of mercy. I'm still convinced that the All Powerful has a soft spot for vampires. We just haven't found the right mix."

"That's a self-serving assumption," said Mikhail.

"Come see me in thousand years," Alu said and disappeared with his consort into the gloom.

"Okay, Ruski," said Jaklin. "Put the lid on it, and let's get out of here."

Finally, Mikhail relented, and again they closed the top, shoveled dirt, and put her tombstone back.

49

More Divine Visitors

That night Jaklin and Mikhail, in their dreams, left Millennium Road and traveled east to the Chateau. Once inside, they looked out at the bridge over the fast-flowing Acheron and saw a woman carrying a child exit the Gates in the wall of the City of God and walk the bridge toward the Chateau. She opened the door that was only accessible from the bridge side. The woman was crying, and the child, a little girl, had a stern look and a fierceness in her eyes that you'd never expect from a baby. The woman was dressed in a flowing white gown, all ruffles and pleats, elegant. A delicate shawl circled her neck and fell to her belted waist.

"I am Velinar," she said. "And I'm here to find and send back Alexandra Marie Eidyn."

"We'll go with you," said Jaklin.

"No. This is my mess, and I've been given orders to pay whatever price it will take to make it right. You're confined to this Chateau and in charge of her little girl's soul until she returns." She handed the baby to Jaklin. "No one is to enter, no one to leave, until Alexandra returns."

"You'll need a guide. Millennium Road can be confusing," said Mikhail.

"Been there before. Spent a while, actually. But I'm not going to

Millennium Road. I'm the cause of all this," she confessed, looking up at Mikhail with tear-filled eyes. "I let Alucius bite me, thinking I could turn him back human. I was a little infatuated, even as an immortal, but it made him worse. Alexandra rectified my mistake, cleaned up my mess, and now it's time to fulfill my debt to her."

"Good luck, and come back safe," said Mikhail.

"I'll not be returning."

With that, Velinar, Prime Counselor, City of God, opened the door to Millennium Road, stepped out, and disappeared into darkness.

"So that was Velinar," said Jaklin.

"Seems we all make mistakes from time to time," said Mikhail.

"And suffer the consequences," said Jaklin.

*

The girl woke tentative at first and was then startled by a scream. She was stepped on and kicked about as she tried to struggle to her feet. She rose but could see nothing. Slowly she was able to make out hysterical shapes about her wrenching their hair and tearing at their skin. The shapes fled, and all she could hear was the cackle of hyenas. She was afraid and started to run, but not in any particular direction. She could only see smoke, smell rot and stink, and feel the sharp uneven rocks and debris at her feet. She stumbled about.

Slowly her eyes adjusted so that she could see dark flames all about her. Someone hit her from behind, and she fell forward into another shape that pummeled her with his fists. She had to fight to get him off, but others were upon her immediately, and she kicked, bit and scratched to get free. She didn't know who she was, why she was there or where she'd been. She could see the smoke of wars in the distance illuminated by explosions and hear the cries of great armies. She saw civilizations swept away, and the hateful shouts of warriors hung in the air. Everywhere the stench of death. She saw herds of great animals driven into ravines and clubbed to death to feed the armies. She heard the hymns of marching soldiers long at battle sung by the mighty voices of millions.

Someone dragged her up and with a great shout shoved her forward into a multitude of forgotten souls. She merged with them, and they ran for an eternity into the glow of a setting sun. She found strength in the shoving and hitting, and they cursed, hated and shouted great slurs at each other. They wielded fire in their hands and threw it at everything that would burn and killed anything that moved. They roamed the Land of Beelzeboul and with cries of great hatred they marched on, and she could see in the distance that it was not all blackness and desolation, not yet. She was behind the lines mopping up from an eternal war.

As the eons came and went, she found herself close to the front where the great destruction was taking place. She stumbled across the injured and clubbed and hated them for being alive, all the while coming closer to where the battle was being fought, where light shone and smoke didn't yet blacken buildings. They tore them down because they stood. They clubbed the walls of homes until they collapsed, set them afire to see them burn and killed those inside. They were a great swarm upon the land, and they killed those quickest who begged mercy, and caught those who ran and ripped and tore their flesh and beat their heads until their brains burst, and they stood among the flames and shouted a great cry of victory for all was theirs, and Desolation was their name.

The girl was lofted into the air where she saw wars in the distance, heard the rumble of magnificent explosions and great awkward machines walking upon the land crushing everything good beneath its mechanical feet. On they went burning and crushing and pounding, and she was consumed by hatred and insatiable thirst for destruction. She sought new ways to defile the countryside, to dig into the dark earth, to grind all above into the rotting ground, to hide forever the order and enlightenment of the ages.

She heard a call from behind her, a foreign desperate voice, the ring of everything she hated. It spoke a single word, that most hated and despised of all words, spoken here among the ruins.

"Alexandra."

She loathed it, she loathed that it had been given voice and turned to crush whomsoever it was that spoke such malediction. She saw a woman dressed in hated white, a blinding flow in the deep darkness lit only by that of wars, and she advanced upon the white glow and struck out at it and hated it and hated the person in it, the white flow of the soul who dared make the pronouncement, "Alexandra." She swung her club to smite the word from the air, to kill the word, to knock it and its hated letters to the ground and crush them into nonexistence so that it could never again be spoken.

But the woman didn't fall under the girl's might. Her blows didn't knock the woman in white to the ground. They didn't still the voice that now said, "Alexandra Marie Eidyn." And a great power overcame her, and she fell to her knees before the woman she hated, and she gnashed her teeth and growled in great hatred in her submission.

"Alexandra Marie Eidyn you are hereby commanded to turnabout and go back from whence you came."

She hated the woman in white for she knew not and cared not from where she'd come for she wished to never return to any place she might have been. But in her groveling and whimpering, she heard a greater voice speak to the woman, one of greater authority that would save her from this voice of sweetness and light.

"Leave this land. You do not belong here and have no dominion or authority over my souls. This soul belongs to me."

But the woman in white was not deterred. "I know I don't belong here and that I have no authority over your subjects, and I can see that she is one of your greatest warriors of destruction. But you can see that I am greater than she, for she cowers before me. I am among the greater spirits of the Universe and even you have no dominion over me but I dominion over you, although I have no authority in this your world. Yet, I will trade my soul for this one. I will take her place, and I will grovel at your feet if you will allow her return from whence she came."

"So be it done!" the great dark voice shouted, pleased beyond measure, he was, and the girl felt herself uplifted, and she stood briefly before the woman.

"Run, Alexandra. Run back in the direction from which I've come. Run with all the strength you have and don't look back. You are to never see what is to be for this has been ordained in Heaven, and so shall it be done."

The girl felt herself running, why she knew not, to where she knew not, and she did run like the wind, but she did look back, no matter the command not to, and what she saw was amazing beyond telling, for a dark image of a giant stood over the crumpled woman, her light dimmed to but a glow, and he beat her with a whip in one hand and a mace in the other, and others came to help him and they beat the woman with such force that it would have crushed anyone but she. They knocked her to her hands and knees and she withstood the blows though she trembled and shook at the great violence that was dealt her and that she would suffer now for all eternity.

The girl ran as she had been commanded although she would have turned back to help, for her heart had been lightened, and she felt great sorrow. She knew not where she was running, but she ran anyway because she could do aught else. Up in the distance she saw a figure, all black but with a pale silhouette who waved to her, and she could but follow, and the dark figure with the soft glow turned and ran before her and motioned again for her to follow, and they ran up an incline to stairs among a giant hole in the dark mountain, and up the steps he went with her following.

Up and up they went, a stairs without end, an eternal climb until she could no longer run, and so he slowed and they walked, and she became weaker and couldn't make the climb and so he returned to her, took her into his arms, withstood her weight and carried her up into a light so bright that it blinded her and hurt so bad that she cried out. It was too much, and she begged him to stop and let her return to the darkness, but he would have none of it, and the light crushed her, and she knew no more.

*

Jaklin and Mikhail awoke from a deep sleep having dreamed of Millennium Road and realized that Missy had return to the Chateau.

"She's alive!" shouted Mikhail.

His voice woke Catherine and the baby, and she ran downstairs just as Jaklin and Mikhail were about to exit through the backdoor.

"What do you mean? Who's alive?"

It was Jaklin who was convincing. "It's Missy. She's back in the Chateau."

And so they dug up Alex's casket again, ripped off the rotting top, there in the dark hour before dawn, only to find that she was still lifeless, still dead as ever.

This time it was Jaklin's turn to wail, and wail she did and shouted disparaging epithets at both Catalin and Velinar. It was then that a ray of sunlight first kissed the gentle cheek of the beloved's face, and she did stir, just a finger, but still.

"Get her inside!" shouted Mikhail, and that they did. A vampire at each end, they carried the casket into the living room and placed it at the center, mud and leaves soiling the carpet.

She again did stir, her mouth working but a single syllable that never yielded sound. The attempt was a priceless joy, and Jaklin hugged Mikhail and they both hugged Catherine. And then she did rise up, as the dead do at times from some spasm of muscle restlessness, but this corpse was again among the Undead.

Although confused and without speech at first, Alex soon regained her bearings. "Where's my cross?" were her first words.

"Call Mary," said Jaklin, searching for her cellphone. Once dialed, she tapped her toe impatiently. "Mary!" she said with a shriek. "Missy, your Alexandra, is alive. Bring her cross quickly." She hung up.

"Why the rush?" asked Mikhail.

"When I wear it here, it's also in my possession on Millennium Road," Alex said.

"What?" asked Mikhail. "It's both places at once?"

"As is the gazebo and Peleş Castle. Since the cross is from the Tree of Life, it has the properties of soul. It can be two places at once, just as are human beings and vampires."

"Why the panic? You're here, you're alive, or undead."

"Velinar is lost to the World of the Damned."

"But she's a divine creature. Others in the Divine World can save her."

"They've abandoned her to the Forces of Hell."

"She was the cause of this. Remember?" said Jaklin. "Let her rot awhile."

"Besides," said Mikhail. "She herself agreed to that judgment."

"But I didn't. You don't know what it's like."

Mary finally arrived. "I knew I couldn't keep it," she said. "But you can't imagine the joy it's been to have it with me all this time. But here. It's ordained yours by Christ himself."

"I do so appreciate you keeping it for me. Perhaps it'll come your way again."

"Why are you taking it to Millennium Road?" asked Jaklin. "Of what use do you believe the cross will be against the great armies of the Underworld?"

"Alu called it the most powerful weapon in the history of the world. Let's see if it's worth its wood."

She immediately fell asleep standing and crumpled to the floor. Jaklin and Mikhail took one look at each other and fell down beside her.

50

Great Evil

They stood inside the Chateau before the door that led to Millennium Road and more recently, they realized, the Underworld.

"You can't go!" shouted Alex. "For the hundredth time. Someone must care for Andra's soul, and you, both of you, will be more trouble than you're worth."

"A likely story," said Jaklin. "I'm faster and stronger than you."

"Jaklin's right. You showed no such skill at the fight in the Ichor Dome," added Mikhail.

"This is psychic space. The Divine World doesn't want even me going. You know how rankled they get. "

"Take just one of us. Me," said Jaklin.

"No! Get over it."

"You're not the boss of us. I want you to know that," said Jaklin.

All three laughed.

"Just saying."

Alex tucked her cross inside her blouse and slammed the door behind her. She headed in the direction of the dark cavern, where the souls of the angel vampires had taken her. She worried that her cross might not work at all, that Alu might have been lying and that the cross might be worthless inside where she was going. She didn't care. She had to do this.

She was the only one to enter the cave entrance in the black mountain and immediately felt the increased grade and her footsteps irresistibly quicken. She could already smell the stench and was losing grip on her mind. She seemed to be dissolving. She could no longer control her speed forward and started to tumble out of control, falling, falling. She didn't record an impact and just became one of many shapes milling about in darkness.

In the distance, the girl saw the great plains of war, the explosions of devices and heard the screams of the innocent and saw the defiling of the dead. She wished to join them, to commit the great carnal crimes of war. But off to the west she saw a dim light, a halo about a mansion on the dark mountainside. She could always wage war but now the light intrigued her and she imagined what great atrocities she could commit to those inside as she climbed the craggy cliff, scampered across the rocks and debris and slinked along the outside of the great dark palace.

The girl found a door to the cellar, broke the latch and crawled inside, felt her way through the dark toward a dim light. She pulled back a partially open stone door, squeezed through into a curious building of halls and open rooms, everything cold black stone, vacant, and yet she heard faint cries of agony. She walked up stairs to the next floor and saw hideous bodies milling about. They paid no attention to her. She stood before open doorways and saw great torture chambers. She entered a cathedral of suffering where souls were chained to walls and spread out on stone tables. Cancerous beasts whipped and beat and abused, and among them walked the Queen of Torture, a magnificent Daemon of Distress urging them on to maiming and decapitation, the searing of human flesh, the main course.

At the far end of the chamber, on a huge throne, sat a pale giant, the Overlord, consuming the tortured and roasted human flesh. The director of all this was a woman, the Queen, once dressed in white but now covered in human grease, burnt drippings of the tortured. Her job was to taste each carcass before passing it on for consumption.

The Queen turned on this new worker, called two of her slaves who slashed the girl with their whips. She was given the task of roasting the victims alive, and the girl could feel her own hatred now, the power of inflicting pain with apathy, turning the Flame of Indifference on the screaming souls until they charred and cracked, and then passing them to the dismemberers.

But the girl wasn't quick enough and although she cried out in hatred and poured the flames and burned the souls, still she wasn't fast enough, for the great consumer had to wait no matter how quickly she worked. And the Queen of Torture came to beat her about the head and shoulders, slapped and shoved her up against the roasting table so that her flesh too seared. She grabbed the girl by her garments to hurl her across the room to the torture chamber that would teach her the price of slowness.

But once she'd grasped the girl's blouse, the Queen stopped for she felt an object beneath it, and her expression changed from utter hatred to one of surprise and recognition. The girl grabbed the Queen's hand where she clasped her garment, and then she too saw and recognized. They heard a great shout from the consumer and they again went about their tasks, but the spell had been broken. The girl looked at the woman. Their eyes met. They connected. The girl turned and ran with the woman, the Queen, right behind, past the screaming and groans of writhing bodies, through the door and along the hall, down the stairs.

They heard the alarm go out, the shouts, the scurry of feet. The girl and the woman weren't quick enough, for the great army that guarded the mansion awoke, and as they exited the mansion they were surrounded, and the Overlord approached. They would now become the eaten. Once again the girl's hand went to her garment and clasped the object underneath. She pulled on its chain and out it came. A pale light it cast in the darkness, and all around cowered and were afraid. They moved forward, and the girl took the woman, not out the main entrance, but down the side of the cliff whence she'd come, and then they were on the plain streaking back along the dark path, the object in her hand lighting the way. It seemed they might escape, although close were they pursued by many.

But a dark figure stepped in their path to the stairs. "You cannot pass," he said. "A deal has been struck, and although it was for just one, you've broken the covenant, and now both are forfeit. Back to the

Halls of Suffering."

The woman stepped up beside the girl, and she clasped the object in the girl's hand also, the two of them sharing the grace.

"I speak the Language of the Cross, and it is one of mercy."

"The cross carries no magic here, and I do not obey such commands. It may lay waste to others, but I obey the ways of the Underworld, and this is an object of a despised realm."

"You may not acknowledge it, but it rules any domain within which it resides. I command you again. Let us pass!" They saw the shape weaken, but the earth trembled and the mountain shook and rocks tumbled from the cliff. Something bigger, more ominous was coming, something neither the girl nor the woman wished to face. They moved forward and although weakened, the shape again moved into their path.

Suddenly, he was cut down from behind.

"This way!" someone shouted.

The girl and the woman fled past the fallen shape and headed for the stairs. Two brave soldiers, a man and a woman, urged them up the stairs while they stood guard protecting their retreat. A flurry of furious daemons flooded the area, but the two fought them off with such speed and agility that one would have not thought it possible. Up the stairs the girl and the woman fled, panic stricken with the two soldiers also retreating but always fighting to push the encroaching army of monsters back off the stairs and into the chasm. They heard the stairs crumble, the destructive force of some magnificent monster of ruin in hot pursuit. On up they went, ever fearful that they were being overtaken.

They exited the cavern and were on the plains of Millennium Road when they heard the cavern crash and crumble in upon itself. No one had followed them out, and the girl wondered at the brave souls who had saved them. Perhaps she'd never know who they were.

51

The Pearly Gates

As they struggled back through darkness toward the Chateau, the girl gradually become aware of her own identity and wondered whom she'd pulled out of the Underworld, hoping it wasn't someone she'd regret liberating. She kept urging the woman forward, trying to gain distance from the Hellmouth.

"Stop!" the woman, said. "I'm ill." Her stomach retched. She burped loudly, projectile vomited, and leaned over gagging with chunks of human flesh hitting the ground. Alex left her to her heaving and just held her, stroked her grease-filled hair and waited for her to finish.

Gradually, Alex came to her senses, and she saw the woman beside her was indeed Velinar. Velinar didn't yet know her, so severe had been her submission and conversion. Alex spotted light from the Chateau and headed toward it. Velinar stumbled and fell. Alex reached to help her.

"Alexandra? Is that you?" Velinar asked.

"We're safe, now that the cave collapsed."

"How did you find me?"

"I didn't. I just wandered onto you."

Velinar rose to her feet, and they struggled forward. The grease and grim seemed to dissolve of its own accord the farther they got from the entrance to the Underworld, and Velinar was beginning to resemble the woman who bit her in what seemed so many ages ago. In fact it had been only a little over a year. Here in vampire psychic space, time didn't seem to be linear. Jaklin had said of her initiation that she trained for years with the Amazons.

Alex looked back one more time and saw two souls emerge from the pile of rubble, both struggling and leaning into each other to stand. She squinted into the darkness for they looked familiar. Could it be?

"Help me, Missy," called Mikhail, "for Jaklin has gotten herself injured."

"You're in worse shape than I am," said a quarreling Jaklin.

Alex flew into their arms. "Never should you have done that. Don't you ever consider the risk?"

They turned back to Velinar who was still struggling to stand.

"Speaking of risk... You might think twice too, Alexandra," said Velinar.

Alex turned on Jaklin and Mikhail. "How could you two possibly be here?" she asked. "You didn't leave Andra's soul alone in the Chateau. Did you?"

"Of course not," said Mikhail. "But you should have seen what happened after you went back to get Velinar. The Gates of the City of God burst open and a flock of angels flooded out. They couldn't cross Acheron, but they hovered over the edge of the bridge and leaned forward to see where you were going. From among them, one stepped forth who was greater than the others. It was a man with no wings standing among angels. He crossed the bridge, opened the door, and I swear to you, Missy, he had tears in his eyes. He had given up hope. He took little Andra from me and would have gone back through the door and across the bridge to the City of God leaving us standing there, but little Andra, small as she is, pounded her tiny fist in his chest until even he turned back to us.

"Go," he said. "God will be with you."

"But who was he?" asked Alex.

Velinar knew. "It was Catalin, of course. He's always meddling."

"We ran," said Jaklin. "We ran as we've never run before. We'd watched closely where you went and knew the vicinity of where you disappeared. We found the entrance, and down we cascaded. And yes, we had bitten off more than we could chew. For, once down there, we had forgotten who we were, why we were there, and were being pulled into the multitude, but then you and Velinar came out of the darkness and we recognized you and we recovered. Although we had no weapons, we fought back the forces of Hell, Missy, and then we all came back up the stairs."

"And yes," said Mikhail, "Jaklin was amazing."

She punched him.

By the time they reached the Chateau, Velinar had recovered. She said, "This will not be the end of it. You must realize what we've done."

"So be it," said Alex as they entered. "It is the end of appeasement. We shouldn't be in the business of buying peace by allowing atrocities against God's divine creatures."

Catalin was inside babysitting Andra. When Alex saw Andra again, she seemed confused. "What is her soul doing here anyway? Please tell me that she didn't die."

"No," said Catalin. "Children's souls stay in Heaven until they are fully anchored to the real world. Obviously, Andra's soul is still firmly planted in Heaven, but she's very much alive in your world."

Alex took Andra from Catalin. There in psychic space, Alex wasn't cold, and little Andra clung to her like a leech.

Velinar addressed him. "We've awakened something from the Depths of Despair that would have been better off left sleeping," she said.

"Mingling with mortals and the Undead is bound to have unsavory consequences. We'll all pay a price." Catalin shook his head and looked terribly dejected.

"Why should we expect repercussions?" asked Alex.

"It's the physics," he said.

"Evil is like entropy," added Velinar. "It just keeps coming."

"At least you're saying 'we' now instead of treating us as a subspecies," said Mikhail.

Velinar stood at the open door before the bridge to the City of God. "Come with me," she said, and they followed Velinar out of the

Chateau and across the bridge. On the other side, the angels gave a great cry of thanks and glory to those who had saved their beloved Velinar.

Velinar tried to take little Andra from Alex, but Andra would have none of it. Velinar said, "Well, perhaps just a little farther. You can't go through the Gates, but just this once, stand before them."

Once among the angels, they fluttered about the three heroes touching them with their hands, their wings causing great gusts of divine air to swirl about them.

And they walked to the Pearly Gates before the City of God and they swung open. And then Jaklin and Mikhail kissed little Andra, and she hugged her mother's neck and kissed her and hugged her again, and allowed Velinar to take her from her mother although her face wrinkled and she cried.

Velinar with the soul of Andra in her arms and Catalin in tow passed though the Pearly Gates with the angels following close behind, and just as they were closing, they got a peek inside. Alex had seen it all before in a dream, but even for her, it was an astonishment. What they saw and those they saw inside was so far beyond describing that even in all the years to come when Alex would try to voice a word to chronicle what they had seen, tears would fill her eyes, her voice would crack and her two companions could only shake their heads yes, they knew, for they had seen it too.

52

Seraph at Shadowrise

Alex, her two companions and great grandmother couldn't wait for the mountain snow to melt, so they could resume their hikes of the previous summer. Sure, skiing was fun, but the baby, hearty as Andra was, would need another year before Alex and Catherine would feel comfortable taking her up in the gondola in the cold wind.

Catherine and Daniel were married after only two months of courtship. They couldn't get enough of each other and didn't want talk of their intimacy to spread beyond the family without ritual sanctioning. They learned two weeks later that Catherine was pregnant, which set not only them in a dither but also the World of Vampires, having reopened the question of whether immortality was really worth giving up a human life.

Now that summer was in full swing, they'd been up the mountain on day hikes to the unusual rock formation called the Sphinx, a natural Carpathian sandstone replica of the one in Egypt, but in miniature. They liked to watch both sunset and Shadowrise from up there, leaning against the Sphinx while eating their evening meal before starting back down to Sinaia. They frequently returned after dark using their enhanced vampire night vision. They considered it a challenge that served to bind them as friends. The three vampires would guide the human couple through the darkness and venture into the night shadows to discuss philosophical issues — the nature of evil was a favorite topic — and wonder the ways of the world. Occasionally, Catherine would invite a vampire friend of many years standing, one of intellectual proclivity, or simply a comical character, to spice up their experience.

So it was that one evening they were up at the Sphinx watching the glowing last lip of a magnificent sun burn itself out at the western horizon and shadows rise up from the valley below to darken the Eastern Carpathians, when they saw on a nearby mountaintop a dark figure spread its cloak as if to become a bat and fly off into the heavens. But in the air above, they saw another object materialize, a winged creature, too large to be an eagle or other denizen of the heavens, descending rapidly. As the dark shape spread its cloak, the angel spread its gold and silver wings to stop its descent and hoover. A lightning bolt struck from the angel to the dark shape, but instead of it crumbling, the angel itself lost strength, fluttered for a second, then plummeted to the ground.

Alex heard a clap of thunder and a long train of echoes off the mountainsides.

"Is that Alu?" asked Mikhail.

"Couldn't be," replied Jaklin. "And that winged creature?" She started to run.

Down the slope they went, and once at the saddle between hills, up the other side. Jaklin and Mikhail were in the lead with Alex carrying little Andra following and Catherine and Daniel struggling to keep up.

Alex saw the dark shape disappear over the ridge as she approached the fallen. She and Jaklin bent over the creature lying on the ground. It was a person, but unlike any they'd ever even imagined. It was phosphorescent, casting its own glow in pale twilight.

Alex noticed the sweet, metallic smell of ozone mixed with burnt creature flesh. The angel had black singe marks across her chest. Alex heard a humming noise and looked up into the clouds at a thousand wings that fluttered over them and quickly disappeared.

Alex held the divine being's hand and consoled it as it took what proved to be its dying breaths. Its glowing wings folded and seemed to dissolve into its back. Slowly, it lost its internal light and became human.

"It's a seraph," said Catherine, once she arrived.

"The war... has begun," the seraph said.

"What war?" asked Jaklin.

The seraph did not respond.

"Who was that?" asked Alex.

"The Great Evil has been turned loose upon the world."

TO BE CONTINUED

www.ingramcontent.com/pod-product-compliance
Lightning Source LLC
Chambersburg PA
CBHW020819180626
46814CB00001B/28